THE COPTIC SECRET

PROLOGUE

I.

The Vatican
August 1510

Father Simon had found the key.

Well, if not exactly "found," borrowed, taken without its owner's knowledge long enough to have it copied. A very expensive process.

Another reason to suspect this man Buonarroti.

Why would an artisan, a mere artist, be entitled to such an elaborate key to his room? The Holy Father had granted other workmen laboring on the new St. Peter's Basilica lodging here at the Vatican. But none had such a costly key if they had one at all.

What need did carpenters, stonemasons and the like have to lock their rooms, anyway? Such simple men had perhaps an extra shirt and a sheepskin to shelter them from the weather, hardly anything worth locking away.

Buonarroti was different.

Five years earlier, he had fled his small studio behind the Piazza Rusticucci, hardly one of Rome's more prestigious neighborhoods, for Florence. Only the command of Pope Julius II and a heated written exchange brought him back to finish the business.

From his return to Rome to the present, *il papa* had granted the man special privilege.

First, Buonarroti's experience was as a sculptor, not a painter.

Second, the man had a foul disposition. Years ago, as a mere apprentice, had he not quarreled with his master, the well-known Ghirlandaio? Even now, he had nothing but harsh words to say about the widely popular Raphael, the architect of the entire rebuilding program. And his shouting arguments with the pope himself were common scandal.

Admittedly, Julius's temper was legendary. At any one time, half the Vatican staff exhibited scars and bruises from His Holiness's cane. So how could he not punish a mere artisan for literally throwing timbers from the chapel's scaffolding at God's anointed pope himself?

Then there was the matter of Buonarroti's piety, or lack thereof. The man attributed his admitted talent not to a bountiful God but to the alignment of planets on the day of his birth some thirty-eight years ago. More pagan than Christian. And there was always the feeling the man knew more than he was telling, that he had some special knowledge gained from sources other than the church's interpretation of the Holy Scriptures, an illicit source that caused him to sneer at church doctrine. Had he not been essential to Julius's plans, the Inquisition might have taken an interest in him.

For all of these reasons Father Simon had become suspicious and sought a duplicate key.

As a member of the Fabbrica di San Pietro, essentially the Vatican's housekeeping organization, no one would think it unusual to see Father Simon in the upper-floor halls of the east wing of the basilica, where many of the workmen were housed. It would not be strange should someone see him doing his job of inspecting the various living quarters.

Still, he paused outside the room, trying to probe the shadows of the corridor, a hallway largely sheltered from the fierce sun of a Roman summer. Once he was certain no one was in this part of the hallway, he inserted the key, fumbled for a moment and pushed the door open.

At first he saw nothing unusual. A bed across from a

small fireplace. At the foot was an oak chest, locked and bound in brass, no doubt to hold the ten ducats a month, the outrageous pay this man had demanded from His Holiness. A rough chair, a table littered with brushes, paint pots and pestles in which to grind pigment.

Then he stopped, unsure of what he was looking at. Figures, forms that . . .

Father Simon felt the back of his neck prickle. Surely he was not seeing what he thought.

Surely.

If so, this man was a heretic at best, a demon at worst.

This man who called himself only by his first name: Michelangelo.

II.

Jabal al-Tarif
Near Nag Hammaddi
Upper Egypt
December 1945

Muhammad 'Alf al-Salman and his brother Hassam Mustafa wanted revenge. Not only did family honor demand it, their grief at the murder of their father had become a hatred simmering like hot coals.

But first the *sabakh*, the soft soil used to fertilize the crops, make them grow in the dry, barren sand. They had ridden the two old camels out here to the mountain where they were using mattocks to dig around a boulder.

The daggerlike blade of Hassam's pick hit something harder than soil but substantially softer than rock. Both men knelt to use their hands to scoop away the surrounding dirt until they uncovered the neck of what looked like a large earthenware jar.

Hassam made a futile attempt to wipe the dust from his

beard. "Perhaps, brother, Allah has smiled upon us. Perhaps there is treasure inside. Else why would someone hide it here at the base of the mountain?"

Muhammad sat back on his haunches. As the older of the two, he made the important decisions. "Just as likely a jinn lives inside."

Ever since childhood, both men had heard stories about the evil spirits that had been captured by heros of old and confined to jars. Those foolish enough to let the malevolent creatures escape had usually lived to regret it.

Hassam pointed a jagged, dirt-encrusted fingernail at a spot just below the neck of the vessel. "But see, older brother, there is a crack. A jinn could have easily gotten out long ago."

Muhammad thought about this. More likely treasure than a jinn. Standing, he used his mattock to break open the jar.

It was instantly obvious the thing contained neither genie nor treasure. Instead, there were thirteen leather packets. Hope of instant riches quickly fading, the two men unwrapped each to find a number of crumbling papyrus books.

"I cannot read them," Hassam said, staring at the incomprehensible writing only dimly visible.

"Of course not," Muhammad snorted. "You cannot read."

"But these marks are unlike the writing I see in the marketplace. They must be in another language."

Muhammad glanced over his shoulder, seeing nothing but the familiar rolling dunes and craggy mountains. "They are old, very old."

"Perhaps their very age gives them value."

"Such old things are forbidden to keep."

Both men had heard stories of their fellow bedouins who had found objects of great age and, supposedly, greater value, only to have them confiscated before the finder could seek a sale to an antiquities dealer in Cairo.

Hassam grinned, showing as many empty sockets as teeth. "Forbidden only if the government knows."

Silently, the two began to fill the sleeves of their billowing robes with the codices.

Chapter One

I.

The British Museum
Bloomsbury
Great Russell Street
London
1842 Hours
Present Day

Langford Reilly was thankful his friend Jacob had insisted he buy a tuxedo for the occasion. From the cab's window, he could see that even a tailored business suit would leave him woefully underdressed. Every man was formally attired. Haute couture dictated the women's gowns. Dior, Chanel, Valentino and smaller houses were well represented in one-off garments that, along with the accompanying jewelry, represented the price of the average home.

All of the guests were invitees to what might be the venerable institution's premier event of the young century. Lang even thought he recognized the faces of a couple of film or television stars whose names he could not recall if, in fact, he had ever known them.

That was the thing about the glitterati: They came and went so fast, it seemed pointless to bother with names. Stardom, trouble with the law or the Politically Correct Police, rehab, cover of *People* magazine, descent to the front page of the tabloids and obscurity. The journey was as swift as it was predictable.

And it made way for new, heretofore unknown celebrities.

Climbing out of the taxi, Lang stopped and stood erect. The classical facade of the world's oldest public museum only hinted at the treasures inside. For years he had promised himself a full day to explore the museum's timeless riches rather than the few hurried hours he had stolen from periodic business trips to London.

There was a gentle push at his back. "Along with you, now, 'r we'll be missing the sodding presentation."

Lang turned, grinning. "Don't worry, they won't run out of champagne or caviar for hours, presentation or not."

Behind him was Jacob Annulewitz, barrister, longtime friend, confidant.

And former Mossad operative.

Son of Holocaust victims, Jacob had emigrated to Israel, serving his military obligation in the intelligence agency where he had met Lang here in London. Though a number of the foreign services were aware of Jacob's connection, few knew his actual specialty: explosives. With equal skill and equanimity, he could disarm a ticking time bomb or build a device that could blow someone's head off without spoiling his necktie.

Jacob returned the smile, a hint of mischief in it. "You're sure of that, are you?"

Lang reached back to pull Jacob abreast so the two could make their way through the tide of visitors entering the museum. "That's what Eon told me, anyway."

Eon.

Sir Eon Weatherston-Wilby, entrepreneur, investor and multibillionaire who had evaded England's near confiscatory taxes by making his fortune in more business-friendly climates. He headed a number of charitable institutions. In addition to his law practice, Lang ran a single nonprofit institution funded by arguably the world's wealthiest, though least known, corporation. The limited number of self-sustaining philanthropic institutions ensured the two men would meet. They had become mutually admiring acquaintances if not fast friends.

Jacob shook off Lang's hand and straightened his cummerbund. "He's the chap that should know. It's all his show tonight. But exactly what are we going to see?"

Lang stepped around a small man in tux jacket and kilts who was holding the hand of a woman wearing some sort of expensive fur. Not even the jacket concealed several strands of diamond necklace. The effect was like a fuzzy Christmas tree.

"Some of the missing Nag Hammaddi Library."

Jacob's immediate disinterest was apparent. "Bloody hell! You mean I got all frocked out to see something I can't even read just to rub elbows with a bunch of toffs? Besides, I can't imagine them looking like anything other than the bloody photographs I've already seen."

Lang stopped at the door to display an engraved invitation to an uniformed guard.

"You're thinking of the Dead Sea Scrolls."

"There's a difference?"

They entered the Great Court. Covered by a dome, it was London's first indoor public square.

"The Dead Sea Scrolls were scraps of parchment found in caves above Khirbet Qumran between 1947 and 1955. As far as is known, all wound up eventually at Hebrew University or Jordan's Palestine Archaeological Museum. Political and academic rivalries kept them from the public for decades."

Jacob snorted. "Cheeky academics! You'd think they'd want to disseminate knowledge, not fight over it like two sodding hounds with a single bone."

The observation was consistent with Lang's experience.

"Anyway, the Nag Hammaddi Library consists of a number of leather-wrapped writings found in Egypt in a jar by two Arabs. They were written in Coptic, that is, in the Egyptian language but with the Greek alphabet. Somehow the old parchment was in pretty good shape, although dating back to fourth-century Coptic Egypt. They took the bound books home and their mother used pages to start the family cooking fire. Seems the two guys were in trouble with the police for avenging their father's death and they were afraid the authorities would discover their find. So they sold a number of the volumes to a Cairo antiquities dealer."

Jacob's hands were restless, the idleness of a smoker denied his habit. Lang was thankful there were enough NO SMOKING signs posted to keep his friend's foul-smelling pipe in his pocket. Finally, Jacob helped himself from a passing tray of champagne flutes. "How many?"

"That's just it. No one knows how many of those near-priceless books there were to begin with."

Jacob smacked his lips, satisfied with the quality of the champagne. "And the subject matter of the books we do know about?"

"Apparent copies of some of the original Gospels, including some not in the Bible, the Gospel of Judas, for instance. This particular work is known as 'The Secret Gospel of James' because it supposedly contains secret revelations made to James by Jesus. There's also the Book of James, or protevangelium, which in many ways parallels the gospels of Luke and Matthew."

Jacob was already searching for another tray when a tall man with collar-length silver hair pushed his way through the crowd, hand extended. "Langford Reilly! I'm truly flattered you could make it to my little party!"

"Eon!" Lang smiled with genuine pleasure as he took the hand. "Wouldn't have missed it."

Particularly since he had business in London anyway.

He turned to Jacob. "This is my friend Jacob Annulewitz. I figured one more body wouldn't matter."

"Not at all," Eon said, shaking Jacob's hand. "Just water down the champers a bit. So what have you been up to?"

"Same old, same old," Lang replied. "Running the foundation and trying to keep my hand in with the law practice."

"Still doing . . . what do you call it? Ah, yes, the white-collar criminal defense. Making sure rich criminals never get their just desserts."

In a single motion, Jacob placed his empty glass on a tray and removed a full one. Eon and Lang helped themselves.

"Better to represent the rich and powerful," Lang observed good-naturedly, "than the poor and oppressed. They pay better. I didn't know you were in the antiquities business."

"Mere happenstance. I came across what might be the only existing parts of the Nag Hammadi Library not in the Coptic Egyptian Museum in Cairo." He shrugged modestly. "Seemed fitting to donate them to the British Museum."

More than fitting. Two centuries of colonialism had given the British ample opportunity to plunder the best of ancient Egyptian artifacts. For years, the Egyptian authorities had been trying to recover some of them, including the Rosetta stone and a colossus of Ramses II.

A bell tinkled behind them.

Eon turned his head. "Ah! My moment has arrived. Time to make the presentation."

"A brief one, I hope," Lang joked.

"I can promise you that, although I fear I can give no such pledge on behalf of the museum's curator."

He spun around on the heels of pumps for which at least one crocodile had perished. "The ceremony, such as it is, will take place in the special exhibit hall, room seventy, the one between here and the Reading Room."

Lang and Jacob merged with the crowd slowly filling a long, narrow room. In the center, a half moon of velvet cord separated an exhibit table covered with a white cloth. Behind the table Eon stood with a portly, bespectacled man whom Lang guessed was the potentially long-winded curator.

A smiling Eon was nodding to familiar faces in the crowd. He raised a hand. "May I have your attention, good people!"

The sound of conversation dimmed to a buzz, then there was silence.

"First, I want to thank—"

From somewhere behind him there was the unmistakable sound of a shot.

Lang and Jacob glanced at each other and began to move toward opposite sides of the room.

One of the uniformed guards stepped into the room, staggered and fell facedown across the velvet ropes. Immediately blood began to puddle from under his head.

A woman screamed.

Eon took a step back. "Bloody hell!"

Four men, two on each side of the room, appeared, each sweeping the room with pistols, each face covered with a black balaclava.

Wordlessly, they motioned the crowd back, including two helpless and unarmed guards. Eon and the curator were more than willing to step away from the draped display case.

The armed men's movements had clearly been choreographed. While two kept Eon's guests covered with their weapons, the other two snatched the cover from the case, removed the contents and slid them into a plastic trash bag before they backed toward the exit. Just before leaving the room, the two other men each took one of Eon's arms, pulling him with them.

There was a second of total silence before bedlam erupted. Everyone seemed to be shouting instructions to everyone else while a man and a woman rushed to the fallen guard. A battery of cell phones appeared. Lang doubted anyone could hear above the general clamor.

He and Jacob nodded to each other as they slid along the wall to the nearest exits in the direction the armed men had taken.

Lang peered around a corner into the Reading Room, restored to the Edwardian furnishings that had hosted the likes of Marx, Gandhi and George Bernard Shaw. Void of their daytime occupants, the empty chairs stood sentinel at the oak tables, casting rigid shadows in the faint overhead light.

At the far end, Lang saw a flicker of movement.

Jacob had seen it, too. He was moving in that direction.

Uncertain what he could do, Lang crossed the room, using the high-backed chairs for whatever cover they offered. The SIG Sauer P226 9mm, a souvenir of his agency days before the law practice, was resting uselessly in a bedside table an ocean away. Even if he had the prescience to bring it, how helpful would it have been against four armed men, with the possibility of hitting Eon? Still, he couldn't simply wring his hands and stand by doing nothing.

He wore his long-ago training like an old but much loved jacket. There were some things never forgotten. Back against the wall, careful not to give a clear target in the dim light nor present a silhouette. The dead guard was evidence that the men who had taken Eon had no reluctance to shoot. The guard had been unarmed, perhaps sacrificed to intimidate the guests. They surely wouldn't hesitate to take a shot at any pursuers.

Lang still had his back against a wall as he took a cautious peek around the next door.

The Egyptian Room. Jewelry, Coptic art, even a reconstruction of a chariot, its metal dully reflecting the indistinct low-wattage night-lights above. The thing was complete with reins and a quiver of javelins. Only the horses and men were missing.

Lang slid into the room.

The chamber reverberated with a shot and plaster inches from his head burst into shards that buzzed past like an angry swarm of bees, stinging his face.

Lang dived under the chariot just as another shot placed his assailant at the far end of the room.

Lang wished the Egyptians had been less efficient in constructing war machines. The cab of the chariot was barely large enough for a driver and archer or spearman. The front was mere framework. The ancient vehicle was constructed to be light and, therefore, fast. The corollary of the design was that it gave little or no cover.

And the man with the gun knew it.

There wasn't enough light to see the gunman but Lang could clearly hear footsteps on the marble floor, footsteps that reached the other side of Lang's scanty hiding place.

He searched what he could see of the exhibit hall for an escape route that would not make him a clear target.

There was none.

He was going to have to do something and do it now.

The footsteps paused and Lang moved.

Rolling from under the chariot, Lang sprang to his knees and shoved. The fragile cart tipped over.

Lang had a blurred vision of a man instinctively throwing a protective hand across his face.

The hand had a gun in it.

Just before the display shattered on the floor, Lang snatched at the quiver, grabbing one of the sharp-tipped spears with his left hand. After quickly transferring the weapon to his right, he drew his arm back to its full length then slung the shaft, shimmering and whining, through the air.

The gunman had risen to his knees, leveling his weapon when the bronze tip hit him squarely in the stomach. Lang heard two things: a shocked grunt and the sound of a butcher's cleaver hacking meat from a carcass.

The gunman dropped his pistol and staggered to his feet,

using both hands to grasp the long shaft. He had an expression of total disbelief as he sank back to the floor as though in prayer before pitching forward, snapping the lance's haft with the crack of old dry wood.

Lang made a dive for the gun, clutching it as he rolled over into darker shadows in case one of the man's companions was nearby.

There was silence for perhaps a second.

Then Jacob appeared, holding a curved sword with a notched tip peculiar to ancient Egypt. He looked down at the crumpled form and turned it over with his foot. "Dare say th' poor sod's the first to die from one of Pharaoh's spears in the last millennium or so."

Lang got to his feet. "Likely, but we need to find the others." He held up the gun, for the first time recognizing it as a Walther PPK, James Bond's weapon of choice. Dated and comparatively small bore but easily concealed. "At least we aren't unarmed anymore. Let's go!"

Jacob put a cautionary hand on Lang's arm. "Don't be so bloody hasty. The odds are still in those blokes' favor."

As quickly as caution would permit, they crossed the Egyptian exhibit and entered a large, empty room. A ceiling-high lifting door identified it as loading space. When he pushed on a smaller door under a lighted EXIT sign, Lang was surprised to find it unlocked.

Perhaps the way the gunmen had entered?

He stared out into Montague Place, the street at the rear of the museum. The sound of a car speeding away from the curb drew his attention to the outlines of the trees in Russell Square.

It was too dark to identify the make or model, but it had its lights out.

Lang exhaled heavily, like someone coming down from the adrenaline high of a losing race.

"They got the sodding book," Jacob said through teeth

now clenched around the forbidden pipe. "What th' bleedin' hell did they want with your friend Eon?"

Lang turned to go back into the building. He planned to check the body on the floor for identification, even though he was certain he would find none.

"I'm afraid we'll know soon enough," he said.

The body was, as anticipated, bare of identity.

Almost.

One packet contained a small wadded bit of paper. The dead man probably was unaware it was there. Lang spread it out on the cold marble of the floor next to the body, squinting in the stingy light.

"I suppose you found the lad's driving permit. Maybe his national health card." Jacob was peering over his shoulder.

Lang held it up. "Too faded to read, some kind of a card. A receipt, perhaps?"

Jacob sniffed. "Not likely the chit from the dining room at the Dorchester." He leaned closer, taking it in his hand. "Looks like . . . like part of a boarding pass."

"A boarding pass?"

"Yes." He turned to catch a different angle of light. "See, you can make out a date and a flight number."

"Swell. Now all we have to do is match an airline with it. Should be no more than a thousand or so scheduled carriers to check."

Jacob handed it back to Lang. "Your bleedin' gratitude is humbling. It's a sight better than nothing."

But not much.

II.

17 Paul Street
Wapping
London
1906 Hours

Inspector Dylan Fitzwilliam had expected the call ever since the immigration people had called him yesterday.

The American, Langford Reilly, was back in London. Every time Mr. Reilly had visited London, some sort of mayhem followed as surely as a contrail behind a jet aircraft. That was why the inspector had a standing request to be notified when Mr. Reilly's passport was swiped through the machine at Heathrow or Gatwick or he appeared under some other name on the face-recognition technology. Admittedly, Mr. Reilly had always been cleared of any crime but he bore watching just the same.

And now, like the bad penny, he was back.

Someone was going to die.

After finishing dinner and settling in front of the telly, Fitzwilliam had dared hope this once Mr. Reilly would depart the UK without coming to the attention of the police. After all, Reilly had been observed visiting some medical supply houses, no doubt on behalf of his foundation, and tonight seemed harmless enough, some affair at the British Museum. With any luck at all, the damn Yank would go back to wherever it was he came from before the bodies started piling up.

But that faint wish had evaporated like smoke the minute the telephone clattered.

A robbery and kidnapping?

Two casualties, one a guard employed by the museum and the other one of the kidnappers? He was less than surprised to learn the latter had died by Reilly's hand. And

Sir Eon Weatherston-Wilby was apparently kidnapped. One of the country's best-known philanthropists.

The media would be on this like another scandal at Buckingham Palace. The difference was that Scotland Yard didn't get pressure when one of the royals acted like Eurotrash.

The inspector felt a migraine coming on, that headache that only Langford Reilly seemed to precipitate.

He got up with a resigned sigh and went to the hall closet. Through the Sheetrock, he could hear the Wilsons arguing again on their side of the semidetached.

"Going out, dear?" Shandon, his wife, asked from the kitchen. "Will you be long?"

"I doubt I'll be any shorter," he replied glumly, the hoary joke they shared.

His mood was not improved when he had to wait a good quarter hour for Patel, his immediate assistant and driver, to pull to the curb. As usual, the man had filled the small BMW with the smell of curry. Nor did Ftizwilliam's disposition improve when the dark face broke into its perpetual grin as though the man enjoyed having his evenings interrupted.

"The British Museum, sah?"

Fitzwilliam swallowed a retort, realizing it would be lost on Patel. "Yes, yes. The museum."

Two blocks of Great Russell Street and Montague Place were blocked off with yellow crime scene tape as was all of Russell Square. Floodlights illuminated the small park with a harsh glare, the edges of which blended into the blue and red flashes of police cars. If anyone in Bloomsbury didn't already know a crime had been committed, they had to be blind and deaf.

Inside, the uniforms had prevented anyone from leaving, a splendid case of securing the barn door long after the horse's departure. Two policemen were seated at a small table in the great court, taking names and addresses of possible witnesses whose interviews would consume days.

"Where's Mr. Reilly?" Fitzwilliam asked one of the constables at the door.

The man pointed. "Right over there, sir."

Fitzwilliam had never seen the man in person before but recognized him from his image on the cameras at Heathrow as well as at least one wanted poster from a foreign country. He watched as a short, redheaded woman in a police uniform took down whatever was being said.

The American was not as tall as the inspector had imagined, shy of two meters. Dark hair with dove wings of silver brushed over the ears. His tuxedo had obviously been tailored; it fit him perfectly. He seemed intent on what he was saying, completely unruffled by killing a man. With a spear, if Fitzwilliam's information was correct.

The man next to him was the Jewish barrister, Annulewitz, pipe in his mouth despite the NO SMOKING signs. Shorter, balding and going to fat. Fitzwilliam had gotten the impression the relationship between the two exceeded a professional one. It had been outside Annulewitz's flat that Reilly had once killed two anonymous thugs, although the fact was never proved. A couple of years later, Reilly had escaped from Annulewitz's law office at the Temple Bar leaving Fitzwillam's men looking foolish indeed.

Lang was just finishing his third recitation of the evening's events when a man in a worn tweed jacket wandered over, the only man he could see without either a tux or a police uniform.

"Inspector Dylan Fitzwilliam," the stranger introduced himself.

Lang extended a hand. "Lang Reilly."

The inspector glanced at the extended hand as though it might explode and stuck his own into his jacket pockets. "I'd appreciate you walking me through what happened."

The man's tone implied he was giving an order, not asking a favor.

"Sure." Lang pointed. "The table where those two police officers are taking names was in the room between here and the Reading Room. Eon was standing—"

"You mean Sir Eon Weatherston-Wilby."

What was the thing the Brits had about titles? Maybe it was the only part of their former nobility that was still noble rather than ammunition for the tabloids.

Lang finished his narrative.

"Perhaps you would be so kind as to take me to room four, the Egyptian exhibit."

Again, more of an order than a request.

A photographer was finishing up taking pictures of a chalk outline on the floor. A janitorial employee, mop in one hand, bucket in another, was waiting to remove what was now a congealed black puddle of blood. The wreckage of the chariot had already been removed, presumably to wherever the museum did restorations.

Fitzwilliam rested an elbow in the palm of one hand while he rubbed his chin thoughtfully with the other. "You attacked an armed man with only a spear?"

"I didn't have a lot of options."

"Why didn't you wait for the police like everyone else?"

Lang detected what could be a tone of accusation. "Because I didn't want them to get away with Eon. Sir Eon."

"Just what made you think they were going to take him farther than this building?"

Lang watched the photographer pack up his equipment. "Why would they take him from where he was otherwise?"

"But they were armed. What did you think you could do?"

Lang was getting irritated at what seemed pointless interrogation. "Ask the man your folks just peeled off the floor there."

Fitzwilliam caught the edge in the reply and changed the subject as well as location. "Let's take a look at the loading door, shall we?"

The door was wide-open, revealing several officers searching the street as well as the square.

"These doors aren't the kind that open from the inside when locked," Fitzwilliam observed.

Having noticed that previously, Lang said nothing.

"That would indicate they were left unlocked, quite likely intentionally."

Lang still said nothing.

Fitzwilliam was scratching his chin again. "What do you make of that, Mr. Reilly?"

"Too bad you can't ask the guard they shot."

The inspector's hands dropped to his side. "Meaning?"

"Meaning someone had to let them in. Killing that someone is the one sure way to make sure nobody knows who they are."

Fitzwilliam nodded slowly. This American might cause trouble, but he didn't miss much, either. "I don't suppose you have a thought as to the identity of the dead man?"

Involuntarily, Lang's hand slid into his pocket, touching the crumpled piece of paper, the half of the boarding pass if that was really what it was. He instantly decided not to mention it. Information was the capital of his former profession with the agency: once spent it became useless.

"Not a clue."

III.

New Mermaid Inn
High Street
Rye
East Sussex
The Next Morning

Jenny Fasting never understood why someone as wealthy as Langford Reilly would choose to stay in a hotel as old as this one. The ceilings were low, the floors uneven, the doorways crooked and the mullioned windows mostly opaque. She had asked him once and he had replied that if the place had been good enough for Elizabeth Tudor, it was good enough for him. Of course, it had been a bit newer when Good Queen Bess had paid a visit to Rye to inquire about an inconsistent source of fish. That was before the river's mouth had silted up, ending Rye's place as a major harbor and fishing center. The inn had been almost new when the Queen visited, having replaced the former Mermaid Inn after the French had staged a surprise raid and burned a good part of the town as well as the hotel. Jenny was fairly certain Elizabeth I had never actually stayed here, though.

That was the thing about the Yanks: they worshiped the old, even old buildings in advanced states of dilapidation. Yanks. A word she understood her boss, Lang Reilly, did not appreciate for reasons that had to do with a dispute over there in America more than a hundred years ago. Something about a War of Northern Aggression. Whatever that was.

Another thing about the Yanks, er, Americans: they were always in a hurry. That was why she had been awakened after midnight last night by a call from London. Mr. Reilly wanted her to meet him in the small laboratory facility his foundation had set up in Rye to serve the institution's needs in the British Isles. Cheaper than London with considerably less traffic. In fact, Rye's main street was still cobblestoned with half-timbered houses just as though the Queen might return.

If he had asked her to meet him anywhere other than the laboratory, she might have been able to fantasize some sort of romantic liaison. Although Mr. Reilly had never been anything more than polite at both the meetings she had with him, he was, after all, single and quite good-looking. And rich. Not the type to show any interest in a drab lab tech like Jenny.

She ran her fingers nervously through limp hair the color of dead grass. One of these days she would replace the thick glasses with that new eye surgery. In the meantime, she would continue to look like just what she was: a lab boffin. A *single* lab boffin.

And there was nothing romantic about being called out of bed to put some stub of paper under an electronic microscope, read it and make a legible copy by breakfast. That was hardly her job. She dealt with the arcana of chemical biology. But Mr. Reilly *was* the boss and if he wanted a jillion pounds sterling worth of gadgetry used to examine a piece of paper, so be it. An airline boarding pass, at that. Seemed he could simply call the airline if he had somehow managed to damage his bleeding boarding pass.

But he was the boss.

That was why she was sitting in the dining room of the New Mermaid, sipping tea that tasted like it had been brewed some time in the distant past, waiting for Lang Reilly.

He appeared on the dot of 8:00, disgustingly wide-awake. He slid into the seat across the table from her, wished her a good morning and ordered kippers and eggs from the innkeeper.

Jenny wondered if anyone, Lang Reilly included, really took pleasure in staring eye to eye with a smoked herring first thing in the morning. Although the dish was as English as afternoon tea, the sight and smell of a dead fish at breakfast was, well, disgusting. Why couldn't he simply have bangers and mash like a working-class sod? Even so, she could not tear her sight away as he deftly stripped the backbone and its comblike rack from the rest of the fish.

"So, what did you find out?" he asked.

Although she knew exactly what she had found, she dug

in her purse and extracted an enlarged copy. "Aegean Air flight 162, seat 24-B. Either the twenty-third or twenty-fifth of last month. The paper was too badly worn to be sure."

He reached for the paper. "Any idea from where to where?"

She shook her head. "I couldn't get a real soul at Aegean Air this early, only serial recordings, but I'll be happy to . . ."

If Jenny had her way, the hottest place in hell would be reserved for whoever invented voice mail and those infuriating mechanical queries that only lead to another.

He smiled as he sectioned a piece of fish. "No need. You've done your job and thanks. You'll find a little gift in your next paycheck."

"Oh, Mr Reilly," she protested, "you don't have to . . ."

She stopped in midsentence. The man at the next table was clearly listening although he was using a copy of the day's *Times* as a prop to conceal his interest. What Jenny was saying sounded like . . . sounded like something quite different than an employer speaking to an employee. She felt herself flush at what the eavesdropper must be thinking.

Lang silenced her with a hand. "Don't deprive an old man of his pleasures."

Pleasures? Old man? She'd give anything to . . . The thought made her blush even more.

"Thank you," she managed.

Fifteen minutes later in his room, Lang stared without comprehension at the copy Jenny had given him. Through long mastery of the corporate telephone maze, he had reached a living, breathing person at Aegean Air. The flight in question had been an A (Airbus) 320-200 from Rhodes to Athens. No, privacy policy forbade disclosing the name of the passenger occupying that specific seat.

A quick call to the States produced a sleepy, "Yeah . . . ?"

"Jimmy?" Lang asked.

"You're calling at fucking two o'clock in the mornin' and you're not sure you have the right person?"

If personality were his only asset, Jimmy Edge would be unemployable. Fortunately, Jimmy was a geek without peer. Unfortunately, his skills were far more useful on the wrong side of the law. Hacking into and altering bank records in his favor had proved far more lucrative than programming corporate computers. Lang had successfully negotiated a plea deal on Jimmy's behalf by which the hacker had provided a complete list of his victims in exchange for probation. The United States attorney had howled like a wounded animal at the court's leniency, but, as one of the larger financial institutions admitted, without Jimmy's help there was little chance their electronic records could be straightened out for years.

"Good morning to you, too," Lang said cheerfully. "I've got a job for you."

"Swell," Jimmy growled, recognizing Lang's voice. "Most of my clients operate during the daylight hours."

"Most of your clients don't operate well in any kind of light, day or otherwise. You got a pencil handy?"

It took less than ten minutes before Jimmy called Lang back.

"He connected from Athens to Rome. Dead end," he announced without preamble. "Passenger's name was Frangelli, address and phone number in Rome. Contact number belongs to a prepaid cell, address is on the Corso. Doesn't exist. No record of Frangelli ever having flown Aegean Air or any major carrier I could call up in a hurry and he's not on Google or any US or European credit records. I'd say you got yourself a real fictional character this time."

"Contact number in Rhodes or Athens?"

"Same cell."

Lang thought a moment. "Thanks, Jimmy. I get any more info, I'll be in touch."

"I can't wait."

Lang terminated the call on his BlackBerry, thoughtful as he put the device back into his pocket. A passenger with no name, a flight between two points so far irrelevant to anything Lang knew. Information, though, could be like a good wine: it increased both in value and quality in time.

IV.

Piazza dei Cavalieri di Malta
Aventine Hill
Rome
Two Hours Later

Gravel crunched as the two men walked side by side along the path. Twin lines of cypress trees pointed like an arrow to the Vatican a mile or so away, creating one of Rome's most famous optical illusions: the trees excluded any lateral view, making the basilica appear to retreat as the observer moved forward.

The piazza had not been open to the public for years.

Neither man was remotely interested in the view, mirage or not.

"Who is this man who cost us one of our brothers?" the elder of the two asked in Italian.

The other man replied in the same language. His accent made it clear it was not his first tongue. "From the guest list, we found it to be an American lawyer named Reilly. He also heads a charitable foundation apparently named after his deceased sister and nephew. He joined the military right out of college and there is nothing but routine payroll records until he entered in law school six years later."

The older man gave a derisive snort. "I doubt he learned

how to use a spear in such a lethal manner in the regular military. Or in law school."

The younger man nodded. "Our council brothers who saw him say he moved like someone familiar with combat, a professional. Fortunately, our brother in charge assigned someone to follow this Reilly person. He went south from London to Rye, where we discovered his foundation has facilities. Apparently he has found some evidence of Brother Lucci's recent journey to Rhodes, the stub of a boarding pass. He was discussing it in a hotel dining room."

The older man's head snapped up. "What else could he deduce from a boarding pass?"

"The reservations were made under an alias, all contact points untraceable."

"But Reilly has the assets to ascertain such a trip was made. Such a man could be a danger. If he discovers our ancient relationship with the island, it could lead him to us."

"We will watch him closely, Grand Master."

The senior thought for a moment. "And what did he have to do with Weatherston-Wilby?"

"As far as we can tell, they only knew each other through their charitable works. I regret I do not have more precise answers to your questions."

The older man gave a chilly smile. "Considering the little time you have had to gather information, you have done well."

"Our brothers are worldwide and cooperative. What are your wishes?"

His companion thought for perhaps fifteen seconds. "This man Reilly could be dangerous. See to it."

Chapter Two

I.

Excerpt from the *London Times*:

Kidnapping Victim Stoned

LONDON—Scotland Yard announced today a grisly discovery next to St. Paul's Cathedral: the body of Sir Eon Weatherston-Wilby, who had been kidnapped the previous evening from the British Museum during a robbery at an affair sponsored by Weatherston-Wilby celebrating his donation of several ancient manuscripts from Egypt.

Police sources who declined to be identified stated the badly bruised body had apparently been thrown from an upper-story window and then subjected to trauma from blunt objects, quite possibly stones found nearby. Police are investigating the significance of a scallop shell placed on the victim's body, possibly by the killers.

An autopsy is under way. Whether the victim survived the fall and was alive at the time of the possible stoning has yet to be determined as has any motive for the kidnapping and murder.

Inspector Dylan Fitzwilliam said, "I doubt the motive was entirely robbery. Since the manuscripts are related to a murder, they would be difficult to sell on the open market."

The inspector did not exclude the possibility the theft was a "contract" job, that is, that the robbers were commissioned by a collector who wished the manuscripts for himself.

The British Museum declined to place a value on the stolen objects.

The abduction of Weatherston-Wilby took place . . .

II.

Delta Flight 1701
Gatwick-Atlanta

Lang Reilly reread the article for the third time. He had only seen it because the airline's supply of *USA Today* had not been delivered prior to the first leg of the Atlanta-London-Atlanta trip the 777 would make that day. For that matter, Lang usually took the foundation's Gulfstream IV to the UK purely as a protest against the Labour government's latest manifestation of wealth envy, a $250 tax on first-class seats.

Right up there in the league with abolishing foxhunting.

The remonstration had been impossible this trip. The Gulfstream's annual inspection was in process and the aircraft grounded for at least a week.

A flight attendant, regulation smile painted across her face, dangled a steaming hot towel in front of him. Without thought, he murmured his thanks and took it.

Lang spread the hot towel across his face as though preparing for an old-fashioned barbershop shave before dropping it on the wide seat divider.

He was lost in thought when the other attendant with an identical smile retrieved it.

Why kill Eon?

If the texts were the point of the robbery, murder made no sense. If for some reason they wanted Eon dead, why take the books? If Eon were complicit in the theft, the thieves might want to eliminate him, but why would he arrange to steal something he was donating? Unless the robbers feared identification, killing Eon was pointless. Lang examined his memory like a student reviewing a text for a final exam. Had Eon given any evidence of recognition? If so, Lang had missed it.

No, none of the possible solutions so far was the correct one.

The only clue was throwing a man from St. Paul's and then stoning him to death if he wasn't already dead. The only purpose for that exercise had to be to send a message.

But what?

And to whom?

Lang slid down the window shade and reclined his seat to the full extent. Perhaps he could get a little sleep before the airline committed the gastronomic atrocity known euphemistically as "an in-flight meal." The only purpose served by airline food, Lang mused, was to ensure the British did not have the world's worst.

He closed his eyes but the vision of Eon being led away would not fade. He hadn't exactly put up a fight but he hadn't gone willingly, either. Lang tried to banish the thought but it was as stubborn as one of Atlanta's panhandlers.

Admitting defeat, he sat up and thumbed through a paperback he had bought at the airport, well aware of his inability to sleep on airplanes. He knew the compulsion to be alert at all times was irrational. If something went seriously south at 37,000 feet, there wasn't a lot he could do about it, awake or asleep.

He began the book, hoping it would banish Eon for the moment.

III.

Park Place
2660 Peachtree Road
Atlanta, Georgia
That Evening

His single suitcase at his feet, Lang was fumbling in his pocket for the key to his condominium. Once inside, he'd take a shower and head for the kennel where Grumps, arguably the world's ugliest dog, would be impatiently waiting.

Why the mutt was so eager to leave what appeared to be, by canine standards, luxurious digs, Lang never knew. Plus the fact the dog always put on a pound or two.

Lang's hand closed around his key ring.

He slipped the brass key into the lock, turned and eased the door open.

Simultaneously, he smelled the strong odor of gas and there was an audible click, a sound like someone snapping a cigarette lighter.

He may have imagined seeing a spark but there was one, visible or not.

Instinctively, he lunged backward, pulling the door shut but not soon enough.

An explosion was accompanied by heat, a burning, searing monster that tried to devour him as it flung him across the hall and against the far wall as easily as a child might toss away a rag doll.

He never heard the snap of bones the impact caused.

IV.

Henry Grady Memorial Hospital
Trauma & Burn Unit
Butler Street
Atlanta, Georgia
Three Weeks Later

Lang was dead.

He was sure.

Otherwise, why would he be visited by the persons he knew were deceased?

On the other hand, being dead meant an end to pain, right? His pain was far from at an end. Sometimes he ached and burned over every inch of his body; at others he could localize his suffering to a leg, an arm, his back. The pain was always red, blurring his dim sight like a curtain of misery that separated him from whatever world he was in, either real or ephemeral.

The only real thing was the pain.

It was like a slowly rising and receding tide. At times he could get his head above it, see the universal light that blinded and feel the agony wash over him. It was all featureless, soundless red. Then, he would be pulled back under into a wet, warm stygian black he had begun to think of as "the Womb," a place where there was no discomfort, only a mellowness and a sensation of floating in space.

That was where the dead were.

As though in a fever dream, he saw his cubicle at the agency's Frankfurt station: a dim, grimy building across from the *Bahnhof*, where he had spent the bulk of his career. He had graduated from college with a liberal arts degree that, outside of academe, proved worthless. When he was looking around for a job, the agency had a certain appeal: lurking in the shadows of Eastern European cities while countering the machinations of beautiful spies . . .

The experience had proved to be more Dilbert than Bond.

After months of training, Lang had been assigned not to Operations but to Intelligence. Instead of glamour and excitement, his daily chores included monitoring a number of Eastern European newspapers and telecasts.

With a single exception, he had never ventured from friendly soil.

Then he had met Dawn, the woman who became his love, his soul mate and his wife. The collapse of the Evil Empire had meant cutbacks in the agency's budget and resulting reductions in force. It had been to please Dawn, though, he had quit the agency and gone to law school. A small matter. He would have invaded hell had she asked.

Once his law practice began to blossom, Dawn declined. A loss of appetite and weight resulted in a visit to the doctor and a death sentence. Lang had watched the daily dying of a woman in her early thirties as she metastasized into a wrinkled crone, a sack of bones with claws for hands. He had visited her hours a day, making promises and plans they both knew would never be kept.

She died with him at her bedside, her cold face shimmering through the tears he made no effort to staunch.

He fell into a hole every bit as black as the one into which he now sank.

But Dawn was here. Not the pitiful skeleton his wife had become but the full-bodied beautiful girl he had married. She whispered in his ear, sorrowful at his pain and reluctant to leave him.

He would have liked to have joined her.

Then there was Janet, his sister, and Jeff, her adopted son, both dead, murdered in Paris. Across the void, he heard her laugh, scoffing at life's inconsistences. Jeff still had his baseball cap on backward, was still clad in drooping shorts that almost reached his ankles. Forever Lang's ten-year-old best pal and frequent coconspirator against the established order.

They both seemed glad to see him.

Do the dead enjoy?

Then there were the people who were alive. At least, he thought they were.

They came only when Lang had his head above the dark tide, when he was in so much pain he could see them only through eyes he could barely open, hear not at all though they seemed to be speaking.

He was fairly certain some of them weren't even there.

Francis, the black priest, Janet's former confessor and Lang's best friend, was there more likely than not, his prayers doing Lang about as much good as they had Janet and Jeff. But Lang appreciated him coming even if visitation of the sick was part of the priest shtick anyway.

Sara, his secretary, came less frequently, for which Lang was grateful. The first two times, she dissolved into tears and had to be led away by a woman in white. The next couple of times she tried to speak but Lang could hear nothing. He was vaguely aware he had an office and a law practice that needed some sort of attention and that was probably where Sara went, but it all seemed very far away, remote from the black tides that engulfed him.

And he was probably dead anyway.

Then there was Gurt, the one he was fairly certain wasn't really there. A couple of years after Dawn died, Lang had been in Rome and taken up where he had left off with Gurt Fuchs, a German national and coworker at the agency.

Tall, blonde and looking like a travel poster for her native country, she moved through a crowd making men stare and women jealous. She had taken temporary leave from the agency to come to Atlanta and she and Lang had lived together for a year or so. Lang had dreamed of marriage and the family he had not had with Dawn. Gurt was not interested. She inexplicably announced she was going back to work in Europe. He had not seen her since.

Not till now anyway.

If she was really there.

Which he doubted.

Either way, they had exchanged more wisecracks than statements of affection. If he could, he would tell her how much he had loved her, although romantic conversation was hardly his forte or hers.

Now it might be too late.

Either Gurt in the flesh or as a chimera would enter the lenslike edge of his vision and stand at the foot of his bed, speaking words that to him were only silence. She hadn't aged since he last saw her, a time span he simply was unable to calculate, so it was unlikely she was real. Reinforcing the idea even more was the child that grasped her hand, a blond little boy with eyes the color of corn-flowers.

There was something vaguely familiar about him, al-though Lang's pain-racked brain simply refused to figure out what. He peered at Lang with the curiosity a child might display toward an insect specimen skewered on pins in an exhibit box.

Then the White Angel would appear and Gurt and the child would leave.

The White Angel, the woman whose face changed fre-quently but who always presaged Lang's return to the Womb.

Lang had no idea how long he had been slipping from one world to the next. He only knew he woke up one morn-ing, really woke up. He could hear voices and footsteps outside his room, fuzzy but sound nonetheless. He could see without the blurred edges at the perimeters of his vision. He recognized smells of a hospital, antiseptic, starch and, he thought, pain.

Father Francis Narumba sat next to the bed in full

priestly regalia, reading what Lang could see was the sports section of the Atlanta paper.

"How're the Braves doing?" Lang asked, the first words he could remember since . . . well, since he wound up here.

Wherever "here" was.

Francis looked up, as startled as if one of the icons on his altar had spoken.

Perhaps more so.

"God be praised! I thought . . ." He smiled. *"Debitum naturae."*

Debt to nature, Latin euphemism for death.

Francis was also what Lang described as a victim of a liberal arts education. Lang and the priest made a game of Latin aphorisms.

"Debemur mori nos nostraque," Lang replied, surprised how easily he did so.

Francis put down the paper and came to stand over the bed. "Horace was right: we and our works may be destined for death, but it looks like you aren't quite due yet."

Lang struggled to sit up only to find he was too weak. That was when he discovered the tubes stuck into the back of his hand.

Francis gently pushed him against the pillows. "Take it easy! *Te hominem esse memento!"*

The line a slave always whispered into a conquering general's ear as he rode a chariot through Rome's streets in a triumph; remember, you are but mortal.

"I may only be human, but I've been here . . . how long?"

"Nearly a month."

"I need to get out and—"

"And what? At the moment you aren't strong enough to get out of bed."

"What happened? I had just come back from England . . ."

"Likely you left the gas on your stove on. When you opened the door, something sparked."

Lang had no trouble remembering his last night before departing for London. He had dropped Grumps off at the kennel and met Alicia Warner, an assistant US attorney and fairly regular date for almost a year, for dinner at a Thai restaurant. The relationship was definitely on the wane. He had the feeling both of them were simply going through the motions before ending it.

The fact she had been kidnapped a year ago in an effort to lure Lang to his death hadn't exactly helped matters.

Lang banished her from his thoughts.

"Grumps?" he asked.

Francis shook his head slowly, not managing to suppress the ghost of a smile. "In an act of Christian charity, I took him in. He repays me by howling at choir practice, snapping at the chairperson of the women's auxiliary and raiding the garbage at the feed-the-poor soup kitchen."

"Centuries of persecution have made us heretics a surly lot. *Vivit post funera virtus.*"

"My deeds may survive the grave but I question if they will survive the bishop."

Lang's ribs ached when he chuckled but it felt good anyway. The fact Francis would give shelter to a mad dog rather than see it put down wouldn't stop him from complaining about being bitten.

He became serious again.

The stove. He hadn't used it the night before he left and he surely would have smelled gas when he came home that night if it had been on.

Then . . . ?

"You were lucky," Francis observed. "For reasons I can't imagine, the angels were watching over you. Somehow you managed to get the apartment door between you and most of the blast. That kept you from burns that would have been fatal. You wound up with surprisingly few burns, but significant internal injuries and broken bones. Happily your skull was too thick to fracture, saving possible brain damage."

Lang smiled weakly. "I'm not sure if I'm being diagnosed or insulted."

The priest glanced at his watch. "I've got a midday prayer service to do but I'll be back this evening."

"That a threat or promise?"

This time Francis chuckled. "Careful or I'll have the folks at Manuel's cater you a meal."

Manuel's Tavern. Quite possibly the funkiest bar in town, the pair's favorite watering hole despite spectacularly bad food. It was a place the Zagat's people would hire Michael Shumacher to drive them past.

"I'll bet the chow here makes Manuel's taste good."

Francis opened the door. "A true miracle."

"Oh, Francis?"

The doorknob in his hand, the priest turned, a question on his face.

"Gurt. I dreamed of Dawn and Janet and Jeff, a number of people who . . . who aren't here anymore. But Gurt . . . she seemed real enough. Did she . . . ?"

Francis face became immobile, the expression of someone unwilling to speak. "She's real enough."

"But . . . ?"

"I'll see you later."

Francis was gone.

More of a retreat than an exit.

V.

Two Days Later

The White Angel propped Lang up enough to eat the equally unappetizing and unrecognizable meal from his bed tray. Its mere appearance made Lang nostalgic for the feeding tube that had been removed just that morning. With totally unjustifiable enthusiasm, she set it before him: there was some sort of mystery meat, into the origins of which Lang feared to inquire, green goo that might at one time have been string beans and a sickly sweet red mass he guessed was Jell-O.

He had discovered a cuisine to rank below airline food.

But it was food, the first he could actually eat rather than absorb through a plastic line.

"Doctor will be so pleased when he makes his rounds," she cooed. "You've really made a remarkable recovery."

"Doctor" was spoken in the same tone as she might have referred to the Deity.

Lang shoved the tray away, surprised at how much of the stuff he had eaten. "That mean I'm going home?"

She looked almost hurt at the suggestion. "Home?"

"You know, the place we sleep at night, keep our stuff. Usually a house or apartment."

She took the tray. "I'd guess you'll be moved out of the trauma and burn ward, probably to a private hospital."

Grady was publicly funded. Unlike most institutions in which the Atlanta/Fulton County government had a hand, it somehow managed to accomplish its function despite continual budget overruns, accusations of racism from both sides, scandals, mismanagement that would make Larry, Curly and Moe look like geniuses and a bureaucracy that could stifle a hurricane.

It did, however, have the area's premier trauma and burn centers and provided practical experience to the residents of both Emory and Morehouse medical schools.

No matter what its qualities, Lang didn't intend to re-main a guest any longer than he had to. And he certainly didn't plan a lengthy convalescence at a private hospital. "But I need to . . ."

The White Angel exited, tray in hand, leaving him to stare at the open door.

It seemed almost preplanned. Seconds after her exit a

slender black man in a suit walked in. "Unnerstan' you doin' much better, Mr. Reilly."

Franklin Morse, Detective Franklin Morse, Atlanta Police Department. He and Lang had a history.

"Who snitched, the nurse?"

Morse made himself at home in the chair Francis had occupied. "Now, that ain' a friendly way to start a conversation, Mr. Reilly."

"I don't recall any of our conversations being particularly friendly, Detective."

Morse sprung out of the chair and began inspecting a list of regulations posted on the back of the door. The man rarely sat still, Lang remembered. His age was at best a guess but he had the build of one of those African marathon runners. Lang would have bet he had run more than one felon down on foot.

Morse spun around to face the bed. "You prolly don' recall any time we had a conversation when there wasn't some sorta mayhem goin' on. Folks jumpin' outta your condo, gettin' murdered, blowin' up your car, stuff like that. Take a whole precinct to keep up with you, Mr. Reilly. Now yo' condo's exploded."

Lang knew the man was perfectly capable of speaking English instead of the dialect he usually chose. "Gas. They say I left the gas on."

The detective flopped back into the chair. "Thass what they say. Question I got, you leave the gas on, why wire a fire starter to the latch?"

Lang stared wide-eyed. "Fire starter?"

"Y'know, one of them gadgets you get what you pull the trigger an' it lights up to start yo' charcoal or fire. Get 'em in any hardware store."

Lang didn't have to think long about the implications of that.

"You found the fire starter?"

"Arson 'vestigator did. What was left of it. Sum'bitch fixed up so's you turns a key and disengage the lock, it clicks. Time you push the door open . . . Boom! A blast furnace. 'Fraid everythin' you had in there is so much ash."

"So you think someone's trying to kill me."

"Don' think it's an April Fool's prank. Lucky it didn't take out none o' your neighbors."

"No one was hurt?"

"'Cept you. Made dust outta the crystal collection the lady 'bove you had, though. Like usual, I don' s'pose you got even a guess who the perp might be."

Lang shook his head. "You're right."

Morse was on his feet again. "This ain' no game, Mr. Reilly. Whoever done that, he gonna try again. Nex' time you might not be the only person hurt."

Lang gestured around the room. "If they were going to try again, this would be the perfect time and place. I've been pretty helpless."

The detective had his back to the room, staring out of the window. From somewhere below, an ambulance's siren wailed. He could hear the mechanical grinding of a garbage truck's insatiable appetite. "Thass why I had a coupla men stationed on this floor."

"I appreciate that, Detective."

Morse turned to face him. "Wasn't you I was worried 'bout, Mr. Reilly. I jes' wanted to make sure nobody here got kilt."

Lang sank back into the embrace of the pillows. "How thoughtful."

Morse shook his head. "Sumpthin' 'bout you. Mr. Reilly, you piss off the wrong people. I jus' wanna find out who 'fore the next body arrives."

"I'm truly touched."

Morse shot a glance Lang couldn't read. "Jus' 'member, Mr. Reilly, this ain' Dodge City. I catch you even spittin' on the street, you are so busted."

"I'll bear that in mind."

"Be sure you do, Mr. Reilly."

Morse didn't look back as he left.

With extra effort, Lang reached the TV remote on the table beside his bed. Reruns of *Everybody Loves Raymond* and *Seinfeld*. Silliness met with canned laughter. A game show and a cooking lesson. The two twenty-four-hour news channels were recounting the latest episode in the life of a movie star Lang had never heard of.

He turned it off.

He'd been right: he hadn't left the gas on. Someone had tried to kill him. Whoever had kidnaped and killed Eon would be a likely culprit. They had moved quickly, putting a plan into play within twenty-four hours and across an ocean. Whoever they were, they had international ties. The thought didn't make him feel any better.

He reached for the phone to call Sara and ask her to go to his place and bring him the SIG Sauer. He took his hand back. If what Morse said was correct, the weapon was likely so much twisted metal.

He needed a replacement and he needed it fast.

Without it, his life depended on the protection of the Atlanta Police Department, the Keystone Kops who had mistakenly shot and killed a ninety-two-year-old woman when the SWAT team had raided the wrong house in a drug bust, who had arrested and roughed up a visiting college professor for jaywalking and who, more than once, had put 911 callers on hold.

No thanks.

Weak or not, he had to get out of here.

Problem was, he was wired in. Two tubes in the back of one hand and a catheter. The two in his hand were easily removed but the other . . . ?

He was reaching for the buzzer to summon the nurse when his hand froze in midair.

He must be hallucinating again.

Gurt stood in the doorway.

Just under six feet, long blonde hair reached below her shoulders. With large, firm breasts, wasplike waist and shapely legs, she had a figure most twenty-somethings would envy.

The same small boy from Lang's supposed dreams stood at her side, his blue eyes locked onto Lang's.

"It was said you might die," Gurt announced, immobile in the doorway.

"Sorry to disappoint you."

Gurt was impervious to sarcasm. It was part of her Germanic nature. "Why sorry? It does me glad."

"I'm glad you've come back."

"I came because I wanted Manfred to at least see his father."

She gently pushed the boy forward.

"His father?"

"Lang, close your mouth. It is most unattractive hanging open."

Now Lang realized why the child had something familiar about him. His face was a small, youthful reproduction of his own.

Lang couldn't take his eyes off the boy who was standing next to the bed, regarding him as though trying to memorize what he saw. "But I don't . . . I couldn't . . . You never . . ."

Gurt seated herself in the chair, fished in a purse the size of a small suitcase and produced a pack of Marlboros. "I left because I was pregnant. I did not want what you call a marriage of a shotgun."

Gurt's mastery of the American idiom was less than complete.

"Shotgun wedding," Lang corrected.

"Why would someone marry a shotgun?"

Lang shook his head impatiently. "You knew I wanted to marry you. That's why it hurt so bad when you left me. I mean, I just turned around one day and you were gone . . ."

His voice trailed off as he remembered his shock and sorrow. Hell, he ought to be angry with this woman who had thought so little of his feelings. He ought to . . .

Whatever.

He was so glad to see her, even more astonished and delighted his dreams of a family might materialize long after he had abandoned them, that his joy would permit no anger. He shook his head slowly, making sure this scene wasn't the result of painkillers.

A son!

He had despaired of ever seeing Gurt again, of having a child of his own. Pain or not, he would have chosen a dozen more broken bones as the price of the elation he felt. Despite his desire for a family, he had always viewed the alleged joy of parenthood as suspect. Midnight feedings, projectile vomiting, nasty diapers. In seconds he had become a believer, a transformation more miraculous than any politician's hundred and eighty degree change of position.

And look at him! Already handsome, intelligence glittering from those blue eyes. In an instant he forgave Gurt the pain of her disappearance, her refusal to consider marriage and anything else she might ever have done or do in the future. He knew it was irrational but he didn't care. He knew it was love for the family that had appeared as though from behind a magician's cape. It was not a time to be rational.

Involuntarily, he reached for the boy, to touch him, to make sure this was no drug-induced dream. The tubes stopped his arms short. The boy, Manfred, stepped into the embrace without hesitation. Lang felt even more delight at the touch of his son's skin, the rigidity of his bones, the knowledge this flesh was of his own.

Ignoring the sign above her head that proclaimed Grady was a smoke-free environment, Gurt lit up, sending a jet of blue smoke into the air. Lang was too happy to chide her about her habit in general and the locale in which she was giving in to it in particular.

She leaned back in the chair. "When I left you, I did not want you to know I had pregnant. I wanted to go back to work—"

"You didn't have to," Lang interrupted.

She nodded and took another drag from her cigarette. "I know. But who wants to be like the women in the building where you live? Not working makes them stupid." She took another puff. "Or they already are. Even though I knew I had a baby coming, I did not want to ask you for help, to look like I needed anyone nor was I willing to give up what could be the only part of you I would ever have."

"By your choice." There was no brittle edge to his tone, only a happy recitation of fact.

"Had you not nearly died, I would probably never seen you again," she said with uncharacteristic emotion. "I would have been very foolish. If you wish me to go, I will."

Instead, he spread his arms again, releasing his son. Cigarette in hand, Gurt came to the bed and embraced him. Lang smelled a mixture of stale tobacco and soap with the smallest hint of some sort of flower fragrance, the one he associated with her. The memories flooded back: Rome, London, Seville, the Languedoc of France. All the dangers they had faced. And the wild, uninhibited, noisy sex. He had missed the former almost as much as the latter.

"Go? Try it and I'll chain you to the bed," he said with a smile.

As though with a will of their own, his hands started moving across her back, down her sides to her hips.

She gently pushed back. "Later. When Manfred is not here."

The first lust he had felt in longer than he cared to remember had not made Lang forget the boy. "No harm in him seeing his parents' affection."

Gurt cocked an eyebrow. "'Affection'? Another minute and you would have had me across the bed."

The growing discomfort from the catheter made Lang painfully aware of how right she was.

He leaned back into the pillows. "Exactly what do you have in mind? I mean, I better be planning on you staying this time."

He was afraid to bring up any arrangement that smacked of permanence. She had left his life twice before when he had.

"Manfred and I will be here at least until the hospital releases you. Longer if you wish."

Lang's eyes were riveted on his son, the child he was beginning to regard as miraculous as any held by one of Rubens's Madonnas. "I can't wait that long. Whoever blew up my condo is going to try again. I'm a sitting duck here."

"What do nesting birds have to do with it?" She was looking for a place to stub out her cigarette. She finally settled on a glass beside the bed before she returned to the chair. "There are men outside that look like policemen."

"They are, City of Atlanta. You lived here a year or so. Would you trust your life to the Atlanta police?"

She gave a toss of the head. "You do not have to. That is one of the reasons I came."

It was not bravado. She had saved his life more than once. After winning the agency's women's shooting competition, she had demanded a face-off with the male champion. She had humiliated him.

"You have a weapon?"

"I had no plans to protect you with a nail file."

"Manfred?"

"He will stay with Francis for the time being."

Francis, keeper of Lang's dog and now Lang's son. The priest was making his bid for sainthood.

Or institutional confinement.

Francis.

Lang recalled his friend's reaction when he had told him he thought he had dreamed of Gurt. "Francis, he . . ."

"He called me hours after you were admitted to the hospital. The doctors were not, er, optimistic."

Lang realized Francis had kept in touch with Gurt, maybe even knew about Manfred. He should feel annoyed, piqued that his friend had kept this information to himself.

But he was far too happy.

And too tired. His first few days back in the world had fatigued him far beyond anything he would have anticipated. He fought the gravitational pull of his eyelids as long as he could.

Then he slipped into sleep.

VI.

Park Place
2660 Peachtree Road
Atlanta, Georgia
A Month Later

Today was the first time Lang had seen his previous home since the blast. He had decided to rebuild section by section, starting with the tiny kitchen. A new wall oven was to be delivered from Home Depot today. So far it had not arrived.

The condominium association had replaced the exterior glass through which was a magnificent view of the city's premier avenue, a long stretch of pavement lined with blossoming trees that pointed like an arrow to the high-rise office buildings of downtown.

That was the only thing unchanged.

Today was also the first time Lang had had Manfred to himself. There had been moments when Gurt had been running errands or absent for some other reason but never far away. Lang's anticipation of the event had been more disturbing than the prospect of seeing his condo for the first time since the explosion. Lang was a newcomer in his son's life. What if the kid suddenly decided he wanted his mother? What if he suddenly got sick, developed one of those childhood diseases that seemed to come and go with the irregular suddenness of summer thunderstorms? There wasn't any *Parenting for Dummies* on the bookstore shelves.

Lang had fabricated a dozen excuses, some very good, why taking Manfred along was not a good idea. He was relieved when Gurt had dismissed them all with an arched eyebrow, an observation that children were not breakable and a reminder Lang had a lot of catching up to do.

The uncertainties evaporated as soon as Manfred put his small hand in Lang's, looked up with blue eyes expressing only pleasurable expectations and asked, "Where are we going today? Can Grumps come?"

How hard could fatherhood be?

Hadn't he been the closest thing to a father his nephew Jeff had? And Jeff had been only a year or so older than Manfred when Janet had adopted him. They had become instant buddies. Manfred would be fine. So would Lang.

Smelling of burned wood and mold, the condo resembled nothing more than some primeval cave. The walls were blackened as though from years of cooking fires. Glass crunched underfoot as he poked at this and that with one of his crutches while holding both the other and Manfred's hand.

The boy made an exaggerated show of holding his nose. "It stinks, Vati."

"Daddy," Lang corrected gently. "In America, I'm your daddy."

He had only about three years to make sure the boy spoke perfect English before he started school.

And it would be the city's best private school. His son was bright and Lang had influence. He would also attend the best of colleges, maybe Harvard. No, someplace more interested in education than politics. Maybe something somewhere in the South. Vanderbilt or Duke, perhaps. Then law school and a partnership with Lang. Or maybe a year or two with one of the mammoth law factories where he'd learn a little humility as well as how to crank out twenty-five billable hours a day. Then . . .

If Gurt would stay that long.

Bobby Burns's comments on the plans of mice and men came to mind.

The boy's face had clouded with the gentle reprimand.

"You're right, though, it doesn't smell so good." Lang agreed with a grin.

Lang was regarding what had been a secretary, a rare remainder from the Charleston workshop of Thomas Elfe, one of pre-Revolutionary America's finest cabinetmakers. It was one of the two or three items he had not sold after Dawn's death. It had housed his collection of antique books and a small group of antiquities. He and Dawn had found it in one of the shops along Queen Street, paid far too much for it and given it a prominent place in the small house he had also sold. Now it was all just so much ash.

He sighed.

Stuff, Francis had said, just stuff, objects that, after all, we only rent during the course of our lives.

Lang had at least pretended to be comforted.

But he wasn't.

Even though he would have gleefully swapped a dozen condominiums at Park Place to learn he had a son, an heir, whoever had done this was going to regret they hadn't killed him.

"Vat . . . Daddy, why did the bad people burn your house?"

A good question. Lang steered his small companion

toward what had been the bedroom. "I don't know. Maybe because they were just that, bad people."

Manfred took in the destruction in the bedroom. "Shit!"

Lang's eyes widened. One of the things he had learned quickly: small children cannot remember to say "thank you" or "please" but they never forget four-letter words.

He couldn't bring himself to rebuke the boy. Instead, he would have smiled had he not been looking at the twisted wire that had been his bedsprings. Squatting sent an electriclike shock of pain from ankle to hip but he wanted to sift through the ash and debris. Sure enough, the SIG Sauer was there, its plastic grip melted into some form of modern art. The heat had set off the bullets in the clip, destroying the firing chamber.

He dropped it, his eye caught by another shine of metal. The small snapshot of Dawn in its silver frame. Miraculously, the glass hadn't even cracked. He blew the dust away and slipped it into his pocket.

"Who's that?" Manfred asked.

Lang sighed again. "Someone I knew a long, long time ago."

"Before you knew Mommy?"

Lang started to simply lie and stopped. He was not about to begin his relationship with his son with untruths. "No, I knew Mommy before I knew her. But there was a time . . ."

How do you explain the complexity of man/woman relationships to a three-year-old?

You don't.

"Let's just say I knew her before I loved Mommy."

That seemed to satisfy him.

He put an arm around Lang's shoulders and squeezed. "I love you, Daddy."

"And I you," Lang said, gritting his teeth against the pain of standing up. "There isn't anything else here worth saving."

A knock at the door.

Lang gave Manfred a gentle shove. "Go open it, will you? It should be men with the oven. Daddy isn't moving so swiftly these days."

Painfully, Lang made his way from the bedroom. From its door he could see two burly men with a wheeled pallet. Whatever was under the shipping blanket was a lot larger than a wall oven.

Lang stopped just inside his front door, watching the blankets come off. Underneath was a huge stove. Six gas burners, grill, two ovens. The thing was larger than his entire kitchen.

"Where you want it?" one of the men asked.

"The enlisted men's mess at Fort Benning, maybe?" Lang responded. "That isn't what I ordered."

The other man looked at a slip of paper before showing it to Lang. "This is what the order form shows."

Lang groaned inwardly.

Home Depot had been founded right here in Atlanta and had grown into the largest home supply company in the world. Its two founders had retired, one bestowing on the city the world's biggest aquarium. The other had purchased the suppurating sore of sports, the Atlanta football team. Only fantasy and hubris could have made him think he could lift the team to a level of mediocrity for which it had vainly struggled for forty years.

Rumor had it that since the founders' departure, the company's service had sunk to the same performance level as the football team.

"I don't care what the paper shows," Lang said. "You can see this stove won't fit into that kitchen."

The man shrugged. "You can take that up with the appliance department. All we do is deliver."

"Well, you can't leave it here."

"Yeah, we can. Fact, we can't take it back without orders from them, the appliance department."

Lang eased the door shut, leaving just a crack. "You're not bringing that thing in here."

With the disinterest Lang thought exclusive to the US Postal Service, the men simply collected the blankets, took the pallet and left the huge stove in the hallway.

Lang almost swore until he remembered the small boy at his side. Instead, he took out his BlackBerry and punched in a number.

"Sara? I need you to call Home Depot, see if you can get someone on the phone with at least a room-temperature IQ . . ."

Outside, a taxi was waiting to take him to meet Gurt and the SUV he had rented until he regained his agility. He hated the lumbering gas guzzler but a more nimble vehicle provided little room to maneuver with in a cast or to store crutches. Lang was unable to drive his manual shift Porsche still garaged here at Park Place. His frustration at having to rely on others tended to make him ill-tempered except where Manfred was concerned. He was impatient for the time he would be mobile enough to play with his son, to take him to a Braves game or any of the things young fathers did.

In the meantime, he kept alert. Whoever had tried to kill him wasn't likely to give up. The only reason he could imagine why they had waited this long was that they either hoped he would become less than cautious or hadn't been able to find him.

He had left the hospital to convalesce in a Trappist monastery in nearby Conyers, a small town east of Atlanta. The quarters had been Spartan, the food hardy if less than sensational. Given the vows of silence of the brothers, the conversation had been less than spectacular, too. He had lived for Gurt and Manfred's daily visits. Still, he appreciated whatever ecumenical strings Francis had pulled to get him into one of the last places on earth any who knew him might look.

Any organization efficient enough to track him down from London to Atlanta, though, would have eyes and ears. Now that he was on the street, they would know it.

The thought was less than comforting.

Once out of the monastery, he, Gurt and Manfred were living on the land Lang called simply "the Farm." The relatively small acreage would have made "plantation" seem not only potentially politically incorrect but pretentious as well. About an hour's drive from the city's southern limit, Lang had bought it some years ago in the name of a dummy corporation. The purchase included a frame cabin of about fifteen hundred square feet, no phone or cable TV. Even better, cell phone reception was spotty when it existed at all. A perfect retreat. It did have good redneck neighbors who took each others' property and privacy rights seriously. They adorned their pickups' rear windows with racks holding at least one shotgun or rifle.

Burglars or home invaders were wise to confine themselves to venues other than Lamar County.

Even better was the ten-acre pond. Manfred had, possibly, never seen a live fish. He squealed with excitement each time he, with minor assistance from Lang, dragged a shiny, flopping bass or bream onto the clay banks. The child had somewhat less enthusiasm for cleaning his catch, something his father insisted upon. Gurt was probably even more thankful than her son when throwing the fish back became the custom. All three had eaten about as much marine life as they wanted for the time being.

Instead of his normal twenty-three-and-a-half-hour daily nap, Grumps showed signs of life, even giving token chase to rabbits he had to know would outdistance him in seconds. He followed Manfred everywhere, a pastime Lang tried to not let annoy him. After all, it had been Lang who had provided the mutt's keep all these years.

But then, what living creature could not adore Lang's son?

All in all, it had been a restful, pastoral period to mend, reacquaint himself with Gurt and get to know his son while bones healed and internal organs returned to their natural locations.

It ended that night.

Not for the first time, Lang was pleasantly surprised by Gurt's adaptability. She had produced a dinner indigenous to the locale: roasted hen with baked sweet potato and collards. As a native Southerner, Lang had been equally delighted and astonished. The green leaves were usually harvested only after the first frost and the unpleasant odor of cooking them normally permeated an entire house. Before he was through marveling at their appearance on the table, she put a small black iron skillet of cornbread in front of him.

Made with buttermilk. It might not have been as good as Lang's mother used to make, but it sure was better than mix out of a box.

He started to ask where she had suddenly acquired such peculiarly Southern cooking skills, thought better of it, and reached for another slice of cornbread.

From his high chair, Manfred inspected the greens suspiciously. "Is it grass?"

Lang was sprinkling the customary green pepper sauce over his own. "It's good. Try it."

With a skeptical eye on his father, the child speared a single leaf and slid it into his mouth, followed by another.

"What is that?" He was pointing to the pepper sauce.

"Hot. You wouldn't like it."

The little boy extended his hand. "Gimme."

Gurt put down her fork. "We say what in English when we ask for something?"

Manfred thought for a moment. "Please!"

Gurt looked at Lang. "He will too hot to eat make it."

Lang had gauged his son's determination and guessed otherwise. He extended the bottle and watched his son dribble a few experimental drops. Then, his tearing eyes never left his father's face as he shoveled the rest of the collards into his mouth.

"He will be a perfect copy of his father," Gurt commented dryly, "too stubborn to admit a mistake."

A trait often attributed to her countrymen. Who else would lose one war and begin another in exactly the same way?

Lang was deciding how well the observation would be received when Grumps leapt up from his customary spot under Manfred's chair and dashed toward the front door, barking.

"Another one of those big rats?" Gurt asked.

Lang was getting to his feet. "Possums. No, I don't think so."

He took a step in Grumps's direction. Through the window, the crescent moon was a diadem on the pond's black velvet. Lang thought he saw one, two, no, three shapes blot out the reflection and dissolve into the night.

What the hell?

The neighbors were definitely not the type to come calling uninvited.

But . . .

Shit!

The cab, the fucking taxicab!

Someone had been waiting, knowing Lang would return to his condo sooner or later. All they'd had to do was follow the cab to the place he had met Gurt and then trail along behind until they were led here. Lang had never thought to look back to see if they had had a tail.

He had ignored agency training. He knew of more than one instance where the omission resulted in no chance to repeat the mistake.

Lang made a dive across the room, knocking the table onto its side among the clattering and shattering of dishes, glasses and silverware.

Gurt knew better than to take the time to ask questions. Instead, she snatched a bewildered Manfred from his chair and darted behind the overturned table as Lang joined them.

A hailstorm of bullets shook the frame house.

Splinters of wood, glass shards and bits of furniture flew through the air as though by the hand of an angry poltergeist. Sharp porcelain bits from the dinner dishes danced and hopped across the floor, all to the accompaniment of gunfire.

Lang snatched Manfred away from Gurt, shielding the child as best he could with his own body.

He alternately cursed himself for his inattention and was grateful to the cabin's prior owner for leaving the ugly but thick oak table.

The sheer helplessness was maddening. The closet where he kept the double-barrel shotgun he used to frighten off rather than harm deer marauding the summer vegetable garden was too far away. He'd never make it unharmed through the fusillade. Gurt's weapon was no doubt in her purse, useless in the bedroom.

It was quiet, the calm of a hurricane's eye, Lang was sure. The only sound was the terrified sobs of the little boy clinging to Lang as though he might fall into the abyss if he let go.

The stillness was more frightening than the storm.

Lang peeled the little fingers loose and handed the trembling child to Gurt. "Try to keep him quiet. I'm going to try to get to the shotgun before they charge the house."

She took her son, jiggling him gently. "It is not likely you will make it."

Gurt the optimist.

Lang was already on his way, crawling commando fashion across a floor littered with a forest of sharp objects. "What else do you suggest, fighting them off with spoons?"

Lang stood and almost fell the last few feet, snatched open the door and was jamming shells into the twin barrels when the bullet-ridden door slammed open.

In a single motion, he swiveled and dropped into a squat, groaning at the pain the sudden movement caused.

He saw only a blur in the doorway framed by the night, a smudge of camo shirt and pants, white face and a weapon.

He pulled one trigger.

The image staggered backward as he was pulling the second.

The twin blasts rebounded from the enclosure of walls and set his ears ringing and his eyes watering from the sting of cordite.

The open threshold was empty. The riddled door moaned as it swung drunkenly on its remaining hinge.

Lang jammed two more shells into place, dragging his cast as he stumbled toward Gurt and Manfred.

Suddenly, the entire outside seemed to light up with a wavering orange glow.

Lang didn't have to guess what was coming. Molotov cocktails, bottles filled with gasoline, fumes compressed by gas-soaked rags for fuses. They would explode like napalm upon impact just as they had when used sixty years ago by Russian partisans against German tanks.

And this cabin was a lot more flammable than any Panzer.

Lang glanced around.

He saw no options.

VII.

Lamar County, Georgia
Five Minutes Earlier

Larry Henderson considered himself a farmer just like his daddy and his daddy's daddy.

In Grandpa's day, cotton had been the crop. He had come home from fighting the Germans to find a combination of boll weevil and long-fibered Indian cotton grown in Texas had pretty much put him out of business. Subsequent efforts at peanuts, soybeans and even a peach orchard had provided a subsistence living, mostly through government subsidies.

Then the BIG CORPORATIONS (Larry always thought of them in capital letters) had bought up thousands of acres on which to not plant anything and the bulk of the county's allotment shares went to them. Gave new meaning to the lines from that old song, "He don' plant 'taters n' he don' plant cotton and them that does is soon forgotten."

By the time Daddy come along, Grandpa had had to adapt. He and Daddy planted corn. Good, sweet corn that fermented in the crick that ran through the property. Boil off a gallon or two and Daddy always said it was the best white in middle Georgia, well aged if the customer got there late in the day.

Daddy sold enough to buy a secondhand Ford every other year to make the weekly run to Barnesville, Hawkinsville and all those other 'villes where the thirst for good white lightnin' was never quenched.

By the time Daddy passed away, the coalition of Baptist preachers and bootleggers wasn't as strong as it used to be and the county went wet. Folks stopped drinking white. Instead, they bought bourbon, vodka, scotch. Government whiskey with the stamp on the bottle's cap.

The corn business was as dead as cotton and it was time to adapt again.

That's when Larry learned about marijuana, that five-leaved devil's weed folks up in Atlanta paid good money for.

The crick nourished the plants the same as it had fermented the corn. And it didn't take half the tending to. It grew like a weed, mostly because it *was* a weed.

Problem was the trouble what went with it. In Grandpa and Daddy's day, the local sheriff would bust up a still every once in a while, particularly around election time. Oh, he'd let word slip out a day or so in advance so everybody could go hide in the woods and nobody got hurt. He even arrested Daddy a couple of times, before he let him go. After all, being jailed for making good whiskey wasn't a shame, not like breaking a real law.

But marijuana was different.

Folks did get hurt.

There were the dealers in Atlanta, the ones Larry sold wholesale to. Their big shiny cars might as well have a sign on them telling the world what they did for a living. He never could see their eyes, because of the sunglasses they wore day or night. How was a man supposed to do business when he couldn't see the other man's eyes?

Larry'd heard stories about how these men would kill someone over a few ounces. He hoped they were just rumors but something in his gut told him not.

And the damn DEA would come down from Atlanta and raise hell. Those stupid McCracken boys, down toward Macon, actually shot a federal man.

Then the shit really hit the fan.

The federals shot one of the McCrackens and confiscated their farm.

How the hell did the government expect a man to make an honest living with his land gone?

Fact is, he couldn't. That's why the McCrackens took to

raiding other folks' farms, stealing their whole crop of marijuana. They didn't much care who got hurt in the process, either.

Larry didn't much blame the McCrackens as he did the federals for fooling around in what should have been a local law enforcement issue, one that could've been handled just like it was in Daddy's day.

No matter, the McCrackens were why Larry kept Daddy's old Remington pump twelve gauge loaded and handy. The blueing had worn off the barrel long ago and the butt plate been screwed back on so many times it tended to wobble. But the bore didn't have a pit in it, shiny and smooth as the day it came from the Sears store over to Barnsville, and constant cleaning kept the ejection mechanism working like new.

Tonight he was glad he'd kept the thing in order.

Momma had been watching her reality shows on the dish TV (there weren't enough subscribers out here to warrant cable). He'd been in the kitchen fiddling with a cranky carburetor from one of the two small tractors and tasting a little bit of the white he still made for home use when from somewhere on the other side of the tree line that marked the crick, somebody was shooting up a storm. A gunshot in the night usually meant someone was headlighting deer to put meat on the table, but what Larry heard sounded like a war.

It would have been none of his business, if he hadn't set out a hundred or so new seedlings near where all the ruckus was coming from, enough crop to make a year's mortgage payments to the bank.

Or maybe buy Mamma something nice.

He shoved the pint bottle in a hip pocket, picked up the Remington, scooped a handful of OO shot from the box, and stuffed them in a pocket.

Mamma was standing by the door. "You gotta go?"

Mamma, Darleen was her name, had dropped out of the

tenth grade to marry Larry when she got pregnant with Little Larry. That had been over twenty-five years ago. Now Little Larry was dead two years, died in some godforsaken place Larry'd never heard of in Iraq. Little Darleen was away at Georgia Southern College, the first Henderson to graduate from high school, let alone go to college.

All because of the marijuana that Larry didn't intend to let somebody else, McCrackens or otherwise, fuck with.

Larry nodded. "Prolly jes' some drunk, shootin' an' raisin' hell."

Neither of them believed that for a minute.

Mamma stepped aside, brushing Larry's cheek with her lips. "You be careful, y'hear?"

He couldn't miss the anxiety in her eyes. "I promise."

Neither believed that, either.

Defending your land was the most important thing a man could do for his family. That's why Great-Great-Grandpa Henderson was staring at the Yankee cannon when he had borrowed a pencil to scribble his name on a scrap of paper and pin it to the back of his homespun shirt before he charged up a hill in Pennsylvania, knowing he'd likely not see Georgia's red clay again. The same reason Grandpa lost two toes to frostbite standing his ground in the snow at a little Belgian town named Bastogne and Daddy had spent two tours in a stinking Southeast Asian jungle.

There hadn't been a war for Larry to go to before he was too old but he would've gone had there been. A man defended his land, either on it or to prevent the other fella from getting to it.

Outside, the katydids continued their argument and a couple bullfrogs down to the pond were trying to get laid by the sound of the baritone calls. Larry glanced at the Ford Galaxie parked in the yard, decided he could get where he wanted to go quicker and quieter on foot and set out at a trot toward the sound of the shots.

A second or two later, he heard footsteps beside him.

Without turning his head, he whispered, "Jerranto, there ain't no need f'you to get inta this."

Jerranto had just shown up lookin' for work a year back at a time Larry definitely needed help with the crop. Not like he could advertise in the paper for field hands to grow what was flourishing down by the crick. The fact Jerranto didn't have a work permit or other papers made it unlikely he'd go to the law.

Jarranto was dark skinned with a doe-eyed wife carrying a baby. Larry neither knew nor cared where they'd come from, though the Mexican accent was a pretty strong clue. He'd given them the old sharecropper's cabin on the other side of the pond and the man worked hard or harder than Larry. He asked no questions, tended to his own business and was happy when Larry gave him part of the cash he got from the folks up in Atlanta.

Larry glanced over his shoulder. The sliver of a moon gave enough light to see a white T-shirt and gleam from the old hammer-firing double-barrel twelve gauge Larry had given him to shoot squirrels and the occasional deer when meat got scarce.

"No need a'tall," Larry repeated. "The federals catch you an' you're goin' back. Plus, Maria's about to have another baby."

There was also enough light to see the flash of white teeth that was an answer. Jerranto spoke enough English to get by but when he just wasn't going to listen, he gave that smile.

The two men could see only the outline of the trees, but the woods here were as familiar as their own bedrooms. They splashed across the crick and came to the edge of the tree line just as the shooting finally stopped.

"Shit!" Larry grunted.

Jerranto called the name of one of those saints he rattled off whenever he was surprised.

VIII.

Lamar County, Georgia

Lang was sliding along the wall toward the remains of the door, using his shotgun as a crutch. He knew the weapon would be no defense against firebombs, but he couldn't stand idle while his son wept with fear.

Instead of the anticipated crash of glass and whoosh of flames, shooting started again, this time the unmistakable boom of shotguns. He peeked through the gap between door and frame and saw the figure of a man sprawled in a puddle of hissing flames.

There was a muzzle flash from his left directed not at the house but at the woods to the right. It was answered both left and right by a barrage of smooth bore replies.

There was a scream and the sound of an engine cranking. Its lights out, some form of SUV crossed in front of the cabin and headed for the twin ruts that served as a driveway, rear end swaying as its tires fought for purchase in the loose soil. From the woods to Lang's left, a figure emerged, took deliberate aim at the vehicle and fired. The SUV swerved drunkenly and smashed into a pine tree.

Then there was silence, a quiet exaggerated by what had gone before. Lang could hear only the hiss of a shattered radiator and Manfred's terrified moans.

Lang took the opportunity to look back into what had been the living/dining room, his anxiety overcoming curiosity. "Manfred OK?"

"He's fine," Gurt answered. "And thanks for asking about me."

By the guttering flames that had ben intended for the cabin, Lang saw the figure, a man, calmly walk to the wreck of the SUV, open the driver's door and snatch out a limp form, which fell into a heap.

At the same time, another man, this one considerably

smaller than the first, became visible approaching from the right.

Lang raised his shotgun. "I wouldn't come any closer if I were you."

There was a snort that possibly could have been a laugh and the first man made a display of leaning his weapon against a tree and raising his hands. "And I'd say 'thank you' was I you."

The man on the right also put down whatever he was carrying and raised his hands, too.

Both kept on walking toward the house.

The first one stepped over a form sprawled across the narrow front porch without giving it any particular notice. He could have stepped out of the film *Deliverance*. He was well over six feet and two hundred pounds, his face tanned by the sun. Blue eyes twinkled from under his John Deere cap. A reddish beard streaked with gray covered his lower face but not the broad lips that were curled into a smile. He was clad in bib overalls. His step had a confidence to it, a manner that seemed to say shooting a couple of men was a normal night's work.

Stereotypes exist. A lot. That's why they keep showing up in life.

The other man was much smaller and looked Latino. His eyes darted back and forth as though anticipating an attack at any moment.

The big man turned back and stooped to examine the body at his feet.

He stood and rolled it over with his brogan. "Ain't nobody I know."

Lang lowered his shotgun. "I'm happy for you."

Behind him he heard Gurt moving toward the bedroom and the gun in her purse.

Both strangers stopped at the door. "Mind if we come in?"

Lang stepped back and they both entered. The larger of

the two surveyed the room. The cabin's thin frame and Sheetrock hadn't stopped many bullets. "Looks like somebody didn't much want you here."

Lang shrugged. "A man makes enemies."

The man in overalls continued to look around, nodding as though understanding a basic truth. "I'd say."

He turned his attention to Gurt as she entered the room, making no effort to hide his admiration. He doffed his cap. "Evenin', ma'am."

She held a SIG Sauer, having left Manfred in the other room despite his howls of protest. Lang felt relief as he saw Grumps slink out from behind the kitchen counter and follow the sounds of Manfred's displeasure. Everybody had made it through OK.

Gurt studied the stranger as intently as he was her. "You are to thank?"

He leaned forward, an imitation of a bear trying to bow. "My pleasure, ma'am." He extended a hand the size of a football. "Larry Henderson. I'm your neighbor."

"And a good one," Gurt said, smiling as she transferred the automatic to her left hand to slip her right into the huge paw.

If Larry noticed the weapon, he said nothing. Maybe pistol-packing mommas were the norm around here.

The little one said something Lang didn't catch.

Larry nodded. "He's right, we need to clean up this mess 'fore daylight."

Perplexed, Gurt glanced from one to the other. "'Clean up'? Should we not call the police?"

Larry took off his cap again and clenched it in a hand, a gesture Lang guessed was a habit. He shifted from one foot to the other like a schoolboy caught passing a note in class. "Well, ma'am, I'm not sure thass a good idea. See, first, we ain' got no phones out here an' . . ." He shuffled shoes the size of rowboats. Then he spoke, staring into Lang's eyes as if seeking an answer to an unasked question. "An', well, I'd soon as not involve the law if you take my meanin'. An' if done, 'tis best done quickly."

Was that a line from Shakespeare? Unlikely. But Lang got the message loud and clear. Whatever Larry was doing was something that the long arm of the law wasn't going to help. The man had just saved Lang's ass by blowing away a couple of unknowns, voting them totally off the island. Now he was asking, almost pleading, not to involve the cops.

"Will not somebody come looking for them?" Gurt asked.

Larry shook his head. "Doubt it. They're all dressed the same like some sorta army an' carryin' those Russian guns . . ."

"AK-47's?"

"Thass the one. Ennyhow, ain' nobody from 'round here. They's from off. I kin take a tractor, tow that car so deep in the woods they's have to send in th' hounds to find it, bury those guys where nobody'd ever look even if they wanted to find 'em. An' I got a feelin' nobody does."

There was a certain logic to what Lang's new friend said. If, as he was certain, these would-be assassins were from the same group that had killed Eon, it was unlikely anyone would be asking questions about their disappearance. Attempted arson, illegal automatic weapons and botched murders would invite the unwanted attention not only of local law enforcement but of the ATF, FBI and other federal and state agencies, not to mention the press. What Lang had in mind could not be accomplished under the scrutiny of an alphabet soup of law enforcement agencies, either.

Larry was looking around the cabin again. "Wouldn't be smart to stay here tonight."

"There is a Gasthaus nearby?" Gurt asked.

Larry gave that sort of bend/bow again. "Why, ma'am, I'd be pleasured if you'd stay with me. Mamma'd love the . . ."

Manfred walked slowly out of the bedroom escorted by Grumps.

Larry gave a grin of sheer joy. "No argument, now. Mamma'd love nothin' more'n than to have a tyke in the house agin."

Hours later, Gurt, Lang and Manfred had been fussed over, looked after and generally made to feel at home in a small but comfortable house while Larry and Jerranto went about work Lang had no desire to question. The living room/dining room featured a wall of shelves filled with books, hardly what Lang expected from what he had seen of his new friend and benefactor. Closer inspection revealed inexpensive and well-worn works of Shakespeare and Milton, some of the metaphysical poets as well as Shelly, Byron and Keats. Somebody in the family had a love of literature as well as shotguns.

He hadn't heard Darleen come up behind him. "Larry's grandaddy's books. 'Fore TV, he read out those book ever night. Larry's daddy did, too. Larry done read ever one of 'em, most two, three times."

That line about done quickly. It *was* from Shakespeare, perhaps *Macbeth*? Lang's surprise must have shown, for she added, "Jus' 'cause Larry couldn' afford college don' mean he's ignorant."

Lang wondered how many college graduates could even name the metaphysical poets.

"Not Tara," Gurt, whose favorite book was *Gone with the Wind*, noted, "but is Southern hospitality I have read of. It really—"

Larry's return interrupted the comment. He stood on a narrow plank porch, using a spade to knock dirt from his shoes before he swung the screen door open. He grinned at Lang and reached into a pocket in the back of his clay-encrusted overalls, producing an unlabeled bottle half full of white fluid.

He proffered it to Lang. "Have a swig. Calm your nerves."

Lang accepted hesitantly. He unscrewed the cap and smelled something like gasoline. "What is it?"

"Georgia white," the man said as proudly as though offering a fifty-year-old Bordeaux. "Made by my family for years." He nodded toward the bookshelves. "Not an eye of newt in the whole process."

Lang was hesitant to try it, but it seemed tactless to refuse the man who had not only saved their lives but also was putting a roof over their heads for the night. Through compressed lips, he let a little trickle into his mouth.

Eye of newt notwithstanding, the brew of Macbeth's witches couldn't have been more potent.

At first, he wanted to spit. Then he was afraid to for fear of setting the place on fire. His eyes blurred with tears as he forced the burning liquid down his throat. He felt as though flames were coursing down his intestinal tract.

Larry was watching every move with the anticipation of someone expecting plaudits. "Well, how was it?"

Lang wiped his lips with the back of a hand and gasped for air to cool his interior. "Just right," he choked.

"Jes' right?"

"It was any better, you wouldn't have wanted to share it. Any worse, it would've killed me."

IX.

Peachtree Center
227 Peachtree Street
Atlanta, Georgia
The Next Morning

Sara looked up from her desk in surprise as Lang hobbled through the door to the suite and made his way to his office.

"You aren't due back for another two weeks," she admonished. "You—"

". . . are giving our clients a bonus."

Lang's injuries entitled him to a prolonged leave of absence from the various courts. The nonviolent nature of the swindlers, stock cheats and other white-collar criminals Lang represented meant most could get bail. Once free, there was little upside to a trial.

Lang could almost hear Sara's jaw click shut as Gurt followed.

If Sara was surprised to see her, she concealed it well. "Hello," she said tentatively.

Gurt was not her favorite person. Even though Gurt had been nothing if not kind and polite, Lang's longtime secretary made little effort to conceal her opinion of Lang and Gurt's previous living arrangements. Lang also suspected a small bit of jealousy. Before Gurt's first arrival in Atlanta, the white-haired grandmother had pretty much run Lang's personal life since Dawn's death. Gurt was a definite challenge to her abundant mothering instincts.

Any hint of hostility fell away when Sara spied Manfred. "And who might this be?"

Manfred bowed slightly and extended a hand. "I am named Manfred Fuchs."

"Manfred *Reilly*," Lang corrected.

Sara's eyes widened as she hastily looked from father to son and back again. She would have been blind to miss the resemblance. "When . . . ? Who . . . ? How . . . ?"

"Sometime ago, Lang and in the normal manner," Gurt said.

"But, but you were never . . ."

"Married?" Gurt smiled. "That is to the biological process irrelevant."

Not to Sara. Lang had often observed that years of membership in a Southern Baptist church made Sara worry too much that someone somewhere somehow was having fun. True or not, he tried not to show his amusement as her religion wrestled with her love for small children.

The latter won.

She fished a cellophane-wrapped peppermint from the bowl on her desk and extended one toward Manfred, who looked at the proffered treat and then at his mother.

Gurt apparently was willing to accept the peace offering. "What do you say?"

"*Danke*, er, thank you."

Sara pulled the candy back. "It comes at a price. Come give your auntie Sara a hug."

For the moment, the Gurt vs. Sara battle was over. Lang had enjoyed the mini drama long enough. He had come for a specific purpose and it wasn't to introduce his new family. He limped into his office and shut the door behind him. Ignoring two stacks of pink phone-message slips, he opened his center desk drawer and reached inside. His groping fingers found a catch and there was a click as a false back popped open. From it he extracted a worn address book. Thumbing the pages, he found what he was looking for and punched numbers into the telephone's keyboard, beginning with the 202 D.C. area code.

He knew the actual phone that he was calling could be located anywhere in the world, connected by a series of shifting random relays that would make any call from the person he was seeking totally untraceable. He waited for the third ring, after which there was only a beep. No voice, no message. He keyed in his own number and hung up.

It took about two minutes before Sara buzzed him. From the noise in the background, she, Gurt and Manfred were having a swell time. "Number one for you. Man named Berkley. Wouldn't say who he's with or what he wanted other than speaking to you. Want to take it or should I tell him you're out of the office?"

Lang was already reaching for the phone to press the button that would connect him. "I'll take it. Thanks."

He pushed the first line button. "Miles! My gatekeeper tells me you wouldn't tell her what you wanted or who you were with!"

There was a slight pause, confirming Lang's guess the call was going through multiple relays. "I coulda told her, Lang, but then I'd hafta kill her. How's it goin' with you?"

"I need a little help."

Again the pause before Miles's drawl. "Damn! An' here I was thinkin' you'd called 'cause you need my wise counsel an' sage advice."

Lang smiled. Miles Berkley was still the same bullshit artist. "Miles, about two months ago a wealthy English philanthropist, name of Eon Weatherston-Wilby, was kidnapped from the British Museum and subsequently murdered."

"I think I remember. Why do all those rich Brits have two las' names, anyway?"

"Same reason Southerners like us have two last names instead of a first and last. Langford and Miles instead of Joe and Frank."

"Damn," Miles said, "an' I'd always thought it was to cover somebody's ass when they weren't sure who the father was."

Lang chuckled. "Like I said, Miles, I need your help."

This time the pause was longer than usual.

"Lang, you know I'll do what I can, but my employer takes a real dim view of sharing information with unauthorized persons."

Or with the rest of the United States government for that matter. "Let me tell you what I need. I believe Eon was killed because of certain ancient documents he had acquired and was donating to the museum, perhaps because he knew what was *in* those documents. I'd like to know where he got them."

Another long pause. "A little out of my bailiwick, Lang."

"Oh, come on, Miles! You guys track large transfers of money like a hen with one chick. I recall, it was you that warned of nine-eleven because you'd noticed a transfer of cash from al Qaeda accounts."

"Shucks, weren't nuthin'."

"False modesty doesn't become you, Miles. If the powers that be had listened to you . . ."

"OK, OK, flattery appreciated."

Manfred walked into the room and froze, awestruck by the view provided by the floor-to-ceiling glass. Lang pointed to a helicopter making a pickup from the roof of a nearby building.

"So, Miles can you help?"

"Officially, no. But I'd like to renew the friendship, Lang. Haven't laid eyes on you in years. You and Gurt still . . ."

Gurt's looks were famous throughout the agency, as was the fact that Lang was the only one of the select members of that group who had ever gotten further than a refusal to do more than have lunch. His post-agency relationship with her was, he was certain, the subject of company gossip.

"We're getting along fine, Miles." He watched Manfred staring outside. "Better than you could believe. Thanks for asking. Now, about Eon Weatherston-Wilby . . ."

"Like I said, I'd like to keep up the relationship with an old friend. You got a cell phone number?"

Less than half an hour later, Gurt was driving the rented SUV back to the residence hotel that would serve as home for the next few days. Lang planned to move frequently until the danger was eliminated.

Gurt was thinking the same thing. "We will live in hotels for how long?"

The prospect of one set of interchangeable living quarters after another was bleak at best. It would be particularly disturbing to watch his newfound son try to understand why he was suddenly an urban gypsy. Not to mention the bribes he would pay desk clerks to take Grumps. "Until we can figure out what to do, learn enough to go after whoever is trying to kill us."

"Kill *you*," she corrected. "Manfred and I were not in the country even when the bomb did your condo."

"Whoever shot up the cabin wasn't making distinctions."

Gurt nodded. "Collateral damage. They didn't care."

Lang pointed to a strip center on the right side of the road. "Pull in there."

Gurt did as she was told, parked in a space perpendicular to the curb and looked up at a sign advertising the best ribs in town. "You have hunger?"

He indicated another neon sign in a window that announced, PAWN! TVS! ELECTRONICS! GUNS! "No, I have a need to be armed."

On the door, a sign informed the entrant that (a) the place was under video surveillance, (b) all firearms must be in cases or holsters and (c) Visa and Mastercard were equally welcomed.

A bell tinkled as Lang entered. A glass case displayed cheap watches and jewelry. Along one wall hung every imaginable form and shape of guitar, trumpet, trombone and several musical instruments Lang didn't recognize. Opposite was a rack of rifles and shotguns.

A man emerged from the shadows at the back of the shop. "Good mornin'! What can I—" He stopped, staring. "Langford Reilly! How have you been, Counselor?"

Lang took a very hairy hand in his own. "Pretty good, Monk. I take it you're keepin' your nose clean?"

"You bet. Not so much as a parking ticket since you got me off." He noticed Lang's difficulty in moving. "What happened to your leg?"

"That's why I've come to take you up on your offer of a favor if I needed one."

William "Monk" Vester, one of Lang's earlier clients.

Also one of the city's more entrepreneurial fences, Monk had been charged with specifying items to be stolen by a cadre of burglars. The case had been airtight with the housebreakers lining up to roll over on their compatriot in exchange for lighter sentences. Lang's only hope had been the incompetence of the Fulton County prosecutor's office. His reliance had been rewarded: somehow the exhibit numbers had become so mixed up it was impossible to ascertain with certainty which object had come from which victim or, for that matter, if the items had been stolen at all.

In Atlanta, Fulton County, it was not only better that a hundred guilty men go free than one innocent man be convicted, it was a near certainty. The district attorney could have screwed up the trespassing prosecution of Attila the Hun.

"Owe you one, sure." Monk's head was bobbing as though on a spring.

Lang suspected the sobriquet came from his former client's resemblance to something simian. The hunched back made overly lengthy arms seem longer still, perhaps long enough to drag on the floor. The hairline seemed to end just above eyes that never stayed one place very long, shifting as though in perpetual search. Thick black hair covered every visible part of his body: his arms, his hands, most of his face.

"So, I'm here to call it due," Lang said.

Again the bobblehead doll effect. "Yeah, yeah, anytime."

"I need a gun and I need it fairly quickly."

The smile vanished into the heavy black beard. The man was clearly torn between doing a service for a friend and the possible hazards. "I dunno. I don't make you wait like the law says, I'm in trouble again, lose license."

Lang stepped over to a glass counter much smaller than that containing the jewelry. "Let's see what you got." He pointed. "Let me see that Browning HP 35 nine millimeter."

"Good gun," Monk murmured as he loped to the other side and turned a key. "Thirteen shots . . ."

"I know," Lang said impatiently, extending his hand.

The feel of the weapon brought back memories. This was the model he had first been issued by the agency before the lighter SIG Sauer with its larger clip had replaced it. Lang pulled back the slide, held the gun up to the ceiling lights and peeked down the muzzle. The grooving was barely worn, the automatic clean, as though its former owner was aware that a well-maintained weapon was a reliable weapon.

He slid the action closed with a distinctive click. "How much?"

Monk pursed his lips and reached over his shoulder to scratch his back, an ape's gesture if Lang had ever seen one.

"Three fifty. For you, an even three."

Lang would have bet Monk had loaned no more than a hundred and a half but he had neither the time nor inclination to haggle. "Done. But I need it now."

Monk produced a sheaf of forms. "ATF requires a background check. Meybbe I can finish before you leave, meybbe three days."

Lang shook his head. "I may not even be in the country in three days."

"No problem. Jus' fill in the forms an' give me a check with a blank date. You don' pass the background check, my ass is so busted."

Gratefully, Lang took the forms and began. "Don't worry. I wouldn't be an attorney if I'd been convicted of a felony."

Monk looked at him, deadpan. "Bein' a lawyer don't mean you haven't been committed to a mental institution or any of those other things."

Lang peeled off an extra fifty after counting off three one-hundred-dollar bills. "To compensate for losing all that sleep."

Then he stopped beside the door, fascinated. He picked up a brass-headed cane, an old-fashioned gentlemen's walking stick. "How much?"

"I'll throw it in f' 'nother twenty-five."

Lang examined it more carefully, noting the head could be detached from the cane itself. "Done!"

Monk stuffed the bills into a pocket without counting. "Say, know the bes' way to get a lawyer down from a tree?"

Here it came.

"Cut the rope."

Whatever happened to blonde jokes?

Browning in one pocket, a box of ammunition in the other, Lang limped outside leaning on his cane and used his arms to pull himself into the passenger seat of the SUV. "OK, got my business done. Let's go."

Gurt didn't turn her head. "As soon as I parked here, the white Chevrolet parked in front of the place that advertises ribs."

Lang was tugging at his shoulder harness. "So? Lots of people like barbecue for lunch."

"No one has gotten out."

Without turning his head, Lang could see two men in the front seat. Neither seemed to be doing anything.

Lang struggled back out of the car. "Wait a minute."

Monk was fading back into the shadows as Lang reentered. "You unhappy already?"

Lang shook his head. "Need another favor."

He told the pawnbroker what he wanted.

Once Lang was back in the SUV, Gurt continued watching the Chevrolet. "And now?"

"We wait."

But not for long.

A bilious green Caddy convertible eased out from behind

the strip of businesses. From the size and gigantic tail fins, Lang would have guessed its origins lay somewhere in the late fifties. Monk had had the car ever since Lang had known him.

The huge automobile stopped just behind the Chevy, blocking it in its perpendicular space. Monk got out and started to go into the barbeque joint.

"Now," Lang said.

Oblivious to the shouts from the barricaded Chevrolet, Monk was entering the rib shack, a man making a quick stop to pick up a take-out lunch. Lang memorized the Chevy's license plate, although he was certain it would lead to a dead end.

Gurt was about to say something when Lang's cell phone pealed. It was Miles.

"What took you so long to get back to me?" Lang asked.

Miles snorted. "I didn't exactly have the full resources of the company behind me, y'know."

"But you did the best you could."

"As always. Where do you want the info sent?"

Lang thought a moment. Miles's reluctance to pass anything along over the phone was understandable. Worldwide, all electronic transmissions sent by satellite were monitored. Since this included well over 90 percent of all communications, Echelon, as the program was named, literally eavesdropped on that part of the world that no longer used wires to transmit messages. It was located in northern England and shared only by the English-speaking nations. The Achilles' heel of the project was the sheer volume of communications. Thousands of computers were programmed to record each message to be searched by other machines for keywords or phrases in a hundred or more languages. Still, the process took a day or so, and "bursts," those messages condensed into a single electronic beep, were not translatable into words.

Keywords or not, Miles was wise to take no chances. Passing out information to the unauthorized was at best a firable offense. At worst, it could lead to criminal prosecution.

"Overnight air to my office."

Lang gave him the address.

X.

Magnolia Motel
US Highway 41
Marietta, Georgia
That Evening

Not the Disneyland Hotel, it wasn't a lot to look at: a room whose faint odor of cheap perfume hinted at a usage by persons who would be acquainted for a short period of time rather than by families. The suggestion was enforced by the fly-specked sign behind the sole desk clerk, IN GOD WE TRUST. ALL OTHERS PAY CASH. The room's scruffy shag carpet, the tattered spreads on the two sagging double beds gave mute testimony that the Magnolia, located on what had once been a main thoroughfare between Marietta and Atlanta, had seen better days.

But the positive aspects outweighed the pervasive atmosphere of sleaze: The proprietor clearly expected cash, a necessity in the hot-pillow trade, thereby leaving no credit card trail for Lang's pursuers to follow. Parking behind the cinder block building lessened discovery of the marital infidelities and indiscretions that Lang guessed were the place's stock in trade. If the moans piercing the thin walls were any indication, business was good.

Lang had produced his money clip and peeled off several bills. The proprietor leered at Gurt with such lust, he seemed surprised when he noticed the child holding on to her hand.

No doubt assuming some sort of perversion was about to take place, he turned his attention back to Lang. "Don' 'low any loud noises. No dope 'lowed on th' premises. Unnerstan?"

Lang assured him he did.

The first thing Gurt had done after entering the room was to put down a suitcase and began stripping one of the beds.

"Now what?" Lang asked.

She was shaking a sheet as Manfred watched. "I wish to rid the bedclothes of any life-forms other than ones I can speak to."

Lang hadn't considered this possibility.

Grumps apparently thought this was some kind of game. He began to bark. The noise next door continued unabated.

Lang kneeled to quiet the dog. He doubted the Magnolia would eject any paying guest but there was no sense taking chances.

When Gurt had made sure the linen was free of unwanted fauna, she put her hands on her hips and gazed around the room. "With you is always first-class, no?"

Lang was in the tiny bathroom, trying to decide if the shower was hygienic enough for Manfred's use. A colony of mildew was prospering nicely on the plastic curtain and a circle of rust decorated the drain. "When you're on the run, you can't always be choosy."

Gurt stuck her head in the door. "And how long 'on the run' will we be?"

Lang wished he knew.

CHAPTER THREE

I.

Ceske Budejovice
Czech Republic
Two Days Later

Judging by the appearance of the customs official at the door to his compartment, Lang guessed the train had crossed the Czech border. He found it as difficult to sleep on trains as on planes. Through eyes that wanted to close, he had been watching the flat countryside slide by, the Eastern European plain north of the Alps and Caucasus which pointed like a double-headed arrow toward the civilizations of northern Europe in one direction and the wealth of Byzantium in the other. Goth, Visgoth and Vandal hordes had marched in one direction; Mongols astride their diminutive ponies and the armies of Ottoman sultans in the other. Invaders from the Caesars to Hitler had come this way, leaving only flat farmlands and meandering streams as their monuments.

Although Lang spoke sparse Czech, there was little doubt what the man in uniform wanted. Lang proffered both passport and ticket and returned to his thoughts. He ran a hand across his face, trying to make his weary mind set things chronologically straight.

The morning after that no-tell motel, he had turned in the SUV, renting another from a different company. Covering tracks was part of agency tradecraft that he would never forget. In his new ride, he'd had Gurt drop him off at the office while she and Manfred set off for one of the malls, a place where she, like most women, could entertain herself indefinitely.

Miles was as good as his word; the overnight air envelope had been waiting for him as Lang limped into the office. He shut the door before pulling the tab that opened the package. Inside were what looked like bank transfer records. From The Bank of Guernsey account of International Charities, Ltd., one of Eon's foundations, to a numbered account in the Ceska Narodni Banka of Prague account of Starozitnictvi Straov of one and a half million pounds. A relatively small amount when Echelon was usually tracking the hundreds of millions that ran through the accounts of fronts for terrorists and narco-traffickers.

Along with the transfer was a note in Miles's oh-so-fine prep school handwriting:

Ran all bank accounts controlled by Weatherston-Wilby or his co's thru computer. Only this one didn't fit normal patterns for last year. Enjoy. Miles.

Lang knew that foundations and corporations had a regular banking routine just as individuals did. People paid their utility bills, for example, on a fairly regular basis along with credit cards, mortgages and the like. In a manner of speaking, so did corporations. Even charitable foundations, such as Eon's, were consistent in the amount of money spent on its good works. A computer, not having a human brain, was unable to understand anything that did not fit its programmed norm and kicked out the fact or data at variance with what it had been told, as more than one major American corporation had learned to its sorrow. For reasons Lang would never even want to understand, the gizmo had flagged this particular expenditure.

Perhaps it was related to the Nag Hammaddi volumes, perhaps not. It was, though, the closest thing Lang had to a clue as to who killed his friend and wanted Lang himself dead.

When he had proposed the trip to Prague, Gurt had wanted to come along. They had argued. Just as correct as painful, she reminded him of at least twice she had saved his life. Her agency training was not only the same as his but years more current. Besides, she spoke several European languages including a couple of Slavic dialects.

"Just what," Lang had asked, "do you suggest doing with Manfred?"

Rather than leave his son without either parent, Lang would let the killers come to him, a risky option at best.

When Lang had thought he had won past arguments with Gurt, he had subsequently learned to his chagrin the debate simply wasn't over yet.

This time her jaw snapped shut and she said nothing.

"We can't very well take him with us," Lang said. "And it's hardly fair to him to risk losing both parents."

"But, we have no place—"

"No problem," Lang said in the same soothing tone he used when urging a jury to discount testimony damaging to his clients. "We can either find a place here in Atlanta or you go back to Germany until this whole thing is over."

For once, he was reasonably certain the argument was done.

In addition to the normal poor service and indifference of the airlines, there were two other problems: First, getting the Browning and its ammunition aboard, either on his person or in his baggage, would be difficult. Second, the explosion and fire at his condo had consumed the false passport and credit card he had used so many times. The real one was in a lockbox at the bank. The reason for the distinction was now unclear. Putting his name on a passenger manifest would be tantamount to sending an engraved announcement of both his departure and his destination to anyone modestly sophisticated in hacking into poorly guarded airline computers.

There was really little choice: He had to take the Gulfstream IV registered to the Jeff and Janet Holt Foundation, the eleemosynary institution Lang had founded with funds he had extracted as compensation from the murderers of his sister and her stepchild. He was its president, implementing its declared purpose of providing pediatric medical services to underdeveloped nations. He took no salary but he did have use of the most luxurious private jet on the market.

And that jet had just happened to be flying a team of physicians to Nigeria the next day. One of them would be picked up in Munich. From there, Lang could take the train to Vienna and thence to Prague. It took far longer but rail transport required no security checks, no identification when buying a ticket. As long as only cash was used, it was untraceable.

There had been only one thing remaining before departure. As always before leaving Atlanta for an indefinite period on an uncertain mission, Lang went to the cemetery. The cab stopped at the foot of a gentle slope with a view of the city skyline. The driver left the engine and meter running as Lang pulled himself up the slight grade, floral paper in one hand, cane in the other. Dawn, Janet and Jeff, the closest people to family he had known in his adult life until now. He was never quite certain why he came here at these times; this time he was more unsure than ever. Somehow, visiting the former family seemed a betrayal of the family he now had. Was it a sense of wrongdoing that had prevented him from telling Gurt where he was going? Had he feared he would offend her? Was the thought he was doing wrong why he had refused to let Manfred come along? Dawn, ever mindful of his well-being, would be happy to know he now had the child she could not give him. Janet had nagged him regularly to seek another mate. Gurt was not one to look over her shoulder. So why the guilt trip?

Kneeling, he unwrapped the green tissue from two dozen roses and placed them in vases attached to the headstones.

Then he had stood, staring at the polished granite for a few moments before going back down the hill.

The train finally eased into the concrete cube that was the Prague railway station. The featureless, massive structure was reminiscent of the country's past as a Communist satellite, its capital city strewn with architecture Lang thought of as Stalinist empirical. Outside the dimly lit interior, he found a relatively undamaged Skoda, a Czech Audi knockoff. Guessing the sign on the roof meant "taxi," he opened the trunk and slid his single bag in next to what looked like the remains of a jack assembly and a spare tire that would have had a hard time even remembering treads.

In front, the driver put down a newspaper and took the last drag from a cigarette that smelled very much like silage. It also smelled very much like the cardboard tubes smoked by the Soviet Bloc defectors Lang had questioned. Cheap, odoriferous tobacco had apparently not vanished along with the Soviet Empire. The evil men do does, in fact, live after them.

"Hotel Continental," Lang said, wondering if the man understood.

They passed tired-looking warehouses with rusty steel doors before emerging onto a four-lane boulevard that followed the gentle sweep of the Vltava River. Ahead, Lang could see Prague Castle brooding on the landscape's only high point. The ebulliently Gothic spires of St. Vitus's Cathedral rose above the ramparts like a crown.

He grinned at a memory: The Defenestration.

In May of 1618, more than one hundred Protestant

nobles had marched into the palace to protest the succession of the notoriously intolerant Catholic Habsburg, Archduke Ferdinand. In the ensuing argument, Ferdinand's two governors were flung bodily out of a window, landing unharmed five stories below.

Intervention by angels, Catholics proclaimed. More likely by the inhabitants of the castle's stables, Protestants retorted. The defenstratees had landed in a huge pile of the morning's soft, still-steaming mucking. Thus began the Thirty Years' War, the only conflict Lang knew that, quite literally, began with horseshit.

Crossing a bridge, the cab came to a stop in front of a glass-and-steel building, just as ugly as the train station.

Lang handed the driver a number of kroner, unloaded his own bag and hobbled into a lobby paneled in light wood. To his left was a shop selling contemporary glassware. On his left, a cigar shop sold Cuban tobacco.

Lang joined a line of camera-toting Japanese at the reception desk. He turned sideways and watched the car in which he had arrived pick up another fare and pull away from the curb. He waited another few minutes before doing an about-face and exiting the way he had come. Trolling his bag behind him with one hand, leaning on his walking stick with the other, he headed south along Parzska. The hum of traffic faded behind him as Baroque buildings with shops on the first floor lined the street. To his right, the sharp angle of the roof of the Old-New Synagogue rose, marking the ghetto, a place that had seen centuries of pogroms long before the twentieth century and Adolf Hitler.

Within another block, he was facing the Old Town Square, a space enclosed by three- and four-story buildings with Baroque facades in fanciful, pastel colors. Lang crossed north to south. To his right was the Old Town Hall with its "new" tower, added in the mid–fourteenth century. A small crowd had already gathered, awaiting the performance of the mechanical figures of the astronomical clock.

Lang paused, a tourist taking in the sights, before selecting one of the crowded sidewalk cafés. He slid into a seat still warm from its former occupant and ordered a Plzensky, one of the slowly matured pilsner beers for which the Czechs are famous. In fact, Lang recalled, pilsner was first brewed only fifty miles away.

Taking his time, he surveyed his surroundings. The place probably looked pretty much the same when Franz Kafka wrote stories of people turning into cockroaches and trials where no accusations were made.

No one paid any particular attention to him. Slowly savoring his beer, he scanned a menu in English before ordering a salami *chlebicky*, an open-faced sandwich served on a baguette. He ate watching the crowd. Still no one seemed interested in him. By the time he had finished and dusted away the last of the crumbs, every table had turned at least once.

He had done what he could to make sure no one had followed him.

Still cautious, he left the square to walk around the block. He paused, seeming to admire toys in a shop window while he checked reflections of passersby. None of the faces were those he had seen earlier today. He returned to the square and entered the huge arched doorway of a blue-tinted building on the south side.

He stood in a cavernous, vaulted space he guessed had once been a stable. A sign at the back advertised a restaurant in the basement below with RED, HOT AND BLUES! LIVE AMERICAN JAZZ AND BLUES NIGHTLY. A stone staircase on his right led to the hotel whose small sign he had noted while he enjoyed his meal. He pushed the buzzer for an antique cage-style elevator. His mending legs could use a respite.

The place had clearly been a private home at one time. On each floor, rooms were angled from a center vestibule so that there had been no need for corridors. Yes, they had a vacancy, the English-speaking lady at the small office announced. It fronted right on the square. Would Lang like to see it?

Minutes later, Lang was in a modestly furnished, high-ceilinged room, poring over the free city map common to most European cities. All its advertisers' locations were prominently marked. Starozitnictvi Staraov was not among them. Returning to the office, Lang had the proprietress run the name through her computer's city directory.

She looked up from the screen and pointed. "It is a dealer in old books. It is to be found in the *Mala Strana*, Little Quarter." She pointed as though Lang could see through the walls of the cramped space. "The area just on the other side of the Charles Bridge."

II.

Piazza dei Cavalieri di Malta
Aventine Hill
Rome
At the Same Time

The older man was looking over the shoulder of the younger, squinting at the computer screen. "You have found nothing, Antonio?"

Antonio shook his head. "Nothing, Grand Master. The American lawyer, the woman, the child—even the dog—disappeared after leaving the pawnshop." He turned to look into the face of the other man. "But I can speculate, should you permit."

"Please."

"We know this man, Reilly, has access to a private jet." He paused long enough to click several keys. A photograph of Lang at the British Museum filled the screen. "We also know that jet left for Africa the day before yesterday."

"Africa? I don't—"

Antonio held up a cautionary hand. "If I may, Grand Master?"

The older nodded. "Forgive my interruption."

"The plane made a single stop en route: Munich."

"And you think this Reilly was on it."

It was Antonio's turn to nod. "I cannot know, of course, but our brothers in Germany are to obtain copies of whatever documents the aircraft submitted to the authorities. We should know before tomorrow."

"That may well be too late. Discovery of the contents of those books would mean disaster."

Antonio was silent for a moment. "We do not know there *are* copies."

"It is a chance we cannot risk. It is better we eliminate this American than to find we have made a mistake. Safer yet, we must silence all but us who might know of the contents of the book. That is why the Englishman died. We must continue to observe the shop from whence they came. If he has found out anything, he will come there."

"It will be done, Grand Master."

III.

Prague
Twenty Minutes Later

The late afternoon sun had sunk enough to put the narrow streets into total shade, making it difficult for Lang to read the tiny print on the map. He was pleased to find he was not lost when he looked up and saw the Old Town Bridge Tower, a medieval defense that guarded the eastern end of the Charles Bridge. He was tempted to take a minute or two to admire the Gothic sculptural decorations of its facade, including the carved kingfisher, personal symbol of the fourteenth-century King Wenceslas of Christmas carol fame.

Then he thought of Manfred, weeping in terror as bullets tore through the walls of the country cabin.

He had no time for historical exploration.

Crowds of tourists wandered back and forth or took pictures of the procession of marble saints that lined the wall along each side of the bridge. Similar to its builder's inspiration, Rome's Ponte Sant'Angelo, the bridge also seemed to be a favorite spot to photograph opposite skylines.

Lang had no time for a Bernini wannabe, either.

Almost a mile later, Lang was leaning on his cane as he stepped off the bridge and began to study the map again. The shop he was looking for should be two blocks down the Nerudova and then right on the street he was seeking, Josefska.

Unlike the Old Town, here the roads were wide enough for automotive travel if barely so because of the lines of parked cars. The pavement began a steep incline toward the castle, now invisible behind nearby rooftops. He made a right turn and stopped suddenly. Directly across from the shop two men lounged against a black Opel Astra. One was smoking a cigarette, the other reading a newspaper. The short street consisted of one or two shops and several restaurants, all closed until the dinner hour. Possibly, the men were waiting for someone, but just like the men outside the pawnshop had attracted Gurt's attention, they set off a well-tuned alarm system in Lang's head. Any anomaly, a dirty, dented car in an upscale neighborhood, a panhandler with shiny shoes, anything that didn't seem to belong where it was, brought agency training to mind like a reflex.

Realizing standing still would make him as just as obvious, Lang developed an interest in the menu posted in a restaurant window before crossing the street and resuming a leisurely stroll. If these guys were, in fact, watching Starozitnicvi Straov, he would certainly attract their attention by entering. As he passed, he noticed a neat sign in Czech, German and English. If Lang was seeing correctly through glass that appeared not to have been washed in this millennium, the latter two announced entry was by appointment.

Lang was about to turn a random corner when he caught his reflection in the side mirror of a parked Renault Megane. He saw himself clearly but also one of the men from in front of the shop, walking casually but at a clip that would shortly close the distance between them.

Lang glanced around. There was no one other than he and the two men on this stretch of street. The weight of the Browning in its small-of-the-back holster was reassuring, but gunfire in this quiet section of town would likely draw the police in a hurry. Involvement with the local cops had no upside. He would be far better off handling this quietly.

The man behind was getting closer. Lang could see sunlight reflecting from the shaved scalp and the single earring so many Czechs seemed to favor. He was big, too. Somewhere north of two hundred, Lang guessed, most of it muscle, judging by the biceps that strained against the restraints of the tight black T-shirt.

Lang increased his speed slightly, swaying like a ship under sail as he used his cane to hobble around another corner. He stopped, turned and spread his legs into a batter's stance.

He didn't have to wait long. Baldy rounded the turn, his eyes searching for Lang in the near distance. It took a millisecond for him to adjust his sight.

Not a lot of time but enough.

Lang lunged forward like a clock spring suddenly released, putting all his weight behind a major-league, go-for-the-fence swing with the walking stick. It landed where it had been aimed, at the bottom of the man's nose, bending the nasal cartilage back against and into the point it became bone. Tissue snapped with an audible pop.

The blow was neither fatal nor particularly damaging but it was one of the most disablingly agonizing Lang knew. Its recipient would be blinded by tears of pain for several seconds at the least.

Baldy's hands flew to his face as he yelped and collapsed to his knees, bringing his head into range of another home-run cut to the side of the jaw.

Baldy fell sideways, lying on the sidewalk as he emitted blood and moans in equal parts.

Looking up to make sure his victim's companion had not heard anything, Lang knelt and awkwardly rummaged through the man's clothes. His fingers closed around a switchblade, which Lange shoved into his own pocket. He had expected no identification and he found none. He was about to give up when his fingers touched paper. He pulled it out and stared.

He was looking at himself in formal garb.

The British Museum.

But how . . . ?

He had scant time to think.

Baldy's friend rounded the corner, grunting in surprise as he saw his pal stretched out on the pavement. If anything, he was bigger than Baldy, big enough to make Lang wonder if steroids were the Czech breakfast of champions.

One thing was certain: they liked knives. Or at least, this pair did.

Another switchblade snicked open, the last of the afternoon sun dancing on a six-inch blade. Lang used his cane to push himself to his feet as the man advanced, knife extended.

He mistook Lang's steps backward for an attempted retreat. Lang didn't understand the words but the tone was clear enough: "Come here, little fish. All I want to do is gut you."

Lang was about to get his twenty-five dollars' worth along with a handsome dividend. Holding the cane in his left hand as he backpedaled as best he could on gimpy legs, he used the right to tug at the cane's knob.

His eyes never left his assailant's; they didn't have to. Instead, he watched his opponent's widened stare as Lang withdrew a good three-and-a-half-foot blade from his gentlemen's walking stick. He had recognized it as a sword cane the second he had touched the brass knob in Monk's shop.

The blade hummed evilly as Lang slashed at the air. "Not exactly what you'd expect from a cripple?"

Evidently so.

It was a lot more steel than the man facing him wanted any part of. He took a couple of steps backward before turning and fleeing.

Bastard probably parked in handicapped spaces, too.

Lang had started to trudge back to the hotel when his BlackBerry buzzed. His office number showed on the screen.

"Sara?"

"It's me, Lang."

"What's up?"

"It's Home Depot. I called like you asked me to and asked that they come get the stove, deliver the wall oven."

Jesus! She could have text messaged him; that was the point of having a BlackBerry. But then, that was Sara, resistant to new technology as a flu vaccine to the virus. When typewriters had become the next buggy whips, it had required a series of threats, promises and finally a raise to convince her to learn basic computer skills rather than retire. E-mail was suspect, subject to electronic whim just as computer files were not to be trusted nor CD's worthy of confidence; they would not cannibalize their information unlike their paper counterparts.

She picked up on the pause. Or perhaps his sigh. "Am I interrupting something?"

"No, no. I was just, er, meeting with some people. Home Depot was delivering a wall oven and . . . ?"

"The man from your condo management company called, complaining about the hall outside your unit being blocked."

"See if you can get the guy who was supposed to install the oven to move it inside."

"Not that simple. They left the stove and delivered a hood to go with it. I called the store. They said that was what you ordered."

Lang sighed. "Who did you speak to, Laurel or Hardy?"

IV.

Thirty Minutes Later

When Lang got back to his hotel, he felt as though Baldy and Co. had succeeded. The still-mending parts, which was most of his body, ached, stung or just plain hurt. He resisted the impulse to stretch out on the bed to relax sore muscles and joints. Instead, he went back to the hotel's small office.

"A favor?" he asked.

The woman nodded. "Surely. Perhaps choose a place for dinner? Call for a driver for a tour of the city tomorrow?" She grinned suggestively. "Maybe arrange for company this evening?"

"Thanks, but no." Lang pointed to what looked like a phone book. "I have a hobby, collecting old books and manuscripts. A friend referred me to a shop here in Prague . . ."

Certain he would never get the pronunciation anywhere near understandable, he wrote out the name. "The sign on the window said 'by appointment.' Could you . . . ?"

She squinted, reaching for an old-fashioned rotary phone.

She spoke what Lang guessed was Czech. He only understood his name and the word "American," a frequent European synonym for "sucker." She handed the phone to him.

"Hello?" he asked tentatively.

"Mr. Reilly?"

He could not tell if the voice, slightly accented, belonged to a man or woman.

"Which of my customers was kind enough to give you my name?"

Lang made the instant decision to go with the truth. Or as much of it as seemed expedient. "Eon Weatherston-Wilby."

"A great pity. You have heard?"

Lang nodded as though the person on the other end could see. "Yes. He gave me the name of your shop shortly before he, er, died. I would very much like to see what you have that might be of interest to me."

"Is there something in particular, some certain type or time period?"

"Something similar to what you sold Sir Eon."

There was a definite pause. "I think it better if we met someplace other than my business."

"I'm a stranger in Prague. Make a suggestion."

"Do you like the food of New Orleans?"

Strange question. "Sure, but . . . ?"

"The basement of your hotel in, say, an hour? If we are to talk, we must finish our business before twenty-one hundred hours. Thereafter, the music makes it difficult to hear."

The line went dead.

How was whoever he had just spoken to going to recognize him wherever they met? He didn't even have the name of the person he was meeting.

Then Lang recalled the sign in the huge vaulted room below the hotel: RED, HOT AND BLUES! LIVE AMERICAN JAZZ AND BLUES NIGHTLY.

Apparently complete with New Orleans cuisine.

New Orleans jazz, too, Lang hoped. He loved Dixieland, the music that had originated in the Crescent City, the Big Easy, that rich gumbo of spirituals, African rhythm and improvisation.

But then, the music wasn't what he had come here for.

An hour later it hadn't begun.

Lang descended a wrought-iron circular staircase to what looked like a large cave. White cloth–topped tables were arranged around a stage to his left, the location of whatever music there would be. Only when he reached the bottom of the steps did he realize the entire room had been carved into solid rock. In days long before refrigeration, such cellars had been used to keep vegetables as fresh as possible. But he had never seen one of these dimensions.

At the bottom of the stairs, a white-jacketed waiter approached.

"Mr. Reilly?"

Lang nodded.

"This way, please."

Lang was less than surprised to be shepherded to the only occupied table. An elderly man lifted watery blue eyes and smiled as he extended a hand.

"Forgive me for not rising, Mr. Reilly, but . . ."

Only then did Lang notice the wheelchair, an old model with a wicker back and a wooden frame that had seen recent polishing.

Lang took the hand, its skin feeling like parchment.

The old man's smile widened, exposing dingy teeth. "You like my antique?" He patted an armrest. "It is old, like me. Handmade when people took pride in the things they produced. I like to think of it as my Chippendale or Bugatti." He motioned for Lang to be seated. "I have the advantage of you, I fear. I know your name but you do not have mine."

His hand slipped from Lang's. "The English pronunciation would be Havel Klaus."

The accent was decidedly British-tinged.

"Your English is quite good."

Klaus leaned back in his seat. "As it should be. I spent most of the war in England, at least that part before Heydrich's assassination. After those brave men died in the crypt of St. Cyril and Methoious, I felt I had to do more. I parachuted in to join the partisans."

It took Lang a moment to draw up the memory. Reinhard Heydrich, Himmler's fair-haired boy, had been the Nazi "Protector of Bohemia." In spite of his brutality, he fancied himself much loved by the people of occupied Czechoslovakia, so certain he drove himself to work daily in his open car. In May of 1942, the result had been an English-made bomb tossed into the passenger seat by Czechs recently dropped near Prague by the English. As intended, the event had been a morale raiser for all of German-occupied eastern Europe.

Cornered in an Orthodox church, the killers had elected to shoot themselves rather than face certain torture. The reprisal was the leveling of one of Prague's suburbs and the execution of every man, woman and child in it.

Klaus signaled the waiter. "But you did not come to Prague to hear the stories of an old man. I recommend the étouffée. Those who have traveled to your New Orleans tell me it is quite good here."

And they were right.

By the time Klaus put down his fork, the room was beginning to fill. Lang had expected the place's patrons to be a young crowd. Instead, most customers looked middle-aged or older.

Klaus was draining the last of his beer. "It would be best if we talked before the band arrives. Exactly what is it in which you have an interest?"

"Do you have anything like the book you sold Sir Eon?"

Klaus chuckled, the sound far deeper than his spare frame should have been able to accommodate. "No, and I doubt there are any more outside of museums."

Lang leaned across the table and lowered his voice. "What can you tell me about the one you sold?"

"Tell?" The old man's eyebrows made snowy arches. "Definitely part of the Nag Hammaddi Library, the Koine Greek, the Coptic Greek that was—"

Lang hated to interrupt, but he wanted to conclude this business before the tables around them were full and the music made shouting necessary to be heard. "I know. I mean, what was the subject matter and where did you get it?"

"Surely you understand my sources are secrets of my trade."

"But Coptic? All the way from Egypt to the Czech Republic?"

"I never said I got it in Prague. I will say that we have to look back in history. By the fourth century, the time these books were written, the western Roman Empire was shattering. The capital was moved to Ravenna, near Italy's east coast, more easily defendable than the ancient city. Thereafter, conquering Franks were calling themselves Caesar though they were not Roman, or even Italian. In the east, Byzantium was flourishing, the city of Constantine. Do you have any idea how long the Byzantine Empire lasted, Mr. Reilly?"

Truthfully, Lang had never given the matter a lot of thought although he considered himself a student of history.

"From, say, the rule of Constantine in mid–fourth century until the Ottoman Turks finally took the city in 1453. It was because of that city's fall that western Europe needed another route to the Orient. Columbus was seeking one when he found the Western Hemisphere."

Lang looked anxiously at the room's growing crowd. The decibel level was climbing noticeably.

Klaus sensed Lang's impatience. "To make it brief, Mr. Reilly, Byzantium, the city we knew once as Constantinople, now Istanbul, was at the center of an empire for a very long time. As the western part of the Roman Empire declined, the east flourished, much more Greek in culture than Roman. Since the pre-Roman rulers of Egypt had been Greek since Alexander's conquest, there was a cultural if not political tie between that country and the Byzantine Empire, an empire that was much of today's Eastern Europe including what is now the Czech Republic. When various parts of the books went on the antiquities black market back at the time of their discovery, it would seem natural to peddle them to some wealthy collector in what, at one time, had been essentially a Greek empire, particularly if that place was not a party to any international treaties regarding the buying and selling of another country's antiquities." He shrugged. "That's only a theory but it is as good a guess as you will hear as to how Sir Eon's book came into my hands."

He continued. "The Nag Hammaddi texts were written by Coptic, Egyptian, Greek Christians, probably a sect we know today as the Gnostics. In AD 367, the pope Athanasius circulated a pastoral letter declaring Gospels not chosen by the Nicene Council of 325 to be heretical. As you know, only four were chosen. The rest were ordered destroyed. Apparently, the Gnostics, or some of them, decided to bury, rather than burn, their copies."

Having explained it to Jacob the night at the British Museum, little of all this was news to Lang. Still, the subject was no less interesting. He forgot the increasing noise level. "Which was the gospel you sold?"

"The Gospel of James."

"James?"

"James, called The Just. He was the first bishop of Jerusalem and the brother of Jesus."

Two questions immediately came to mind. "Brother? I didn't know Jesus had a brother."

Klaus's face wrinkled in a smile. "Then you haven't read your Bible. He had a number of siblings. Mark refers to them in chapter six, verse six."

"I never knew that, either. But then, I grew up Episcopalian."

"You were not supposed to know. The existence of siblings presents a problem for the church. First, the doctrine of Mary's perpetual virginity. Multiple children contradict that idea. Second, having brothers and sisters of the Son of God running about is a bit inconvenient."

Lang forgot the background noise and leaned closer. "How do they explain away what the Bible says?"

"The church, particularly the early church, was a master of . . . what do you Americans call it? Spin. Yes, they were spin masters. I think the standard argument goes something like this: Joseph, Mary's husband, is not mentioned in any gospel by the time Jesus reaches maturity, most likely died. He was, therefore, considerably older than Mary, a man who outlived his first wife who was the actual mother of all of Jesus's half siblings."

"Pretty lame. My next question is, what did the Gospel of James say?"

A shrug. "I do not know. As I said, it was written by Coptic Greeks and I do not read Greek nor understand Egyptian."

"Then how did you . . . ?"

Klaus held his empty glass up to a passing waiter. "How did I know what I sold Weatherston-Wilby was genuine? I assure you, he had it vetted thoroughly before the transaction was complete. The provenance was impeccable if . . ." He searched for a word. "Not entirely normal."

Lang was silent for a moment, pressing circles into the tablecloth with the bottom of his glass. "I sure would have liked to know what it said."

The old man smiled again, this time creating enough wrinkles to make him resemble one of those Chinese dogs, a shar-pei. "Then I am a fortunate man. I thought the copy I made would have no value other than the satisfaction of having it translated so I, too, would know its contents."

Lang simply stared at him, remembering Gurt's admonition about closing his mouth.

Klaus laughed, a sound like footsteps crunching in dry leaves. "You are surprised, yes?"

"Astounded would be more like it."

"And how much is your astonishment worth?" He saw the expression on Lang's face. "I am, after all, in the business of selling old books and manuscripts."

"Certainly not as much Sir Eon paid. And I'd like to come to your shop, see how legible your copy is."

The old man shook his head slowly. "Only those patrons I know well visit my shop." He waved a blue-veined hand in the air. "Much of my merchandise is . . . well, of difficult pedigree."

"Provenance, you mean?"

Klaus nodded.

Swell.

Lang was doing business with a dealer in stolen rare books.

"But I am a reasonable man. Selling the copy is like, like . . ."

"Finding money on the street."

"Yes, money on the street, say finding five thousand US dollars."

Lang folded his arms. "I'm not that curious."

Klaus nodded again, acknowledging the haggling had begun. "And just how curious are you?"

"About a thousand dollars."

"I have enjoyed the supper, Mr. Reilly." He pushed back from the table and swung the wheelchair around toward the elevator, stopping only to offer over a shoulder, "Many museums will want a reasonably priced copy."

The copy had gone from being self-educational only to a desirable museum exhibit. The prospect of money had been known to work even bigger transformations.

As Lang had suspected, the old man had intended to

make additional dollars with a copying machine all along.

Lang motioned for the check, studiously ignoring the wheelchair rolling across the dining area. He was almost ready to get up and go after Klaus when the old man folded first.

He spun around and rolled back to the table. "We Czechs have a saying: Stubbornness deprives all of a fair bargain."

Lang grinned. "We Americans also have a saying: A fool and his money are soon parted."

"Thirty-five hundred."

"Fifteen hundred."

At two thousand dollars, the two shook hands.

"Give me the money and I will see that your copy is delivered to you."

What had he just said about a fool and money?

Lang shook his head. "Tell me where to meet you so I can look it over and the cash is yours. As soon as I can get it out of an ATM."

Klaus looked puzzled, then brightened. "ATM? Here we have Bankomat. Bring it to my shop in the morning. With two thousand dollars, you will have become one of my customers I know well."

Lang went to his room with the vison of Klaus hunched over a Xerox machine all night.

As the waiter deftly snatched the cloth from the table Lang and Klaus had vacated, he stopped and removed an object not much larger than a penny from the bottom of the table. He walked to the men's room and opened the door to the sole stall. Inside was a man who exchanged a wad of kroner for the thing from under the table.

V.

A Few Minutes Later

Once in his room, Lang used his BlackBerry to call Gurt. Ostensibly, he was calling to make sure she and the little boy were keeping on the move. He really wanted to speak to his son. He had thought he had experienced loneliness before but never had he suffered an absence as he did being away from little Manfred. Surely, he told himself, he would finish his business here in Prague in time to be home tomorrow night. His conversation might well be picked up by a tap on Echelon, but whoever wanted him out of the way probably already knew he was in the Czech Republic.

"Lang?" Gurt could have been in the next room, not an ocean and half a continent away.

"We are weary of this all the time moving. I have decided to visit Manfred's *Grossvater*."

Grandfather, Gerhardt Fuchs, a former East German official and the subject of Lang's only venture into Soviet territory while with the agency. Few people knew Fuchs was now living in the resort town of Baden-Baden in the Black Forest. Gurt, also aware of Echelon and the possibility of its being compromised, didn't mention the location.

"Do you need to? I was just getting acquainted with my son."

Lang regretted the words as soon as he had spoken them. If anyone was qualified to gauge how safe remaining in Atlanta was, Gurt was that person.

"*Our* son," Gurt corrected. "It is more without danger if we leave."

How do you argue with that?

"Let me speak to him."

Manfred gave a thorough description of his exploits with Grumps and his latest visit to the local International

House of Pancakes, a place the child equated with heaven itself. Lang had to admire his mother's courage in taking an active three-year-old to a place where containers of sticky, multicolored syrup were not only within reach but easily opened as well. As the child stopped for breath in his excited narrative, Lang was convinced his son was intelligent and mature beyond his years, an observation which uniformly drew his skepticism when voiced by other parents. The inconsistency never occurred to him.

Gurt took the phone back from a reluctant Manfred. "We were having lunch with Uncle Fancy when you called."

Uncle Fancy. The conjunction of the hard and soft consonants of the priest's name defeated the three-year-old tongue, hence the sobriquet, one Francis bore with good humor.

"Put him on."

"On what?"

Gurt's Teutonically literal mind and her difficulty with the American idiom was both one of her most endearing and annoying qualities.

"Let me speak to him."

"How's my favorite heretic?" Francis's bass boomed through the ether.

"Fine," Lang replied. "I hope to be home soon. I need your advice."

"Tell me you've seen the light, Paul on the road to Damascus. *Veritas praevalebit.*"

"More like Demosthenes holding the light in search of a single honest man. Don't fire up the incense yet. The truth I'm looking for is more church history than religious . . . I think."

"You know I'm available anytime . . . particularly if single malt scotch is involved." He became serious. "I've learned not to ask, but Gurt really believes she and the child are in some sort of danger."

It was an invitation to explain. Doing so might well expose the priest to the same people who had employed Baldy and Co.

Lang said nothing.

Francis began again. "You might be interested to know I've been summoned to Rome for a convocation of African and African American priests. Church business, but I thought you and Gurt, Manfred, too, for that matter, might want to come along. As well as you know the city . . ."

"Thanks but no, not at the moment. Gurt's leaving to visit with her father for a few days."

"Perfect! That leaves you free to come along. I think she might trust me with your behavior."

Lang didn't want to hurt his friend's feelings, but he couldn't very well explain why he didn't have time for optional travel. "I'm pretty busy right now, Francis. We can talk about it when I get back, probably tomorrow."

Francis didn't do so well hiding disappointment. "It's not for another week. Perhaps then."

Lang had gotten what he sought: affirmation the priest was going to be available to answer questions about James the Just, reputed brother of Jesus. "Let's hope. Now, let me speak to Gurt again."

The additional conversation did little but make him aware of the hole in his life that was the absence from Manfred and Gurt. He could not remember ever being so impatient to get home. He fell asleep almost immediately after terminating the call, but not before mentally marking the toy store he had passed. There were a number of items in the window that might interest an exceptional three-year-old.

VI.

Old Town Square was empty of yesterday's tourists. Anyone following Lang would have been obvious. The sole traffic on the Charles Bridge was a woman with a head scarf on a bicycle, its handlebar basket full of baguettes that still had a freshly baked aroma.

Ignoring leg muscles still in denial from yesterday's excursion, Lang took a circuitous route to the bookseller's shop. The neighborhood was just awakening to the new day. A few merchants were rolling up steel mesh blinds as restauranteurs swept already spotless sidewalks. A woman exited from somewhere down the row of Baroque buildings, pushing a pram. No Baldy. Unwilling to take unnecessary risks, Lang took another lap around the block, this time trying not to be obvious as he scanned windows and doorways.

He finally stopped in front of Klaus's business, taking a final glance left and right. Pushing a button beside the door, Lang was rewarded with the sound of pealing bells from within. A minute passed, then another. Lang tried again with the same lack of result. He took a step back and looked at the upper-story windows. European shopkeepers frequently lived above their stores. Perhaps the old man was still upstairs, unable to hear.

More from frustration than because he expected success, he used the head of his cane to rap on the door. To his surprise, it swung open a couple of inches.

Klaus had not impressed him as a careless man, the sort who might forget to lock up. Holding the cane in his left hand, Lang used it to push the door wide, his right hand on the butt of the Browning in the small of his back.

The only available light was that coming through the shop's filthy display window, a light filtered by an accumulation of dust. He could make out silhouettes: a table, a counter running the length of one wall, but little else. His left hand searched the wall until he found a switch. The single overhead bulb did little more than chase the pervasive shadows into corners where they waited sullenly. Startled, Lang snatched the Browning up only to grin sheepishly at his own reflection in a dozen or so old-fashioned glass bookcases, each crammed with leather-backed tomes. The room had an overlaying musty smell of prolonged disuse. But there was something else, too, an odor that was familiar yet not quite remembered clearly enough to identify.

Lang went to the foot of a staircase and peered into the darkness that inhabited the area above the fifth step. There must be an elevator here somewhere, the means of a wheelchair-bound man to ascend to the floors above.

But he saw none.

Instead, as he looked closer, he could make out the faint impression of a shoe's print in the dust that coated the stairs.

But how . . . ?

Lang went to the doorway of the shop and looked outside. Next to the store, massive oak doors were flanked by a brass plaque with names and individual buttons. That was it, of course. The shop had a street entrance, but also access to the apartments above by an elevator that served all units from a common foyer. Klaus, if he lived above, could enter his apartment by elevator or his shop from the street.

OK, so how did a cripple leave a footprint?

Lang went back to the stairway, wishing he had thought to bring a flashlight. He placed a tentative foot on the first step and, using the cane, brought the other up to the next.

Progress was slow and got even slower when he ran out of what poor light there was and had to feel his way with the hand holding the pistol while using his cane to push upward. Each riser sent an ache from hip to ankle.

More than once, he was tempted to shout upward, to tell the antique-book dealer he was here. After all, Klaus had seemed eager enough for the money. Something else, perhaps his agency training or some sixth sense gained by experience, told him he did not want to announce his presence to everyone in the building any more than he wanted to confine himself in an elevator.

He reached a small landing. Light leaked around three edges of a door. Lang put his head next to it and listened. The only sound was of an occasional automobile passing in the street below.

Lang gently pushed the door open. The smell from downstairs grew stronger.

With the door halfway opened, Lang could see into a short hallway, its stone floor partially covered by an Oriental runner.

In a single motion, he was in the hall. He pulled back the slide, cocking his weapon as he swept right and left.

"Mr. Klaus?" he called in a low conversational tone. "Mr. Klaus, *dobry den?*"

His answer was a silence that seemed to intensify the longer he waited.

The first door off the hallway was to his left. He nudged it open and looked into a bathroom from the last century. A claw-footed tub with the usual European shower hose filled one wall across from a toilet with an overhead water tank. He eased the door shut and tried the next one up the hall. A tiny kitchen contained a small box of a refrigerator, a two-eyed gas range and a microwave. There was barely room for a short wooden countertop and a doorless cabinet filled with mismatched dishes. Through the kitchen, he was looking into part of the dining/living room. A floor-to-ceiling window allowed cheerless sunlight through gauzy curtains.

If Klaus made the sort of money Eon had paid him, he certainly didn't spend it on luxurious living.

Browning held in an extended hand, Lang stepped across the kitchen's cracked linoleum and into the room. Klaus was seated near a corner. Now Lang recognized the odor he had been unable to identify: blood.

Blood soaked the old antiquarian's shirt, blood filled his lap. Blood was puddled on the worn carpet. Blood that was already turning brown and dried into a crust along the jaw-to-jaw slit in the neck.

Lang swept the room with his weapon. Books, manuscripts, scrolls and stacks of loose paper occupied every horizontal surface. And dust.

Either in an unsuccessful defense or death throes as Klaus suffocated or bled to death, the wheelchair had smashed into a sturdy, tufted sofa, knocking a wheel off the axle. It was wedged between the dead man and the upholstery.

Lang surveyed the room. The copy he had come for could be in plain sight and still invisible. It would take hours if not days to sort through the material in this room alone, not even contemplating the shop downstairs and the remaining room at the end of the hall, a room he guessed had been the old man's bedroom. And Lang was fairly certain he didn't have hours. Sooner or later an unanswered phone, a missed appointment, something would result in a visit to this apartment and a grisly discovery.

Lang stepped to a battered end table and looked down on what appeared to be an atlas in a language he couldn't identify. Under it were two rolls of parchment held together by a rubber band.

He was so intent on making at least a cursory search, he barely heard the creak of a floorboard.

Gun outstretched, he whirled.

Too late.

The heel of a hand from behind him hit his wrist, sending the Browning spinning across the room.

A forearm was around his neck, closing his air passage. Another hand held a knife, a long switchblade. Like Baldy's. Probably like the one that had killed Klaus. His attacker's body was jammed against his, making it impossible to use the sword in the cane.

With one hand, Lang dug and clawed at the forearm that was squeezing off his air. With the other, he held off the knife. It was an unequal contest; his assailant was too strong.

Letting go of the choking arm for an instant, Lang drove his elbow backward, jamming the point into a stomach rigid with muscle. There was a grunt and an exhalation of air, but the grip around Lang's neck grew tighter.

A gray fog was growing at the periphery of Lang's vision, a sure sign of oxygen deprivation. The only real question was whether Lang's throat was going to be cut like Klaus's before his air-starved brain went blank.

Unless he did something and did it quick.

But what?

VII.

Hartsfield-Jackson International Airport
Atlanta, Georgia
8:31 P.M. EST
The Previous Evening

Gurt was watching the man who was watching her.

She was quite accustomed to men staring before hitting on her. But this one was pretending to be engrossed in a newspaper, so engrossed that he had been holding up the same page for the last twenty minutes.

She had first noticed him when she and Manfred had arrived at the gate. Not the gate from which they would actually depart, but one chosen almost randomly as a precautionary measure. Just in case someone like the man with the newspaper showed up. She had little doubt he would hang around the departure area until she boarded the flight to . . . She flicked her eyes to the electronic board behind the check-in booth. To Paris.

That was, of course, one of any number of places she and her son were not going tonight.

The flight to the City of Light was scheduled to push back from the gate in seventeen more minutes. She had deliberately chosen Atlanta's leading airline, knowing its storied inability to make an on-time international departure. She supposed that, being a company based in the languid South, posted arrival and departure times were informational only; that is, the plane would definitely not depart or arrive *before* the time given. How long thereafter was slightly less predictable than the stock market, future interest rates or the next professional athlete to be accused of steroid use. Experience had taught her that taking an international flight on this airline to connect with a foreign carrier's schedule was a guarantee of time to be spent in unplanned places.

But she was not connecting and what she had in mind would work only with a dominant if inefficient airline.

Between scratchy announcements of varied reasons the Paris flight would be predictably delayed, she attempted to keep a wide-eyed Manfred entertained. Or at least from becoming a nuisance to passengers already irritated by the airline's endless supply of excuses. Walks up and down the concourse or following the lights of planes until they disappeared into the night sky worked for the moment. Whenever she left the gate area, her watcher moved to a position where he could see. Several times he muttered into a cell phone.

She surmised she was not the person her minder's superiors were really interested in. They wanted Lang. She was merely someone who might be going to meet him and therefore worth keeping under observation in case Lang slipped his tether. Perhaps they didn't actually know where he was, a fact she doubted. For all she knew, whatever organization the news reader was working for had already hacked into the airline's reservation system. If so, no wonder they had a man to see where she was going after periodic and less-than-subtle tails for the last few days, tails she had regularly evaded. She booked the flight under her own name. The agency's paranoia as to possible adverse publicity regarding unnecessary pseudonymous travel required it when not on agency business.

Excuses finally exhausted, first-class boarding for the Paris flight was announced. Holding Manfred's hand in one of hers, Gurt rolled her suitcase on board with the other. As anticipated, the flight attendant barely glanced at the two boarding passes before both Gurt and her son were ensconced in large, comfortable seats with leg room large enough for an normal adult. It only took a few minutes before a man stood in the aisle, looking from Gurt to his boarding pass and back again.

"You sure you're in the right seat?" he asked, his tone indicating the answer he expected.

Gurt took a long look at the slip she held in her hand. "Flight one seventeen, two A and B."

By this time the flight attendant had arrived. "Wrong flight, honey. This one goes to Paris."

Gurt stood, feigning both surprise and embarrassment. "I am so sorry." She bent over to unbuckle Manfred's seat belt before retrieving her bag from the overhead compartment. "I hope I have not caused . . ."

The displaced passenger's eyes were fixed on the place the top button of her blouse was fastened. "No trouble at all. Hope you make your flight."

Gurt took her time, standing aside as the other passengers trooped aboard like cattle into a pen. When the last one was through the door, she led Manfred up the passageway to the gate area. As she had expected, the man with the newspaper was gone.

She calmly walked down the concourse to the flight she had planned to take all along. She had also planned on the fact its departure would be delayed.

There was something to be said for predictability as a substitute for punctuality.

VIII.

Prague

Lang felt weakness in his knees as he struggled to gasp air through the stranglehold. The knife's blade was inexorably moving toward his throat. He was smaller than his opponent to begin with; his partially healed injuries had tipped the scales even further.

He leaned backward.

The man behind him reflexively took a step forward, the better to balance dead weight.

That was when Lang brought the heel of his shoe smashing into the arch of the other man's foot.

Metatarsal bones crunched like dry twigs.

Simultaneous with a yelp of pain, the grip around Lang's throat relaxed slightly and he went totally limp. The sudden gravitational pull against the loosened grasp dropped Lang to the floor like a sack of concrete.

Fighting the urge to stop long enough to fill his lungs, Lang rolled across the planks and the worn carpet toward where he had last seen the Browning when it was knocked from his hand.

A bellow of rage made him glance backward. Baldy, his

ruined nose covered in a dirty bandage, glared through a pig's bloodshot eyes. He was unable to put weight on his crushed foot. He was padding across the floor on his knees, the switchblade extended.

He swiped at Lang, the blade glittering like a streaking comet in the window's light. As Lang jerked back, before Baldy could draw back again, Lang was on his feet, delivering the hardest kick he could muster to the side of his enemy's head.

He may as well have used a pillow. Baldy wagged that shiny, shaved head like a boxer shaking off a hard right cross and came on, muttering something Lang was happy he could not understand. The intent was clear enough.

Lang gave ground, his eyes searching for his missing weapon, until he felt the wall at his back. His hand touched the top of a chair. Baldy made no effort to dodge as Lang raised it above his own head to bring it crashing down on Baldy's.

Unlike the brittle furniture of cinema, the wood did not shatter or even crack. It did, however, lay Baldy out flat for about a two count before he used a table to struggle to his one good foot and came on, dragging his other.

Talk about hardheaded determination.

Lang slid along the wall as Baldy continued, the knife making small circles in the air. Lang stopped. He waited until his assailant was almost within striking range. Then, leaning back on his left leg, he swung his right in an arc, the foot-sweep common to judo, jujitsu and any other number of martial arts. His foot knocked Baldy's out from under him.

The man crashed like a felled oak, the hand not holding the knife swiping at Klaus's wheelchair as though for support. The wheelchair did, in fact, shatter like furniture in the barroom fight scene of a B-movie Western.

The old man's body was dumped unceremoniously on the floor like a discarded doll.

Lang had no time to observe the niceties. His seemingly

invincible opponent was struggling to his feet once more. He considered a retreat to the kitchen in hopes of finding a knife of his own, but Baldy was between him and the doorway. From its location, Lang guessed the only other exit led into Klaus's bedroom. Baldy could simply wait in the hallway and dispose of Lang at his leisure.

The he saw it: the Browning's butt half hidden under the folds of a carpet kicked over in the present struggle.

Baldy saw it, too, and he was closer.

But with his injured foot, he was also slower.

Lang was going to bet his life on it.

Reaching behind him, Lang picked a book from the table and threw it as hard as he could at the right side of Baldy's head. There was nothing wrong with the man's reflexes. He ducked to his left, away from the pistol. Lang dove for it, a swimmer's racing dive onto a hardwood floor.

The impact knocked the breath out of him and sent colored spots spinning in front of his eyes as partially healed bones and muscles protested the impact.

Gun in both hands, Lang rolled onto his back just as Baldy leapt at him, knife outstretched.

The Browning jumped in Lang's hands and he forced its muzzle down for a second shot.

He saw the brass shells spin through the air, reflecting the light; he smelled burned gunpowder. But he never recalled hearing the shots, some sort of reaction of the mind to block out some sensations while magnifying others.

He also saw Baldy, sitting splay-legged on the floor. The knife was beside him but the man was intently inspecting two growing red Rorschach blots on his chest that could be seen even against the black of his T-shirt. Shakily, he got to his feet, glaring at Lang with unmistakable hatred. He said something Lang guessed was in Czech, took a half step and did a face-plant on the floor.

Lang circled warily. He fully expected the man to get up and come at him again.

Pressing the gun's muzzle against the shiny scalp, Lang listened for breath for a moment before feeling for the carotid artery. There was no pulse.

Lang felt nausea rising in his throat. He could not ignore the irony: In all the years he had spent with the agency, he trained in the art of killing but never had. Since then, he had been forced to take perhaps a half dozen lives in defense of his own. Justifiable or not, he would never get used to it.

Swallowing pure bile, he hastily looked around the room. The sound of the struggle and the gunshots surely had caused someone to call the police. It was definitely time to leave. He started for the door when two things stopped him in his tracks.

Among the wreckage of Klaus's wheelchair was a purse, the old-fashioned cloth kind that snapped shut, the sort of thing in which a woman might keep in her handbag with her change in it. Lang did not recall seeing it; but, then, he hadn't had a lot of time to look around. Either way, it was empty.

There was another item, one he was sure had not been there before: a sheaf of papers in one of the shattered arms of the wheelchair. The arm was hollow. A quick inspection showed a series of characters Lang recognized as Greek. The old fox had likely had the copy of the Book of James with him last night, concealed all along, no doubt planning to make more.

Lang took one last gaze around before he left the room to the growing sound of sirens. He stepped over Baldy's body. Distasteful or not, Lang was thankful a couple of 9mm slugs finally stopped him.

He was fresh out of sharpened wooden stakes.

Chapter Four

I.

The Rectory
Immaculate Conception Catholic Church
48 Martin Luther King, Jr. Drive
Atlanta, Georgia
8:34 P.M., Two Days Later

Lang waited until Francis's housekeeper removed the last of the dinner dishes. An expectant Grumps followed her into the kitchen.

"You sure you won't have any trouble with the diocese, letting us, me and the dog, stay here?"

Francis was halfway to a sideboard and the bottle of single malt scotch it contained. "I'm sure the bishop would agree it is better to have the apostate where the church can keep an eye on them. If we had watched Luther a little more closely, it would be a better world."

"Only if you happened to be a papist."

Francis snorted and lifted the bottle to show the label to Lang. "Precisely."

Lang followed the priest and the bottle into a small study. Books lined the three windowless walls. "I'll have to admit, this is one of the last places anyone would look for me."

Francis was tinkling ice cubes from a silver bucket into glasses. "No argument there." He handed one of the tumblers to Lang. "And you are sure someone is after you? This isn't a manifestation of paranoia produced by a troubled mind?"

Lang sank into a leather club chair. "Want to go down to my country place and count the bullet holes? And you should see the burned hole in the sky that was my condo."

Francis sat and took a sip, shaking his head. "In the vulgate, your ass is always in one crack or another. I gather that's why Gurt left?"

Lang nodded. "Pretty much. Neither of us want to take chances with Manfred."

Francis thought this over a moment. In the years of his close friendship with Lang, he had learned Lang would tell him all he wanted known in his own time. "From what you said before supper, it has something to do with scripture or one of the apostles."

"I think so. Specifically, James. Was he the brother of Jesus?"

The priest stared into his drink for a moment before rising to pull a well-worn Bible from the shelves. "That's been the subject of debate. Matthew 13:53–56 says"—he opened the book—"after the young Jesus astonished the various priests at the synagogue, it was asked, 'Where did this man get this wisdom and these mighty works? Is this not the carpenter's son? Is not his mother called Mary? And are not his brothers James and Joseph and Simon and Judas? And are not all his sisters with us?' Mark has almost the identical language at 6:6." He thumbed the pages. "Plus, Luke 2:7 speaks of Jesus as Mary's firstborn son, an implication she had others later. In Galatians 1:19, Paul tells us, when he traveled to Jerusalem, he 'saw none of the apostles except James, the Lord's brother.'"

Lang took a drink. "I understand that poses a problem to you bead slingers, both from the point of view of having the siblings of the Son of God unaccounted for and the doctrine of the continuing virginity of Mary. I also understand the church contends all those siblings were from a previous marriage of Joseph."

Francis sighed as he returned the Bible to the shelf and

sat. "*Vexata quaestio,* a vexing question. It is certainly possible they were *half* brothers and sisters. St. Jerome taught in the fourth century that they were only cousins."

"*Veritatem dies aperit.*" Lang grinned as he lifted his glass.

Francis rattled ice cubes, a melodic chime against the crystal. "Time may reveal the truth but two millennia haven't shed a lot of light on this one. It is also possible that the writers of those gospels meant brothers and sisters in the sense we are all children of God."

Lang left his seat for a refill. "The Gospels were written in Greek originally, were they not?"

"So I understand."

"I don't know the language, but I seem to recall it has a very specific word for 'brother,' *adelphos. Anepsios* for cousin. If the writer had meant cousin or half brother, he had the words to use."

Francis's faith and Lang's lack of it had been the cause of endless spirited but friendly arguments. In fact, religious debate was second only to Latin aphorisms as an entertainment medium. Both men respected the other's intellect; both practiced a profession involving logical advocacy and argument. Nonetheless, Lang was careful never to demean his friend's beliefs or go past that ill-defined point where Francis might perceive insult or threat. Conversely, the priest never tried to convert Lang to anything that could be described as organized religion and managed to keep his mouth shut about aspects of his friend's life of which neither the priest nor the church approved. The boundaries made the friendship both interesting and pleasurable.

Francis waited until Lang had finished pouring before refilling his own glass. "I'm not sure I understand what all this has to do with your present problem. It's an old dispute, one that I'm sure sent any number of heretics to the stake. But we don't do that anymore. I'd be surprised if anyone, even the most devout, were trying to kill you over the James-brother-of-Jesus thing."

Lang was back in his chair, legs crossed. "Someone sure didn't mind killing my friend Eon."

Francis nodded his agreement, sending the light dancing on the beads of the rosary he wore around his neck. "True, but that involved rare documents, something of actual cash value. Have you ever considered the fact that he and that man in Prague . . ."

"Klaus."

". . . Klaus. That they both were killed because of what was *in* those old papers?"

"That was why I wanted a copy. I figured if someone was willing to kill anyone who had access to them, there must be something the killers don't want known. If I can find out what that is, I may be able to find out who they are."

It had worked before. The secret of the enigmatic painting by Poussin, a seventeenth-century French artist, had led him to the shadowy Pegasus organization.

"If you live long enough."

"Spare me your optimism."

Francis was looking into his glass, debating a third scotch. "And you have this copy of the book?"

"In my safe-deposit box until I can find someone to translate. I made yet another copy."

Francis had decided another wee libation might do no harm. "I'm sure there's someone at Emory . . ."

"There is, but he's on sabbatical until the end of the summer. I don't intend to let it out of my sight when it's not in the lockbox."

"You could make another copy, send it to someone."

"And risk their life? Remember, two people who had that book are dead. That's why I'm keeping it close at hand."

Francis gestured toward the bottle; Lang shook his head. "So, you don't plan to find out who these people are for some time?"

Lang had thought of that but couldn't come up with an

alternative. "If you have any suggestions, don't let your priestly humility keep you from speaking up."

"Humility's the Dominicans' shtick. Come with me to Rome. Like I told you, I'm leaving next week. Sunday, actually."

Lang started to protest but the priest raised a silencing hand. "It works." He held up a finger. "First, you can bet your heathen soul there'll be someone at the Vatican who can read that book of yours, Coptic Greek." He held up a second digit. "Second, you can share my room *in* the Vatican. You don't get much more secure than that even if your pals figure out where you've gone."

Lang wasn't wild about the idea but he didn't have a better one.

Half an hour later, he was staring at the ceiling of the rectory's small guest room. He would be glad to get out of Atlanta. Being here without the warmth of Gurt's body next to him made his hometown an alien and lonely place. Worse was knowing that Manfred would not be exploding through the door at the first hint of morning, ready for the day's adventures. Even Grumps, stretched out beside the bed, was staring morosely into space. Lang was sure he was thinking of his missing playmate.

Gurt and Manfred had just entered his life, what, a couple of weeks ago? Far too short a time to miss them as much as he did, he told himself unconvincingly. He intentionally replaced growing self-pity with anger. Who were these people that made it necessary to be apart from his son and lover? What was it in that ancient text that made it necessary to kill any who possessed it?

Well, Francis was right about one thing: if any place on the face of the planet would be sure to have scholars of ancient Greek-Egyptian, the Vatican would be it. Lang hoped he would learn the secret of the Book of James before his pursuers discovered where he had gone.

He hoped.

II.

Delta Flight 1023
Sunday Night

Lang's dislike of flying was enhanced by the stingy dimensions of a tourist-class seat. They hadn't expanded any since his agency days when travel was always by the most economical means possible. Apparently the Catholic Church subscribed to the same idea. The only difference was that now the airlines no longer served complimentary drinks to economy international passengers, but charged five bucks for those beverages that could only be sold to adults. He had offered to pay for an upgrade for Francis rather than suffer the discomforts of tourist-class travel, but the priest had pointed out that it would be bad politics for any of his fellow clergy to see him luxuriating in accommodations designed for adult-size passengers. The same reason excluded use of the foundation's Gulfstream.

There had been some small comfort in having Francis confirm that politics played as large a role in the clerical world as the secular.

Both men finished a meal of what had been charitably described by the flight attendant as chicken marsala, the only alternative to the mystery meat Lang had seen being served to other, possibly less perceptive, passengers. Lang and Francis put down the post-9/11 plastic utensils that had been largely ineffective in dismantling the rubbery fowl. They reclined the few millimeters allotted each tourist-class seat. Lang opened the novel he had bought at the airport bookstore only to realize he had read it years ago. The publisher had reissued it with a different cover. Now he was stuck with futile attempts to sleep sitting inches away from perpendicular or the in-flight movie, a G-rated animation suitable for small children and the easily amused simpleminded.

He had forgotten how dismal economy travel could be.

He turned to Francis, who looked disgustingly comfortable. "So, tell me about James."

Francis blinked and shook his head as though he had been asleep, a possibility Lang hadn't considered given the circumstances. "James? James who?"

"Jesus's brother, James the Just, I think he's called."

Francis was unsuccessful in stifling a yawn with the back of his hand. "What do you want to know specifically? The Catholic Church and you heretics differ on a number of details."

"Try the truth."

The priest smiled. "You really know how to put a fella between an ecclesiastical rock and a hard place. As you know, we believe in the perpetual virginity of Mary, which by definition excludes the possibility of Jesus having any full siblings."

"Who came up with that idea?" Lang asked.

Francis shrugged as much as possible in the cramped confines of his seat. "I'm not sure. The idea probably originated in an obscure second-century text called *Proto-Evangelium of James*. Like the Jews, the early Christians felt anything sexual was unclean. It would be impossible for the mother of the Savior to be defiled. Since she was perpetually a virgin, she could not be the mother of Jesus's so-called siblings."

"Convoluted reasoning, I'd say."

Francis nodded. "Perhaps, but then how reasonable is it that a man would rise from the dead?"

Exactly what Lang had been thinking. How could a religious devotee also do the Vulcan mind-meld? *Star Trek* or witchcraft? "OK, but what about James the man?"

Francis was on firmer ground. "There were two Jameses who were the original disciples. But they are always designated as James the son of Zebedee, brother of the apostle John, and James the son of Alphaeus, also known as James the Lesser."

"James the Just wasn't an apostle?"

"Someone literally had to stay home and mind the store. If Jesus was pursuing his ministry and Joseph, husband of Mary, had, in fact, died by then, who was to support the family?"

A question of such practicality, Lang was surprised he had never considered it.

"In fact . . ." Francis produced a pocket-size Bible and quickly thumbed the pages. "Ah, here, John 7:2–5 makes it clear than none of Jesus's brothers seemed to believe in him. In fact"—he flipped the pages again—"Mark 3:20, 31–35 tells us that, when his family heard of his healing the sick and casting out demons, they went to restrain him. People were saying Jesus was out of his mind. I'd say it would be a fair guess that the family was less than pleased to have an itinerant preacher for a brother. In fact, you may recall it was his inner circle of disciples that buried him, not family, although his mother may have been present according to the Gospel of John. I'd also guess that having a family member crucified, a death reserved for traitors to Rome, was a bit of a humiliation."

"James wasn't a disciple, but he became the first bishop of Jerusalem?"

Francis put the little book back wherever it had come from. "True. How did James go from alienated brother—or half brother—to ardent apostle? I'd speculate it took something pretty dramatic. Like, maybe, Jesus's post-crucifixion appearance to James, which Paul mentions in 1 Corinthians 15:3–8."

"But why James? I mean, why not one of the original twelve disciples?"

Francis shook his head. "Part of some divine plan, I'm sure."

"Unsatisfactory response, but a safe haven. C'mon, Francis, you can do better than that!"

Francis pursed his lips. "I'm sure the church has an

answer, but if I had to speculate . . . well, the Gospels tell us Christ selected Peter to continue his ministry, his church, as it were . . ."

"Upon this rock . . . ?" Lang interjected.

Francis rolled his eyes. "They say even the devil can quote scripture, but, yeah. Anyway, I'd postulate that Peter, at least at the beginning, pretty well had his hands full spreading the word. He needed someone to handle things at home in Judea and who better than a . . . a close relative of Jesus himself."

"OK. What else can you tell me?"

"It will please you to know there is no rest of the story, at least not in the Bible. The time line of the New Testament ends just about there with Acts 15. We *do*, however, have a historical reference by Josephus."

"The Jew historian turned Roman citizen?"

"The same. He tells us James was reputed to be so pious, to pray so much that his knees were like those of a camel. He also refers to James as 'the brother of him that was crucified, held by some to be the Messiah.' I believe this is the closest thing to a contemporary mention of Christ that exists."

Lang stretched his legs as far as the limited space allowed, an unending quest for comfort. "You said that was the end of the story. What became of James?"

Francis made no effort to suppress a yawn. "Martyred. He was stoned by a mob outside the Jerusalem temple and then thrown from the highest part of the building. Or vice versa."

Lang sat straight up, legroom forgotten. "Stoned and thrown from a building? That was the way Eon was murdered."

"Now there's a coincidence."

Lang shook his head. "I don't think so. A bullet would have been quicker and easier. Besides, when's the last time you heard of death by stoning?"

Francis's lips tightened. "You're saying someone killed

your friend in the same manner as James? Why would they go to that much trouble?"

"If I knew that, I might have a good idea who these people are." Lang thought for a moment. "Were any of the saints martyred by having their throats cut?"

Francis was silent a moment, reviewing the ever-ingenious ways in which early Christians were dispatched to meet their God. "I suppose that could be said of Matthew. He was hacked to death with a halberd. But why . . . ?"

Lang was thinking, calling up details of the murder scene in Prague. "Does a purse mean anything to you?"

The priest was clearly puzzled. But then, his friend frequently asked questions that made no sense at the moment. "A purse?"

"Like an old-fashioned woman's change purse."

Francis ran the palm of a hand across his jaw. "As perhaps related to St. Matthew?"

Now it was Lang's turn to be baffled. "A purse would be related to a particular saint?"

"All saints have symbols; most, several. In medieval times, the clergy were the only people who could read and, of course, no one knew what the various saints looked like. So, they were identified to the common person by symbols. Matthew's was a purse, since he had been a toll collector. But he is also symbolized by a winged man or a lance."

But neither a lance nor a winged man had been in Klaus's home.

Something else was emerging from Lang's memory, something he had read. From experience, he knew no amount of effort was going to make it clear. It would come in its own sweet time.

The newspaper, the *Times* account of Eon's death. It had mentioned something that at the time seemed a non sequitur, a totally irrelevant fact.

A seashell? No, a specific kind of shell . . . a scallop shell!

If the purse hadn't belonged to the old man, if the killer had left it behind as a symbol of the saint whose death resembled his . . .

"What was the symbol for James?"

"A shell, the sort of shell the oil company uses as its logo. I can understand your interest in James, since it was supposedly his gospel that was stolen, but why the sudden curiosity about saints in general? I'm not optimistic enough to think a conversion of the heathen is taking place. Even God recognizes the futility of some of his miracles."

"Just thinking."

Francis removed the pitifully small pillow from behind his head and gave it a couple of emphatic thumps as though it were capable of being fluffed. "Think on. I'm going to try to get some sleep."

In minutes, Lang was left alone with his thoughts and the sound of soft snores.

III.

Leonardo da Vinci International Airport
Fiumicino
The Next Morning

Lang felt as wrinkled as his clothes when the 757's engines spooled down and he stood to retrieve his single bag from the overhead rack. Francis stretched and yawned, looking disgustingly rested. Sleep of the innocent, Lang supposed. In minutes, they were immersed in the up-and-down ramps, twisting corridors and general confusion of Rome's international airport. An indifferent woman in uniform slid their passports through a scanner and impressed the documents with a barely legible stamp. As in most European Union countries, customs consisted of merely walking through the gate marked NOTHING TO DECLARE.

Then the real task began: navigating from one terminal to the next to the rail station, a structure resembling a huge Quonset hut housing four tracks. The trains ran only north to the city and there were no reserved seats. Lang and Francis boarded along with a group of American college students whose chatter seemed far too cheerful for the morning's early hour.

Francis checked his ticket for the fourth time. "Remember, we're getting off at Trastevere, not Termini."

Termini was the main Rome rail station, the ultimate destination of all trains from the airport. Trastevere was one stop short, the station nearest the Vatican.

Lang shoved his bag into the overhead rack and sat in one of the two-by-two seats underneath. "How could I forget?" he asked good-naturedly. "You've been reminding me ever since we landed."

Francis slid into the seat beside him. "How will we know when we're there? I mean, neither of us speak Italian."

Lang rubbed his eyes, still stinging from lack of sleep. "Look out the window. There'll be a sign announcing the name of each stop."

Patience, Lang told himself as the train groaned to life and began to pick up speed. Francis had never been to Rome, let alone the Vatican. The priest was as excited as a child the night before Christmas.

Lang's eyes saw uncut grass between rusty rails, discarded rolling stock and the rear of shabby buildings. His memory painted Dawn, his wife, with cruel realism as she squealed in delight at every crumbling structure, certain she was viewing temple ruins rather than storage sheds displaying years of deferred maintenance. It had been their only trip together, their sole excursion before the doctors had found the death sentence she carried within her. Two years later, it had been here in Rome that Lang had renewed a relationship with Gurt. This local train might be passengers only but, for Lang, it carried a lot of freight.

They were the only passengers disembarking at Traste-vere.

Just as well. There was only one vehicle available, a small and nearly shabby Fiat with a Vatican license plate. Lang was forever surprised at the lengths to which the world's wealthiest organization went to comply with the Christian dictates of humility.

Outside the Holy City, that is.

Inside St. Peter's, wealth equal to the gross national product of most of the third world's countries was displayed to anyone with the price of a ticket to that part of the Vatican's treasures open to the public. Only an imagina-tion uninhibited by lengthy digits could encompass what was not on display.

The docility evidenced by the church's choice of trans-portation was not reflected in its operation. The man was definitely a grand prix aspirant. Lang marveled at the calmness with which Francis chatted with the driver as the Fiat charged down the narrow alleys of what had been Renaissance Rome's working district. Last night's wash flapped overhead in the morning's gentle breeze that would later become a listless wall of heat. Although Rome itself was a city of neighborhoods, Trastevere was even more independent, viewing with distrust anyone from as far away as the next piazza over. It was this attitude that had convinced Lang to choose lodging here while he was investigating what would later be revealed as the Pegasus organization.

The Fiat squeezed through an intersection to a cacoph-ony of protesting horns, reminding Lang that Roman driv-ers took traffic directions such as stop signs as advisory only. Seemingly unaware of their imminent peril, Francis continued his chat with the Italian version of a kamikaze.

If Lang had ever had questions about the depth of his friend's faith, they were dispelled now.

The testosterone-charged competition that is Rome

traffic continued as Lang found a handhold and gripped it for dear life while trying to ignore the blasts of angry horns, used far more often than brakes.

He felt a wave of relief as the little car careened around a bus, missing its massive front by inches, and turned onto Via del Conciliazone, the divided boulevard that ends in the circular embrace of St. Peter's Square directly in front of the basilica. This would be the first time Lang had been in the Papal States since the Julian affair, a near-disastrous venture that took place in the little-known necropolis upon which the Vatican itself had been built.

Scattering pilgrim and tourist alike, the Fiat plunged across the square, stopping only at a barricade along the left or south side of the cathedral. A Swiss guard in full purple and gold sixteenth-century regalia carefully checked Lang's and Francis's passports against a printed list on a clipboard.

Satisfied he was dealing with legitimate visitors, he stepped into a booth beside the entrance and returned with two laminated badges.

"Be sure you wear these at all times," he cautioned in stiff English before waving them past.

Minutes later, Lang and Francis were shown into second-story dormitory-style rooms located the equivalent of two or three city blocks east of the basilica with a view of St. Catherine's Gate. Below, Swiss guards came and went.

"Must be close to their barracks," Lang observed.

Francis joined him at the window. "Barracks, mess hall, parade ground and armory, according to the official guide-book. Celebrated their five-hundredth anniversary in oh six. That's a long time protecting popes."

Lang stepped back from the window. "Who are the Swiss Guard, anyway?"

Francis chuckled. "If you're looking for a job, forget it. You have to be between nineteen and twenty-five, single, of good moral character, a Swiss citizen and a practicing Catholic."

Lang tsk-tsked, shaking his head. "Too bad. Those unies are real chick bait. Do they actually guard the pope or is their function ceremonial?"

"They really do guard him like our Secret Service does the president. A lot of them died when Charles V of Spain sacked Rome in 1527. Clement II really pissed him off. The pope barely managed to escape. Three days of the customary burning, looting and raping."

"Ah, the good old days when the winner didn't have to worry about political correctness."

A gentle tap at the open door interrupted the conversation. "Father Narumba?"

A young black man in a cassock stood in the doorway. "Excuse me, Father, but the meetings are about to begin."

Francis glanced at Lang. "Just as well. The conversation was rapidly degenerating. Lang, are you . . . ?"

"I'll be fine," Lang assured him. "I've got something to do here, too, remember?"

Lang took the time to douse his face in water as cold as the small bathroom's basin could provide. On the way back out, he slipped, a towel rack being the only thing that prevented what could have been a nasty fall. Puzzled, he glanced around the bathroom for the source of the water he now saw on the tile floor. A drop on his cheek directed his gaze upward to a brown, soggy stain on the ceiling. The plumbing probably hadn't been checked since running water had been installed to update what Lang guessed was a very old building.

Minding his step, he went back into the bedroom. He changed into a clean shirt, decided his rumpled pants could go another day and stepped into the hallway. Only then did he realize he had no key to the room. And the door had no lock.

Lang didn't know whether to feel stupid or embarrassed. This was, after all, the Vatican, where saving of souls took precedence over material objects.

Nonetheless, Lang went back into the room to make sure he had left no valuables. Practicality was hardly a sin.

Rather than risk getting lost in miles of hallways, Lang retraced his route. His memory from the Julian affair proved correct: the *scavo archaelogica* was almost directly across from the point he and Francis had checked in with the Swiss guard minutes ago.

Keeping a lookout against the possibility some irresponsible soul had again entrusted the morning's driver with a car or other potentially lethal device, he crossed the narrow passage and opened the door.

He entered a small room divided by a counter bearing colored brochures of the Vatican, the necropolis underneath and several of the Vatican's museums.

A white-haired man in a short-sleeve shirt, the first person Lang had seen without a uniform or clerical adornment, looked up from what appeared to be the sport pages of *La Repubblica*. "The last English tour of the necropolis has already left," he said.

"I'm not here for the tour, but thanks for the information."

The man frowned as if Lang's disinterest in being shown through the ancient Roman cemetery was a disappointment. His eyes came to rest on the visitor's badge. "Then, how may I be of service?"

His tone said he had no such intent but Lang smiled pleasantly. "I was sent to this office to find someone who can translate Coptic Greek."

It was clear the old man was weighing the possible position in the Vatican hierarchy of the person who had sent this American against the bother of interrupting his perusal of the soccer scores.

The unknown prevailed.

"That would be Father Strentenoplis." He pointed the way Lang had come. "Archives, across the way."

Lang thanked him and left.

The next person Lang met escorted him down a short corridor to an open door. Inside was a desk supporting neat stacks of paper beside a computer screen, behind which sat a man with a chest-length beard. He wore a simple black cassock adorned only with a gold cross on a chain around his neck.

He looked up and smiled with tobacco-yellowed teeth. "Come in," he motioned. "Come in, sit." He pointed to a single wooden chair.

Again, Lang was amazed at how easily Europeans recognized Americans.

Or they automatically addressed anyone who looked like they had just gotten off an airplane in English.

"Father Strentenoplis?" Lang asked.

The man stood. He was well over six feet. The beard, Lang saw, was streaked with silver, hiding the entire lower part of his face. The beaklike nose was striped by threads of red, those tattletale burst capillaries of the heavy drinker.

"Is me!" He was still gesturing for Lang to sit.

"B-But," Lang stammered, noting the cross had two cross members "You're . . ."

"Greek church, one you call 'orthodox.' Is true! Who read ancient Greek better than another Greek, no? You are surprised I am here at center of Western church, no?"

Lang sat. "Well, yes."

Father Strentenoplis also sat. "Is age of ecumenicalism! No longer argue over number of angels dancing on head of a pin. Your pope need expert in ancient and Coptic Greek, my patriarch in Istanbul want expert on medieval German, read heretic Luther. Even swap, yes?"

Lang nodded, the man's enthusiasm contagious. "Sounds fair to me."

The priest gave the doorway a surreptitious glance before he reached under the desk and produced a small pouch and a stack of rolling papers. For an instant, Lang thought he was about to roll a joint. He was relieved to see he was only preparing a cigarette. He rolled it with one hand, using the other to extend the tobacco and paper across the desk.

Lang shook his head. "No thanks."

The father lit up, instantly dispelling Lang's long-held belief that his friend Jacob smoked the foulest tobacco in the world.

"You come see me about ancient Greek, yes?"

Lang reached inside his shirt, producing the sheaf of papers. He peeled off one of the two copies. "I was hoping you could translate."

The priest held the cigarette between his lips, squinting through the rising column of smoke. Lang wondered how many times he had set his beard ablaze. He held the papers flat with one hand, producing a pair of half-moon glasses with the other. He scanned the first couple of pages.

"I have not seen before. Is gospel I read about, the one where man get killed in England, no?"

"Sir Eon, yes. The Gospel of James."

The priest looked up from the papers, staring at Lang.

"I found where Sir Eon got that. The man who sold it to him made copies."

Father Strentenoplis nodded slowly as though answering a question only he had heard. He exhaled, sending smoke into his beard where tendrils wafted upward as though from a brushfire. "St. James first bishop of Jerusalem, first Eastern bishop. Is liked, esteemed, more by Eastern church than by Western."

Lang resisted the temptation to fan away the smell of the cigarette. "You can translate, read Egyptian with Greek letters?"

He was happy to see the butt finally stubbed out into a small ceramic dish. "Is Greek, no? Should have by tomorrow morning."

Lang left, certain he wouldn't get the smell of whatever tobacco the good father smoked out of his clothes for days.

If it was tobacco.

Lang was on his way to his room when a familiar buzz came from a pocket. Sara.

"Lang? The people at your condo are really getting annoyed."

Why not? His unit had been a hole in the side of the building and now the interior hall was filling up with unwanted kitchen appliances.

"You did what I suggested?"

"Of course. I placed the charges in dispute with the credit card company. Just like you said, that got Home Depot's attention. They called yesterday and promised to come get the stove and hood. And deliver your oven."

Why did he think the matter didn't end there? "And?"

"Now there's a stove, a hood and a bidet sitting in your hall."

IV.

The Vatican

Lang returned to his room the way he had come. After a sleepless night, the single beds looked inviting. But first . . .

He took out his BlackBerry and punched in Gurt's number. He was aware of Echelon, but what were the odds of this particular call being selected for a closer look or listen? Even less were the chances that whoever had killed Eon had a way to hack into that system.

He realized he was simply rationalizing a chance to speak to his son.

Manfred had spent the morning with his mother and grandfather, hiking in the nearby Schwartzwald, Black Forest. Lang smiled, recalling how much the Germans loved to tramp through the woods for no other reason than being there. He had often theorized two world wars might have started accidentally by what began as an overzealous stroll through the Ardennes.

Yes, he had had fun, but when was Daddy coming to take him back to Grumps?

Soon, Lang assured him.

With a child's insight, Manfred insisted on a specificity Lang was unable to give.

Gurt rescued Lang by taking the phone. "I also would like to know when you will be able to come."

Lang told her what had happened since their last conversation.

"You are without a clue," she observed.

"I should know something more when I get the translation back tomorrow," he said with an optimism he did not entirely feel.

The conversation ended with more promises to Manfred than Lang felt he could keep.

When he hit the end button, he sat morosely on the bed. When would he see his son again? Would Gurt legitimize the child by marrying him? With his home destroyed, where would they live? All of these seemed far more important than some ancient gospel the collators of the Bible had decided not to include. Lang wanted nothing more than a peaceful life with the family he had found so suddenly.

But there could be no peace as long as someone wanted him dead. Anger at these unknowns who had threatened not only him but his son began to grow, a rage made greater by lack of a specific target. The only real clue was the murders of Eon and Klaus, each with biblical overtones. Who but some fanatical religious group would take the pains to relate cold-blooded killings to the martyrdom of saints?

If only . . .

He forgot everything he had been thinking of and stared at one of the two small chests of drawers against the far wall. The pulls were plain, round copper or brass disks.

But one was slightly larger than the others.

Intrigued, he sat on the floor, staring at what, moments before, had been a mundane, ordinary piece of metal. He opened the drawer. Each pull was secured to the inside by a bracket and a screw. He fumbled in his pocket for a moment before he came up with a dime. It fitted the screw head well enough to turn it.

Moments later, he was looking closely at the bit of metal in his hand, a fine mesh rather than solid like the others. Using a thumbnail, Lang pried up part of the tiny screen. He was not surprised to see a miniaturized listening device.

He instinctively glanced around the room. The thing could have been installed at any time but the battery life on something that small would only be a day or so. It was a safe guess the very unknowns against whom he had been raging had put it there. He resisted the impulse to grind the tiny thing under his heel. To do so would only alert its installers it had been found and encourage replacement with one he might not locate.

Instead, he carefully reinstalled it.

Then he began a meticulous sweep of the room. The phone was dis- and reassembled. The plates on all three electrical sockets were removed and replaced. Even the overhead light fixture received attention. There are only a limited number of places a bug can be placed and escape notice.

Satisfied, he took another longing look at the beds. No nap now. With doors without locks and his unidentified enemies aware of his location, sleep could be suicidal. He yawned. One of the little bureaus could be placed in front of the door and . . . and what? Without a weapon, it mattered little whether he heard a potential assassin or not.

Then he remembered something Francis had said just before he left.

Lang went back out, this time turning east toward St. Catherine's Gate. He crossed the area where he had seen the guards from his window and entered a building distinguishable from its neighbors only by a flat roof rather than the sloping red tiles common to the Vatican's buildings. Long wooden tables ran the length of a beamed room, reminiscent of a medieval banqueting hall. Clearly the mess. Across a hall was a smaller room, one stocked with the sort of general wares one would expect in an American drugstore, the commissary. Lang selected a baseball cap emblazoned with a helmet and what he guessed was a Swiss Guard logo. It was the smallest one he could find, one he hoped would fit a certain three-year-old head.

As he paid for his purchase, he asked the young, crew-cut man behind the counter, "Where's the armory?"

The kid didn't even look up from counting change. "Outside, turn left. Second door, first room on the right."

The armory was perhaps fifty feet long, its walls hung with halberds, swords and shields. An open gun rack ran down the middle containing enough rifles to start a small war.

As long as that war was fought in the first half of the last century. The rifles were bolt-action Mausers, the standard weapon of Germany's World War II infantryman.

A lone Schmeisser, automatic pistol, of the same vintage lay on top of the rack.

Lang stared stupidly at the far wall where a rack held both matchlock blunderbusses and flintlock muskets. The modern-day Swiss Guard must keep their own weapons instead of drawing them as needed from the armory. It made sense: The contemporary guard was unlikely to find itself opposing a siege by an enraged European monarch. These days, even royalty had to contend with budgetary constraints. A war of aggression would have to compete with national health care, an increasing dole and a parliament unlikely to reduce a litany of benefits to which voters had become accustomed. Rifles and heavier small arms weren't needed for the required duty, guarding the person of the pope rather than the bulk of the Papal States that had finally succumbed to the unification of Italy in the nineteenth century. Easily carried and concealed weapons would be all the modern guard required. The very sort of weapon Lang had planned on "borrowing."

Short of mugging one of the men in uniform, he clearly wasn't going to succeed.

With a sigh, he left the room and walked out into the increasing heat, which seemed to aggravate healing muscles already cramped by the long flight.

Outside the Vatican's walls, he stopped to buy a bottle of water. He all but emptied it before covering two blocks. He stuffed it into a back pocket. Since Rome was connected to a series of aquifers, even the little fountains, those consisting of no more than a pipe a foot or so above the street, provided sweet, cool and potable water.

The crowd around St. Peter's made it impossible to notice a possible tail.

Crossing the turgid green Tiber by the bridges over the Isola Tiberina, he could see the ruins of the massive Theater of Marcellus in the ghetto, the area in which medieval Rome's Jews were required to live and be locked in each night. There was much less foot traffic and he took his time, pretending to marvel at the old buildings. He even doubled back a couple of times without revealing anyone interested in his destination.

He hoped his memory held up because he knew his destination would be difficult to find. He turned left onto the Via del Portico, a convoluted route but one that would reveal anyone following him.

Navigating largely by the sight of the synagogue, one of the area's tallest buildings, he turned south, back toward the river. Every time he visited this part of Rome, he was impressed with the diminishing number of Jews. The narrow, winding streets, some of the oldest habitable quarters and location had made the neighborhood desirable to the city's young and affluent. He could only hope the man he had come to see still lived at the same address. He would be well past ninety by now.

He turned north on the broad Lungotevere dei Cenci and walked two blocks along the river before stopping to admire an apartment building that had maintained its ancient facade while the interior had been renovated. Still nobody paid him attention. Two quick steps carried him into a narrow alley. At the end stood a three-story structure he remembered from years ago.

Lang was relieved to see the name still beside the list of doorbells, faded but legible: BENSCARE. Lang pushed the button and waited. He tried again with the same result.

He was about to make one more attempt when a voice crackled from the speaker. The words were unintelligible, but the tone indicated a question.

"Viktor, it's Lang Reilly," he said, his mouth close to the speaker to avoid having to shout. "You and I did business years ago."

There was a heavy metallic thump as a bolt slid back and Lang stepped inside. The marble foyer was only large enough to contain doors to the two lower apartments and a staircase. There was no elevator. Renovation had not reached this far yet.

Leaning heavily on the stair rail to take as much weight as possible off protesting muscles and joints, Lang climbed to the top, the third floor, and knocked on a worn wooden door.

The door swung open and Lang was looking at an elfin little man whose long white hair reached below his slumped shoulders. Inside, klieg lights, lamps, reflective umbrellas, tripods and camera gear occupied every horizontal surface.

The man was still working, although he had to be well into his nineties. Even more amazing than handheld worldwide communication.

Lang knew Viktor Benscare had lived and worked as a professional photographer in this same apartment since 1922, the same year a certain lantern-jawed Fascist named Benito Mussolini had come to power. During the war years, Viktor had developed a profitable sideline: forgery. He had created passports for partisans as well as for Jews seeking to escape deportation to the death camps while the nearby Vatican inexplicably had not even murmured a protest. Due to the Italians' lack of fervor in enforcing their German comrades' racial edicts, his semicelebrity status as Rome's most famous portrait photographer, a non-Semitic name and, no doubt, well-placed bribes allowing him to tinker with birth records, Viktor had survived the Holocaust. With the fall of the Axis powers, his sideline boomed. He provided identities for those displaced persons who had lost theirs and for those who could not afford to retain their own in view of the Allied war crimes tribunals. When Europe settled down to its usual semipeaceful bickering, he had worked for the Camorra, the Neopolitan crime families, a loosely knit organization far exceeding in size, power and wealth its Sicilian counterpart.

During the Cold War, Viktor had been steadfastly neutral, equally happy to create a Russian driver's license or a British national health card. Several times, Lang had arranged for passports and supporting documents for a recent refugee from one of the workers' paradises when, for whatever reason, the agency was unable to do so.

Lang pushed the door closed behind him. "Viktor! You haven't aged a bit!"

The Italian smiled with teeth far too perfect and white to have originated in a mouth that old. "The quality of your sheet of the bool has no diminished, either." He led the way to a pair of chairs and began removing camera lenses from the seat of one. "An' you no come here causa you wanna you pi'ture made. Still, good to see one mora ol' frien' not dead." He motioned to the now empty chair. "Come, seet an' hava a glass a Barolo."

Lang was far too tired to be drinking anything alcoholic, but he acceded rather than wound feelings. When Viktor returned with a bottle and two glasses, he cleared another chair, sat and lit a cigarette. The smell was slightly better than the caustic odor of chemicals that pervaded the apartment. Lang watched the cigarette as he and his host discussed the relative merits of the wines of Tuscany versus those of Piemonte. Once the tobacco was stubbed out, the appropriate amount of time would have passed for the banter that precedes business in Italy.

As anticipated, Viktor cleared his throat as he ground out the butt. "So, you wanna what?"

"A passport."

The forger nodded. "OK."

"How much?"

The forger shrugged, a matter of such little consequence it was hardly worth discussing. "Thousand euro."

The old fox had raised his prices quite a bit since Lang had done business with him. "I'll pay when I pick it up."

Viktor shook his head. "Same as usual. Half now, half when you get."

Lang pretended to consider. "All right, but only if you can do one more thing."

The Italian waited, making no commitment.

"A gun. With ammo."

The old man's eyes widened, sending thick white brows into a single arch. "A gun? Canna do! You know—"

"I know you have connections and I'm willing to pay well."

That put a different complexion on the matter.

"How well?"

"Depends on the gun. A pistol, preferably an automatic I can carry in my belt."

"You coma back tomorrow, meybbe . . ."

Lang didn't even consider returning to the Vatican un-armed. "Today for the gun or we have no deal, Viktor. Of course, if you don't want the business . . ." Lang stood as if to leave.

Viktor was on his feet with an agility surprising for his age. "No, no! You go outside, meybbe see a church, old temple. The Colosseum. You come back . . ."

"In two hours," Lang finished for him.

Outside, Lang's stomach growled loudly, a reminder it had been a long time since his last meal. At the same time, he caught the aroma of a nearby restaurant. An hour and a half later, he had enjoyed zucchini blossoms, stuffed with mozzarella and anchovies and fried in yeast batter. He hadn't had the peculiarly Roman/Jewish dish in years. Tired or not, he had permitted himself a beer, pic-colo, small.

Now he needed cash, probably more than his limit at an ATM.

Crossing a little piazza, he looked around. An old woman pushing a baby pram, two priests. He entered a bank just before it closed for the afternoon hours when most busi-nesses, museums, even churches in Rome, and most of It-aly, shut down until four o'clock. It took a few minutes with personnel irritated at being detained from lunch to work his way up to someone with authority to phone the States and arrange for a cash transfer. Lang was aware the transaction was likely to be picked up by Echelon. It was unlikely, though, that a transfer this small would draw notice. Pocketing a roll of euros, less fees, Lang checked his watch, noted that two hours and sixteen minutes had elapsed and returned to Viktor's apartment.

This time he was buzzed in on the first try.

Viktor was grinning as he handed Lang a paper bag. "Eet is as you weesh!"

Lang nearly dropped it from the unanticipated weight. He peered inside and blinked, uncertain he was really seeing what he thought: an M1911 .45 Colt, the standard US military sidearm for nearly sixty years.

"Ees automatic as you weesh!" Viktor was beaming. He held up an extra magazine. "An' have extra boolits!"

"Yeah, but I didn't want something used by George Custer."

"Who Custer?"

"Man who couldn't count Indians."

The gun was as heavy as it was notoriously inaccurate. With its box clip holding only seven rounds, it was also short on firepower. On the positive side, the Colt's large caliber reputedly could stop an elephant. If the shooter could hit it. The gun was much sought by collectors but hardly by anyone whose life might depend on it.

Lang pulled the slide back, checking the barrel. At least the grooves were distinct, unworn. The thing must have been left over from the occupation of Rome in 1944 when some GI traded it for booze or sex, the two major incentives of soldiers in all wars.

"Untraceable, also," Viktor noted.

"I don't care if it's registered to the pope," Lang replied, knowing that touting the weapon's few attributes was a means of gaining advantage in the oncoming haggle about price. "How much?"

"Onlies two thousand euro."

Lang shrugged and handed the gun back to Viktor. "Too much."

Happily, the forger had no idea of how badly Lang needed a weapon immediately. Also in Lang's favor was the fact that Viktor's supplier would expect immediate payment, not a return. An anonymous tip to the police by the gun's former owner that Viktor possessed a prohibited firearm would be certain if the .45 wasn't sold as promised.

Viktor crossed his arms. "I stretch my neck for you, Lang."

"OK, fifteen hundred including the passport."

Lang was more than willing to pay the two thousand. That was not the point. Like most Italians, Viktor admired the art of bargaining. Lang would have lost face had he simply paid the first price offered.

Fifteen minutes later, Lang felt the reassuring weight of the Colt in his belt under his shirt as he left Viktor's apartment. He had had his picture taken for a passport that would be ready about this time tomorrow.

He was returning to the Vatican by the most direct route possible. This included crossing the multilaned Lungotevere dei Tebaldi.

Even during the afternoon recess, automobiles, buses and scooters clogged the boulevard. There are unwritten rules of crossing a street in Rome: If a driver knows a pedestrian has seen him, the vehicle continues, insane speed undiminished. The wary street-crosser stays in the crosswalk, eyes down, pretending to see nothing but the pavement in front of him.

Observing the rule, Lang was about to step off the curb when an alarm went off in his head. Agency training, intuition, blind luck. Something was out of place, an aberration like an open front door in an affluent neighborhood.

There was no one behind him, nothing . . .

He saw them.

Two workmen, one approaching from his left, the other from his right, their gait timed so that each would reach him simultaneously. Restoration and construction is always in progress in Rome, but work sites, like businesses, closed for the first part of the afternoon and it was not likely that the two were out for a stroll in the midday heat. And their clothes, though worn, were clean, none of the city's yellow dust or grainy grime that came from working with old stone.

Street crime in Rome tends to limit itself to picking pockets or snatching purses. Neither of these two looked the type. They lacked the furtive movements. Besides, pick-pockets and purse snatchers rarely operated in tandem.

Lang's hand went to the heavy weight in his belt. No, that wouldn't work. Shots would draw the carabinieri or *polliza* that were never far away. Just having the gun was a serious crime, and Lang didn't enjoy the thought of being imprisoned where his enemies could easily reach him. The two workmen knew that, too. A quick stab with a knife and they would continue on their way before anyone knew what had happened.

Where the hell had they come from? A picture of the two priests flashed across Lang's mind. Like most people, when he saw a priest, a cop, a soldier, he tended to see the uniform, not the face. He had failed to notice the two priests outside the bank, two clerics dressed in full cassocks that could easily conceal the clothes he now saw.

He took a look up and down the street, busy no matter what the hour. Of course there wasn't a taxi to be seen and the nearest bus stop was a block away. A dash across the street could prove as fatal as not moving.

In Rome, there were two types of jaywalkers: the quick and the dead.

Turning slowly, the moves of a man uncertain where he was going, Lang began to limp back toward the ghetto. There, if he had to use the .45, he had a better chance of getting lost in the winding streets.

The two workmen peeled off in unison, making no effort to conceal their intent to follow.

As Lang would have said during his years with the agency, he had a tactical situation.

V.

Schlossberg
Baden-Baden, Germany
At the Same Time

Gurt had thought the hike would have tired Manfred. Perhaps it had been the conversation with Lang. For whatever reason, the child had been cross all morning. He had complained about the same breakfast he had eaten without comment every day. He grew tired of his favorite toys.

Gurt had even allowed her son a rare interlude with the television. She usually forbade more than a few minutes of sitting in front of a device she suspected rotted brain cells, as witness the women she had met in the States who sat in front of the thing all day while their husbands pursued cardiac arrest at jobs that allowed them to meet the women's demands. Usually trophy second wives who shared Lang's condo building could speak only of the morning dramas that never seemed to reach conclusions.

What were they called? Something to do with washing, although Gurt had never seen anyone bathing the two times she watched the mindless action. Laundry shows? No. Never mind.

The same women spent afternoons with cooking demonstrations on TV when the only thing they made for dinner were reservations.

Even the magic box had not calmed Manfred.

Gurt was a loving mother, but she did not subscribe to the irrational thought that a child should be given a choice between obedience and "time out." When discipline was called for, she applied it, usually to the seat of Manfred's pants. It was old-fashioned but effective to make markets, airlines and other public places more enjoyable. Unfortunately it had gone out of style in America.

Gurt's father looked up from his *Süddeutsche Zeitung*, speaking in English as Gurt insisted whenever Manfred was present. "Why not take the automobile into town? You may find something to amuse him there."

Not one to cater to irritable children, even her own, Gurt gave the idea consideration. Inflicting a whining child on someone else, even a grandparent, was selfish, another concept long dead in America. But it might work. Baden-Baden liked to call itself Europe's vacation spot, as indeed it had been when crowned heads from Portugal to Russia had visited in the eighteenth and nineteenth centuries to partake of the mineral baths that supposedly had curative powers. The custom dated back to the first-century Romans who had founded the town.

European royalty was notably lacking these days, but tourists still came to take the baths, lounge in the Belle Epoch hotels and gamble in the Rococo casino that sat like a gem on green velvet in the narrow meadow that was the valley of the river Oos. The river, though scenic, would hardly rate the status of a creek in the US.

Gamble.

Also horse racing.

Horses.

Manfred loved to watch the horses as they were put through their morning exercises.

Gurt took her son by the hand. "Come, Manfred, we will go see the horses."

That suggestion, along with the hint they might have lunch in whatever American junk food spot had recently opened, brightened the child's disposition to the extent he forgot his usual complaints when buckled into the child seat that occupied most of the backseat of the ancient but pristine Volkswagen.

The road, a snake of pavement, wound around steep hills. Gurt had driven enough here that she knew every bend well enough to reduce driving to an almost subconscious level.

Certainly her mind was not completely on the task at hand.

Why was it, she asked herself, that women are ultimately stuck with the job of nurturing the children?

Because if men did it, no one would ever grow up.

Still, it wasn't fair that Lang was doing something exciting in Rome while she was reduced to taking a tot to watch horses. Of course, she admitted, she had not given Lang the chance to experience his son's early days, his first step, his first word. Perhaps she had been a bit overly independent, too fearful her freedom would be compromised.

That was when she noticed the big Mercedes in the rearview mirror.

Rich people were fairly common in the area, so expensive cars were no surprise.

But this one was flashing its lights and blowing its horn as though to pass.

"Car make noise," Manfred observed, twisting his neck to look out of the rear window.

In itself, again no surprise. The wealthy were frequently in a hurry.

But pass?

The ribbon of asphalt had few straight stretches and fewer shoulders. The outside of each turn was lined with flimsy-looking Armco barrier and the inside tended to climb vertically.

There was a bump from behind that nearly tore the steering wheel from her hands.

Manfred began to cry.

Who is this maniac? Gurt wondered, fighting to regain control.

Then she remembered the hail of bullets at Lang's country place and the fiery ruin that was his condo. The man at the Atlanta airport. Whoever wanted Lang dead was perfectly willing to use his son to get to him. And her.

But how . . . ?

She mentally kicked herself. Airline reservations were easily hacked. All someone had done was ascertain she had flown into Frankfurt. Her passport would have been registered at customs and immigration, a passport that listed Baden-Baden as her address. *Dumkopf!* Working and living in Frankfurt, she could have listed it instead. For that matter, her employer could have provided her with papers with any address in the world, rules notwithstanding.

Now these people had her actual address and were trying to either run her off the road or get her to stop.

Another not-so-gentle tap on her rear bumper emphasized her problem.

Reaching to the floor, she retrieved her purse with the agency-issued Glock she had stopped to pick up upon her arrival in Frankfurt to replace the one airport security mandated she leave in Atlanta. The people in the Mercedes wouldn't expect her to be armed. If they pulled out to push her to the edge . . .

No, that would only invite return fire. No gunplay, not with Manfred in the car.

The BlackBerry? Doubtful she could take her eyes off the road long enough to dial. And the hilly terrain made the use of cell phones an iffy proposition.

Think.

Her agency training had taught her any number of mundane objects could be used for self-defense. She opened the glove box. Only insurance documents and a couple of road maps. Tire tools? In the trunk. The people in the Mercedes would be on her before she could even get to them.

She took her eyes off the road long enough to glance around the interior of the VW.

Then she had an idea.

VI.

Rome

It was obvious Lang's pursuers were gaining on him even if they were taking their time about it. He turned a corner and spied a trattoria, a small, usually single-family-operated eatery specializing more in home-type cooking than the formal fare of a *ristorante*. Outside, a waiter in an apron stained with tomato sauce was bussing the five tables with paper tablecloths.

Lang remembered his own lunch. It gave him an inspiration.

"*Dove il cabinetto?*" he asked.

The waiter was still protesting that the restrooms were reserved for paying customers as Lang stepped around him and went inside.

Now Lang had to rely on luck. If this place was like a thousand others, the single-sex toilet, the kitchen and a few more tables would all be in the back. There might even be an exit to another street.

The downside lay in the local knowledge of the two behind him. If they knew there was no other exit, all they had to do was wait for him to come out.

His plan was to draw them in.

Sweeping aside a curtain, Lang was in the tiny kitchen. The chef, in grease-splattered white, looked up from a four-eyed gas stove on which artichokes were frying. He started to say something but then gaped as the waiter and the two workmen charged in behind Lang. Everyone was close enough to touch everybody else.

In a single motion, Lang snatched the wooden-handled skillet from the stove and heaved its sizzling contents into the face of the first man.

He screamed, clutching his face as though tearing away the frying skin would end his agony.

Lang continued a swing. The huge iron pan slammed against the head of the second man, who dropped to his knees with a moan, then collapsed to the floor and lay still.

The chef and waiter stared openmouthedly as Lang walked back to the front of the place where an older man stood behind a butlers' desk on which were several credit card machines.

"You might want to rethink your menu," Lang said as he went through the door to the outside. "Some people just can't tolerate fried food."

VII.

Baden-Baden

It was difficult to keep one eye on the tortuous road and the other on the rearview mirror but somehow Gurt managed.

"Manfred," she said as calmly as she could above the clatter of the VW's four cylinders at full rpm, "unbuckle your seat, get out of it and lay down on the floor."

"But Mommy . . ." the terrified child protested.

"And do it *now*."

Gurt was using that I-am-about-to-turn-you-over-my-knee tone that the little boy had learned meant the time for negotiation was over. She could only hope that small three-year-old fingers were equal to the task.

The Mercedes moved toward the left-hand lane, a position from which it could easily utilize its superior weight to push her into and perhaps over the Armco. She twitched the wheel to the left to block the move and took another jolt on her bumper. At the same time, she saw Manfred slip out of his seat and disappear onto the floor.

Just ahead was a sharp right hairpin around a hill, a turn so acute the Mercedes would lose sight of her for an instant.

Beyond that was a short straightaway at the end of which two driveways led to houses hidden from the road by conifers. If she could just slow the larger car a bit, she might make it to those driveways and someone might be home, someone with a landline telephone to summon the authorities. Or, if not, at least she and her child might find a place to hide in the woods.

It was a big *if*.

One hand on the wheel as she entered the turn, she reached back and grasped the child seat. Manufactured to provide protection in case of a crash, the thing must have weighed a ton. The thought of what her pursuers might have in mind for her and her son gave her an extra boost of adrenaline and she tugged the seat free.

At that moment, the angle of the hairpin blocked her view of the Mercedes. She frantically rolled down her window. It seemed to move with glacial speed. Once open, she shoved the child seat through it, watching it hit the pavement and bounce just as the larger car exited the curve.

The result was far more spectacular than she had dared hope. The hood of the big auto dipped in a sudden application of brakes to avoid the object coming through the windshield. The violent locking of those brakes along with the centrifugal force of the corner broke whatever adhesion had existed between tires and pavement.

Gurt exhaled in relief as the front of the sedan spun to its right, too far over for the driver to correct in time. Panicked to stop the skid, he followed instinct rather than physics. He fought the wheel in the opposite direction instead of applying gas to regain lost traction. The car, already as loose on the pavement as a raindrop on a windowpane, simply swung the other way and planted its radiator into the Armco with a protesting shriek of metal that Gurt could clearly hear.

As she lost sight of the Mercedes behind the next rise in the road, a cloud of steam obscured the front end.

She was going the have to take the long way home and make an immediate departure, but, at least for the moment, she and Manfred were safe.

What was it she had been thinking? That she envied Lang the excitement? He always said to be careful what you wish for; you might get it.

VIII.

The Vatican
A Few Minutes Later

When Lang reached the top of the stairs on his way to the room he shared with Francis, the hall was packed with priests. They were excitedly chattering in at least four languages Lang recognized. As far as he could tell, the center of attention was in the direction of his room. Fearing something might have happened to Francis, Lang easily shouldered his way forward. He was somewhat more aggressive than your average priest.

When he reached the front of the crowd, he almost slipped again. More water. The Vatican plumbing had struck again.

But water wasn't what had drawn all the attention. It flowed from the open doorway of the room next to Lang and Francis's. Standing on tiptoe, Lang could see it coursing down the far wall. The sheet of water had washed away the white plaster, revealing a painting, a fresco.

A large bearded man in biblical dress stood, poised to throw a rock. His face was twisted in rage. Hatred, pure and simple. His other hand held a large key. Around him, other men were in the process of throwing rocks, stones or anything else at hand.

Their object was another man who cowered against the walls of what Lang guessed was a palace or castle. One hand was raised in supplication while the other arm dangled at an angle indicating it was badly broken. His face was streaked with blood, yet he wore an expression of serenity hardly in sync with his situation. He was surrounded not only by rocks but also what could have been the contents of a nearby trash dump: pottery shards, sticks and even a seashell.

Lang was about to ask the man next to him a question when the entire hallway went silent as though some cosmic switch had been flipped off. Lang's eyes followed the turning of heads to the left. At the end of the hall stood a figure in a cardinal's red robes. Priests parted like a black sea as the newcomer approached the spot where Lang stood.

"Cardinal Benetti," Francis whispered at Lang's elbow. "The Holy Father's personal secretary."

Lang had not noticed his friend's arrival. "What . . . ?"

Francis put a finger to his lips as the cardinal spoke.

"There will be no word of this outside these walls," the man announced before repeating the message in French, Italian, German and Spanish and again in Latin. "I speak for the Holy Father," he added before closing the door to the room and disappearing in the direction from which he had come.

"What was all that about?" Lang asked.

"I'd say it was about letting what's here stay here," Francis said.

"Playing dumb doesn't become you," Lang observed. "You know what I meant."

Francis nodded toward their room as the priests began to disperse like spectators after the game is over.

Inside, Lang and Francis sat on opposite beds.

"Well?" Lang demanded.

Francis drew a breath and shook his head slowly. "I'm not really sure. A challenge to church dogma at best, heresy at worst."

Neither possibility particularly worried Lang. The Inquisition, indulgences, insistence the universe revolved around the earth had all come and gone, the greatest damage being a tad of soon-forgotten ecclesiastical egg on the church's face. It was obvious, though, that Francis took what they had seen seriously. The endless if friendly debate of the church might not be wise here.

"OK," Lang said, "let's start with the mural, fresco, whatever. What's so amazing about it?"

Francis gathered his thoughts and began. "You recall the discussion we had on the plane about saints and their symbols?"

"Sure. After all, it was just last night."

"Think about what you just saw."

"Looked like an old-fashioned lynch mob to me."

Francis nodded slowly. "Yes, yes I'm afraid it did."

Lang was taking off his shoes. "I still don't get it."

"The symbols, Lang. Remember what the symbol for James was?"

"A seashell, a scallop shell. Like the one next to the poor bastard being stoned." Lang's face lit up with recognition. "St. James! But he *was* martyred by stoning, right? What's blasphemous about that?"

Francis was staring at the floor. "The other man, did you see what he was holding?"

"A key, a big one. He was going to throw that, too?"

Francis managed a weak smile. "Hardly. The key is the symbol for St. Peter."

Lang paused, shoelace in hand. "St. Peter led the mob against James the Just? They were both Christians. That makes no sense."

Francis nodded slowly. "It does in a way, I suppose. See, at the beginning, right after the Crucifixion, Jesus's followers took up his ministry. Most believed Christianity was a sect, a subspecies of Judaism. That meant to be a Christian, you had to be a Jew, be circumcised, follow the dietary and other laws. James the Just opposed that idea, saying anyone, Gentile or Jew, could be a Christian as long as they ate no meat that had been bled out, sacrificed and avoided fornication."

"Clearly he won out. With the possible exception of the last part."

Francis nodded. "Clearly. As the first bishop of Jerusalem, James gave Peter his orders. Like any good soldier, Peter died obeying those orders not two hundred yards from where we sit."

"Then, someone just made up the bit about Peter leading a lynch mob."

Francis stood and went into the bathroom. Lang could hear him over the running water. "It's hard to believe someone just imagined that."

Lang raised his voice to be heard. "Go down to the Sistine Chapel. I doubt Michelangelo ever saw people falling into hell."

"At least there was some theological basis for the idea."

"But none for the fresco?"

Francis emerged from the bathroom, toweling his face. He reached to his throat and began to remove the studs attaching his clerical collar to his shirt. "*That* is what worries the church. That fresco could very well date back to the time of the rebuilding of St. Peter's. Who knows what heresies might have been around then?"

"And for every heresy, the possibility of truth."

Lang propped a pillow behind his back and stretched out. "Someone faced the problem before. They plastered right over it. Why not just do it again?"

"I'd guess when that painting was obscured, there weren't newspapers and television. Word gets around pretty fast these days, and, will of the Holy Father or not, news of the discovery of an unknown fresco will get out, particularly if it's dated back to the rebuilding of the basilica. Could be attributed to Raphael or Michelangelo, far too big for a cover-up. Besides, the church is no longer in the business of concealing things."

"Right. Tell me what day the Vatican's secret archives will be open."

"It already is open to accredited scholars."

"Accredited scholars" being defined as those whose loyalty to the church is unquestioned.

But Lang felt this wasn't a time for argument. Instead he said, half joking, "You could always just give it an acceptable twist."

Francis looked at him blankly.

"You know, like how the church defaced or tried to destroy nearly every Roman monument in this town. The marble and steel support rods were stripped from the Colosseum to build the 'new' St. Peter's and I doubt Trajan was the one who put a statue of St. Peter on the top of his column."

"I doubt we'd have the Colosseum today if it hadn't been preserved for use as a church at one time. And as for Trajan . . . One of the early popes, Gregory I, I think, was so taken with the depiction of the emperor comforting the widow of one of his fallen soldiers, he ordered not only the column be preserved but prayed Trajan's soul be released from hell where all pagan souls went."

Lang had never heard this before. "And?"

"And we still have Trajan's column and Gregory had a dream in which God told him he had released the emperor's soul but please not pray any more heathens out of hell."

Lang sensed the dark mood the fresco had inspired in his friend was lifting. "Just for the sake of argument, what if there really were some truth to the painting?"

"Peter is the founder of the church. It would change more than I can imagine. Christianity's premier saint exposed as a murderer. It could tear the church apart, something the more conservative members would never permit." Francis carefully placed his collar and studs on the top of one of the dressers. "Word of that fresco gets out, there'll be a brief stir among the usual skeptics. The faithful will continue. It would take more than a fanciful painting to convince anyone Peter killed James. Did you have anyplace in particular in mind for dinner?"

Even if his curiosity was far from satisfied, Lang was glad to drop the subject that had so bothered his friend. "I understand there's a really good seafood restaurant near the Pantheon, La Rossetta. Do you get priest discounts in this town?"

His BlackBerry buzzed.

He felt uneasy when he saw it was Gurt calling. She wouldn't be phoning after speaking with him only a few hours ago unless something had come up.

"Yes?" he said curtly.

Then he listened for the next two minutes before saying, "I agree."

He ended the call.

Francis was studying his face. "Trouble?"

"Yeah, sort of."

Had it been any woman but Gurt, Lang would have been overcome with anxiety. Gurt was not exactly your typical damsel in distress. The description fit her worse than a double-A bra. A deadly shot, she had run out of fellow agency partners with whom to practice martial arts, men and women. She had caused too many injuries.

And, as she was quick to point out, she had saved Lang's ass more than once.

She certainly hadn't called to worry him, to distract him from what he was doing. That wasn't the way they both had been trained.

But the training hadn't included a small child, his child.

"What sort of trouble?" Francis asked.

"Er, a car accident, nothing serious."

"Then why do you look worried?"

Because I am, Lang said only to himself.

Real worried.

"You need to leave Rome?"

"As soon as I finish some business."

IX.

Piazza dei Calvalleri di Malta
Aventine Hill
Three Hours Later

Late every afternoon, a phenomenon takes place in Rome:
As the sun edges westward, it tints otherwise ordinary
buildings a color somewhere between sienna and ochre.
There is no hue exactly like it elsewhere, a fact disputed by
Sienna, Florence and several Tuscan and Umbrian hill
towns. Their afternoons are dismissed as either too red or
containing not enough yellow by any native of Rome whose
opinion is sought on the subject.

Dispute notwithstanding, the two men who had one of
the city's best views from the window next to them paid no
attention. Instead, they listened closely to the hissing of a
recording device, interrupted by voices.

"The fresco has been found," the younger man said. "I
had come to believe it existed only in rumor."

The older man shook his head. "An unfortunate time. It
will only encourage the American to get whatever copy he
has translated if he has not already done so."

"Why else would he have gone to see the Greek priest,
Strentenoplis, other than seek a translation?"

The older man thought for a moment. "See to it. See to
the Greek, also. But do so without leaving a trail for the
police."

"And what of the Jew, the forger?"

"See to him also. We want no path for the authorities to follow. The American no doubt wanted papers of some sort. Watch the place against the possibility the American returns there. He must be eliminated quickly by any means other than violence in the Holy City. We cannot risk the gospel's message becoming known."

"We have located the German woman and the American's bastard child. I should know shortly. If we can take them captive, we may have this Reilly come to us."

The old man stood. "You are doing God's work. In his name, bless you."

"Thank you, Grand Master," the man said, trying to suppress the resentment bubbling in his chest.

Today he had lost two good knights, one with burns that might cost him an eye, the other with a fractured skull. It had been bad enough to lose the hired help in Prague and the men in the United States who had mysteriously disappeared after finding Reilly's place south of Atlanta. But he had only a limited number of soldiers, knights, who were even remotely competent to deal with the American. Or who, for that matter, had even fired a gun.

It was easy enough to give orders; not always so simple to carry them out.

God's work or not.

X.

The Vatican
The Next Morning

Notwithstanding taking the middle of the day off, offices in Rome generally open between 9:00 and 9:30 A.M. As far as Lang could tell, the Vatican was no exception.

After showing his pass to the Swiss guard still dressed in the uniform designed by Michelangelo, he was admitted to the *scavi* and walked a short way down the hall to Father Strentenoplis's office. The door was closed. Lang knocked briskly, waited a moment or two and knocked again without result.

He pushed gently. Like most of the doors here, it had no lock. It swung open. The space looked the same as it had the day before. Smelled the same, too. Whatever the good father smoked, it clung to the walls like paint.

Lang considered looking through the papers on the desk and decided against it. He had the remaining copy of the gospel, so there was no need to try to retrieve the one given to the priest and the priest hadn't expected to have a translation until now.

The problem, of course, was, where was the priest?

Lang shut the door behind him, went down the hall and stopped in front of an open office where a very short nun sat on a very tall swivel chair. Her feet barely touched the floor as she pecked at a keyboard with the hesitancy of someone not entirely comfortable with the machine.

Lang stepped across the threshold. *"Mi scusi, parlal' inglese?"*

She spun around in the chair, bathing him in the most radiant smile he had ever gotten from a seventy-year-old. "Of course I speak English, but thank you for asking! Most of your countrymen take it for granted that everything and everybody speaks English, and, if not, the problem can be cured by progressively raising the voice. How may I be of service?"

"Father Strentenoplis, I had an appointment with him . . ."

She sniffed disdainfully. "You are early. He rarely is in his office before ten thirty."

Lang's suspicions about the priest's drinking habits were confirmed.

"It's really important I see him. I'm leaving Rome this afternoon . . ."

She turned the chair to face the monitor. "He is a visiting priest, staying in one of the apartments the Holy See keeps for such purposes. We have no phone number." She scowled at the screen as though the omission were its fault. "He must use a cell phone."

Lang shifted his weight back and forth. "Do you have an address?"

"Of course! We keep the scoop on all our visitors. Is not that what you say in America, 'the scoop'?"

Not in the last thirty years.

"Ah, here! Do you know the Via de Porta?"

"'Fraid not."

She pointed. "As you leave St. Peter's Square, turn right on Porta Cavalleggeri. It's a main drag. Then left on Via del Crocifisso. De Porta will be on your left." She wrote something down on a piece of paper. "Here. You want apartment nine at number thirty-seven. A piece of cake, as you would say!"

Lang thanked her and left, wondering how she had acquired so many outdated American idioms.

There was nothing wrong with her directions, though. Father Strentenoplis's street was one of those Roman alleys so narrow Lang doubted the sun touched it more than a few minutes each day. The building was a former palazzo converted into apartments by the high taxes of the Socialist state. A massive arched wooden door could easily have accommodated a carriage and mounted outriders. A more human-scale Judas gate had been cut into one side.

Lang surveyed the list of doorbells mounted beside the entrance. He pressed number nine with no result.

The good father was probably sleeping off the night before, in no shape to hear the buzzer. And Lang had a plane to catch.

He pushed all the buttons.

He got two garbled responses he could not have understood even if he had spoken Italian.

"Now is the time for all good men to come to the aid of the party," he said.

The door's latch buzzed open. Someone had been expecting a visitor and the electronics were as unintelligible inside as they were out.

Lang stood in a vaulted stone vestibule even taller than the door. To his right was a shallow set of marble stairs that wound around an old birdcage elevator before disappearing into darkness above. In front of him was the private interior piazza that had once contained a garden secluded from the noise and smell of the street. Rather than fountains and flowers, it was now a parking lot for tenants' cars. Over a field of Fiats and Volkswagens, Lang watched a man in coveralls emerge across the courtyard, no doubt the servants' entrance in better days.

He acceded to joints already aching and took the elevator. He feared he might have made a poor choice as the contraption groaned its way to the third floor, the fourth in the US. The door creaked open and he could see the number nine in the dim light of low-watt bulbs in sconces.

A series of knocks were fruitless. Lang inhaled deeply as he tried the lock, remembering the blood-soaked apartment in Prague. He stepped back and visually checked the lock, its bolt visible where the door had shrunk from its frame. Less than a minute's application of a credit card and there was a gratifying click. He pushed the door open.

"Father Strentenoplis?" he called.

No response other than the wheezing of an overworked window air-conditioning unit.

A sagging curtain leaked enough light from the room's only window to see two weary club chairs facing a short sofa across a plain wooden table on which rested a Compaq laptop and a stack of papers. A crucifix over the sofa was the only effort at decoration. Two steps down a short hallway a door opened into the bedroom: a single bed, a small bureau resting on three legs on which a clean clerical collar and studs waited and a curtained alcove. If the priest had slept here last night, he hadn't made up the bed. Beyond the rumpled sheets was a doorless entrance to a small bath. On the sink was an open tube of Grecian Formula.

Father Strentenoplis cared about his appearance.

And Lang was feeling more and more like a burglar.

Recrossing the room, Lang slid the curtain back. Behind it was a single rod on which several cassocks hung beside two black suits, a pair of jeans and two golf shirts. Two pair of black wingtips, one each of brown loafers and Nikes paraded across the floor in a neat line.

Lang started to close the curtain when something on the floor gleamed in the dim light. He stooped and scooped up a cross on a gold chain, a cross with a third cross member. A Greek cross. He frowned. Not something Father Strentenoplis would leave behind. With it in his hand, he walked over to the apartment's second window, one across from the bed. Closer examination showed the catch on the cross's chain still closed. The chain was broken.

Lang carefully placed the cross and chain on the bureau and crossed the short hall into a minuscule kitchen. The heel of a baguette lay on the counter next to the sink along with a chunk of hard pecorino, cheese made from ewe's milk, and a sliced pear, its edges already turning brown, a typical Italian breakfast. A coffeepot sat on one of the stove's two gas burners. It was still warm to the touch.

Father Strentenoplis hadn't impressed Lang as a man who would leave a meal prepared but uneaten and he certainly wouldn't leave a gold cross.

Lang went back into the living room and turned the computer on. Nothing but a blank screen. He tried several booting-up procedures but the screen never wavered from its unrelenting blue. Had its main drive been removed?

He was leafing through the papers when he jerked his head up. Footsteps in the hall. He slipped the .45 from his belt and cocked it. The sound receded and he eased the hammer to half cock and made certain the safety was on. Cocked and locked.

He returned to the papers, but found nothing he could read.

A broken chain, opened hair dye, unfinished breakfast. It was beginning to look like Father Strentenoplis had made an unplanned departure.

Why?

Perhaps the priest had taken another route between his apartment and the Vatican and Lang had simply missed him. Possible but Lang didn't think so. He would certainly go by the office again. There was nothing further here.

At least nothing tangible. Lang had a feeling, a gut vibe that if someone had made the good father disappear that person could still be around.

He took the stairs rather than making himself a stationary target on the elevator.

They came for him there.

Between two floors, two men were waiting on the landing. Each looked as though he might have had a career as a professional wrestler. Each carried a gun with a very visible silencer. Each held his weapon at arm's length as though fearing it might bite.

Amateurs, Lang guessed.

But it doesn't take a professional assassin's bullet.

And there wasn't anything amateurish about the footsteps

Lang heard behind him. Get your quarry in a cross fire, as professional as you please.

"Ah, Mr. Reilly," said one of the men below him, speaking in accented English, "we need to speak with you."

"Throw the guns over the bannister and we'll chat all day."

The man who had spoken smiled. It wasn't a nice smile, either. "Just put up your hands where I can see them."

Lang sensed, rather than heard, whoever was at his back upstairs getting closer, closer than anyone who knew what he was doing would be if he planned to shoot. The plan was to distract him while someone grabbed him from behind. Then dispose of him in some manner honoring a saint.

Was a saint ever shot?

He was thankful he had cocked the .45. There was no time to do so now. He raised his left hand, his right brushing his back a little slower. His only defense was they had no way to know he was armed.

A soon as he felt the Colt clear his belt, he whirled as he lifted it. Over its muzzle he saw two astonished faces. One turned to crimson mush as the big gun bucked in Lang's grasp. The impact knocked the man into a spin and over the railing. There was a wet-sounding impact as he hit the floor below.

The roar of the .45, rolling up and down the stairwell like a departing thunderstorm, momentarily transfixed the men below. Someone yelled and a door slammed.

A spitting sound and something unpleasant buzzed past Lang's ear.

Using his other hand, Lang grabbed the gun arm of the remaining assailant above him on the steps and yanked him to the side as he stepped behind him.

Now he had a shield. Or so he thought.

There were the coughs of two silencers and the man went limp.

Lang was holding a lifeless body, one that had taken bullets meant for him.

The dead weight was pulling Lang off balance. He had the right gun for bluff and bluster but not marksmanship. All he could do was fill the air with lead and hope. He pointed the automatic in the general direction of the two remaining men and emptied the clip. Chips of plaster and stone filled the staircase like shrapnel. One man cursed and dropped his weapon to try to staunch a river of red coursing down his arm.

Lang would have bet the wound was inflicted by flying debris rather than accuracy with the heavy pistol.

The remaining man fled.

Lang looked around him. A stinking fog of gun smoke filled the staircase. Shell casings glittered on the stairs like a field of gold nuggets. The man he had held was stretched out headfirst, his arms reaching for a discarded weapon, a Beretta 9mm. Another dead at the bottom of the stairs. Blood made abstract patterns against the gray stone walls and stairs.

It wouldn't take the police force's resident rocket scientist to figure out what had happened and Lang was the only person left to question. He started down the steps as fast as his gimpy legs would go. The bottom was in sight when he heard the pulsating wail of sirens. From the sound of them, they would arrive at the front door about the same time he did.

Time for Plan B.

He turned and fled back upstairs.

Minutes later, the stairs became a busy place very quickly. A photographer was firing off a flash from every angle. Two men in uniform picked up shell casings, using a grease pencil to mark the location of each. A man in a suit was kneeling beside a body with its head pointing downstairs. Another put on latex gloves before picking up a Beretta.

Several more uniforms were standing to the side doing little but observing.

Inspector Manicci, in charge for the present, watched from the top of the staircase.

The assembly stopped as one as a priest came down the steps. No one observed that his cassock swept the steps rather than ended at the ankles or that the clerical collar was a size too big. The absence of the usual rosary was not noted. Instead, all of the men nodded politely with the courtesy toward the church shown by all Italians, whether churchgoing or not.

The priest stopped, shocked, at the sight of the dead man. Kneeling, he began reciting in Latin. No doubt a prayer for the dead. At first the men on the stairs exchanged uncertain glances. Then, one by one, they decided it was time for a cigarette break outside.

A few minutes later Deputy Chief Police Inspector Fredrico Hanaratti arrived, blue lights flashing on his dark blue Alfa Romeo. His driver parked squarely in front of the massive doors. No matter. No one was going to be leaving anytime soon. One of the uniforms escorted him inside, explaining what had been found so far.

And that some priest was slowing up the investigation.

The inspector hunched his shoulders and started up the stairs. He would put an end to this interference, priest or not.

Except there was no priest.

"Interview everyone in the building," Hanaratti ordered, "including the priest."

But he was not to be found.

Twenty minutes later, a deputy inspector reported the discovery of another, much smaller entrance/exit across the piazza. It lead onto another street.

Just inside the doorway were a clerical collar and a cassock.

CHAPTER FIVE

I.

Alitalia Flight 171
Between Rome and Atlanta
Four Hours Later

Lang luxuriated in the first-class seat as he accepted his second glass of champagne. Well, Spumante, a discrepancy more than compensated for by being able to actually extend his legs while he enjoyed it. The past few days hadn't exactly been the rehab his surgeon had recommended. Wriggling his toes in the thick airline-issue socks, he gazed down on the rugged Alpine region below, replaying his last hours in Rome.

After a hasty exit from Father Strentenoplis's apartment building and shedding priestly garb, he had headed back toward the Vatican, stopping only long enough to dump the .45 from the Ponte Vittorio Emanuele into the sluggish green Tiber.

He had not even considered returning to Viktor's to collect his passport. It was too likely the men he had encountered in the ghetto yesterday had observed him coming in or out of the building. That they knew about the priest only strengthened this supposition. He would need to find translation of the gospel elsewhere, preferably somewhere someone wasn't trying to kill him.

He had used his BlackBerry as he walked to call up Delta's stored number. With surprising accommodation, they booked him on that afternoon's flight on Alitalia.

He had no sooner disconnected than the device buzzed, this time showing his office number.

"Sara?"

"It's me, Lang. You all right?"

Just swell, Sara. Twice in as many days, somebody has tried to kill me. I've been forced to seriously burn one man, maybe crack the skull of another and shoot one more to death. I'm not forgetting being responsible for yet one more getting his throat slit and the disappearance of a priest. I'm a one-man plague, but I'm just peachy keen. "What's up?"

"I thought you'd like to know, a Larry Henderson called last night. Says he knows you. He's in the federal pretrial detention center in Macon on what I gather are a number of charges related to growing marijuana. He's got an arraignment in front of a magistrate coming up."

Larry Henderson.

The name was familiar but just out of his memory's reach. Lang was puzzled for other reasons, too.

"I'm still on medical leave of absence from the various courts, I don't practice outside the Atlanta area and I sure as hell don't defend dope dealers. None of this is news. What's special about this guy?"

"He said to remind you of your house in Lamar County."

It all came back to Lang like a yo-yo on a string. Shit! A real pain in the ass when you owe someone, really owe them, and they come around to collect. Especially when your own plate is full of assassins who want you dead.

On the other hand . . .

"Have someone tell Mr. Henderson I'll drive down to Macon tomorrow. Call and make arrangements with the Fed Bureau of Prisons people."

Lang terminated the call and made another, this one to Gurt.

"There's been a change of plans," he told her.

When he got back to the Vatican to throw his few clothes into his single bag, Francis was waiting for him. The priest was sitting on one of the twin beds, fingering the rosary in his lap.

"Lang, what have you gotten into?" were the first words he said.

"You already know as much as I do," Lang replied, crossing to the small closet and taking out a pair of slacks. "What brings this up?"

Francis hesitated before answering as though carefully constructing an answer. "That Greek Orthodox priest you asked to translate for you, the one visiting from Istanbul . . ."

"Strentenoplis."

"Father Strentenoplis. He was found an hour ago."

Lang felt as though he had tried to swallow something without chewing, something very large. "Found?"

"In the Tiber."

"He fell into the river?"

Lang knew better.

"Not unless he was carrying the hundred-pound anchor tied to his legs."

"Who . . . ? I mean, you can't just throw somebody tied to an anchor into a river in broad daylight without a couple hundred witnesses. Somebody must have seen it."

Francis arched an eyebrow. "And what makes you think it was done in daylight?"

A warm coffeepot, a clerical collar with studs on a dresser, a breakfast not eaten.

But Lang said, "Lucky guess?"

Francis shook his head. "A dozen or so people called the police. Of course, each had a different idea of the make of the truck they used, its color, even how many people were involved."

"And, of course, nobody got a tag number."

"Oh, they did, all right. According to Vatican security, the Rome police found the truck abandoned. It had been stolen." He stood, staring at Lang intensely. "Lang, you're not telling me something."

Lang laid his suitcase out on the other bed and began transferring shirts and underwear into it from the bureau. He was acutely aware someone in addition to Francis was probably listening. "More than one something, Francis. Unless you want to end up like Father Strentenoplis, I'm doing you a favor." He stopped in midpacking. "The anchor, it's the symbol for . . . ?"

"St. Clement. He was tossed overboard at sea tied to an anchor."

Lang zipped his bag shut. "Crude but efficient. Even considering the Tiber is, what, ten feet deep? I'll see you when you get back."

"You're going back to Atlanta?"

A fact the eavesdroppers either knew or would soon.

"It's a starting place."

Francis stood. "Lang, please. Drop this search for a translation of that gospel. It's not worth your life. Give it to whoever wants it. No more killing, no more . . ."

Lang gave his friend a bear hug. "Always the man of peace, Francis. Problem is, I wouldn't know who to give it to or that they'd call off the dogs if I did."

Lang's thoughts were interrupted by the flight attendant extending a pair of tongs holding a hot towel. He mopped his face and dropped the towel onto the seat divider to be collected by the same set of tongs.

One of his problems was he had no real clues as to who it was that wanted him to drop the matter of the Gospel of James. The obvious answer was some fanatical religious splinter group of Catholics. Problem was, which one? He couldn't name them all. He could eliminate the Pegasus organization as having too much to lose in the event of his violent death. Besides, Pegasus's killers were professionals. The men who had made attempts on his life, at least in Rome and Prague, hadn't been, a fact for which he was extremely grateful. There was no way to tell whether the bombing of his condo had been the work of a true pro or some Timothy McVeigh wannabe. Ever since the tragedy in Oklahoma City, anyone could mix up an explosive mixture of sulphur nitrate from recipes on the Internet. And this particular bomber hadn't had to. Natural gas had worked just fine.

A comforting thought.

He had no clue, nothing other than the untranslated gospel and the hope it would help identify those who were more willing to kill him than have it see daylight.

He pushed his seat back to a near-reclining position, punched a series of buttons on the in-flight entertainment system and began watching some mindless comedy.

II.

Macon
Bibb County, Georgia
The Next Day

Larry Henderson had thought he might be in trouble when Jerranto found the man on Larry's property. Clearly from the city, the trespasser was all dressed up in blue jeans newer than Larry'd seen in a long time. Shiny new boots, too. Had a pair of binoculars around his neck, a camera with a long lense and a book with pictures of birds in it. He said he was a bird-watcher, come down to the crick because he heard some kind of woodpecker was there.

What man would tromp around with rattlers and cottonmouths just to see a woodpecker?

Hadn't made sense then.

But it made a lot of sense now, to Larry's misfortune.

Particularly as the man was close to two things Larry'd just as soon keep folks away from: the current crop of marijuana and a couple shallow graves containing the men who had shot up the house belonging to that Atlanta lawyer.

After he thought about it, Larry decided the man's story smelled like a mess of catfish that had been out of the water too long.

And he was right.

Two days later, the federals were swarming all over the place like fire ants when somebody's kicked over their hill. It took them less than a minute to find the crop, as if they knew where to look.

Now Larry was in deep shit.

More specifically, he was in the federal pretrial detention center in Macon.

Good thing that Atlanta lawyer, Lang Reilly, told him he'd be happy to return the favor if Larry ever needed it. Just out of curiosity, Larry had Googled him one night when there was nothing on TV. Reilly had five or six pages on him.

Reilly had defended the previous mayor of Atlanta aginst all kinds of corruption charges and got him off with a couple years for tax evasion. He'd also pissed somebody off big-time, had his house blown up, in addition to the men who shot up his place.

Whoever was mad enough at Reilly to want him dead wasn't any of Larry's business. He'd done Reilly a huge favor and now he was asking to be paid back.

Larry was just sitting down to his prison lunch of peanut butter sandwich, french fries and strawberry Jell-O when two of the guards came over to his table in the mess hall.

The man had to holler to be heard above the noise of a couple hundred men all talking at once. "You got a visitor, Henderson."

Although he knew it was routine, Larry's face burned

with embarrassment when one of the guards snapped on leg shackles while the other watched. None of the other prisoners seemed to notice anything but the food left on Larry's plate.

Larry shoveled as much of the sandwich as he could into his mouth and followed the lead guard, the other one behind him. His fellow inmates were welcome to the Jell-O, but he hated leaving the fries even if it was the fifth time in as many days they had been featured on the noon menu.

They went down on an elevator and through a series of doors that hissed shut before the next one opened; then he was led into an eight-by-eight room divided by a metal table at which were two chairs. In one of them was the lawyer Reilly.

Lang stood and extended a hand as the guards removed the shackles and withdrew. Larry's bright orange jumpsuit was less than becoming.

"'Lo, Larry. How goes it?"

Larry looked around the room. "Stone walls a prison do not make, but this sucks."

Richard Lovelace? The value of a liberal arts education: recognizing cavalier poets.

Dumb question, anyway. Lang started over. "Looks like I'm going to have the chance to repay the favor."

"'Preciate anythin' you can do." Larry sat in unison with Lang. "Guess you know the federals impounded all the cash I had. All the cash *Momma* and I had," he added bitterly. "I ain't astin' for charity, but . . ."

Lang waved his hand. "You're not getting charity. You're allowing me to repay a debt, a very big debt I owe you on my behalf as well as my family's."

Larry felt better already. The Hendersons had never been rich, but they'd never been beggars. This lawyer might be from Atlanta, a place so evil they let women dance naked in bars, or so Larry heard, but Reilly talked like he had the same principles as people in Lamar County.

Lang slipped papers out of a briefcase and handed them across the table. "Here's a copy of the indictment. Basically, you're accused of growing marijuana for purposes of distribution. That encompasses several other crimes such as transporting for sale, sale, etcetera."

Larry's heart sank as though suddenly cast in lead. "I done it. I'm guilty. How long'll I be in jail?"

Lang shook his head with just a trace of a smile. "You may or may not have done it, but you aren't guilty till a jury says you are. Tell me exactly what happened."

And Larry did just that. Starting with the bird-watcher whom he vaguely connected with his problems, he finished with the raid on his home.

"Can you tell me the exact date you found this person on your property?"

Larry scratched his jaw, thinking. "Was a Tuesday, 'cause Momma has her hair done ever Tuesday. An' it was a Tuesday, las' Tuesday, I was arrested."

Lang glanced at the papers from his briefcase. "And the indictment was handed down thirteen days after you saw the bird-watcher."

"You reckon he had anythin' to do with it?"

"I reckon he had *everything* to do with it."

"Shoulda shot him when I had the chance."

If past experience was any indication, he wasn't kidding.

Lang put his elbows on the table, making a steeple of his fingers. "If you'd shot him, you would have been in a lot more trouble than you are now."

"It's for sure *he* would be. Look, how long will I have to spend here?"

Lang puffed and blew out his cheeks. "Frankly, I have no way to know. If you're found guilty, or decide to cooperate . . ."

"Cooperate?"

"I'm sure the DEA boys would be delighted to know to whom you sold, stuff like that . . ."

Larry shook his head. The Hendersons weren't tattlers, either. "Not gonna happen."

Lang stood, snapping his briefcase shut with finality. "That is, of course, up to you. But in any scenario, we are a long way from talking prison time, a very long way."

"But if I done it . . . ?"

Lang leaned across the table, lowering his voice. "The government is a long way from even getting to whether or not you did what they say. A bit of advice: drop 'I done it' from your vocabulary. Second, remember, there are men in here who will swear you said just about anything so they can trade for a lighter sentence."

Larry watched the guards unlock the door and Lang start to leave. Slightly skeptical men would actually bear false witness against each other for their own benefit. There must be some very bad people in here.

"Lang . . ."

He turned back from the door, a question on his face.

"If you can, meybbe when you come down this way to be in court, if it ain't too much trouble . . ."

Lang grinned. "C'mon, Larry. Spit it out."

"Momma. It's jus' she ain' never been alone an' . . ."

Lang chuckled. "I think I can assure you she won't be now. Even as we speak, Gurt is at your house making arrangements to move into your son's old room until all this is over."

Lang had never seen a man in a prison jumpsuit happier.

III.

Lamar County, Georgia
7:28 P.M.
That Evening

Lang needed to take a walk. He'd eaten a great deal more than he had intended. Starting with a tomato aspic salad, he had been served with a panoply of fresh vegetables "from the garden," homemade corn bread, ham with redeye gravy and peach cobbler for dessert. Feeling slightly guilty, he had left Gurt and Darleen to do the dishes at the latter's insistence despite the glare he got from the former. Manfred, in a blatant effort to postpone bedtime, had wanted to come along, which meant Grumps, recently liberated from the boarding kennel, had included himself.

The stroll, though pleasant, had a purpose other than a futile effort to settle the results of gluttony in his stomach. Lang headed slowly but purposefully along the dirt drive leading to the highway. He took his time. He stopped to watch Manfred chase the few early fireflies that ventured out into the fading light and Grumps's futile attempt to extract some small animal from its lair, a hole the dog was rapidly expanding. When he could see the state road, he stopped. He was not surprised a Ford sedan in plain wrapper was parked on the shoulder. In most federal dope busts, the DEA would keep a constant watch on the premises in hopes of snaring others who might be involved.

At least that was the reason usually given.

Lang suspected a more sinister motive might be to prevent intentional damage to property that the federal government would surely seize as contraband once Larry was convicted.

Either way, the inexhaustible assets of US law enforcement would be guarding Gurt and Manfred even if that was not the intent. They would also be protecting the very lawyer who already had a plan to defeat them in court.

He grinned. Is this a great justice system or what?

Although he couldn't see them, he would bet several other agents were serving as dinner for gnats and mosquitoes in the surrounding woods where they could survey the house from different perspectives.

He turned, took Manfred by the hand and started back. The fact the feds would predictably keep Larry's farm under surveillance, at least for a while, was the reason he had asked Gurt to propose staying there to Darleen. That and the hope the people who wanted him dead wouldn't guess he would return to the place they had nearly killed him earlier.

Or, at least, it would take time before they did.

He had picked up a two-man tail upon his arrival at the Atlanta airport. He had made no effort to keep them from hearing the directions he gave the cabbie before climbing into the backseat.

The cab got lost twice largely due to the driver's unfamiliarity with the city's streets and inability to understand Lang's directions. He could only imagine the growing frustration of his minders as the hack turned and doubled back several times in what must have seemed a random pattern.

He had been grateful when the taxi had made it to Francis's church downtown. The following Chevy parked across the street before Lang could get out.

After paying the fare, he had entered the church, walked through to the rectory and then to Francis's bedroom. There he found the Browning he had concealed before departing for Rome. He helped himself to the key to the aging Toyota the diocese provided his friend and exited to the garage behind the church.

The Chevy had still been parked as he drove away in the anonymous Toyota.

He could only hope Gurt had shaken whatever tail might have been assigned to her.

The next morning he had rented a car and driven to Macon. On the way, he stopped in Barnesville, the county seat, and made arrangements to rent office space from a law school acquaintance. He was now a country lawyer with a single client.

His thoughts returning to the present, he walked back to the house. He listened with half an ear to his son's chatter, mostly soliciting assurances that a fishing expedition to the pond was on tomorrow's agenda. Making only the vaguest of promises, Lang examined what few facts he had.

There was something in the Gospel of James that someone very much wanted suppressed, wanted enough to kill anybody who might reveal it. His only lead to who that someone might be was the gospel itself. The longer he waited to get it translated, the greater the possibility his mysterious assailants would find him. Worse, the greater the chance they would find his son.

But where to get the documents put into readable form? A search had shown no more than a handful of universities listed someone knowledgeable in Coptic Greek. As a consequence, any trip to one of these schools would be both obvious and transparent. He didn't want some unknown professor to be the next victim.

Reaching into a pocket, he produced his BlackBerry and called up a schedule of foundation travel for the next two weeks. He scanned past the usual European and South American destinations. Damascus, Karachi, Istanbul.

Istanbul. What did he recall about Istanbul?

That it was, had been, the place whose Orthodox patriarch had sent Father Strentenoplis to Rome. There had been, Lang vaguely remembered, patriarchs in Jerusalem, Antioch, Alexandria and Constantinople during the Byzantine Empire. But today? He started to call Francis before realizing the priest would be somewhere between Rome and Atlanta at the moment. Instead, he took the device in both hands, using thumbs to enter an e-mail to Sara.

An hour later, he lay in the four-poster beside Gurt. Her restlessness told him she was not asleep.

"You sure Darleen doesn't mind us camping out with her?" he asked.

"She will have disappointment when we leave. Correction, she will have disappointment when Manfred leaves."

Superficially, Lang found it perfectly understandable that anyone would be delighted to have the little boy around. Realistically, he found it difficult to accept that a middle-aged woman would want a small child underfoot.

As if reading his mind, something she did with disturbing regularity, Gurt rolled over to face him. "With her husband in jail, she is quite happy to have company. She has not been alone since she was seventeen. It has been a long time since she had a child in the house."

Perhaps Lang had underestimated the maternal instinct.

By the dim light from under the door, he could see Gurt's outline resting her elbow on the bed, her head in her hand. "She would be happy to keep him here . . ."

The slow curveball.

". . . so I may help you find those who would harm his father."

The fast break, down and away.

"Are you sure that's smart, leaving a three-year-old with a woman you hardly know?"

Gurt took a moment, composing an answer. "We talk, Darleen and I. She is a good woman. She was not, I would know it. Besides, did you not say there are federal agents nearby?"

"US Marshals, I'd guess. But they're not here to guard Manfred."

Gurt moved her arm, placing her head on the pillow. "How long would we be gone?"

Lang noted the plural. Gurt had already made the decision that his son would be fine in Darleen's care. He let it pass. "I'm not sure. I'll know more tomorrow. I've got a doctor's appointment and I'll drop by the office. Between Sara and Francis, I should have some idea then."

Long after her regular breathing told him Gurt was asleep, Lang wondered how she could be so certain his son would be fine left with Darleen. His only consolation was that the child's mother had done without his input for the last three years. That thought was less than comforting for more than one reason.

IV.

Buyukada
Princes' Islands
Sea of Marmara
Turkey
A Week Later

The call of the muezzin from the balconies of a dozen minarets were clearly audible across the water even though the mosques themselves were no more than needles against the silhouette of the shrinking Anatolian shoreline. The electronic enhancement of the five-times-a-day summons to prayer had increased their range if done little to give the flesh-creeping wails any melodic quality.

From his position at the stern of the ferry, Lang had watched as the ship passed Seraglio Point with its Topkapi Palace, home of the Ottoman sultans. And what a view those rulers of the near east for four and half centuries had enjoyed: the mouth of the Golden Horn to the Bosphorus, separating Europe from Asia. One city, two continents. Idly, he noted a Russian supertanker, high in the water as it made its way north back to the oil fields of the Black Sea.

He recalled the international friction these crafts had caused for years. The Russians, unwilling to hire a local pilot, would not suffer the oil spill resulting from one of the ships going aground less than a mile from Turkish shores on either side.

The foundation's Gulfstream had deposited Gurt and Lang at the customs house behind the main terminal at Istanbul's Ataturk Airport, where they had purchased visas for sixty dollars (euro or New Turkish lira would have been equally acceptable) and been welcomed to Turkey. As anticipated, there had been no customs. Both Lang and Gurt's weapons were available if needed and the copy of the Book of James was inside his shirt. A taxi, equally ambivalent as to currency, had taken them to Karakoy, the swarming anthill of piers from which ferries departed. Travel by water was Istanbul's preference when possible, avoiding the crowded streets and confining alleyways. Lang had noticed about half the women covered their heads; half of those with gaily colored scarfs, others with the full-length, long-sleeved black dress, their heads and faces covered by the traditional burka from which only the eyes were visible.

"Roaches!" Gurt had hissed, making no effort to conceal her scorn for women submitting to a male-dominated society.

Turkey was about 90 percent Islamic, mostly Sunni. Its constitution, however, mandated a secular government, freedom of religion and abolishing the fez and other religious dress in its universities. It was the only Islamic democracy in the world. This was beginning to slip, bit by bit. The country's new president, devoutly religious—

A tug at his sleeve. "Come see!"

Lang followed Gurt to the bow section just as the ship's whistle announced its arrival. Lang saw white two- and three-story buildings ringing a small harbor sheltering hundreds of small boats, a number of them scooting across the sapphire surface like so many bugs. Towering over the activity were green hills with houses stacked along the edges like merchandise on store shelves.

"I don't see any cars," Lang said.

"Motor vehicles are forbidden," Gurt replied. "Other than police or garbage trucks."

Gurt had read the guidebook. Or she had been here before in her past life during the bad old days of the Cold War on some mission neither of them was eager to discuss. This was Lang's first visit to the former capital of the eastern Roman, Byzantine, then Ottoman empires. These islands took their name, Princes', from the fact that the sixth-century emperor, Justin II, had built a palace here. Later, the scattered monasteries served as a place of banishment for overly ambitious members of the royal family or public officials, frequently in addition to blinding, slicing off a nose, having the tongue cut out or castration.

The Byzantines knew how to ensure neither a person nor his potential heirs would ever become troublesome again.

With the advent of steamboat service from the mainland in the late nineteenth century, the islands' beaches and wooded hills became popular resorts as well as home to a number of expatriates such as Leon Trotsky.

Lang noted a number of horse-drawn phaetons obviously waiting for the ship to dock. Bicycles zipped in and out of both equestrian and pedestrian traffic.

"Hope there's one of those carriages left for us," he said, turning to follow the stream of disembarking passengers.

"A bicycle would do you more good," Gurt teased.

Lang took her hand, leading her between a group of giggling high-school-age girls, none of whom wore scarfs. "Some other time when I have a few less broken bones."

"Perhaps a horse?"

"I try to avoid anything that is both bigger and dumber than I am."

As they stepped off the gangplank, Lang inhaled a potpourri of odors: coffee and baking bread, frying olive oil mixed with the pungent smell of horse dung, all blended with a trace of freshly cooked sweets. He and Gurt were standing in a village of shops, restaurants, small inns and businesses the purpose of which was unclear to anyone who did not read Turkish. Outdoor *lokanta*, cafés, were filled with customers sipping sweet apple tea from small, hourglass-shaped glasses. The mood, both of those just disembarked and those already there, was one of a holiday. Everyone seemed to be speaking at once.

He could have been standing in the center of a number of beach resorts worldwide.

Suitcase in one hand, Gurt's hand in the other, he shouldered his way through good-natured vacationers to where a pair of well-fed horses were harnessed to one of the carriages. The driver, dressed in jeans and golf shirt, held a sign with Lang's name on it.

Francis, who had arranged the visit to their destination, had thought of everything.

"Monastery of St. George?" Lang asked.

The driver nodded and said something in Turkish, gesturing they should climb in. Lang knew better than to attempt to assist Gurt aboard. She resented any effort, no matter how courtly, that suggested she, as a female, was due any treatment not owed to a man.

Without any perceptible signal from the driver, the horses trotted through the town's streets, hooves playing a syncopated rhythm against the pavement. With no change of pace, the coach began a climb up the hills. Absent vehicular traffic, the road could have been a highway from another century. Large villas shared ocean views with smaller cottages and a few hovels that had not seen paint nor repair for ages. Even these were draped with purple and blue bougainvillea.

At each dip or hollow, the driver applied a protesting brake handle to keep the speed at a manageable level.

They reached the crest, a narrow ridge dropping almost

straight down on either side. The view was as spectacular as it was unobstructed. In the distance, the Turkish mainland was only a suggestion in purple. Other islands were set like emeralds in a placid ocean. Lang was so enchanted with the scenery, he hardly noticed an increase of breeze on his face. A squeeze of his hand brought him back to his surroundings. The phaeton was headed downhill fast enough to make him uncomfortable and the body of the thing was swaying dangerously, leaning first one way toward the deep valley on the right and jagged rocks lining the coast hundreds of feet below to the left.

Local custom or were they riding with a madman?

He leaned forward to speak to the driver.

Before he could say a word, the man bent over. With a grunt, he snatched loose a pin and the wagon's tongue and horses were gone, a blur as the carriage careened past. Then the driver hurled himself onto the only grassy shoulder Lang could see and rolled to a stop. Lang saw or imagined a smile on his face.

There was no other place to jump without a fall of hundreds of feet.

It was clear the rig was not going to make the next turn where the road disappeared around a stand of trees.

As happens when events move too fast to comprehend, Lang's mind went into slow motion.

The brake handle loomed before him.

Hand on the back of the driver's seat, Lang leaned forward. He couldn't reach the handle.

The bend in the road was rushing toward him, a giant mouth open to devour the carriage and its passengers. The speed increased, slow motion notwithstanding.

Seeing what he was trying to do, Gurt grabbed him by the belt, allowing him to fully extend.

His fingers brushed the wooden handle. Leaning as far as he could, he still could not close his hand around it.

Just ahead, the pavement ended in open space.

V.

Buyukada
A Few Minutes Earlier

Emniyet Polis Inspector Mustafa Aziz stood behind his desk and tried to calm the man down long enough to understand what he was saying. Something about being bound, gagged and hidden in the woods just off the road after he had been forced from the phaeton he drove for a living. He had picked up the fare, supposedly to take him to one of the island's beaches, and then been forced at knifepoint to surrender his rig.

Obviously, something was missing. In the first place, why would someone be stupid enough to steal horses and carriage on a small island where search and detection would be all but certain? Second, the man had not been robbed of his money, little enough to make robbery an unlikely motive. Third, crime on the island consisted almost entirely of pickpockets, small-time theft and an occasional burglary.

He winced at the last part. The dearth of crime was why he would serve his last few years before retirement in this political backwater, guarding tourists and vacationers against purse snatchers. A beautiful place to work but hardly a place he could regain the reputation he had once enjoyed.

There had been a time when the young Aziz had a career as full of promise as a fruit tree in bloom. Then there had been what he mentally referred to as the Mohammad Sadberk Affair.

Sadberk had been prominent in Turkish politics, distinguished enough that not only Aziz's *emnit polist*, security police, were alerted when his wife reported him missing but the *Yunis*, Dolphin, rapid-reaction force as well. The politician had reputedly been on a fact-finding excursion to southeastern Turkey and there was reason to fear Kurdish rebels had taken him hostage. Stellar police work, a tip deemed fortunate at the time and plain luck led young inspector Aziz to a shabby resort on Turkey's southern coast.

Certain of fame and promotion, Aziz had not paused to consider the improbability of Kurds, or any other terrorists, choosing a hideout in an area favored by European tourists on all-inclusive, hundred-euro-a-day beach vacations, particularly since retreat by the suspected abductors across the Iraq border at the other end of the country would all but have guaranteed the end of pursuit.

Instead, Aziz had assembled a sizable force of police to surround the small inn a few streets back from the beach. He had not forgotten to include members of the press to record what would certainly be the turning point of his profession as a policeman.

And indeed it was.

Kevlar-clad *Yunis* smashed through a door as the cameras rolled. Their focus was on Sadberk, lipsticked and clad only in the finest French lace panties, and his companion, a young boy.

Although the Turks wink at a number of the Koran's prohibitions, homosexuality is not greeted with the same secular blind eye as, say, alcohol. Sadberk was politically ruined and his powerful friends outraged at what they viewed as an overzealous investigation to ruin a man who, like Aziz, had had a bright future.

The inspector had been transferred to *turizm polist*, tourist police, where his main duties had been to sit in the Sultnahmet district office in view of both the Blue Mosque and Hagia Sophia, writing endless reports of lost or stolen cameras, wallets and passports. Even this had apparently not been enough for Sadberk's cronies. A year later, Aziz was exiled to Buyukada as though he had offended some Byzantine emperor.

Exiled or not, he intended to do his duty even if all that was involved was a pair of horses and a carriage, more likely borrowed than stolen. But first he had to calm the driver into coherence.

One again, the distraught man went through his story: a passenger had taken his rig at knifepoint. No, he had never seen the man before. In fact, the robber appeared foreign.

Aziz ran the tip of his index finger across his mustache. "Foreign? How?"

"He didn't speak at all, just gestured. He just didn't look like a Turk to me."

"Well, what did he look like?"

The driver shrugged as though saying it was the duty of the police to know such things. "Just under two meters, dark hair, brown eyes. Heavy, perhaps a hundred or more kilograms."

In other words, almost any adult male on the island.

"Did you get any idea where he was going?"

The man shook his head, bewildered. "On a small island?"

This time Aziz's hand went to his bald head. "No, no. Where *on the island*?"

A blank stare. "How would I know?"

Aziz leaned back in his chair and glanced at the stucco ceiling as though seeking the patience to endure this dolt a little longer. He was about to refer the man to someone for a description of his lost horses, one Aziz could easily imagine: long neck at one end, tail at the other, four legs each . . . when the phone on his desk rang.

Ordinarily, Aziz would have let someone else pick it up, it being unbecoming to his rank of inspector (albeit the only one on the island) to answer his own phone. Today, he would rather lose face than continue what was clearly a pointless conversation.

"Inspector Aziz," he announced.

He listened for a few minutes before thanking the caller and hanging up. "I think we have your horses and carriage," he said grimly.

VI.

Buyukada

Either he would find a way to grab the brake handle or Manfred would be an orphan in the next few seconds. Lang considered simply jumping until a good look at the stony ground told him the price of such a move at this speed would be much the same as following the carriage over the edge. The driver had known where the last spots soft with grass and loose sand were when he jumped.

Better to try something else.

If he could.

Lang unbuckled his belt, holding both ends in one hand. The first and second tries missed. On the third, he got the loop around his target. He threw his weight back as hard as he could, praying the belt would hold. Alligator was decorative but not as strong as the more plebeian cowhide. Muscles still healing sent a jolt of pain up his arms and across his back, anguish that brought tears to his eyes.

Still, he held on and pulled as Gurt, both arms around his waist, pulled him.

He heard the scrape of the wooden shoe against the metal rim of the wheel and felt the vibrations but the speed seemed undiminished. Then the curve was not rushing at them quite so fast.

One wheel bumped slowly over the edge and they were stopped, literally hanging over the edge of a very long drop. Three hundred or so feet straight down, the Sea of Marmara gnashed its rocky teeth in a swirl of creamy foam.

Gurt let go of Lang and started to step down to the ground.

Gravel crunched and the phaeton shuddered, edging an inch downhill.

Gurt froze in midstep. "I think the balance is not so good."

"Too good," Lang said, arms frozen to the belt still looped around the brake. "We move an ounce of it and we'll be in the water."

"And so? We stay here until someone come by and can help?"

Another movement by the carriage, slight though it was, answered that question.

"I don't think we have that long," Lang said needlessly.

As though to confirm the observation, a sudden shift in the breeze made the light rig lean another inch or so. Damn pity they weren't in a sturdy farm wagon. At least the top was down rather than adding to the potential sail area. Both Lang and Gurt remained still as statues as the rig swayed slightly in the breeze. At some point, gravity was going to claim it.

And them with it.

Almost afraid to move his lips, Lang said slowly, "I'm going to count to three. On three, we jump."

"And my bag? My clothes and makeup?"

Gurt might insist on being treated like a man, but she was still female.

"Were I you, I'd think more about whether you're going to be alive to use the replacements."

"But I do not know I can replace them here."

Lang repressed a sigh, trying not to reconcile Gurt's feminine worries about clothes and cosmetics with her ability to shoot a helicopter pilot in his aircraft from the ground as she had done during the Julian affair. To a man, women would be the last great unsolved mystery on earth.

Instead, he began to count, eliminating further discussion. "One, two . . ."

As though choreographed, two bodies leapt from the phaeton, hitting the hard surface of the road with a single thump. Lang's vision turned red, punctuated with blotches of color as his still-healing body responded with a jolt of pain that would have taken his breath away had not the impact already done so. There was a buzzing in his ears as he struggled both to suck air into his lungs and not to black out.

He fought his way to his knees, reaching behind him to make sure the Browning was still in its holster at the small of his back. Gurt was already on her feet, hand extended to him. "You are OK, yes?"

Lang took it and stood gingerly, determined not to show his discomfort. "I don't think anything's broken that wasn't already."

Together they stepped to the edge. Other than a single wheel spinning in the surf as if still on its axle, the phaeton had vanished.

A sound behind them caused both to spin around. Lang's hand was on the butt of his weapon.

They were looking at a small cart pulled by a donkey. Sitting on the board provided for the driver sat a man with a full beard. He was dressed in a black robe and a tall hat was on his head. He was regarding them curiously as if they might have dropped from the moon. For an instant, Lang thought he was looking at the reincarnation of Father Strentenoplis.

A monk from the monastery?

"Do you speak English?"

The man nodded gravely. "A little."

"You are from the monastery of St. George?"

He nodded again. "That is where I serve my church and my God, yes."

"That was where we were going when . . ." Lang trailed off, unsure how or if to explain.

The priest pointed to the top of the next hill. "It is there. You cannot see it because of the trees." He stepped down from his perch. "One of you may ride . . ."

Taking a closer look at the wagon, Lang saw it was full of fish and vegetables, no doubt from a market in the town below. "No, no, we wouldn't . . ."

Gurt led Lang to the cart. "My friend here is—was—hurt."

The man gave Lang the sort of look he might have used in appraising a new donkey. "When your carriage fell over the edge?"

Gurt and Lang started at each other as he continued. "I saw it as it was, was . . . balancing? Yes, balancing before it fell into the sea. I was not near to help and I feared if I made myself known, you might turn and . . ." He pulled a cell phone from the folds of his robe. "But I did call for help."

From whom, a sky crane?

As if on cue, Lang heard the pulsating wail of a police siren. A small white car with blue stripes emerged from a grove of cedars sculpted by the wind. A bar on top flashed red and blue.

Lang forgot his aches and pains for the moment. Arrival of the local police rarely heralded change for the better. It was certain the weapons he and Gurt carried would create problems if discovered. The last thing they needed was to be confined in the local jail where potential assassins could easily locate him. Visions of the prison of the 70s movie, *Midnight Express*, came to mind with all of its dark horror of filthy cells and brutal guards. At least that particular building had been converted to one of Istanbul's more luxurious hotels.

The car came to a stop amid swirling dust. The driver was in uniform, the passengers in mufti. A short bald-headed man with a mustache got out, holding his police creds in his hand. He was dressed in what Lang guessed might have been the only suit and tie on the island. From the backseat emerged a younger man wearing what looked like American jeans and a long-sleeved dress shirt open at the collar.

The policeman pointed and asked a question Lang could not understand. The younger man replied in the same language, shaking his head.

The policeman gave a smile that wrinkled his round face but didn't reach his eyes. "I am Inspector Aziz," he said in almost accentless English. He did not extend a hand. "This man had his horses and carriage taken at the point of a knife. He tells me you are not the guilty person."

A good start.

"Your passports, please." The policeman's hand was outstretched.

Lang, always suspicions of both police and such requests, toyed with the idea of claiming both documents had been lost along with their baggage. He decided the ensuing problems with having no official ID outweighed his reservations. He and Gurt handed them over. The inspector flipped through both of them, squinting at the date of the recently purchased visas.

"You have had quite a bit of, of . . . excitement since your arrival in Turkey." To Lang's discomfort, he slid the passports into a jacket pocket. "Perhaps," he continued, "you would be so good as to tell me who you are and what has happened here."

Lang explained.

The inspector ran a finger across his mustache, a gesture Lang guessed was more reflexive than intentional. When Lang had finished, the dark brown eyes narrowed. "No attempt was made to rob you or the lady?"

Lang shook his head. "No."

"And you had never seen this man, the driver, before?"

"No."

Again, the finger ran along the mustache. "What possible reason, then, would the man have to risk his own life by jumping from the carriage and leaving you to fall to your deaths in the sea?"

Lang shrugged, eyebrows raised at a question without an answer. "I have no idea, Inspector."

The Turk studied Lang's face carefully, his disbelief clear though unspoken.

The car's radio exploded in a rash of static and words. The uniformed driver acknowledged the message.

"They have recovered the horses," the inspector announced to no one in particular, "but there is no information about the man who took them."

Lang pointed to the hill where the monastery was supposedly hidden by trees. "Inspector, I, both of us, would like to continue on our way if you have nothing further." Lang held out a hand. "And I'd like our passports back."

Aziz seemed to actually notice Gurt for the first time. Perhaps it was an excuse to ignore Lang's request. "How long will you be in Turkey?"

Lang shrugged. "We want to see someone at the monastery. After that . . . well, there would be no reason to stay."

The policeman gave that chilly smile again and patted the pocket into which the passports had disappeared. "There are many reasons, Mr. Reilly. Have you ever taken a cruise up the Bosphorus? Seen the Blue Mosque or Topkapi Palace? Shopped at one of our bazaars?"

Lang held out his hand again. "Inspector, our passports. We cannot even get a hotel room without them."

Instead, Aziz handed over a business card. "Should you have problems without your papers, have your hotel call me."

Lang's patience was wearing thin. "You have no right to—"

The Turk snorted. "You are not in America, Mr. Reilly. Here, your *rights* are what I say they are, certainly as far as your passport is concerned. When I have finished my investigation, it will be returned to you. For that reason, I suggest you keep me aware of where you might be found. In the meantime, take the time to enjoy these islands and Istanbul."

It looked like they would have little choice.

Gurt, Lang and the priest watched the police car until it

vanished among the trees before the latter spoke. "It is but a short trip up to the monastery. Come, we all can sit and have something refreshing to drink."

Lang smiled tightly. Once again, he didn't see any other options.

VII.

Buyukada
Twenty Minutes Later

Inspector Aziz sat behind his desk, glaring at the two passports as though ordering them to give up their secret.

The American, Reilly, and the Fuchs woman simply did not pass what he referred to as the smell test. The more a person's story varied from the inspector's personal experience, the more it smelled like meat left too long in the hot sun. Reilly and the woman would have him believe they had come to Istanbul and the Princes' Islands simply to visit the monastery of St. George.

Implausible but possible.

Of all of Istanbul's sights, a twentieth-century cloister ranked near the bottom. Still, there was no accounting for the quirks of Christians in general and Americans in particular.

It was the next part that defied belief.

For someone to risk not only apprehension for theft of the horses and rig but also chance breaking their neck to jump from the carriage to kill two tourists made no sense at all. In the first place, the felon had a knife—the owner of the phaeton had seen it. Why not use it?

For that matter, a gun, perhaps a rifle, would have done the job. The fact a firearm was not employed indicated the would-be killer probably had no access to one, no way to evade Turkey's stringent gun laws.

In short, an amateur rather than a professional criminal. But jumping from the carriage?

The only answer Aziz could come up with was that the unsuccessful assassin had somehow known his prey would be difficult to kill in the close quarters a knife required. That would suggest two things: first, Reilly was not your ordinary tourist and, second, whoever had tried to kill him knew it. If that supposition were true, then who was he?

The policeman spun his swivel chair to face the monitor and keyboard behind his desk. A few taps brought up the Interpol Web site. He entered the password both for Turkey and himself. He now was into the international police organization's list of criminals and suspects.

He entered Lang Reilly's name and was rewarded with immediate results. Mr. Reilly, an American lawyer, had been suspected in the deaths of two street hoodlums in London several years ago, although there was insufficient evidence to bring him to trial. A few months past, he had killed one of the men who had kidnapped a wealthy British philanthropist. Aziz moved closer to the screen, squinting. Yes, that was what Scotland Yard's report said, killed an armed gunman . . . with a spear.

Hardly your average tourist.

The Fuchs woman did not appear at all.

But Reilly would bear watching. If he were up to some illegal purpose, Inspector Aziz would make sure he was the person to apprehend the American. Reilly just might be Aziz's own passport, one back to the mainland.

VIII.

Monastery of St. George
At the Same Time

The buildings had been erected less than a hundred years ago but the place still had the air of its medieval cousins. From the outside, its most noticeable feature was the Orthodox, or Greek, cross atop its domed roof. Inside was the familiar four-sided open cloister surrounded by a roofed colonnade along which black-clad monks blended with the afternoon's shadows and passed just as silently. From somewhere inside, melodic chants flowed on air scented by the courtyard's multiple rosebushes. It could have been built in the early twenty-first century or the first part of the twelfth.

Lang found comfort in such anachronisms. They gave a sense of timelessness that said no matter how great the world's problems, civilization would endure and continue. By contrast, the individual's woes diminished.

Gurt set the her glass on the stone bench they shared while waiting for the prior. "*Stra*, he called it?"

She referred to the priest who had escorted them here and insisted they take some sort of refreshment.

Lang ran his tongue across the back of his teeth. "Somewhere between wine and grape juice, I'd say." He drained the last of it. "A drink for the abstemious."

Gurt looked at him with that expression that said she had no clue what he had said.

He changed the subject to one they both had intentionally avoided till now. "How do you guess they knew we were in Turkey? For that matter, they even knew we were coming *here*."

This time she was on familiar turf. "Francis, Father Fancy, used his church contacts to arrange for us to meet the patriarch of Istanbul, did he not?"

"It was the only way I knew to get us in to see about getting the book translated."

"Perhaps his conversation was overheard."

"Not likely. I insisted he use e-mail. In Latin."

Gurt stood and stretched, her hands above her head. "Perhaps Latin is not as dead as you think."

"Meaning?"

She shrugged. "Meaning someone understood it, someone with a way to read the e-mails."

"That doesn't help a lot. In this day and time, hacking into someone else's computer is as common as housebreaking. Reading Latin, though . . ."

The conversation halted as a portly man in a black robe strode purposefully toward them. Had he not had a long beard, he could have been a priest or monk from the Roman Church.

He stopped in front of them, extending a hand. "Mr. Reilly? Ms. Fuchs? I am Father Stephen, the prior. The abbot, who is also the patriarch you seek, is at the library of the school of theology on Heybeliada, another of these islands."

Lang shook hands and waited for Gurt to do so before he asked, "Do you know when he will be back? I thought we had an appointment . . ."

The monk held up his hands, palms out. "I fear not. Although the school itself has been closed for years, scholars still gather at the library. His Holiness enjoys a good theological argument and tends to forget the time. He may return quite late."

Lang looked around the cloister, aware that some European monasteries allowed guests. "Any chance we could stay here for the night?"

The prior shook his head. "You, yes. The chapter forbids women in the cells."

Gurt's look said it clearly: Muslims were not the only sexists in Turkey.

The monk had also seen her expression. "It is an ancient rule, Ms. Fuchs. Both historically and today, men join monastic orders to pray and serve God with their full attention. For that reason, we have neither television nor radio. Only religious books are allowed. Women, particularly attractive ones such as yourself, are one of the distractions they wish to avoid."

Gurt appeared mollified if not satisfied.

The prior continued. "You may find it difficult to find lodging here. This is the peak of vacation season and the few hotels tend to fill up. I suggest you return to the mainland, where you are more likely to find rooms. The ferry to the mainland quits running at eight o'clock."

"But," Lang protested, "the patriarch, we need to see him!"

"He will be here tomorrow until about noon. He then leaves to go over to Istanbul for the baptism of a friend's grandson at the Church of the Savior in Chora. Although quite small, it contains some of the most beautiful of Byzantine mosaics. You might want to meet him there."

Lang had really wanted to stay at the monastery. Anyone who didn't belong would be obvious. Plus, another ferry trip would be sure to give whoever wanted him dead another try. At least in the city, he and Gurt might be able hide in the cosmopolitan crowds. They would certainly stand out less than on these remote islands.

"Please tell him we will look forward to seeing him at the baptism. I'll need only a few minutes of his time."

IX.

Side Hotel and Pension
Utanga Sok 20
Sultanahmet
Istanbul
Early Evening

The hotel was a small, simple place with a limited menu served on the rooftop terrace. From their table, one of only ten, Lang and Gurt had a spotlighted view of the Blue Mosque, Hagia Sophia and the Egyptian obelisk that marked what had been the center of the Hippodrome, Byzantium's third-century 100,000-seat stadium. They trusted the owner, also the maitre d', to select dinner. They shared a huge plate of fish shish kebab with sides of *imam bayildt*, literally, "the imam likes it," small eggplants stuffed with tomatoes and onions, followed by an oven-baked rice pudding served cold. The bottle of white Doluca wine, though astringent, did not go to waste.

The proprietor had shown a special interest in them since their arrival. Lang guessed few Americans stayed here, let alone those without passports. No papers meant formal registration was unnecessary as well as impossible. In short, the money for their room would go straight into the owner's pocket without notice to the tax man. The owner hovered nearby as Gurt looked up from a city map similar to those given away by hotels across Europe, one sponsored by local merchants and restauranteurs. "Is the Grand Bazaar open at this hour?"

The proprietor shook his head sadly. "No, madam, most shops are closed by now." He brightened and gave Lang a wink. "But the place itself is open. There are a number of restaurants, coffee shops and even a mosque that never close. You can shop the windows and it will cost you nothing."

Lang gave Gurt a sharp look and a slight shake of the head as the hotelier continued, pointing, "Go left to Yerebatan Cad. You will see a stone there that is all that is left of the Million, an arch built by the Romans. Go left again. The street becomes a different name several times but it will take you to the bazaar."

Lang watched as the man scooped up the remaining dishes and headed toward the stairs down to the kitchen. "Are you nuts?"

With an air of innocence that didn't quite fit, Gurt raised an eyebrow as she fished a pack of Marlboros out of her purse. She shook one out and tapped it slowly against the tabletop, a habit Lang inexplicably found sexy.

She lit up with a match from the table and inhaled deeply. "Nuts? What makes you think so?"

Lang glanced at the adjacent table. Its occupants were smoking, too. For that matter, he was the only customer who wasn't. Almost every man he had seen on the streets had a cigarette dangling from his lips or fingers. The Turks obviously liked to smoke. Maybe there was something in the local water supply that prevented lung cancer and emphysema. On second thought, the only water he had seen consumed had been from bottles bearing French names.

"What makes me think so?" He lowered his voice. "Just a few hours ago, somebody tried to kill us. Now you want to go out at night and wander the streets?"

"Wander? We will not 'wander.' We have directions."

"But—"

"But what? We arrived by twice switching taxis from the ferry to make sure we were not being followed, then one of those, those . . ."

"*Dolmus.*"

It had been an early fifties Chevrolet from which the seats had been removed and opposing benches installed behind the driver. They drove set routes. Cheaper than cabs, more regular than buses. They rarely moved before they were filled with passengers, hence the name, *dolmus,* Turkish for "full."

She wrinkled her nose at the memory. "The man next to me was almost in my lap and had not bathed recently."

"And couldn't take his eyes off your bustline."

"Perhaps his wife wears one of those horrid black things and he was angry I was not."

Lang was fairly certain he could distinguish anger from lust. Still, from what he had read, Muslim men could be offended by an excessive show of legs, arms or other female anatomy. Perhaps Gurt's sundress with the scoop neck had trespassed across some line. He let her continue.

"Anyway, we agreed we had not been followed. When we got here, we had no passports, so the owner had to phone the police. That means we are not in the police register as we would be had our papers been in order. Whoever might be looking for us cannot chop into—"

"Hack into."

"Chop, hack, what does it matter? *Machts nichts.* They cannot find us as easily as if we had registered in the normal manner."

"So?"

"So, why not have a look at the Grand Bazaar?"

There was a flaw in her logic, Lang was certain. He just couldn't find it.

She stood, stubbing out her cigarette, and delivered the clincher. "I am going. If you wish to accompany me, come along."

Lang knew Gurt was more than capable of taking care of herself. Even so, there was something in him, perhaps the mixed curse/blessing of being born Southern, that would not tolerate letting a woman go out alone at night on the streets of a strange city, even one who had saved his life more than once with skills decidedly unladylike.

Outside, the streets were well lit and populated. The number of fellow pedestrians thinned more and more the farther they got from Sultanahmet Square. Lang's hand went to the small of his back when a man stepped out of a doorway.

"Good evening," he said in perfect English. "You are enjoying your stay in Istanbul?"

He had a closely cropped beard and a recent haircut. The linen suit he wore without a tie fit snugly. In the shadows cast by streetlights, Lang could not be sure it was too tight to allow a shoulder holster.

Rather than risk offense on the slim chance he had approached them for some legitimate purpose, Lang responded, "We are, thank you."

Lang tensed as the stranger reached into a pocket. Then he handed Lang a business card. It was too dark to read the small print.

"Saleem Moustafa," the man said, extending a hand.

Lang knew better than to give a potential assailant a chance to grab his right arm. Gurt had moved back a step or two, too far away for the stranger to assault both at the same time. He noted her purse was open and her hand in it.

"Lang Reilly," he said.

The man matched their pace for a few moments before he said, "I think the old city is best seen in the evening. Would you agree?"

Lang shrugged. "I haven't seen it in the daylight yet."

"Oh, a recent arrival?"

Lang stopped, careful to keep Moustafa between him and Gurt. "I appreciate your thoughts, Mr. Moustafa but . . ."

The man smiled widely. "My brother has Istanbul's finest rug shop. If you will just come with me . . ."

If this was cover for someone to follow them, it was less than brilliant.

"No thanks. We're not in the market."

Moustafa was not to be shed so easily. "I assure you, Mr. Reilly, no other shop in this city . . ."

Lang stopped, turning to face the man. "Thank you for the opportunity but no."

Moustafa gave a slight bow, smiling. "Then, a pleasant stay to you."

He was gone as abruptly as he had appeared.

"You suppose he really is a rug merchant?" Lang asked.

Gurt shrugged. "Perhaps, since he is now talking to a couple behind us. But the man across the street does not seem to be selling anything and he has been with us since we left the hotel."

Lang bent over, pretending to tie a shoe. The man on the other side of the street turned to study street numbers. The man, like Moustafa, wore a suit, this one with a tie.

Lang tried to see the man's shoes. Footwear told a lot. A woman, for instance, did not plan on long walks if she was wearing heels. A man who spent a lot of time on his feet was unlikely to choose loafers. This man had on lace ups with thick soles that Lang guessed were rubber, which made it easier to follow someone without being heard.

Wordlessly, Lang took Gurt by the elbow, steering her into one of the endless alleys that intersect streets in Istanbul's older areas. They stood in darkness as the man fidgeted, trying to decide what to do. Looking as casual as possible, he lit a cigarette and crossed the street, pausing only briefly before entering the alley himself.

Only a true amateur would enter where he could not see on a surveillance job. Or someone supremely confident.

Gurt knew the drill from years of agency practice. She kicked over a trash can, stomped her feet and made whatever noise she could. The effect was to distract the watcher who had now become the prey. As he left the lights of the main street, Lang silently slipped from the shadows behind him. A sweep of the foot and the man stumbled, his arms flailing to give him balance. In one step, Lang grabbed both hands, pulling them back behind the man's back. Before he could protest, Gurt was rifling his jacket pockets.

She stepped back, holding a pistol in one hand and a wallet in the other. Jerking the man's arms upward until he grunted in pain, Lang frog-walked him to the edge of light from the street. Gurt held up the wallet. Something was shining, reflecting the light. Something like . . . a badge.

A policeman's badge similar to the one the inspector had displayed that afternoon.

"Oh, shit," Lang muttered.

Gurt had seen it, too. Holding the weapon up, she removed the magazine and emptied it of bullets before returning it and the wallet to their owner.

Lang let go of the man's arms. Even from the back, he could sense the anger.

"Sorry," Lang said. "We had no way to know . . ."

"Cowboys!" the policeman spat. "You Americans are cowboys, attacking a man on the street!"

"Attacking someone who was following us," Lang corrected. "The next time you shadow somebody, you might let them know you are the police, not a potential mugger."

"I may have you both arrested!"

Lang shrugged. "You may but only after you admit you did such a poor job following us. Had we been criminals, you could well be dead."

The cop made the motions of dusting himself off, more to give his hands something to do than a necessity. Lang's observation had quenched some of his anger. He tugged at his jacket and straightened his tie. "In the future, be more careful."

"I'd say Inspector Aziz thinks we must be up to something," Lang observed, watching the angry policeman return the way they had come.

Gurt zipped her purse shut. "That causes us no problem."

Lang wasn't so sure. "The next person following us may or may not be a cop. There's no way to be sure."

"Nor are we sure there will be a next person. Now, let us go to the bazaar."

Once more, Lang was amazed at Gurt's ability to seamlessly switch from possible danger to shopping opportunities. Was it just her or were all women like that?

Two more rug merchants approached them before they reached their destination, each nicely dressed, each speaking fluent English. Lang found it disconcerting to be accosted by strangers whose motive could vary from sales to murder.

They reached an ornately arched gate next to the Nuru-osmanley Mosque where men made ceremonial ablutions at faucets set in a row before entering to pray. The bazaar itself was a labyrinth covered by a painted vault. Founded by Mehmet II shortly after the Ottoman conquest of the city in 1453, it had grown from its origins as a warehouse to the world's largest market.

The first corridor they entered was, according to several signs, Kalpakcilar Caddesi, a phrase that meant nothing to Lang or Gurt. Wider than many of the city's streets, it was lined with tiny shops whose windows displayed gold and diamond jewelry. These all appeared to be closed. On the right were bays and halls of establishments selling rugs, brass, glassware, leather goods, water pipes, bolts of textiles and many objects Lang could not readily identify. Contrary to what the hotelier said, many of these were open, their proprietors leaving their wares long enough to aggressively seek custom from passersby.

Lang was instantly alert. The constant movement of people made perfect cover for someone wielding a knife. Gurt sensed the potential, too. Without speaking, she joined him along the southern row of stores so the shops themselves protected their left flank, obviating the possibility of having to fire across their bodies should the need arise.

Dividing their attention between the ambling crowd of visitors to the market and the goods on display, they passed a small café as several young men were emerging. They all were bearded and wore the small, embroidered caps and vests common to Muslim men in the city.

One gave Gurt obvious attention. He took two steps toward her and snatched at the shoulder strap of her purse. Before his hand closed, Gurt gave his extended arm a chop across the elbow that elicited a yelp of pain and a quick retreat.

His comrades found this immensely funny. The would-be thief was now an object of ridicule, having been bested by a mere woman. Either to show off to his friends or from annoyance at the put-down, the purse snatcher flushed, stepped closer and drew back an open hand as though to deliver a slap.

Lang never even considered intervening. He knew what was coming.

The young thug had counted on the submissiveness of Muslim women. What he got was somewhat different.

He let out a surprised yelp as he found himself both air-borne and upside down, followed by a thump as he hit the floor. He was still gasping for breath when Gurt delivered a kick to the groin that might permanently adversely effect any sexual endeavors.

One of his fellows made the mistake of rushing to his comrade's defense. He was greeted with a nose-shattering right hook that would have done credit to a professional boxer.

The rest of the group grumbled for a moment as if about to do something as painful as their two cohorts. Apparently they simultaneously recalled previous engagements.

Whether their collective memory had been jogged by Gurt or the approach of a uniformed policeman, Lang would never know. He did know having the cops arrive was rarely a good thing. This one, though, was doing a poor job of masking a grin that wouldn't go away.

"I apologize," he said in heavily accented English. "I have had problems with those, those . . . hooligans before. They steal what they can in the bazaars and frighten the tourists such as yourselves." He nodded to Gurt. "I would think at least two of them will go elsewhere." He watched as the last of the group disappeared around a corner. "I am . . . what? Shame, yes, shame for my city."

Gurt, not even breathing hard, smiled. "We are nothing but well treated here."

"I have been impressed by how very courteous you Turks are," Lang chimed in.

Except for one very bad apple on the Princes' Islands who tried to kill us.

The policeman made no effort this time to conceal a grin. "You have . . . what do you say? Teached them a lesson."

As he left, he couldn't resist taking one last look at the tall blonde woman who had physically beaten two men. Islam, Lang guessed, didn't have many Gurts.

An hour later, Gurt and Lang left the bazaar. He was carrying a box containing a pair of garish carpet slippers Gurt had insisted he buy. She had enjoyed haggling with the shopkeeper far more than he was going to enjoy the shoes. Where in Atlanta do you display red, blue and green footwear? Answer: at home where no one you know will ever see them.

She had purchased a pair of purses that had probably never seen France despite the double-C brass clasp of one of Paris's more chic fashion houses. As she had noted, the price had been right, an opinion she might change if they fell apart in a week or so. One thing was certain: the Atlanta Chanel store would collapse in laughter if asked to honor any supposed warranty issued by its Grand Bazaar branch.

They exited the way they had come in. They were greeted by the wavering wails that were calls to *yatsi*, the fifth and last prayers of the day, from the adjacent mosque.

They were also greeted by a group of scruffy-looking young men just outside the gate.

Two or three of the young hoodlums from inside and two or three Lang and Gurt had not seen before. It was a safe guess they weren't there to apologize.

But how?

Easily enough. Of the multiple ways in and out, only four led toward the part of town where tourists would be likely to stay. Several faced toward the slope that lead to the Spice Bazaar and the Golden Horn beyond. With one man with a cell phone covering each of the probable gates, the gang could quickly assemble at a place across Lang and Gurt's path.

Lang cursed himself for not considering the fracas inside might be continued. The two young men had received injuries to their pride far more serious than Gurt had inflicted on their bodies. Being not only physically beaten but also humbled by a woman was an insult few Muslim men would ignore. Nor would their friends let them.

Lang's hand went to his back, where the steel of the Browning reassured him. Undesirable as shooting their way out might be, it was preferable to what these hoodlums had in mind. Explaining weapons to the police was not why he and Gurt were here.

There had to be a better way and it was right in front of him.

Taking Gurt's left hand, he snatched her toward the mosque.

Inside, rows of arched windows of intricately designed panes were black with the night in stark contrast to the lighter tiles set in intricate and abstract patterns. The dome with its supporting arches must have contained thousands of them. A wooden calligraphic frieze ran above the gallery of the square prayer hall. There was little time to admire the city's first Baroque mosque. Men were kneeling on the floor facing the *mihrab*, or niche indicating the direction of Mecca. A few latecomers screamed in outrage at the violation of their sanctuary by the presence of a woman in the men's prayer section and an indecently clad one at that.

Time to change plans. It was clear he and Gurt would find no refuge here. Lang shot a glance over his shoulder. Two of the gang were already coming through the door. Neither had stopped long enough to remove their shoes. A third entered, saw Lang and Gurt and shouted as he pointed.

The mosque went silent as the murmur of prayer stopped. First one, then a second man stood to glare at the new set of intruders. Suddenly realizing their mistake, the young men from the bazaar started edging their way back toward the entrance. It was already blocked by several infuriated worshipers.

Lang and Gurt made a dash for a doorway on the opposite side of the building. Behind them, they heard enraged shouts. Apparently sacrilege by believers or infidels was equally egregious.

A glance over his shoulder told Lang that a dozen or so shoeless and angry Muslims were in pursuit. Weaving in and out of alleys, he and Gurt tried without success to lose the men behind them. In a few blocks, Lang realized they were close to the hotel. Letting a mob know where they were staying was among the last things he intended to do. They had just rounded a corner and come into view of the Blue Mosque when he spied another small inn. Without hesitation, they entered, ignoring the openmouthed clerk behind a reception desk.

Gurt headed for the stairs and took a stride up only to find the passage blocked by a red-faced man pushing a cart loaded with baggage. Above him were several Asian men and women.

Swell.

A great time to encounter one of the Japanese tour groups that occupy budget hotels the world over.

There was no place to go but down.

At the bottom of a short flight of stairs was a door, which Lang jerked open and stopped, staring.

He was looking at water.

Not a puddle or an indoor pool but a span of black water that stretched as far as the light from the doorway let him see. He made out rows of Corinthian capped columns under multiple arches that faded into the gloom.

What had he read in the guidebook on the plane?

The sixth-century Byzantine emperor Justinian had built a cistern underneath what was then the royal palace, the present location of the Blue Mosque, as a source of water should the city come under siege. He recalled something about eighty thousand cubic meters. There had been a great deal more information, but it hardly seemed relevant as he heard angry shouts above. He only wished he could recall if the book had mentioned the depth.

The yells were growing closer and he could hear footsteps on the stairs. Both he and Gurt could swim if need be.

It was only waist deep.

He and Gurt waded blindly until they reached the nearest column. Lang measured by wrapping his arms around it. Not wide enough to hide them if the men behind them had a flashlight. They moved farther away and stood silently. The sound of an occasional ripple told Lang they were not entirely alone in this amazing pond. The realization sent cold fingers of apprehension down his backbone, a chill he tried to persuade himself was merely the coolness of the water.

What creatures inhabited the cistern, living in water and darkness? His imagination conjured up a number of very unpleasant possibilities: Some heretofore unknown species of piranha? Crocodiles? Somewhere he had read about freshwater sharks in a South American lake.

A small splash inches away made him flinch. Fish. The water was full of fish. He could feel small bodies nudging his clothing. The story of how they got here would be an interesting one.

The door through which they had entered opened, casting a rectangle of light floating on the water, illumination that did not reach them. Lang could hear voices. From the tone, he guessed there was an argument about who would volunteer to wade into the cistern to search it.

There were a couple of splashes as at least two men entered the water.

Lang leaned over and whispered into Gurt's ear.

Both slipped under the surface and began to swim, her hand holding on to his shirt. She still had the bag with the counterfeit purses in the other. He made sure each stroke stayed beneath the surface where it would not make a sound.

When he had to come up for breath, he stood, listening. The splashes of pursuit seemed no farther nor nearer. Sound would be unreliable here. The water, the multiarched ceiling would echo each shout, each splatter so that it would be impossible to be certain either of its direction or proximity. Lang could only retreat back below the surface and hope he didn't run into them by mistake.

The good news was that the men behind him were just as disoriented as he.

When he surfaced for his next gulp of air, all was silent. Lang checked the luminous dial of his watch and counted off five full minutes. Beside the occasional piscine splash, he could hear his own teeth chatter. The chill factor of the water was becoming uncomfortable.

Gurt's sneeze echoed from the stone walls.

The sound brought shouts and more splashing although it was impossible to be sure of the direction.

Lang thought the sounds and resulting echos might be getting more distant. Then, only silence punctuated with an occasional ripple pressed on Lang's eardrums, a quiet so heavy it had a sound of its own.

They, too, were listening.

After another sneeze had potentially betrayed his and Gurt's position, Lang whispered, "We can't stay here."

"OK, you plan to go where?"

Lang's foot touched something on the otherwise smooth bottom. He stooped and picked up something of stone. About the size of a softball. There was no light to determine exactly what it was or whether it had fallen from the centuries-old roof or was part of something else.

It really didn't matter.

He waited until a voice, then another bounced off the walls of the cavernous lake. Making the best guess he could as to direction, he hurled the stone the opposite way. He was rewarded with yells and sounds of men trudging through the water. He was certain now they were going away from him and Gurt.

He wanted to wait a few minutes, let them put even more distance between them.

"It is not safe to stay," Gurt grumbled. "If we remain longer, we'll have pneumonia."

"Better pneumonia than lynched. Come on."

Instead of risking returning the way they had entered, Lang searched the inky dark until he thought he saw a tiny blur of light. Hands outstretched to prevent colliding with columns, they slowly waded toward it. From ten or fifteen feet away, Lang recognized light around the edges of a door. They climbed out of the water shaking like spaniels with the chill.

Lang tried the door. "It's locked."

He could feel Gurt's hand over his as she checked out the lock by touch. "Is an old one. Do you have a knife?"

"Will a credit card do?"

"Try it."

After several minutes of sliding the card up and down the frame without finding the locking mechanism, Lang said, "I can't find the damn bolt."

"Perhaps it is simply swollen shut from the moisture, not locked."

"No, I can see light around the edge."

"Try a hard kick."

Lang gave the door a blow with his foot and it moved slightly. With a second, it swung open, its rusted locking mechanism dangling. Climbing a few stairs put the pair in the lobby of a another small hotel. Lang could hear each step squish water from his shoes. In his imagination, a fish leaped from a pants pocket. The clerk and two guests stared bug-eyed at two people, fully clothed, dripping wet and calmly walking through to the street.

Lang stopped at the door, unable to resist turning to the guests. "Lovely swimming pool but not very well lit."

Once back in their own hotel room, Gurt held up one of her two new purses, wrinkled as prune. "Ach! It has become ruined!"

Lang looked at the box with his carpet slippers in it. It was hemorrhaging red dye. Destroyed, no doubt.

He wouldn't have to wear the damn things.

"Ah, well, it's an ill wind . . ."

Gurt's glare told him he had been speaking out loud.

He hoped she hadn't understood what he meant. But when he climbed into bed, instead of the noisy and joyous sex that usually followed a close call, an expressionless back was turned to him.

X.

Church of St. Saviour in Chora
The Next Morning

The taxi had careened along the road paralleling the Theodosian Walls, four miles of fortified gates, towers and moats that had sealed off the city from the landmass from the Sea of Marmara to the Golden Horn. For a thousand years, their red tiles and yellowish limestone had resisted sieges by Attila the Hun, Russians, Bulgars, Arabs and even the armies of the Fourth Crusade.

The twin-domed Church of St. Saviour was unimposing compared to the massive mosques that dotted the city. It did, however, contain one of the finest displays of Byzantine mosaics.

Lang was glad they had come early enough to give them time to see the genealogy and life of Christ in the north and south domes, the chronology of the life of the Virgin, Christ's infancy and ministry, all done in tiles no bigger than the nail of his little finger. Like many artists, the fourteenth-century remodeler of the church, Theodore Metocites, had an ego. He had included a scene of himself presenting the finished building to Christ.

Styles change; human nature does not.

Outside in the small walled garden, guests were arriving for the baptism. There were none in obvious Muslim dress. The chatter of multiple conversations slowed, then ceased as a tall man with a flowing white beard appeared among a number of younger priests. From his black vestments, tall hat and Greek cross, Lang surmised he was seeing the patriarch, an assumption fortified by each guest bowing their head for the holy man's touch and blessing.

Lang was unsure exactly how to approach the churchman with his request. He need not have worried. The patriarch stopped in front of him and smiled.

"You must be the American, Lang Reilly," he said in slightly accented English. "You were the friend of Father Strentenoplis?"

Lang nodded. "Yes, Your Holiness."

The old man shook his head sadly. "May his soul be with God. One of our American friends in the Roman Church was kind enough to contact someone at the Vatican who called my office here about your visit. Has it been a pleasant one?"

Other than nearly going over a cliff and being chased by a mob from a mosque.

"Yes, sir."

"I understand you have a document in ancient Greek you wish translated."

"Actually in Egyptian Greek. It's supposed to be one of the Nag Hammadi books."

The patriarch held out a hand, age spotted and ridged with blue veins. "May I see it?"

Lang reached into his shirt, thankful he had wrapped the pages in a waterproof bag to protect it against sweat. Last night's excursion would have ruined it otherwise. "It is a copy."

The old man smiled again. "So I see. Or its authors chose to use bond paper available at any copy store."

Lang was always relieved to know he was dealing with someone with a sense of humor. "I have reason to believe some people don't want its contents known."

A chuckle like the sound of dry logs burning. "Some people would suppress all knowledge. Our brothers in Rome once had that reputation. On the other hand, our church, the church of Constantine, preserved the wisdom and science of the ancients, tolerated their religions, when the Western church had declared science and the old gods heresies. Be assured you will get an accurate translation in that tradition."

"Thank you, sir. Without being unappreciative, might I ask when the translation will be complete?"

The patriarch handed the pages to a priest at his elbow. "There are only a few pages. I see no reason why you cannot have it in two days. Three at the most. In the meantime, enjoy this marvelous city. You might start right here with this fine collection of mosaics the Ottoman Turks were kind enough to preserve."

He saw the look of skepticism on Lang's face. "Preserve them they did. When Constantinople fell, all churches were converted to mosques, frescos and mosaics plastered over. In 1922 when French and English occupation ended, Ataturk's constitution proclaimed a secular state. The remaining Christians here simply removed the plaster. The artwork had been preserved far better than if it had been left exposed. I believe you Americans would refer to that as the law of unintended consequences."

Indeed.

Lang and Gurt watched the old man walk away, stopping to bless all who wished it.

"How long the translation takes does not matter while the policeman holds our passports," she observed.

"That," Lang said, "is why our next stop is the American consulate. Let's see if we can bring a little pressure on Inspector Aziz."

XI.

Buyukada
Princes' Islands
At the Same Time

Inspector Aziz normally didn't read the routine daily reports of police activity, but this one had caught his attention.

Last night there had been two seemingly unrelated incidents: A young hoodlum had tried to snatch the purse of a tourist in the Grand Bazaar. By the time the policeman had reached the trouble spot, the perpetrator had a very sore groin among other possible injuries. One of his associates had a bloody nose. Both inflicted by the woman, not her male companion. The woman, tall and blonde, spoke English with a decided accent. The man was American. The young thugs got away but, in the reporting officer's opinion, had been duly punished anyway.

A weak excuse for not doing his job, but that was some other inspector's problem.

An hour or so later, a couple fitting the same description had disrupted the evening prayers at the nearby Nuruosmaniye Mosque. At the same time, a gang of young men had entered the mosque, apparently in pursuit of the couple. The couple had escaped both the infuriated worshipers and the band of street criminals.

A lot of guesswork rather than police work but interesting. The man he had assigned to keep watch on Reilly and the woman had reported nothing unusual other than the fact they had spotted him, thereby rendering his surveillance useless and he had therefore gone home to dinner. Aziz would make sure the next assignment for that fool would be chasing pickpockets in the narrow confines of the Spice Bazaar.

He smiled. Disturbing the peace as well as disrupting a religious assembly were petty crimes but crimes nonetheless. Just cause for investigation and interrogation. He ran a finger across his mustache. There was no doubt in Aziz's mind who the couple were. As was so often the case, the female would appear to be deadlier than the male. But Interpol had no record of her. The very fact a woman of such capabilities had left no paper trail suggested a number of interesting possibilities. One did not naturally come by the ability to turn an opponent's size and weight against him. Such things were taught, taught by the military, police and intelligence services.

The latter raised some vary interesting questions. Turkey's borders with Syria, Iran, Iraq and Russia had made the country a center for espionage for the last three decades. Could it be that Aziz was about to uncover something of international significance? He had no idea what. But did it matter as long as he received the credit?

He had every right to have Reilly and the woman detained and questioned about the affair at the mosque. Perhaps he would discover exactly what their business in Turkey might be. Possibly he would uncover something that would finally get him back across the Sea of Marmara. Besides, a pair of sore balls and a bloody nose were the least of the problems they might cause. Turkey, like other countries wedged between conflicting political structures, had learned spies had a genetic disregard of the laws of their host country.

He reached across the desk and began to shuffle papers. He had written down the name and address of the hotel that had called about admitting them without passports.

XII.

Side Hotel and Pension
Thirty Minutes Later

Gurt and Lang had returned to their hotel to leave their weapons. The security level at American embassies and consulates in this part of the world would surely have detected firearms and neither wanted to have to explain why they were armed.

Gurt was gazing out of the window. "We will not make it to the consulate, I think."

Lang was emerging from the bathroom where he had taped one gun under the sink. The other he had stuck to the bottom of a drawer. The popularity of *The Godfather* had made underneath the toilet tank top the first place anyone looked.

"Why not?"

"There are two police cars outside."

With perfect timing, there was a frame-rattling knock on the door.

Lang opened up and looked into the faces of two officers. The flaps on their holsters were undone as if they expected trouble.

Lang bowed deeply, gesturing. "Do come in, gentlemen. It was so very kind of Inspector Aziz to send two men to return our passports."

Neither seemed amused.

"Come with us," one said gruffly, peering past Lang into the room.

Lang continued the charade, giving Gurt time to make sure there was no scrap of tape, no clue something had recently been concealed. "Oh, that won't be necessary. He doesn't have to return them in person. Just drop them off at the front desk."

Cops are not known for their sense of humor and these

two were no exception. The one who had spoken grabbed the front of Lang's shirt. "I said, come with us."

As close as the two stood to each other, it would have been relatively easy to disable and disarm both. That, however, wasn't going to get the passports back or make the inspector any more cooperative.

Lang held up his hands, a gesture of submission. "OK, OK! I'm coming."

They drew the attention of the three or four people lounging in the lobby/reception area as they were herded through and stuffed into the backseats of different police cars, separated from the front by the wire mesh common to law enforcement vehicles. One behind the other, they descended to the Golden Horn, crossed the Galata Bridge and entered Istanbul's commercial center, Beyoglu. Dominated by the Galata Tower at its highest point, it had been first settled by Genoese traders and merchants in the thirteenth century, soon to be followed by Jews fleeing the Spanish Inquisition, Arabs, Greeks and Armenians. It was also here that the European powers established embassies to further trade with the Ottoman Empire. Except for the fourteenth-century tower, the area could have been the center of any modern city.

None of this interested Lang as much as their possible destination.

Both police cars stopped in front of a building distinguished only by the white star and crescent on a field of red, the Turkish flag. Inside, they were subjected to inspection by a metal-detecting wand. It chirped merrily at Lang's watch, belt buckle and the change in his pocket. The offending items removed, it beeped again, at what Lang could not guess. The attendant seemed satisfied. They were marched up a staircase carpeted with a runner showing more thread than weave. At the end of a hall, the two policeman stopped and knocked on a door. Inside, Inspector Aziz sat behind a scarred and dented metal desk whose twins could be found in any police station Lang had ever visited. On its surface was a thin manila folder. On top were the passports. At his elbow, a cracked cup was filled with cigarette butts next to a rotary phone. There was no other furniture in the room other than the chair the inspector occupied. From the total absence of personal effects, Lang gathered the inspector only had temporary use of this office.

Aziz nodded and the two policemen stepped outside, closing the door behind them.

The Turkish policeman said nothing, staring first at Gurt, then Lang. It was a basic interrogation technique, one intended to unnerve the subject. Lang made a conscious effort not to shift his weight as he stood there, looking out of the single window behind the desk. The view was of a brick wall.

Realizing his ploy wasn't working, Aziz moved to another. He opened the file and pretended to read.

"You have an interesting record, Mr. Reilly. Suspicion of a couple of homicides in London . . . Definitely killed a man there a few months ago."

Lang was not surprised. The price of the information age was the death of privacy. He was sure the inspector had entered his name into any number of crime-reporting systems. "The English haven't seen fit to detain me."

The Turk's brown eyes flicked up from the paper. "Presumption of innocence, fair play and all that, I suppose." He leaned forward, resting his elbows on the desktop. "Here in Turkey, our laws are quite different. You may be detained with or without such suspicions."

"I'll bear that in mind before I commit any crime in Turkey."

Aziz turned his attention to Gurt. "And you, Ms. Fuchs, how is it you have an American passport, but your primary language is not English? Surely you must be able to speak English to be an American."

"Try calling customer service at any public utility," Lang said.

Aziz gave him a glare that could have burned the wallpaper had there been any. "Well?"

"I was born in Germany," Gurt said, leaning forward and resting her hands on the desk.

It was a natural gesture but one that showed monumental cleavage. Aziz was clearly fighting to keep his eyes on her face.

"East Germany," she continued, appearing oblivious to the conflict between the policeman's eyes and his professionalism. "I fled to West Germany a few years before the wall came down. I got a job with an American company . . ."

This could be shaky ground, Lang thought. They had no way to know how much the inspector had learned. It was a safe bet that Gurt's employment with the agency wasn't to be found by browsing international police sites. Still, some long-ago cover story, some forgotten identity might jump up, alerting this detective to some perceived inconsistency in her story.

Aziz managed to shift his gaze to Lang. "And last night at the Grand Bazaar?"

"A couple of young men attacked us. One of your officers witnessed the whole thing."

Aziz ran his index finger across his mustache as he turned to Gurt, struggling to keep his eyes above the neckline of her blouse. "So I heard. Just where did you learn to defend yourself like that?"

Gurt, still leaning over the desk to the man's distraction said, "It gives good exercise to join the many judo classes in the United States."

"And in these classes, they teach you to disrupt religious services?"

Gurt and Lang exchanged bewildered looks.

"I'm not sure we know what you're talking about, Inspector," Lang finally said.

The policeman glared first at him then at Gurt. "Do you deny you entered the Nuruosmaniye Mosque during prayers last night?"

Lang shrugged. "Is it a crime to enter a mosque?"

"It is if you in any way interfere with worship."

Lang shook his head. "We know nothing about any disruption of any mosque. Unless you have evidence to the contrary . . ."

Aziz smiled. "We are not in the United States, Mr. Reilly. As I think I mentioned, I can hold you on suspicion."

"Then you better call the consulate and tell them we won't be coming," Lang bluffed.

"Consulate?" For the first time the inspector seemed less that certain of what he was doing.

"The American consulate," Lang continued. "We were on our way there when your men showed up. We were going to see what our government could do about your taking our passports on a mere whim."

Aziz's eyes darted from one to the other. His computer search had revealed not only Reilly's potential criminal past but also that he was a very rich individual, head of an international charitable foundation. The rich were usually well connected. The last thing he needed was to cause an international incident. He would not only never get off Buyukada, he might well wind up shoveling horse manure from the roads there.

Best not to let these infidels see his indecision. "I remind you, Mr. Reilly, you are in my country, not yours. I will return your passports when my investigation is complete."

"Investigation of what, some disturbance in a mosque?"

"We know nothing about any mosque," Gurt chimed in, drawing the inspector's eyes back to her.

Had another button on her blouse come undone?

The inspector made a decision.

"Go to your consulate, then. I will find witnesses to the incident in question. If they cannot identify you, your passports will be returned."

"In the meantime, we're free to go?" Lang asked.

Aziz sneered. "You will not go far without your papers."

He was answering the ring of the phone as they left.

Gurt and Lang tried not to hurry down the hall or stairs. Once outside, they dashed to the first cab they could find.

Lang handed the driver a wad of Turkish lira. "There's more if you can get us to the Side Hotel in a hurry. A big hurry."

Once underway, Gurt was rebuttoning her blouse as she spoke. "Once we get our, er, possessions, where do we go?"

"The airport and the first flight out of Turkey."

"We can do this before he finds out you slipped the passports off the desk while he was staring down my shirt?"

"You're right. The airport is the first place he'll look. I don't understand why the man is so interested in us in the first place and I don't want to stick around long enough to find out."

They were silent for a second or so before Gurt said, "The agency has perhaps a safe house here. A favor or two is owed me at the Frankfurt office."

She produced a BlackBerry and keyed in a series of numbers.

As if in response, Lang's BlackBerry buzzed. He sighed when he saw his office number. He was afraid to guess what Home Depot might have left on his doorstep this time.

"OK, Sara, what got delivered now?"

"Lang? I wasn't calling about that. I wanted to remind you, you've got a preliminary hearing in Macon day after tomorrow."

"Macon?"

"Macon. Federal court. Larry Henderson. A narcotics

charge, y'know? Like the ones you said you'd never take. The one case in which you don't have a medical leave of absence."

"I'll be there."

But first he had to get out of Istanbul.

XIII.

Piazza dei Cavalleri di Malta
Aventine Hill
Rome
At the Same Time

The room was dark. Heavy curtains blocked the bright sunshine of a summer day in Rome. The only light came from the monitor of a computer, tinting the faces of the two men in front of it a bluish color.

"He has disappeared," the younger of the two said. "Or at least neither he nor the woman have submitted their passports to register in any hotel."

The older man was scanning a list of names on the screen. "Or they are using false papers. Have you checked to see if they are perhaps staying at the monastery?"

The younger shrugged. "The monastery, too, must register its guests."

"What about the airport?"

"No airline has booked a flight for them."

The older man shook his head. "What do you suggest?"

"We believe he came to Istanbul to have the book translated by someone who can read the ancient Greek. That is what led us to keep watch on the island where the monastery is located . . ."

"And we had an incompetent to do the most important task this order has faced in centuries!" the other man snorted.

"Grand Master, by the very nature of our order, men who are skilled at such work would be excluded."

The older man put a reassuring hand on the other's shoulder. "You are right as usual, Antonio. Please continue."

"Since Reilly and the woman were not on the island long enough for a full translation, they must be planning to return. This time I have gone outside the order to procure the service we need. The man is a professional."

"One outside the order is not bound to silence about our affairs."

"True, Grand Master. This man, the one waiting near the monastery for Reilly's return, believes he is being paid by a certain organization from Sicily."

The older man gave a grim smile. "You have done well. Let us hope he succeeds."

XIV.

United States Consulate
Mesrutiyet Cad 104-108 Tepebasi
Istanbul
Thirty Minutes Later

Gurt had shown her creds to the marine guards, enabling she and Lang to bypass the building's metal detectors after all. Lang was grateful. He was well aware of the spools of red tape that would have been required to explain the weapons they had retrieved from the hotel as they departed. She gave a name to a receptionist and they were ushered to an elevator.

Jim Hartwell operated under the title of assistant trade attaché, the somewhat shopworn label given the agency's local chief of station. His status meant he had been around a long time, certainly during those years when Lang had been married to Dawn and out of touch with the covert world shared by Gurt and Hartwell. What else they might have shared was none of Lang's business. It was clear he had a thing for her. Whether he had lusted from afar or a lot closer than Lang would like to think was going to remain a mystery.

Lang waited patiently while the agency man and Gurt swapped news about mutual acquaintances and reminisced about past assignments. The tailored Italian summer-weight wool suit, the currently popular solid-color power tie and handmade wingtips that had to have come from Milan cost more than a month's pay for a chief of station in anyplace other than a major embassy. His hair was expensively cut and streaked with silver in just the right places. His teeth, which he displayed often, could have served as a commendation for any orthodontist. Lang doubted he had gotten his tan from being outdoors. His appearance, his diction, told Lang Hartwell was one more rich kid who had sat down in the lap of luxury at birth and whose family had accurately assessed his abilities and potential for damage to the family business. Like so many wealthy American dynasties, they had either successfully persuaded or threatened him into "public service," an euphemism for whatever available government job that did not entail sweat or dirty fingernails. If he managed to be something other than a total disaster, politics would be the next step.

As the preliminary pleasantries drew to a conclusion, Lang decided he didn't like Jim Hartwell very much.

Then Gurt outlined the purpose of the visit.

Hartwell tapped his teeth with the stem of a briar that looked well used despite the NO SMOKING signs that adorned every American government outpost from Abu Dhabi to Zwolle.

If there was an American outpost in Zwolle.

"Let me get this straight," the agency man said, staring out of the window of his second-floor office. "You want me to arrange for you both to get out of Turkey by diplomatic means, never mind that Turkey is an important ally of the United States."

"It is a particular police inspector that is no ally," Gurt said.

"Getting people out of places is something your employer routinely does," Lang added, "even when they aren't particularly eager to leave."

Hartwell shot him a glance. "Not as routinely as you think. We got burned a couple of years ago."

He referred to an incident when a suspected Muslim extremist had literally been snatched off the streets of Milan for interrogation in Egypt, where the definition of torture was somewhat looser than in Europe. An outraged Italian government had indicted in absentia the agency personnel suspected. Only the US's refusal to extradite had prevented a very embarrassing trial.

"You will not do it?" Gurt asked.

"I didn't say that. I'd have to get authorization."

No matter what branch of government, buck passing was the standard credo.

"In Belgrade I did not wait for authorization," Gurt said.

Lang suppressed the urge to ask what had happened in the Yugoslavian capital. He was fairly certain he wouldn't like the answer anyway.

Hartwell studied his manicure. "You're asking me to risk my ass."

"As did I."

Apparently satisfied with cuticle depth and nail length, Hartwell turned his attention to a cluster of diplomas on the wall, all from smaller Ivy League schools.

Lang felt a growing annoyance. He started to say something and clamped his jaw shut. Was he giving way to an irrational emotion because he had had to watch Gurt utilize her sexuality on the Turkish cop and now she was doing the same thing, albeit in a different way, with this empty suit who might be a former lover? Or was it because there had been a time when a chief of station was answerable to nobody below the director, a congressional investigating committee or, occasionally, God? Those days had disappeared with the Berlin Wall. Feather merchants had replaced decision makers. Small wonder tiny nations like Bosnia or North Korea took delight in sticking a thumb in the eye of the American eagle. Small nations or those of the Middle East that actually were no more than tribes with flags.

Hartwell slapped an open palm down on the desktop with a whack that made Lang forget his irritation.

"I've got a way, I think."

There was a brief silence as though he were awaiting applause for what might be his first idea in a long time.

"There's a marine helicopter that leaves almost every day for the embassy in Ankara, diplomatic mission carrying sensitive papers and the like. I might be able to get you space on it."

"Last time I looked, Ankara was still in Turkey," Lang drawled.

Hartwell glared at him, then smiled, bearing those magnificent choppers again. "There's international service from Ankara."

"To where, Kabul or Islamabad? We need to get to someplace where there's service to the US."

Hartwell, still smiling, shrugged. "Best I can do."

Gurt, anticipating Lang's reaction, held out a restraining hand. "Cannot the Gulfstream land in Ankara?"

"Gulfstream?" Hartwell asked, chagrined to suddenly realize he might be dealing with someone important.

The Gulfstream, of course.

Lang had allowed himself the luxury of being too busy disliking the man to think clearly. He stood and took the BlackBerry from his pocket. "Is there anyplace I can have a private conversation?"

Coming around his desk, Hartwell crossed the room, opening a door that had blended so well with the paneling Lang had not noticed it.

"Our conference room. Soundproof, swept daily," he said proudly.

In a few minutes, Lang returned. "I forgot. The plane is in Damascus. We're building a couple of children's hospitals there. Just tell me what time."

Hartwell picked up a phone on his desk, muttered into it and said, "In about two hours."

Lang did some geographical calculations. "That should work."

"One more thing," Gurt announced sweetly. "A very special favor for an old friend."

Hartwell suddenly looked as if his lunch had disagreed with him. "I thought . . ."

"Just a truly little thing." Gurt was holding thumb and forefinger an inch apart. "We need to stop at the monastery on the Princes' Islands. They have something very important for us to pick up."

The agency man looked from Gurt to Lang and back again, just now realizing they had agreed to keep this part of the agenda for last. "Impossible! This isn't the States where helicopters fly pretty much where they want. We have to clear every flight days ahead of time. Besides, like most European countries, helicopters are restricted over certain areas. I can't . . ."

Gurt clucked her sympathy. "It does me so sad, to think that everyone in the agency will hear about Belgrade. It is a very amusing story."

Not to Hartwell. Lang watched eyes grow as the man inhaled deeply. The effect was like a balloon being overinflated. No doubt he was seeing a political career slosh 'round the bowl and down the hole.

"You wouldn't . . ." he finally gasped. "I mean, it's been so long."

"Still funny," Gurt insisted. "I can now see you. When . . ."

Hartwell held both hands up, surrendering. "All right, all right! I'll think of some diplomatic reason . . ."

Minutes later, Lang and Gurt were sitting in what might have been a lobby had it been somewhere else, waiting for their flight.

"OK," Lang said, now fairly certain whatever had happened in Belgrade had comic rather than sexual overtones. That, of course, did not exclude the possibilities of the latter in some other locale. "What happened?"

Gurt made a sound that could have been a laugh or a snort. "That would be telling."

XV.

Buyukada
Princes' Islands
At the Same Time

Levanto had no idea how his new client had done it. In fact, he had only an unconfirmed suspicion who his client might be. All he knew was that a man he had never seen before had appeared at the gates of Levanto's summer villa, the one in the hills above Palermo, with an introduction from Levanto's last client and a briefcase. The briefcase contained a number of interesting items: a Turkish passport, a ticket for connecting flights from Istanbul back to Palermo, a map and, most important, three quarters of a million euro in fifties and hundreds.

By the nature of his profession, Levanto dealt exclusively in cash but usually half before, half after the job was complete. The stranger was perfectly willing not only to front all the money but to ensure that the tools of Levanto's trade arrived.

This latter promise made Levanto a little uneasy. The Walther WA 2000 was fragile. Its extreme accuracy, perhaps the best in the world, did not tolerate abuse well. One hard jolt, a few minutes exposure to blowing dirt or grit and the barrel could be off a thousandth of a centimeter or the delicate telescopic sight skewed less than that or the chamber's seal compromised. Either way, the tiniest misalignment deprived the weapon of its accuracy of nearly a mile. That was why it was generally shunned by military snipers.

The rifle weighed over eighteen pounds. That and its distinctive bullpup configuration made it difficult to conceal from even the most casual baggage inspectors. Plus Levanto would not dare let the handpicked .30-caliber Winchester magnum ammunition out of his sight. An abrupt change in temperature or humidity could cause alterations in the casing so minuscule as to be visible only under a microscope but big enough to make several yards' difference in accuracy. In Levanto's business there was no substitute or compromise. The bullet either hit the target in the exact place intended at a bone-shattering 800 mps or the shooter was just one more amateur who was better off hunting wild animals or other targets not likely to shoot back.

Levanto customarily stalked his targets, noting routines and schedules. That way he could choose the optimum time and place to do the job. Not on this assignment.

He had declined the offer of a private jet to Istanbul, preferring to make his own travel arrangements using one of the many passports from a library of documents he had accumulated. Caution was job one. He had then taken a late-night boat ride to what he had guessed was an island. The truly peculiar feature of the whole trip was the horse-and-buggy ride to a small cottage. Daylight revealed the house was between a copse of trees and a cliff with a view of the ocean. On the other side of the trees was what

looked like a church. Whatever it was, there was an unobstructed view of the front entrance from the cottage's
second-story window.

From the other side of the room, he could see the ocean.
The two views were the most attractive part. The rest of
the chamber consisted of a double bed and a few pine
pieces. Against one wall was an iron staircase that, Levanto
guessed, led those who wished to enjoy the sun in privacy
of the flat roof.

Less than a kilometer to the church. Child's play. The
only difficulty was the breeze from the water: it tended to
shift abruptly. Even the slightest change in direction or
velocity could affect accuracy. Fortunately, the distance
from the upstairs window to the church's entrance was so
short a slight variation in wind would present far less of a
variable than a much longer shot.

A man would come to this church in the next few days,
a man who could be recognized from several photographs
showing him on a street, getting out of a cab, talking to a
tall blonde woman. Levanto guessed the man had been
unaware the snapshots were being taken.

Once the job was complete, Levanto was to simply walk
out of the house to where a tethered horse would be already harnessed to a wagon. He would leave the rifle. It
was both untraceable and replaceable. He was left alone to
set the rifle's bipod and adjust the telescopic sight. There
was nothing more to do than wait and Levanto was a master at waiting.

XVI.

Sea of Marmara
Two Hours Later

The earphones did only a modest job of filtering out the noise of the Sikorsky H-60K's rotors. Lang was uncertain if the helicopter was in its Black Hawk or Seahawk configuration, but he recognized the aircraft as the US military's workhorse medium transport chopper of the 1970s through the '90s. Its age showed. The metal bench seats that ran down both sides had been polished to a gloss by generations of rear ends. Although not a pilot, Lang recognized the avionics up front were long outdated. He didn't want to think about the hours on airframe, engine or rotor vanes. All in all, the craft exemplified the Marine Corps' frequent complaint that the equipment it received was that no longer wanted by the army or navy.

Below, the water was a cerulean blue, its surface marred only by creamy arrows, wakes of ferries shuttling between mainland and islands. Lang had trouble relaxing enough to sleep on airplanes. Helicopters frightened him. Things that flew were supposed to have wings, right? No one could convince him that the rotor blades served both as wing and propeller. It just wasn't natural.

His anxiety abated slightly as good, solid terra firma slipped beneath the aircraft.

Across from him, Gurt hardly noticed the slight turbulence caused by the difference in temperatures between land and sea. She didn't even look up from the week-old copy of *USA Today* she had found somewhere. Lang didn't need the cautionary instructions to fasten his seat belt that came through the headset that made onboard communications possible without screaming. He had never removed it. As the craft settled to the round, Lang was trying to squelch his envy. How could she be so serene in the face of the total disregard for the laws of nature shown by helicopters?

The crew were equally indifferent. The pilot and copilot, wearing visored helmets, had obviously become inured to this breach of the law of gravity. The courier, a marine sergeant with webbed gun belt and a battered briefcase chained to his arm, looked bored as did the similarly armed escort beside him.

The world's statesmen thought with Descartes-like logic: I am a diplomat; therefore my communications are important. Important enough to require four marines and a helicopter that probably gobbled a thousand or so dollars an hour of taxpayer money, all to deliver documents that likely had the same security needs as yesterday's comic pages.

And decidedly less amusement value.

Slightly less than a kilometer away, Levanto slipped behind the stationary rifle mounted on a table just inside the window. He could see the markings on the helicopter easily, but he peered through the scope to make sure.

United States Marines?

Nobody had mentioned a helicopter to him, much less one of a military nature. He had no intent of reneging on a deal made; it would be the end of his business. But he certainly would have increased his price had he known the job involved shooting at US Marines. He could only hope the first bullet would be the only one necessary and he would have time to escape amid the ensuing confusion.

He began to inhale deeply in preparation for that long instant during which he would hold his breath, the moment he squeezed the big Walther's trigger.

Then he stopped in midbreath.

The helicopter was discharging its passenger or passengers, if that was what it was doing, from the side facing the church.

The side he couldn't see!

Raising his face from the scope, he looked around the church for some place of concealment from which he could fire. Years of practice made him calm. There was always an alternate possibility and only amateurs acted in haste. He had not survived in this business by letting changing circumstance lead to panic. It would take him at least five minutes or so to set up and stabilize his weapon and reset the telescopic sight even if he could find a suitably level surface. Any such location toward the church would increase the distance to where the horse and wagon were supposedly waiting. No matter: a contract was a contract and his reputation for fulfilling each would be irreparably damaged if he didn't perform this one.

But he couldn't shoot through the damnable aircraft even if he could see his target. And there were no topographically acceptable places to shoot from without time for serious readjustment of the sight. Even then, he had no guarantee his designated target was on board. He might well be risking exposing himself for nothing.

The rotors began to spool down. The helicopter was going to remain on the ground. At least for a few minutes.

That gave Levanto an idea.

Ducking by reflex to avoid the breeze created by the slowing blades, Lang and Gurt stepped to the door of the monastery, where a group of openmouthed monks stared as though they were watching a spaceship land. Behind them, Lang could see the patriarch.

"I welcome you to our home," the prelate said, raising his voice above the dying engine whine, "though I never expected such a, er, sensational arrival. If you will come with me . . ."

They walked in the shadows seeping across the cloister and entered the building on the far side. Again, the whiff of roses. The patriarch opened an elaborately carved wooden door and ushered them inside. They were standing in an office that could have been anywhere, another anachronism considering where they were.

The patriarch stepped behind a battered desk and handed Lang two sheaves of paper. "If you have a moment, I would like to explain."

"Please."

The churchman extended one of the packets. "There are two books of James. The first, of which parts of several copies exist, is called the Protoevangelium. It closely follows the gospels of Matthew and Luke. I suspect the early church fathers discarded it when they were compiling the New Testament simply because it added little beside the fact its author showed a surprising ignorance of Palestinian geography and Jewish customs. It is likely the creation of someone who was neither an eyewitness nor had access to reliable tradition. That is not what you gave me to translate."

Lang waited, trying not to show his impatience.

"The other, what you have, is known as the Apocryphon of James, a postresurrection conversation between Our Lord, James and Peter. It also exists in various fragments in several languages. Since at least the first part was supposedly written by James, the original would have been in Aramaic, later translated into Greek with perhaps a Hebrew version in between. The one you have is the first complete copy, certainly the only one I know of that contains formerly missing lines. I took the freedom, er, liberty of noting those for you." He handed over the second bunch of papers. "I fear there are those who might cause you trouble for what those lines contain."

Tell me about it.

Gurt started to say something and thought better of it, edging toward the door. "We have a hurry to get to . . ."

The patriarch smiled. "Americans are always in a hurry, perhaps so is the whole modern world."

Lang tucked the papers into his belt. "How much do we owe you for your time in translating these?"

The man seemed genuinely surprised. "Owe? As a debt? I owe you for allowing me to see a copy of such rare documents, so rare I suspect I will hear much about them soon." He paused a moment. "Of course, if you wish to make a donation to the monastery . . ."

Levanto reached the top of the staircase and pushed gently against the trapdoor to the roof.

Stuck!

He shoved harder with the same result.

Cursing softly in Sicilian Italian, he scampered back down the stairs and glanced around the room for a tool. The butt of the Walther was the obvious choice, but to use it to batter the stubborn hinges of the door to the roof would be to risk damage to the delicate sight and firing mechanism.

His eyes fell on a pair of pine chairs with woven reed seats. In a step, he had one of them by a leg, smashing it against the floor. All but the leg he held splintered.

Mounting the staircase again, he jabbed the chair leg against the recalcitrant trapdoor. His effort was rewarded when one of the boards came loose, then another.

Lang and Gurt were crossing the cloister again, accompanied by the patriarch. Although every instinct told him to hurry, Lang could not have enunciated a rational reason to do so. The Gulfstream would be waiting in Ankara and they would be out of Turkey before Inspector Aziz knew they had left Istanbul. Experience, though, had taught him that not only was he who hesitated lost, he was usually terminally fucked as well.

Fidgeting, he consulted his watch as the kind old man explained the Bible story depicted in a panel of mosaics. The cleric was clearly taking delight in delivering a tour of the premises. Gurt was enjoying it, too, despite her earlier inclination to make haste. Lang's Southern rearing made him loath to appear rude by cutting the patriarch short. He still could not have given a reason for his urge to hurry other than a belief in the quote from a brilliant if semiliterate Confederate general that it was best to git while the gittin' was good.

Levanto used the chair leg to pry open the remaining parts of the trapdoor. He waited cautiously to make sure the noise had attracted no attention before he pulled himself up. A second later, he was on the roof. A pair of folding lounge chairs and a plastic table confirmed his guess the place was used to take in the sun. More important, he could now see over the helicopter and into the space between it and the church's entrance. When the passengers returned to depart, he would have a very brief gap in which they would be in view. The question now was whether it would be enough time to sight the rifle in time and confirm the chopper's passenger was the intended target.

It would be close but possible.

Gurt and the patriarch stood just inside the doorway as he explained something to her. Lang waited impatiently behind. The helicopter pilot, seeing them, turned over the starter and the rotor began a slow circle.

Gurt finished the conversation and preceded Lang outside as the rotor's blades blurred and the ship became light on its skids.

Through the scope, Levanto could see there were actually two passengers; a man and a woman. Avoiding the temptation to let his view linger a little longer on the woman, a tall and very shapely blonde, he switched to her male companion and smiled. There was no doubt: he was looking at the man in the photographs.

Obligingly, the target stopped long enough to say something to someone behind him, someone Levanto could not see. Levanto used perhaps a tenth of a second of the unexpected time to make a minor adjustment to the scope to compensate for the increased wind on the rooftop and estimate the prop wash from the blades. He inhaled deeply, exhaling and beginning a slow, gentle squeeze of the trigger.

Almost at exactly the same time as the Walther's recoil thumped against Levanto's shoulder, something whirled across the scope, something large and blurred. Without thought, he chambered another round.

Lang was never quite sure of the exact following sequence. Gurt climbed aboard with him a few feet behind. There was a clang of metal on metal, the unmistakable whip crack of a rifle and the whine of a ricocheting bullet that buzzed past Lang's head like a hungry mosquito. By reaction rather than plan, he lunged for the aircraft's open door, colliding with the marine escort who was fumbling with the holster on his webbed belt. Both men tumbled to the floor as the ship lifted off.

Lang struggled uncertainly to his feet. He was about to wonder if any damage had been done to injuries still healing when the pilot's head dissolved, splattering blood and brain tissue across the windscreen and cockpit.

It was unlikely Lang would forget any of what happened next, but what stood out was the calm assurance with which the copilot grasped the controls in front of him with one hand while wiping the gore from his helmet's visor with the other. Use of this ship as a messenger service might be wasting the taxpayers' money, but the man's piloting skill was worth every dime.

The Black Hawk/Seahawk was vibrating slightly as it banked sharply left and climbed. Holding on to a series of overhead straps that reminded him of a New York subway car, Lang made his way forward.

He had not had time to put on the headset. "What . . . ?" he screamed at the copilot's back.

The copilot's answer was to hold up a hand, signaling to stand by. Lang guessed he was on the radio, seeking instructions from the consulate.

When he had finished, he turned slightly in his seat, pushing the boom mike away to speak to Lang. "Dunno. Somebody took a shot through the rotors before shootin' the lieutenant." He pointed to a bank of incomprehensible dials and gauges. "Doesn't look like he hit a vein, the hydraulics that angle the blades so we can control the ship. He did take a nick outta one of the blades, though. That's what's causing the vibration. I'm gonna try to get the lieutenant to the nearest hospital."

Lang glanced at the blood-soaked corpse reclining in the pilot's seat. He caught himself before saying something to the effect the lieutenant was in no hurry. Instead, he waited for this thing to shake itself into pieces in midair.

Levanto cursed for the second time in less than thirty minutes. Unbelievable! His first shot had been deflected by the helicopter's rotor blades. By the time he had worked the rifle's bolt and recentered the sight, moves he had practiced hundreds of times, he knew he had less than a good chance of hitting the pilot as the ship lifted into the air. He had, though. And with a killing shot. Yet the helicopter had not spun out of control as he had anticipated. He had not seen a copilot but clearly someone had taken charge quickly despite what was possibly the best shot of Levanto's career, a feat he suspected his client would not fully appreciate.

For an instant, he contemplated a third try, one for the

helicopter's engine. His discipline overrode his anger. At this range, such an attempt would serve more to divulge his location than to bring the chopper down. Best he keep his rendevous with the horse and wagon.

To Lang, the trip back seemed much shorter than the outbound leg. He did, however, have time to think. Perhaps too much time. Despite the parts of the radio conversation he could hear and the consensus of the three remaining marines, he was certain this was not a terrorist plot to kill the pilot in an attempt to intercept communications between the consulate in Istanbul and the embassy in Ankara. Muslim jihadists had bigger goats to fry, more important infidels to kill. Or just more important than a marine lieutenant. And there were certainly more significant messages to intercept and bigger things to blow up than a single helicopter. Like schools, churches and other places the innocent might gather.

All in the name of peace, Islam and their Prophet.

No, the bullet that had nicked the rotor blade had been meant for him.

The thought wasn't exactly self-flattery. Or comforting.

A glance forward showed splatters of red congealing into mud brown. That could just as easily have been his blood, his brains. Although this wasn't the first time such a thing had happened, he felt the sourness rising in his throat. Because the bullet had been meant for him or because it had found someone else, he could not have said.

In what seemed like seconds, the helicopter was dropping onto a pad on top of what Lang assumed was a hospital, an impression enforced by the crew of white-clad men surrounding a gurney. They removed the lieutenant under the cocked and ready weapons of the remaining crew. While everyone else was attending to the mortally wounded officer, Lang took Gurt's arm, leading her away from the group.

"What?"

"Get your bag. We're leaving."

"Leaving?"

"There're always taxis around hospitals. One can drive us to Ankara."

"Why did we not do that before?"

"Because the police were watching us. There was good chance they would have followed a cab, stopped us before we got far. I doubt they've had time to figure out where we are now."

"Once the inspector finds we have left the city, the police will question cab drivers until they find the one who has driven us to Ankara."

"By that time, we'll be halfway home."

CHAPTER SIX

I.

Over the North Atlantic
That Night

For once, Lang's flight-induced insomnia was a benefit. He had left Gurt snoring gently in the Gulfstream's stateroom. As is so often the case, proximity to sudden and violent death had stirred a passion that had resulted in wild and noisy lovemaking shortly after the stewardess cleared the dinner dishes. In fact, it had taken some restraint to wait until the woman had discreetly retreated to the galley before both made a dash for the plane's bedroom as they undressed en route. Now Lang looked around in case some of Gurt's more intimate garments might yet be decorating the seating area.

Occasionally Lang wondered if he and Gurt were the

subject of gossip among the crews of the world's biz jets. He didn't necessarily care, he just wondered.

But not tonight.

He was far too engrossed in the translation he held in his lap. He was surprised at its length, only a few pages. It seemed very little to have cost the lives lost since its discovery. He reread the first lines. It seemed to be a letter.

> Since you asked me to send thee a secret book which was revealed unto me and Peter by the Lord, I could not refuse thee. I send this with wishes. Peace be with thee, Love from love, Grace from grace, Faith from faith, life from Holy Life. But inasmuch as thou art a minister of the Salvation of Saints, endeavor earnestly and take care not to recount this book to many—this which the Savior did not desire to recount to all of us.

Us? Who was "Us," Lang wondered. The disciples? No, hadn't Francis suggested James, this James, Jesus's brother, had not been a disciple, that he had probably stayed at home to run the family business?

The ever-annoying indefinite antecedent.

But he read on.

> This book was revealed only to Peter and me, James, brother of Our Lord.
>
> Now we were sitting altogether at the same time, and remembering what the Savior had said to each of them, whether secretly or openly, they were setting it down in books. And I was writing what was in my book—lo the Savior appeared after he had departed from us and five hundred and fifty days after He arose from the dead. And we said unto Him, "Have you gone and departed from us?"
>
> And Jesus said, "No, but I shall go to the place from

which I have come. If thou desirest to come with me, come."

They all answered and said, "If Thou biddest us we will come." He said, "Truly I say to you, no one will ever enter the Kingdom of Heaven if I bid him but rather because you yourselves desire it. Let me have James and Peter that I might speak with them privately."

"Coffee?"

Lang was jolted back into the present. The stewardess was standing in front of him, holding a tray with a pot and a cup and saucer with the foundation's logo on it.

Coffee would ensure he didn't get even a few minutes sleep but the woman had clearly made fresh brew just for him.

"It's decaf," she chirped.

Tell my nerves that. They can't distinguish. And how can anyone be that perky at this hour of the night? But no sense being churlish.

"Sure. Thanks for going to the trouble."

He had hoped she would pour a cup he could leave ignored on the coffee table before him. Instead, she hovered like a sommelier uncertain of his wine selection.

He took a sip. "Thanks. I really appreciate your going to the trouble."

She flashed him a megawatt smile. "That's what you pay me for."

True, he mused as he watched her retreat to the galley, but how many employees ever gave it a thought? Setting the steaming cup down once she was out of view, he resumed reading.

And when He called us two, He took us aside and commanded the rest of them to busy themselves with that with which they had been endeavoring.

When we were alone, the Savior said, . . .

Lang noted the next twelve lines were highlighted in yellow, the missing lines, he assumed.

> *"It is time that James lead my church."*
>
> *And Peter protested, saying, "Lord, didst thou not say, 'Upon this rock I shall build my church,' meaning me? Hast thou not called my name as Cephus, the rock?"*
>
> *And the Savior answered unto him, "Didst thou not thrice deny me as was prophesied? Would a master have a servant that denied him?"*
>
> *And Peter grew wroth, saying, "Lord, who would serve you better?"*
>
> *And the Savior answered, "James," whereupon Peter became even more angry, demeaning James as a coward and one who had not forsaken his family to follow the Savior as had Peter.*

Lang reread the lines before continuing. The rest contained homilies on reaching heaven, the duty to spread the word and assurances the unknown "they" would reach heaven. Nothing to really distinguish it from the known quotes attributed to Jesus.

On the last page, the patriarch had also highlighted several lines with a note in the margin:

> *This last part obvious not written by James but added. Thank you for your promised donation.*

Shifting in his seat, Lang read the final paragraph and jerked up straight with surprise.

> *And after the Savior departed, Peter considered these words and his anger increased so that by the second day his anger could no longer be contained. And he went forth, seeking James. And when he had found him in the temple in Jerusalem at prayer, he threw him from the*

temple to the ground below. And Peter accused James of stealing the Savior's affection from him, saying to those who had gathered, "Look upon the face of a man who has betrayed our Savior." Whereupon they stoned the Lord's brother.

Lang reread the paragraph to make sure there was no mistake. Peter, the supposed anointed leader of the early church as usurper and murderer? He recalled the expression of rage on the saint's face as depicted by the mysterious fresco. No wonder the spectators had been ordered into silence. That an early gospel had noted James, not Peter, had been chosen, let alone what amounted to a theological coup . . .

And the missing lines . . . well, they could set the church back on its velvet-slippered heels! Since the pope claimed his title through Peter by apostolic succession, the pontiff and all before him would be no more than pretenders. Apparently someone already knew of those lines, someone like whoever had painted that picture in the Vatican, someone like . . . like the people who wanted him dead. The papers in his lap might have been the first the patriarch had seen that included those lines but they existed somewhere else, too. Or had existed. The question was, where? If he could ascertain who knew of Peter's wrath at being essentially demoted, he would have the answers he needed.

There was, he supposed, a way to find out.

But first, he had business back home. More important, he had a son he felt he hadn't seen in forever.

II.

United States District Court for the Middle District of
  Georgia
Macon, Georgia
Two Days Later

Courthouses, hospitals, prisons and other institutions
trafficking in human suffering have a certain intimidating
air about them. In the case of the former, this is not by
accident. To induce apprehension if not outright fear is the
first commandment of government. That is why judges
wear black robes, like priests of some somber but powerful
religion whose acolytes speak in mystical tongues, words
like "hereinafter," "alleged" or "tort feasor." The courthouse lobby might be marred with some form that is "art"
by the loosest of definitions, smears of color chosen by the
lowest bid. An alternative might be a plaque commemorat-
ing someone or some event in most cases otherwise forgotten.

The courtrooms themselves are interchangeable. This is
particularly true with the federal judiciary because the
taxpayers who fund the cheerless decor are spread from
Alaska to Florida rather than concentrated in a single
county where local voters are likely to note and complain
about excess.

Lang sat alone at counsel table, pondering who had decided the apricot carpeting went with the dark-stained
wooden paneling. Who had been responsible for choosing
the slime green plastic cushions that did little to mollify
the painfully hard wooden chairs? He was convinced that
somewhere in Washington, D.C. was a Bureau of Vile Taste,
a permanent board that furnished federal courts and other
places where justice was dispensed, or, just as often, dispensed with.

He turned at the sound of an opening door behind him.

A young man was wheeling into the room a small cart loaded with files, each of which was stuffed to the limit with papers. An assistant US attorney, no doubt. And a very junior one. Lang glanced back at the slim attaché case he had brought. Lawyers who worked for the government equated quantity with quality. Of course, so did many of their private-practice counterparts. If you generated enough paper, there was bound to be something good in there somewhere, right?

The young man parked his cart at the other counsel table and walked over, hand extended. "Sam Roads."

Lang stood and shook. "I bet they call you Dusty."

The assistant US attorney stopped in midshake. "How'd you know?"

"Same way I'd guess if your last name was Waters, you'd be called Muddy. I'm Lang Reilly."

The assistant US attorney smiled. "Coulda been 'Country.'"

Lang nodded. "Or 'State' or 'Federal' but it's always 'Dusty.'"

Dusty eyed Lang's single attaché case and his grin faded into suspicion. "You have a reputation even this far from Atlanta."

Lang's turn to smile. "Calumnious lies, I swear."

Dusty wasn't so certain. "You ready?"

Before Lang could reply, the door opened again, this time admitting Larry Henderson with a burly US marshal on either side. Detention life didn't look like it agreed with him. The man had lost a dozen or more pounds. His color was that ashlike complexion Lang associated with inmates of much longer duration. It was as if the gray of prisons' concrete walls rubbed off on those they contained. He wore a Day-Glo orange jumpsuit and a pair of leg shackles.

He smiled when he saw Lang, probably the first friendly face he had seen since Darleen's last visit. Lang felt a twinge of guilt. He guessed those visits had been limited during the time Manfred had been staying with her.

Larry's escorts moved to the courtroom's door and Larry hobbled toward counsel table.

Lang spoke cooly to the marshals. "The leg irons need to come off."

"Not till the judge comes in," growled one of them.

It was hardly a major issue, but Lang knew the importance of not acceding to the slightest infringement of clients' rights. Likewise, he was aware of jailers' tendency to intimidate their charges whenever possible. "The rules say restraints come off in the courtroom without a specific order to the contrary. Don't make me file a formal complaint."

The guard who had spoken before shot Lang a poisonous glare before producing a key and removing the shackles. Lang caught a satisfying whiff of a muttered, "Goddamn smart-ass Atlanta lawyer."

From her private entrance, the judge appeared on the bench like magic. Short blunt-cut steel gray hair, little if any makeup. Before sitting, she fluffed her robe, the sole feminine gesture she would make. Although he had never seen her in person, Lang had done his homework on Judge Linda Carver. Like all federal judges, she was a political appointee, this one from the Reagan administration. She had served as one of the then rare Republicans in both the state senate and house as well as vice chair of the Georgia Republican Party. Although never as important in the appointment process as the politics, her legal abilities were reflected in the fact she had been a partner in a major mid-Georgia law firm when female associates, let alone partners, had been rare. Even though her experience had been more in the boardroom than the courtroom, she had surprised a number of unwary lawyers with a knowledge of evidence, procedure and the other arcanum of the trial practice. She had a reputation of being fair but hard-assed, the description usually given to a judge who suffered fools poorly and the unprepared worse.

Judge Carver lowered half-moon glasses from her forehead and studied the papers in front of her before looking up. "You are Mr. Langford Reilly?"

Lang, still standing, nodded. "Guilty, Your Honor."

A trace of a smile flickered and disappeared across the judicial countenance. Score one small point for the good guys.

"Welcome to the middle district, Mr. Reilly. I understand you practice mainly in Atlanta."

Lang wasn't the only one who had done their homework.

"You have already met Mr. Roads, I see."

"Yes, ma'am."

She was still scanning the papers in front of her. "We are here today for a formal arraignment, plea and scheduling. Is that you gentlemen's understanding?"

"And application for bond, Your Honor," Lang added.

Roads was on his feet. "Your Honor, the defendant is charged with trafficking in narcotics, a serious felony . . ."

She silenced him with a frown and a cocked eyebrow. "Have a seat, Mr. Roads. It's customary to hear the defendant's plea before a bond application."

Flustered, the assistant US attorney sat back down and began thumbing through one of the file folders.

Judge Carver began reading the charges, a long, repetitious list of misdeeds and offenses. When she finished, she looked up. "How does the defendant plead?"

Lang was still standing. "Not guilty, Your Honor."

There was a tug at the back of his suit jacket. Larry had a question.

"May I confer with my client?" he asked the judge.

After receiving an affirmative nod, he knelt beside Larry.

"I done it, done what they said. I unnerstan' from the

folks down to the jail you get a lighter sentence, you admit what you done."

"I didn't say you didn't do what they charge," Lang whispered. "I said you were not guilty. Believe me, there's a difference. Besides, if we have to, we can change our plea."

"But how—?"

Lang held out a hand for him to be quiet. He understood Larry's discomfort. His fate in the hands of a system he did not comprehend, he understandably relied on what he knew usually worked: honesty and candor, two traits virtually unknown to the judicial system.

"Do we still have a 'not guilty'?" the judge asked impatiently.

"We do, Your Honor. Now, if I may, I'd like to ask the court to set bond. Mr. Henderson is a lifelong resident of Lamar County, where he was born and grew up as did both his father and grandfather. He owns considerable real estate and has family there. As far as I know, this is his first brush with the criminal justice system. He has been incarcerated since his arrest. I don't understand why he wasn't promptly brought before a magistrate a week or so ago."

It never hurt to point out your client's rights had already been compromised.

Judge Carver was scanning the file in front of her, presumably verifying what Lang had said. "It says here your office informed the clerk you were out of the country. For once the glitch wasn't in the system."

Whoever kept the file on this case did a more meticulous job than Lang was used to. He made a mental note to go easy on the righteous indignation in the future.

"Mr. Roads?"

Dusty was already on his feet. "The government opposes, Your Honor. Mr. Henderson was using his 'considerable property' to grow marijuana. Under the law, he stands to forfeit every square foot of it as contraband. He has no incentive not to flee."

Lang started to reply but the judge silenced him with a wave of the hand. "Bail is set at one million dollars, cash or property. Does Mr. Henderson possess a passport?"

Lang looked at Larry, who shook his head.

"No, Your Honor."

"Very well, then. He may bond out anytime after this hearing."

Dusty half stood. "But—"

"And, Mr. Roads, don't even think about the government interfering with Mr. Henderson putting his real estate up as collateral. You might be able to condemn it as contraband under the law, but not unless and until he's convicted. Understood?"

A hangdog. "Yes, ma'am."

Judge Carver glanced at her watch, seemed satisfied the time so far had been well spent and said, "Now, then, scheduling. Mr. Reilly, what do you propose?"

With his client about to be freed on bond, there was little incentive for a speedy trial. In fact, just the opposite. "Motions in ninety days, trial in six months?"

Again, Dusty was about to stand. The judge waved him back into his seat. "A little prolonged, Mr. Reilly. All motions will be filed not later than sixty days of today." She consulted a computer terminal on the right corner of the bench. "We will begin striking a jury sixty days thereafter."

"That's mighty quick, Your Honor," Lang complained mildly.

"We move a little faster here in the middle district, Mr. Reilly. We don't have the caseloads judges have where you practice. Anything else gentlemen? No?" She stood. "Good. I'm glad we're all in agreement."

Then she disappeared.

Dusty intercepted Lang in the hallway. "Don't suppose you're interested in discussing savin' the taxpayers the cost of a trial, seein' if we can make a deal?"

Lang shifted his briefcase from his right hand to his left and punched the elevator's "down" button. "You're right, I'm not."

Dusty studied his face a moment as if trying to ascertain if he were serious. "You shittin' me? Your man was growing marijuana, acres of it. We got witnesses, photographs. He's guilty as hell."

The elevator door pinged open and Lang stepped inside. "Maybe. Question is, can you prove it?"

Dusty's expression of incredulity was erased by the closing door.

Lang was certain of the course his defense of Larry would take. There would be no point in challenging the government's case but every reason to prevent them from proving it. The bird-watcher was the obvious starting point.

III.

Piazza dei Cavalleri di Malta
Aventine Hill
Rome
Later that Day

There were perhaps a hundred seats in the priory chapel, Santa Maria del Priorato. Through the arched doorway, men draped in the black hooded robes of next door's Dominican church entered singly or in small groups. Inside, the ancient stone walls were decorated not with figures of saints but with coats of arms bearing the family names of European royalty as well as those of more contemporary princes of international commerce. Instead of large stained glass, the only windows were small and high up the walls as if the builder had wanted to limit not only access but light as well. The impression was that this place could be converted to a fortress in very little time. Through the open door could be seen the famous view of the Vatican. Closer, obelisks and other military trophies were placed around sculpted rose gardens and the tomb of Piranesi, the man whose name had become synonymous with detailed pen-and-ink architectural drawings and who had redesigned the church in the eighteenth century.

When the last man entered, the doors swung silently shut on well-oiled hinges. Overhead lights gave a dim, buttery illumination that softened the old stone walls and flooded corners with shadows. General conversation muted to a few murmurs, then went silent as a single figure proceeded down the center aisle toward the block of marble that was the altar. No doubt it was a combination of the light and his dark floor-length robe that gave the illusion he was floating rather than walking. Just before reaching the altar, he turned, pulling back his hood. A full head of silver hair reflected the light into a golden halo.

He looked around the small church like a man just now deciding what he was going to say before he spoke in Italian. "Brothers, welcome and thank you for obeying my summons on such short notice."

There was the sound of people shifting in their seats, the sound of impatience.

"We are faced today with a peril greater than any we have seen since the Ottoman Turks stood at the gates of Vienna four hundred years ago. It consists of heretical documents defaming our blessed St. Peter, holding the rock of our church up to scorn, opprobrium and ridicule, challenging his and subsequent popes' most holy position as head of the one true faith."

Angry mutters rippled through the assembly.

"No!"

"We cannot permit it!"

"I will describe this calumny in more detail shortly," the speaker continued. "First, though, let me remind you of the nature of our order. Most of our brothers, over 95 percent, view their membership as a great honor with the responsibility only of generosity. They have no idea of what we do and lack the strength of will to do it themselves. Without them, though, we would not receive the funds necessary to exist as an order. I mention this because, in less than two weeks, the annual gathering of the entire order will take place. Bankers, stockbrokers, merchants will fill this place for the fellowship and pleasure the order gives them. Under no circumstances must the danger to which I allude still exist. Knowledge of that danger, and the means we must use to combat it, could mean not only the end of our order but also Christ's church as we know it."

He was silent for one, two seconds, letting the urgency of his message sink into the minds of his audience.

Then he continued. "As you know, nearly two millennia ago, the church fathers met at Nicaea to establish commonality of beliefs including the text of what would become the New Testament. The decisions were made and all texts and their copies not included were ordered destroyed as heretical. Until very recently, I had thought the only remaining copies were safely in the Vatican's most secret archives, preserved solely for study. Such is not the case; one has surfaced.

"I will not burden you with the content of this document but only the fact it presents a danger to Holy Mother Church. It and any who may become aware of its blasphemy must be destroyed. Regrettably, this has included some otherwise devout Christians such as one Greek Orthodox priest and, just hours ago, a patriarch of the same faith who somehow let himself become ensnared in this hideous apostasy."

"Greek or not," someone in the back shouted, "they were fellow Christians!"

There were several more comments against a background of unhappy muttering.

The speaker held up his hands for quiet. "I tell you this,

my brothers, only to emphasize the severity of the danger we face. My purpose today is to involve all of you in this most holy crusade to protect the very foundations of the church."

"We are not assassins," a voice protested.

"No," the speaker agreed, "but we all gave the oath of allegiance to the holy church, to oppose her enemies and to obey the orders of our superiors."

"We didn't give an oath to kill," another person said.

"Obedience to one's superiors includes anything that superior, with God's help, deems necessary for the good of the order."

No one could muster an argument against that logic.

Satisfied there would be no further disagreement, the speaker continued. "Here is what we must do . . ."

IV.

Park Place
2660 Peachtree Road
Atlanta
Two Days Later

Lang had to do something about completing the restoration of the burned-out shell that had been his home. Letters from management imploring action had turned into pleas from the condominium association invoking sympathy for his fellow residents' property values. Now he was receiving angry demands citing association rules. Management had called his office almost daily as unwanted and unordered appliances arrived from Home Depot. Repeated calls from Lang's secretary, Sara, to the company had elicited promises to remove not only the bidet, dishwasher and huge stove but also two shower stalls, two sinks (one porcelain, the other stainless steel), the newest in minimum water usage toilet and a giant gas barbeque grill that would have been at home on any patio that included a football field. Instead, each arrival of the delivery truck heralded the appearance of more home furnishings that had already overflowed Lang's small unit and the building's basement storage area as well.

The company's explanation was always the same: a computer glitch, a gremlin in the system who had, so far, eluded whatever efforts Home Depot had exerted. Lang guessed that somewhere a contractor was sliding into bankruptcy as item after item failed to materialize at one job site after another while the supply company's posse chased fruitlessly through cyberspace. As is often the case, technology had replaced reality.

It had become clear the problem wasn't going to get solved by phone. Besides, Lang was eager to prepare the place for sale and look for more spacious quarters for his new family before the homeowners' association filed suit. He had an even greater incentive to find a new home: Now that Judge Carver had prohibited any forfeiture action by the government, the US Marshals Service had lost interest in surveillance. The farm was no longer secure.

He would have to at least begin making repairs to the condo to mollify his neighbors. He could hardly consult with a contractor without pointing out the work he wanted done. The problem, of course, was the condo was an obvious place to keep under observation by those who had tried to kill him.

Wearing jeans and a shirt, Gurt pulled the rented SUV under the porte cochere, surrendering the vehicle to an acne-faced young man in a white shirt and black clip-on bow tie who fidgeted impatiently while she released Manfred from the constraints of his kiddie seat. Hand in hand, mother and child entered the building.

Moments later, a man walking a very ugly dog turned in from the sidewalk. His stooped back and deliberate step gave a sense of age's infirmity, an impression difficult to verify since the pedestrian wore a cap pulled low on his forehead and the collar of his shirt turned up as if to ward off a chill despite the warmth of the day. Whatever his decrepitude, the greeting by the concierge at the desk evidenced he and the dog belonged in the building.

After an elevator ride, Lang and Grumps exited facing a rather poor reproduction Boule chest topped with a worse reproduction of a Ming vase. Even the flowers it contained were silk, not real. Lang knew the condo association's decorator was gay. Strange he had an affinity for reproduction of any sort.

The building's elevators opened onto a sort of foyer with a condominium unit around each corner. Two steps to his right brought Lang to his door where Gurt, Manfred in hand, was talking to a burly man in a sport shirt and slacks, no doubt the contractor the condo association had recommended.

"Mr. Haverly?"

Lang extended his hand to have it encased in a bear's paw. "Mr. Reilly. I was just describing to your missus here what our options might be. You understand we're pretty much starting from scratch."

"Pretty much, if that," Lang replied hurriedly, before Gurt could correct the man's perception of her marital status. "Even fixed up, the place is too small. I'd like to get it done on a reasonable budget as quickly as possible, put it on the market."

While Haverly seemed to be considering this new twist, Lang leaned over and unlocked the door. He shoved it open, releasing the odor of things burned.

Manfred made an exaggerated face, holding his nose. "Phew! Still stinks!"

Grumps snorted his disapproval before taking tentative steps inside.

Lang waited a second for Gurt to join in, grateful when she didn't.

Haverly's eyes were taking in the empty shell of what had been Lang's home when the contractor's cell phone beeped.

"Yeah?"

He turned to Lang. "One of my men's downstairs, says there's a delivery truck from Home Depot."

Lang's sigh was lost in the sound of his grinding teeth. At least this time he would meet face-to-face with a flesh-and-blood employee instead of a sympathetic but totally unhelpful telephone voice.

He handed Grumps's leash to Gurt. "I'll be back in a minute."

Seeing his expression, she shook her head. "Remember, the man is only doing his work. It will do no good to gnaw him."

"Chew him out."

"That either."

Lang used the elevator ride to try to cool off. Gurt was right: Blasting a mere truck deliveryman wasn't going to solve the problem. Maybe he could hold the truck hostage, maybe . . .

The elevator doors wheezed open and Lang stormed into the building's lobby. And stopped as though he had hit a brick wall. The cool marble was empty except for the doorman and the concierge who were staring at him as they might a man suddenly gone mad. There was no truck waiting on the other side of the glass doors, no one waiting for him here.

"Is there anything wrong, Mr. Reilly?" asked the door-man, whose expression said he thought, yes, there *was* something very wrong with Mr. Reilly.

"A delivery truck," Lang stammered, "And an associate of Mr. Haverly . . ."

"Mr. Haverly?" the concierge asked, a note of concern breaking through his professional calm like a rock jutting above the surface of an otherwise placid ocean. He looked out onto the empty circular driveway. "Delivery truck?"

Oh, shit!

Lang urged the gracefully smooth rise of the elevator to greater speed. It seemed to take hours to reach his floor. When he arrived, only Grumps was there to meet him.

Gurt, Manfred and Haverly were gone.

V.

Park Place
Seconds Earlier

Gurt was never certain where they came from, the two men with guns. Two things were clear: they knew this Mr. Haverly and they had been waiting for Lang to leave the floor.

Her first thought was for Manfred's safety and her second the Glock. The latter dissolved when one of the men took her purse, emptied its contents and stuck the gun in his waistband.

Wordlessly, the second motioned her outside the condo and to the freight elevator where Haverly was holding the door open. Even as frightened as she was for her child's safety, her professional training did not desert her. She watched the two men as the elevator sank below the lobby toward the underground parking levels of the building. They were clearly tense, if not nervous. Each had his finger on the trigger of his weapon. A professional would have his trigger finger along the barrel of the pistol where it could be moved in an instant but not cause an accidental firing in the meantime. A professional would never have left her purse and its contents on the floor, a clear indication she had not left voluntarily. Someone experienced in this sort of thing would want to cause as much uncertainty as possible, delay any pursuit. Neither were accustomed to handling firearms; neither had experience in an abduction.

That was both the . . . What was it Americans said? *Ach, ja*, the good news and the bad news. Nervous amateurs were likely to overreact. Or act hastily. On the other side, these men might not be aware of what a person, a mere woman, could do with bare hands if given the opportunity.

And she was going to do her best to see they did just that.

"Where are we going?" she asked in a trembling voice. "Please, let the child go. I'll come peacefully. Please don't hurt him."

"Lady," one of them said as the elevator came to a stop, "you and the kid do as you're told and neither of you get hurt."

She recognized the line from an old movie she and Lang had watched on television. But these men were not Hollywood actors, and she didn't believe men abducted people without purpose. And she was pretty sure what that purpose was.

Drama had never been Gurt's forte, but she was going to play the part of a terrified female to the best of her ability. She might even manage a tear or two. No one would recognize the difference between tears of terror and those of rage. In the meantime, she would access what assets she could muster.

Like the BlackBerry in the pocket of her jeans.

Haverly stood beside the open rear doors of an unmarked white van. All but the front seat had been removed. Gurt stopped until she was roughly shoved from behind.

"Remember, lady, you try something and the kid gets it."

She recognized the gun pressed against her son's head as one of the Heckler & Koch P9 "blowback" models. Its muzzle size suggested the .45-caliber version made for the American market who found the European 9mm either suspect or too puny. The child's eyes were wide with fear and he was manfully fighting back tears. It took considerable effort for Gurt to restrain her rage at the terror inflicted on her son. These men might be amateurs, but that didn't mean they wouldn't do as they threatened.

She climbed into the back of the van, sitting splay-legged with her back against the side. Manfred huddled against her, momentarily shielding her left side from view. She reached into her jeans pocket, felt the BlackBerry and prayed the keys she was punching by touch alone were the right ones.

VI.

Park Place

Lang inhaled deeply, forcing himself to be calm. He knelt, ignoring the pain the move shot up his leg, an abrupt reminder his healing still had a way to go. Compact, lipstick, purse, stuff Gurt would never have left behind voluntarily. They had tried to grab her and Manfred once before, the episode in Baden-Baden.

Now they had succeeded.

They.

He had been gone, what, five minutes at the most? Perhaps not time for them to clear the building.

Leaving Grumps in the hollow shell of the condo, Lang was tempted to take the stairs. But no matter how quickly he moved, the elevator was going to be faster descending twenty-four floors. Even so, the trip seemed to last an eternity. When he finally burst out into the lobby, he made for the concierge.

"The contractor, Haverly, has he come through here?"

The man gave him a look that clearly said he already thought Lang had gone nuts and this merely confirmed it. "Haverly? Haverly Construction? Haven't seen him in weeks."

"But he was just here, looking at my unit."

"I don't think so, Mr. Reilly."

"Then who the hell was . . ." Lang made himself pause, swallow hard. "There was a man on my floor, claimed to be Haverly. Just how the hell did he get in? He had to come right past here."

The concierge shrugged, unperturbed. "Not necessarily. The building can be accessed from the parking levels."

Lang was dumbstruck. It had never occurred to him that the security apparatus that represented a substantial portion of his condominium dues could be short-circuited so easily.

"You mean just anyone can drive down to parking and enter?"

"They would show up on the security cameras' tapes."

Swell.

By the time tapes were reviewed, someone could walk off with half the building. With any luck, that would include the faux Boule chest and Ming vase. Silk flowers, too.

"You're telling me no one watches the cameras?"

The man behind the desk was adroit in blame shifting. At some point in his life he clearly had been employed by some level of government. Or Home Depot's customer service. "You'll have to take that up with the security office, Mr. Reilly."

"Screw that. There's no time!" he spat.

He started to dash for the elevator and to the parking areas when he saw a white van drive from that direction and stop at the traffic light where the drive met Peachtree Street.

He yelled over his shoulder, "Is there any work going on in any of the units today?"

All workmen had to check in and out with the concierge.

The concierge opened a desk drawer and took a brief look at a legal pad.

"Hurry up, dammit!" Lang exploded.

"No, not today."

Instead of the elevators, Lang charged outside where an elderly woman was being helped from her massive S-series Mercedes Panzer by one of the carhops. She fumbled with a cane while a second was opening the trunk. Only yards away, the traffic light turned green and the van turned right into traffic.

"Excuse me!"

Lang was in the Mercedes's driver seat, knocking the woman one way, her cane another. Before anyone could protest, rubber was shrieking against pavement and the two carhops diving out of the way, forgetting the poor woman. She sat on the pavement, middle finger extended. In the car's mirror Lang could read her lips as she shouted, "Fuck you, asshole!"

Not his grandmother.

The big car fishtailed onto the street just as the light turned red again. Lang was far too intent on the white van to hear the yells and curses of the carhops as they dusted themselves off and inspected minor abrasions caused by impact with concrete.

Granny had to get up herself.

Lang's impulse was to force the van over to the curb. He resisted. It was a fair assumption that Gurt had not gone with the occupant or occupants of that vehicle willingly. They had likely been armed and they certainly now had her Glock, too. Putting the kidnappers in a position where shooting would endanger not only Gurt but also Manfred. Instead, Lang dropped back, allowing one or two cars between him and the van. He only hoped he wasn't spotted.

Then his BlackBerry chirped. A quick glance showed Gurt's number.

He fumbled for the Bluetooth earpiece, and put it in place. At first he heard nothing, then, "This van is uncomfortable."

He started to reply before realizing she wasn't speaking to him. She was verifying that she was in the van.

He heard a man's voice, but the words were indistinguishable.

"Can't one of the three of you . . ."

He missed the rest, but he got the message.

The van continued with the normal flow of traffic. Lang could only hope that a series of turns didn't betray the tail. Instead, the van entered I75-85, heading south. A few exits later, it turned onto the ramp for I20 West. Lang was trying to guess where they might be going.

Birmingham?

His answer came a few minutes later when the van turned off the interstate. Lang knew the exit well. It was the one for Fulton County–Charlie Brown Field, the place the foundation kept the Gulfstream.

As if in confirmation, Gurt's voice said, "Why are we going to Charlie Brown Airport?"

Again, the unintelligible response.

At the terminal building, the car took a right turn. Lang knew the road led to only one place: Hill Aviation, the only fixed-base operator on this side of the field. The asphalt was slightly above the level of the airport itself, giving him a view of the ramp area in front of Hill. A stretch Lear was taxiing on the tarmac. Nothing unusual about that. Except the identification letters, what would have been the N number on an American plane. Foreign countries, including all of Europe, used letters only.

Lang felt a jolt of panic. They were going to try to get Gurt and his son out of the country. If he was going to stop them . . .

The van turned off the road and down a slope to the FBO. Lang followed.

His turn must have alerted someone the van had been followed, for it spurted ahead to the gate in the security chain-link fence. Not waiting for someone inside to verify their identity, the van smashed through the fence as though the steel links were made of paper.

By the time Lang followed, the Lear was already moving toward the van, its clamshell door yawning open like the mouth of a predator about to feed. Helpless, Lang watched three men hop out of the van and herd Gurt, holding Manfred's hand, aboard.

The door closed just as the Mercedes reached the plane, already in motion. Lang was tempted to ram the fragile hull but knew that such action could rupture an auxiliary fuel cell, engulfing the Lear in flames.

Instead, he watched the plane lumber away like a waddling goose, slow and clumsy on the ground but a picture of grace and speed in the air.

Well, sitting here wasn't going to do any good, and he doubted the two cars with the flashing yellow lights of the airport's hired security were going to be a lot of help, either. By the time he explained what had happened, the Lear would be in the air, miles away. He didn't think the plane had the fuel capacity to cross an ocean without at least one stop, but where? The flight plan mandatory for flights at jet altitudes would reveal that information, a plan from which no aircraft in US airspace could deviate without risking attention from air force F-18's. But how long would it take to secure the information? The very fact he had followed the van through the pitifully inadequate security fence would cause the rent-a-cops to hold him until police arrived.

A half a mile away, a small Cessna lifted into the air from runway nine and gave Lang an idea.

He stood on the Mercedes's accelerator, pleased to find power under the hood proportional to the car's bulk. He sped after the slow-moving Lear, trailing two light-flashing cars behind on the taxiway.

Inside the Lear, Gurt and Manfred had been forced into two of the four forward-facing seats, two and two separated by a narrow aisle. Behind them, a pair of small sofas faced each other across a small table of plastic faux wood, their backs molded into the curving hull of the airplane. The interior had no personal touches. It was as cold as a hotel lobby. One of the pilots stooped to enter the cabin from the cockpit. He whispered something Gurt could not hear to the man who had identified himself as Haverly. Both men were looking at her.

Not a good sign.

Haverly squatted beside her seat. "Ground control tells us some idiot is following this plane in a car. I think we both know who that idiot might be."

Gurt said nothing, trying to hide her satisfaction.

Haverly handed her a cell phone. "Now, you call Mr. Reilly, tell him if he doesn't call off this absurd chase, the little boy will be dead before takeoff."

Gurt made a decision. She shoved away Haverly and produced her BlackBerry. "This you have heard, Lang?"

"You bitch!" Haverly snarled, grabbing for the BlackBerry. "They were supposed to search you! No wonder he tracked us so easily. I should have killed you and taken the boy."

Gurt wasn't listening. Instead, she was staring at the tiny screen of the BlackBerry. She read the two lines and deleted them just as Haverly snatched it away. As she knew he would, Lang had a plan.

The taxiway was too narrow to pass the jet, blocking its way. Lang had considered driving off onto the unpaved shoulder but discarded the idea for fear the Mercedes's weight might mire him in soft soil or mud. Now that he had been able to communicate with Gurt, he had a slightly modified course of action in mind. He ground his teeth in impatience waiting for the Lear to reach the end of the taxiway, the place it would have to swing wide to the right to align itself with the runway.

Haverly, or whoever he was, was still standing over Gurt when the plane began a slow swing to the right, just as Lang had predicted. She pushed Manfred down in his seat, a move that attracted Haverly's attention. He drew her Glock from his belt.

"What th' hell you think you're . . . ?"

Lang saw the plane begin its slow turn and slammed the gas pedal to the floor.

The most vulnerable part of any modern aircraft is the nose wheel. It is lighter than the other two gears so it can easily be moved as a steering mechanism by pressing one rudder pedal or the other. The landing, or main, gear are hardy shock absorbers, designed to take the impact of the worst landings while the pilot holds the delicate nose gear off the round until it can be lowered somewhat more gently.

That was Lang's target.

With a whip of the wrists, the Mercedes was around the front of the Lear, describing a semicircle. The arc came to an abrupt end when the steel of the German car smashed into the nose wheel strut, snapping it as though it were a dry twig.

Haverly had reached out a hand to steady himself as the aircraft began its swing onto the runway in anticipation of takeoff. Suddenly the plane pitched forward and down, throwing him off balance.

Gurt moved.

Pushing up from her seat, her left hand grabbed his right wrist, swinging the Glock harmlessly upward. Her right fist impacted just below his sternum with all the force of her full body and legs behind it. With a whoosh, Haverly doubled over. Still holding his right wrist, she yanked down, her left foot on his, tumbling him onto the floor between her and the other two men seated behind on the sofas and effectively blocking their line of fire.

She had to hope the two pilots were unarmed.

"Mutter!" Manfred screamed from somewhere behind her.

She whirled in the narrow aisle just in time to see one of the pilots lunge for her.

He was met with a smashing blow. Its impact was not quite as loud as the crunch of nose cartilage. Nothing is more temporarily disabling than a sudden, unexpected and severe dose of pain. He sat suddenly, his face puzzled, perhaps contemplating his sudden and involuntary rhinomycosis as a flood of crimson dripped from his chin.

Now the aisle was blocked from the cockpit side, too.

The man who had called himself Haverly was on all fours, trying to get up. The Glock was still clutched in his right hand. Gurt brought the heel of her left shoe down on his wrist. Howling with the pain of a potentially shattered ulna, he let go of the gun only a split second before her right foot caught him under the chin at the end of a kick that would have done credit to an NFL punter.

She dived for the floor as a shot, magnified by the confines of the aircraft's cabin, rang in her ears. She had to divert any gunfire from where Manfred was wailing in fright. Glock now in her possession, she thumbed off the safety and she rolled behind a seat as the one next to it disintegrated under a hailstorm of bullets.

On her stomach, she pushed herself back into the aisle and aimed at an indistinct form blurred by a cloud of cordite-stinking smoke. The Glock jumped in her two-handed grip, her ears by now deaf to the gunfire. Somewhere toward the back of the Lear, she made out a face, its eyes crossed as if trying to focus on the neat red hole between them before it pitched forward and disappeared.

Now silence pealed in her ears, loud as the gunfire itself. Cautiously, she peered around the edge of one of the sofas. Not five feet away, Haverly and the other man who had been in the condo were looking back at her. The Glock came up and both men raised their hands. They had had enough.

But she had not. Alternating the Glock's muzzle from one man's chest to the other, she quickly stepped over to where Manfred's cries had become moans. If there was so much as a scratch on him . . .

Haverly read her mind. "We weren't going to hurt him, honest."

Gurt savored the fear that was emanating from her former captors as she might enjoy the bouquet of a fine wine. She had to battle the impulse that sought retribution for the ordeal her child had suffered both here and in Baden-Baden.

"Your weapons, throw them here. Left hands only!"

With shaky hands, they did as they were told.

Only then did she allow herself to move her eyes to where Manfred was on the floor, scrunched up behind a seat in a tight ball that seemed to deny the existence of a skeletal structure. He grabbed for her desperately and climbed into the open arm, the one not holding the Glock.

Other than understandably terrified, he was fine.

A sound behind her caused her to spin. The pilot, copilot, she was never sure which, with the broken nose still sat on the floor, his hands futilely trying to staunch the flow of blood. Behind him, the other crew member was reaching to open the cockpit door. His hands flew up in surrender the moment she faced him.

"Er, ma'am, someone is outside. Shall I open up?"

She heard it for the first time, a beating on the aircraft's hull along with muffled shouts.

"*Ein augenblick*, a moment, please." She motioned to Haverly and his man. "Your pockets, empty them there." She indicated the low table between the sofas. "*Schnell*, quickly!"

She allowed herself a tight smile as she watched them rush to comply. She had not been conscious of the German she tended to speak when excited.

Unlike any professional on a similar mission, these men had papers, perhaps identifying papers, on them. Even a pair of passports in a language she could not read.

She stuffed them into a pocket before turning to the crew member. "Open the door."

Lang waited nervously as the door opened. A man in a

pilot's uniform was the first thing he saw, suddenly pushed aside as Manfred, a small missile, launched down the stairs and into Lang's arms.

He raised a tear-streaked face. "Vatti, I was so scared!"

VII.

Rectory
Church of the Immaculate Conception
48 Martin Luther King, Jr. Drive
Atlanta
That Evening

Exhausted, Manfred slept where he had gone to sleep on the floor of the small library, his head resting against Grumps's flank as the dog continued his nearly perpetual nap. Lang and Gurt shared a leather settee. Across from them, Francis occupied a leather wing chair. All three held glasses of scotch, varying only in degrees of dilution by ice cubes. The two men puffed on Montecristo #2's, the fat *pyramidos* Lang had shipped from Cuba via the French West Indies on a regular basis. The ashtray in front of Gurt displayed filters, tombstones of Marlboros. A stratus cloud of tobacco smoke hung against the ceiling.

Francis puckered his lips, ejected a shimmering blue smoke ring and watched it expand. "Must have been some kind of a scene at Charlie Brown this afternoon. Local TV news even got most of it right: Attempted kidnapping by some kind of foreign agents, maybe Islamic terrorists, ritzy airplane, woman foils plot. Never did quite explain the why of it, though."

Lang took a long sip from his glass followed by a lazy puff on the cigar. "FBI sees a motive in it."

Francis chuckled, a low warm sound. "Let me guess." He held up both hands, two fingers of each extended to make quotation marks. "Son of wealthy local philanthropist object of kidnap. Child's mother, father foil plot with quick action. One dead. Film at eleven. That about it?"

"As far as the fibbies are concerned, yeah." Lang got up and crossed the room to a small bar, helped himself and tinkled ice cubes into his glass. "They'll spin a few wheels trying to ID the real owner of that Lear jet—or what's left of it." He looked at Gurt, eyebrows arched. "Next time, try not to trash the interior of expensive aircraft."

She was reaching for the cigarette pack on a small table. She shook it, frowned and fished in her suitcase-size purse for another pack. "And you did good to the entire front end and nose gear?"

"Anyway," Lang continued, "I'm sure the plane is registered to some untraceable shell corporation. They'll never find out who those bozos really are."

Gurt looked up as she shook a cigarette out of the new pack. "But we know."

Both men stared at her.

"We do?" Lang finally managed.

She took the unlit cigarette from between her lips. She was mining that huge purse again, this time producing two passports. "I relieved our Herr Haverly and his friend of these."

Lang took them in his hand, studying the front of each. "Some kidnappers, carrying ID like that! Hardly professionals; might as well have had name tags. I don't think I've ever seen . . ."

Francis set down his drink and came to look over Lang's shoulder. "Those are *Vatican* passports."

"The pope is trying to kill us?" Gurt asked incredulously.

Francis took the documents from Lang. "Let me have these. It's a bit late to be calling Rome right now, but I can promise you I'll be burning up the line to the Vatican foreign office first thing in the morning." He put them down on the bar and turned to face Lang. "Perhaps there's something you're not telling me?"

Lang inspected the tip of his cigar. He had intentionally not told his friend about the James translation just as he had kept secret several past theological discoveries, particularly what he referred to as the Pegasus matter. Francis was a good friend and devout in his faith. Such matters would only cause him pain and doubt.

He was also a good enough friend to know when Lang wasn't being entirely candid. "Well?"

Lang took a healthy swig from his glass as though that would anesthetize his discomfort. "The Gospel of James, the Nag Hammadi book I mentioned . . ."

Francis ignored the growing length of his cigar ash, letting it finally fall onto the floor. "And?"

"It states that Christ reappeared to the apostles, including James, for the purpose of removing Peter as the leader of the early church. Peter got angry and killed James."

"Like the fresco we saw at the Vatican that day," Francis said.

Lang was thankful the priest was so calm about something that contravened everything he had been taught.

"So, why does that mean people would want to harm our child?" Gurt asked.

Francis shook his head slowly, wearied by the things some do in the name of faith. "Peter was the rock upon which Christ founded his church. To make him into not only a petty political squabbler but a murderer . . . well, it would certainly rewrite the days of early Christianity as we know it, cast doubt on the validity of other gospels. It would be like . . . like discovering George Washington was actually in the pay of the British. Peter, his view of what the church should be, formed the very basis of the church we have today. The church, the papacy, the sacraments, a great deal of the ritual, all of it. There are some in the church, some of the ultraconservatives, who would deny there is any truth whatsoever to your book. And some who would do anything to suppress it."

"Including killing someone?" Lang asked.

"We're not proud of it, but that's what the Inquisition was all about: crushing heresy by killing heretics. Anyone who thinks that mentality doesn't still exist among some ultrareactionaries is kidding themselves." Francis gave a sad little smile. "You already have your answer. Find those who feel that violently about it and you have your assassins."

"Makes sense," Lang mused aloud. "Leaving clues at murder scenes that related to the martyrdom of various saints. Would have to be religious zealots. Problem is, who?" He turned to Francis. "And you?"

Francis gave a deep sigh. "Faith is not knowledge; it is belief in what we cannot know. What I believe is that Our Lord walked this earth and I intend to follow him, no matter who did so first, Peter or James. On an intellectual level, I know that *all* gospels were written after the Crucifixion, the closest perhaps seventy years later. There are discrepancies as there would be in any history after the fact. One gospel has Jesus born in a barn, another in a house and a third and fourth don't mention the birth at all. Who is to say your Nag Hammadi book is correct and Matthew, Mark, Luke and John are wrong?"

"But the fresco . . . ?"

Francis shrugged. "The Vatican, like all of Rome, is full of fanciful art as we discussed about the Final Judgment in the Sistine Chapel. The imagination of some Renaissance artist, no matter how talented, is nothing more than that, imagination. Don't worry about my faith, my good friend; worry about who is trying to kill you."

VIII.

Atlanta Headquarters
Federal Bureau of Investigation
Richard Russell Federal Building
The Next Day

Lang and Gurt were at a table in a windowless conference room. Manfred sat quietly beside her, crayon in his fist as he obliterated the pictures in his coloring book in a maze of hues that were not greatly different from the contemporary art hanging in the building's lobby. She was unwilling to let him out of her sight and Lang had realized early the futility of trying to persuade her otherwise.

The incident at Charlie Brown yesterday involved an attempted kidnapping, clearly the turf of the federal government. The fact that an aircraft, an instrument of interstate, if not international, commerce was involved only strengthened their territorial claims. The local cops could do little but complain that a homicide, a state offense, had occurred. For the moment at least, the investigation would be conducted by the FBI, not the Atlanta police.

Before arrival in the US, the the Lear had filed an international flight plan originating from Ciampino, Rome's other airport, used by private and charter aircraft. It had made two intermediate fueling stops. The registration had led to a dead end, a company based in the Chanel Islands where corporate secrecy was a major export.

In short, the FBI, so far, knew less that Lang and Gurt.

The matter would be handled in a professional, not an Inspector Clouseau–type, manner.

Lang got up and walked over to the window, taking in Atlanta's railroad gulch, a scar of empty space that had once been the locale of two rail terminals. The stations and tracks were long gone, leaving a spaghetti bowl of overpasses above kudzu-lined parking lots. At the far end, the

Georgia Dome's canvas roof rose like a poisonous mushroom. If view were any criterion, the bureau did not rank high in the federal pecking order.

He turned as the door behind him opened and a chubby-faced young man entered with slender file under one arm.

He plopped his burden down on the table and extended a hand. "Special Agent Kurt Widner. I want to thank both of you for coming down here today."

He sat, opening his file. "Mr. Reilly, would you mind returning to the reception area?"

Lang would have been surprised if he had not been asked to retire. Basic interrogation procedure required each witness to be interviewed out of the hearing of another. In this case, the practice was reduced to form over function. He and Gurt had had plenty of time to decide what would and would not be said. Lang retraced his steps down a short corridor to the receptionist's area, a windowless room as bleak as the conference room. The picture of the president and the copy of the Constitution ubiquitous to federal offices were the only decorations. The room contained but two chairs separated by a small table of cheap laminate. Both chairs were occupied. The bureau was unusually popular this morning.

Lang looked around, uncertain of what to do.

"I can borrow a chair from the conference room," chirped the receptionist from behind her sliding plastic window.

Lang turned and saw a smiling black woman. "Thanks. If you'll unlock the door, I'll save you the trouble. I know the way."

There was a buzz as the dead bolt slid back and Lang reentered the hall he had just left. The receptionist was a new hire, he guessed. The few previous visits he had made here had been characterized by security measures far beyond what was necessary to protect whatever investigations were under way. Or Fort Knox. Locks on every door, every door locked, every visitor thoroughly vetted, scanned and escorted. The bureau either took itself very seriously or suffered mass paranoia. Or both.

One door was ajar. Not surprisingly, it bore the name of Special Agent Kurt Widner. He had not shut and locked his office, intending to go between here and the conference room as he checked facts on his computer while interviewing Gurt and Lang. A metal government-issue desk occupied most of the space, crowding a desk chair on one side and a small metal chair with a shiny vinyl seat on the other. There was hardly room for the squat iron safe in the far corner.

A small hinged frame contained picturers of an attractive woman and a child of undeterminable sex. Lang smiled. Ever since the Hoover days, the bureau had been big on just this sort of homey touch. So great had been the pressure on agents to enjoy familial bliss that Lang had heard of single or divorced agents who displayed pictures of strangers or other people's kids rather than risk the director's disfavor. Strange, considering Hoover himself had never married.

The photos shared the desktop with a computer and several files. Lang hefted the chair with the vinyl seat and was about to leave when his eye caught a label on one of the folders.

DEA CO-OP. And in smaller letters: LAMAR CO. GA.

Still holding the chair, Lang backed into the hall and looked both ways. Empty. He could get in big trouble, both with the fibbies and the state bar, for what he was about to do. The upside was that he was about to have some real fun.

He stepped back into the office, shut the door and began to skim the file, an outline of a joint investigation between the Drug Enforcement Agency in middle Georgia and the Atlanta FBI. Mere coincidence he had found this? No, not really. Bringing in agents both from Atlanta and a different branch of law enforcement whose faces would be unknown in Lamar County made sense. If there was luck involved, it was that Special Agent Widner had gotten careless. Lang would have liked to have taken notes, but there simply wasn't time. At some point, Agent Widner was going to come back here or the receptionist would come looking for him. He scanned the file a second time, making sure of the relevant details.

On the way back from the federal building, Gurt and Lang discussed their separate interviews. From the questions asked, it seemed clear the feds were clueless as to the identity of the would-be kidnappers. Lang gathered that, whoever they were, they were being less than cooperative when questioned. But they were in custody and would be indefinitely, hopefully long enough for Lang to discover who had sent them before they tried again.

In the meantime, Lang had to find the would-be assassins. Trying to kill him was real personal. Attempting to harm his new family was even more so.

But first, Lang would be busy with another matter.

IX.

United States District Court for the
  Middle District of Georgia
Macon, Georgia
A Week Later

The drive to Macon had seemed endless even though only eighty miles of interstate separated it from Atlanta, where Lang and Grumps had become indefinite guests at Francis's rectory. No one followed Lang on a few aimless excursions from the interstate. Before leaving, he had verified his still-unknown enemies were still in the custody of the

feds in Atlanta. Whoever they were, they apparently did
not have endless reinforcements.

Surprisingly, Gurt had offered little argument when a
European vacation–bound friend of Lang's had offered the
use of a cottage on the grounds of the High Hampton Inn
in the mountains near Cashiers, North Carolina. She
would scrupulously avoid the use of credit cards, ATMs or
anything else that might leave a record of her presence
there. Happily, other than homemade quilts, tacky handi-
crafts and overpriced junk that every roadside stand proclaimed to be "genuine mountain antiques," there was
nothing to buy. The accommodations were rustic at best,
the hotel's food wholesome if unappetizing. But the view
was magnificent, the climate temperate as compared to
Atlanta from June until September. Best of all, a number
of young mothers and their broods summered there while
their husbands labored during the week in Charlotte, Atlanta, Birmingham or a dozen other southeastern cities.
Manfred had more playmates than he ever had and Gurt
could watch for strangers who would stand out like a missing plank in a picket fence.

Francis was still trying his Vatican contacts to learn
more than the names of the men in the Lear jet but so far
without success. Lang got the impression the delay was
more attributable to red tape than stonewalling. Not even
the Holy Father was immune to bureaucracy and this one
had had two millennia to become entrenched, immovable
and unhelpful.

Lang eased the Porsche into a parking lot, thankful he
had mended enough to manage the car's manual transmis-
sion. His two-block stroll to the courthouse reminded him
he had also healed enough to resume his regularly scheduled workouts.

Sam "Dusty" Roads, the youthful United States attorney, was already in the courtroom, accompanied by an
older man whom Lang recognized as a senior US attorney

from the northern division. His name eluded memory's grasp. Dusty's greeting was decidedly less enthusiastic than his previous one.

"What the hell are you trying to do, Reilly?"

Lang put his slim attaché case down on counsel table and smiled. "And a good morning to you, too. What I'm trying to do is to have my client acquitted."

"What you're going to do is get yourself sanctioned," the older man growled. "Subpoenaing a federal agent, demanding sensitive FBI files . . . In case you didn't know, the bureau isn't involved in this case. The DEA is."

The smile never left Lang's face. His experience was that the greater the government bluster, the better chance he was on track. And a senior US attorney hadn't driven down here for the ride. "Thanks for enlightening me."

"You may think this is some kind of a joke, Reilly, but—"

He was interrupted by the door opening. All three men turned to see Larry Henderson timidly peering into the courtroom like a mouse trying to decide if it was safe to leave its hole.

Lang motioned. "C'mon in, Larry. Us lawyers were just exchanging pleasantries."

Freed of leg irons since he was out of jail on bond, Larry nonetheless traversed the room with uncertain steps and sat next to Lang. He wore a suit with a tie narrow enough to serve as a shoestring, something Lang guessed had belonged to his father. Before the two could exchange greetings, the marshal appeared to herald Judge Carver's ascension to the bench. The judge nodded a no-nonsense "good morning," sat and began to thumb through the case file while the court reporter wound paper into her machine.

After a full minute, the judge looked up. "We are here today at the defendant's special request for an early hearing on the defendant's motion to suppress evidence, specifically any marijuana allegedly taken from the premises of the defendant. Do I have that right?"

Al Silverstein, that was the man's name, the US attorney from Atlanta, Lang recalled as he stood. "Yes, Your Honor."

Silverstein was on his feet before Lang could sit. "Before we begin that, Your Honor, the government has a motion to quash a subpoena served on an FBI agent and a subpoena duces tecum calling for the production of certain sensitive documents from the bureau."

Was that the ghost of a smile Lang saw around the judge's lips? "I am well aware *all* documents from the bureau are sensitive, Mr. . . ."

"Forgive me, Your Honor, Silverstein."

"Yes, well, what's the connection between a Drug Enforcement Agency prosecution and the FBI, Mr. Reilly?"

Lang knew better than to give the government time to mount a defense by showing his cards before he had to. "The defendant believes that will become self-evident as this hearing progresses."

"But, Your Honor," Silverstein argued, "the very point of our opposition to letting Mr. Reilly proceed with this, this circus, is that both the witness he has subpoenaed and the records he seeks are both irrelevant and potentially harmful to ongoing investigations."

Judge Carver touched her lips with her pen, thinking. "This is a nonjury hearing, Mr. Silverstein. I determine what is or is not relevant. You may object at the appropriate places. If you like, I can order the transcript sealed."

A sealed transcript was not what Silverstein had in mind, but he knew better than to risk provoking the judge's impatience. He sat with a deflated, "Very well, Your Honor."

Round one to the defense.

The judge was looking at Lang. "Mr. Reilly, you have a statement?"

"No, Your Honor, but I would like to make one at the conclusion of this hearing."

"Very well. Proceed."

Lang placed a hand on Larry's shoulder. "We call Mr. Larry Henderson."

Larry went to the witness stand with nervous steps, shoulders slumped as he swore to tell the truth. He sat as if the chair contained thorns rather than a cushion.

After the preliminary questions as to his name and residence, Lang asked, "Do you recall any unusual incident the week before you were arrested?"

Larry nodded. "Uh huh."

"You'll have to give us a yes or no, Mr. Henderson," Lang said gently. "The court reporter can't get a nod or an *uh huh.*"

"Sorry. Yes, I did."

"And that was?"

"Fella came onto the property, said he was lookin' f' some kinda woodpecker."

"A bird-watcher?"

"I guess. Had binoculars and all."

"The binoculars would have allowed him a good look at your property, right?"

Lang paused a second and, as anticipated, Silverstein was on his feet. "Objection! Calls for a conclusion."

A point, if not a round, for the defense. The objection would serve only to emphasize those binoculars.

"Sustained. Mr. Reilly, try not to ask your client to speculate."

"Yes, Your Honor." Then, to Larry, "Ever seen him before?"

Larry shook his head.

Lang pointed to the court reporter.

Larry took in a breath. "Sorry. I ain't never spoke in court before. No, I never seen him before."

"Since?"

Larry looked at him quizzically, not understanding the game in which he was participating. "In the hall."

Lang's voice dripped incredulity. "In the hall? Here?"

"Right outside that door."

"Your Honor, we have Special Agent Kurt Widner under subpoena. Would you have the marshal ask him to step in here?"

She nodded to the marshal.

Silverstein stood, one last attempt. "Your Honor, I must renew my previous objection. As you noted earlier, this is a prosecution by the DEA, not the FBI . . ."

"And as I noted, Counselor, I will determine what is or is not relevant. Your continuing objection is noted."

Widner preceded the marshal into the room, somewhat less rosy cheeked and cheerful than when Lang last saw him.

"Thass him!" Larry was pointing. "Thass the same man."

"You certain?" Lang asked.

Larry nodded vigorously. "Absolutely."

"Let the record reflect the witness has identified Special Agent Widner of the Atlanta office of the Federal Bureau of Investigation as the man 'bird-watching' on the defendant's property two days before the defendant was arrested. Your witness, Mr. Silverstein."

The US attorney made a show of reviewing his notes before he said, "No questions at this time, Your Honor, but we reserve the right to cross-examine Mr. Henderson later."

"So noted. Another witness, Mr. Reilly?"

"The defense calls Special Agent Widner. As he is an employee of the government we ask we be allowed to cross-examine."

"Granted."

If Larry had been a nervous witness, Widner approached the witness stand with the reluctance of a man climbing steps to the gallows.

After the preliminary stating of his name and employment for the record, Lang got right down to business.

"You a bird-watcher, Agent Widner?"

The answer was sullen, almost hostile, just as Lang would have wanted it. "Sometimes."

"How long have you pursued that hobby? No, don't look at Mr. Silverstein. I want *your* answer."

Now a hangdog demeanor. The man knew what was coming. "Meybbe six months."

Lang turned to face Judge Carver. "Your Honor, I served a subpoena duces tecum on the government regarding a certain memo. I'd like it produced before we continue."

Silverstein rose slowly. "Again, Your Honor, we object as to relevance." Dusty Roads tugged at his sleeve and they exchanged whispers. "Plus as an interoffice communication, we contend it's privileged and not subject to production."

Agent Widner and Silverstein were not the only people who had a good idea where all this was headed. Judge Carver leaned forward, hand extended. "We need more, not less openness in government. The memo, Mr. Silverstein."

Silverstein made a show of digging in his litigation bag before asking, "May we have a brief recess, Your Honor? I'd like to confer with Mr. Reilly."

The judge gave a half glance, half glare at both lawyers. "For what purpose?"

This time it was Roads who responded. "We think we have a very attractive offer for Mr. Reilly's client."

The judge again looked from one lawyer to the other. "Fine. Mr. Reilly, I want to remind you this court is not bound by any agreement as to sentence upon entry of a plea of guilty. I'm sure the same is true in the northern district where you practice."

"Understood, Your Honor."

"Five minutes, then."

And she was gone.

It was almost surprising what a change the brief hearing had wrought in the dispositions of the government's lawyers. Both Silverstein and Roads were all smiles. Both extended their hands.

"Lang, we're prepared to reduce the charge from possession with intent to distribute to simple possession," Silverstein said. "Eighteen to twenty-four months, a reduction for participating in a rehab program, 10 percent off for good behavior and your man walks."

"You're kidding," Lang said. "Nice try, having your 'bird-watching' special agent stumble onto my client's property but it won't wash. The fact one agency makes a discovery and another prosecutes the crime won't work, fruit of the poisoned tree. A warrantless search is still illegal whether made by the FBI or the post office unless you can show probable cause, which you can't. If you think Judge Carver is going to swallow the bird-watching crap, you might try and sell her the state capitol building. Particularly in light of that memo suggesting, what was it? Oh, 'interagency cooperation.'"

A great deal of congeniality drained from Silverstein. "There's no way you could have known about that memo legally. How'd you find out?"

"A little bird I was watching on my own."

There was a chuckle, choked back to what sounded like a snort from Larry.

Silverstein began to flush red from the neck up. "You can't . . . If I find out you came by that memo in any way that's illegal . . ."

"By the time you find out how I learned about it, you'll be too busy denying it existed. Or too busy handling appeals when the news of the DEA's scheme is made public."

For a second, Lang thought the man was going to choke. "You can't . . ."

"Last time I looked, the First Amendment was still in effect. I'd guess the media would love the story."

Silverstein took a deep breath. "OK, OK! I'll make a deal: your man walks and you forget you ever saw the damned memo."

"How soon can you get the paperwork complete to release the bond and put my client on the street?"

"I'll order his release immediately."

No one had noticed Judge Carver's return to the bench. "You can pick him up at the jail as soon as he changes out of his prison jumpsuit." She smiled. "The government can't afford to give them away as souvenirs to former inmates."

Both government lawyers began repacking their briefcases.

"Not so fast, Mr. Silverstein, Mr. Roads. The court wants a word with both of you."

Her tone indicated it would not be a pleasant word, either.

Outside the jail an hour later, Larry was jabbering joyfully like a child on Christmas morning. "I can't believe I'm really outta there!" He grasped Lang's hand. "We few, we happy few! We band of brothers!"

Lang was unsure his victory equaled that of King Henry at Agincourt nor that he wanted Larry, the classics-reading marijuana farmer, as a brother.

His enthusiasm undiminished, Larry continued. "Don't unnerstan' how you done it, Lang, I really don't."

"Do you care?"

"Guess not. All I know, next time I need a lawyer, I know who to call."

Lang suppressed a groan.

"If it's any comfort to you, I'd bet Judge Carver is still reaming Silverstein and Roads a new asshole, giving them a lesson in constitutional law they won't soon forget." He pointed. "Car's this way. I'll drive you back to the farm." Lang extended his BlackBerry. "Want to call your wife?"

"I done it from the jail. She says to give you a big kiss for her."

Now there was an unattractive picture. "Maybe we'll let her do that herself."

They were perhaps halfway to the parking lot when Larry asked, "One thing: You had a motion to depress the stuff they took from my place, the marijuana. What was that all about?"

"If the government came by evidence illegally, that is, trespassing without a warrant, then that evidence can't be used. If they couldn't use the marijuana, then they can't prove you grew it or even that there was any."

Larry nodded, no doubt agreeing with the wisdom of such a rule. "But it was the FBI . . ."

"That's what we call 'fruit of the poisoned tree.' Once evidence is obtained illegally, it can't be made legal no matter who wants to use it."

"But if—"

The BlackBerry chimed. With a little luck, the interruption would end the lecture on evidentiary jurisprudence.

An e-mail from Francis:

Got the information you wanted. Or at least all I'm going to be getting.

X.

Piedmont Driving Club
1215 Piedmont Avenue
Atlanta
Three Hours Later

Until succumbing to an attack of political correctness in the 1990s, the Driving Club had been Atlanta's most exclusive men's social organization. Founded in the late nineteenth century, it had provided a place for the city's upper-crust gentlemen to drive their four-horse carriages outside the dusty and noisy town limits. Now midtown surrounded the property and views from its dining rooms were filled with high-rise condos and office towers. It was not unusual to see collared priests dining with members, although clerics were more numerous at the club's golf facility south of the airport. The food was mediocre on the chef's best days but small, private dining rooms, part of the original structure, were available on request.

It was the latter feature that had suggested the club to Lang. He was seated across an expanse of white linen, picking at a Cobb salad while Francis finished a short and disappointingly uninformative recital of what he had learned.

". . . And both the men whose passports Gurt took were American but had been at the Vatican for twelve and eight years."

Lang turned half of a hard-boiled egg over before spearing it with his fork. "We knew they were Vatican passports. They were, are, priests?"

Francis used his knife to probe his broiled snapper for bones. "Seem to be important ones. Word was they were being recalled to Rome as soon as the diplomatic office can get the feds to release them."

"Recalled? I thought they'd be in custody until a trial was held. I mean, kidnapping isn't exactly a misdemeanor."

"They claimed they had held Vatican passports and as such were on a diplomatic mission at the time. The Vatican's foreign office confirmed it."

Lang put his fork down, egg untouched. "Diplomatic immunity?"

Satisfied the fish was safe for consumption, Francis took a tentative bite. "Apparently."

"You telling me the pope condones kidnapping, not to mention attempted murder?"

"Not at all. I'm sure the foreign office has apprised him of what's happened. I'd guess he has his own discipline in mind."

"Like what? I haven't heard of any renegade priests being burned at the stake lately."

Francis shrugged before taking a larger forkful of fish. "I'm afraid the Holy Father doesn't always confide in me."

Lang put his fork down, salad forgotten. "Is it possible the pope *doesn't* know what's going on here? I mean, maybe these guys, these priests, have friends in the Vatican foreign office, pals who could act in the pope's name without him ever knowing about it."

The prospect troubled Francis enough that he stopped chewing long enough to think that over. "Possible, I suppose."

"Possible but not likely, you mean."

The priest shook his head and swallowed. "The Vatican, like any country, could have bad people in its bureaucracy."

This, coming from Francis, was a big admission. "Careful, there, padre. I wouldn't want to see you cast out as a heretic."

Lang returned his attention to his salad, surprised to see the half egg still on his fork. "OK, what else did you find out?"

"Not much." Francis used the edge of his fork to sever another piece of snapper. "Both work with the Knights of Malta."

The name had a familiar ring. Lang searched his memory during two bites of salad including the half egg. "Isn't that an honorary society for the really big hitters, men who donate really *big* bucks to the church? They dress up in funny costumes with big hats with feathers?"

Francis smiled. "I take it your information comes from *Godfather III?*"

"Yeah, that's it. The movie starts by showing this guy, Michael Corleone, being initiated into this high order of the church and keeps flashing over to where across town his hit men are simultaneously taking out members of a rival gang."

"Hardly an evenhanded depiction of a very old order of the church."

"It's Hollywood. They don't have to be evenhanded, just sell tickets. But what would an honorary association . . ."

Francis held up the hand that didn't have the fork in it. "Whoa there! The Knights of Malta is not just an honorary association."

"I suppose you're going to tell me about it, *homo multerum litterum.*"

"Only if you're interested. But remember, *Davus sum, non Oedipus.*"

"I'm not asking you to solve the riddle of the Sphinx like Oedipus; just tell me about the Knights of Malta."

Francis was staring at someplace above Lang's head, his forehead wrinkled in thought. "Best I can recall, they were founded in the late eleventh century as a monastic order, Order of St. John, to minister to the sick of Jerusalem, then held by the crusaders. Their order was answerable only to the pope himself. The first religious order of chivalry. Only the sons of titled nobility need apply. As the Holy Land came under attack from the Saracens, the order morphed into a military organization. When the Muslims ejected them from the Holy Land, they occupied the island of Rhodes from the early fourteenth century until the sixteenth when the Turks successfully besieged it. The order wound up on Malta, which they made into an island fortress. That's how they came to be called Knights of Malta. Their real name is still Order of St. John."

Lang paused in his unsuccessful effort to cut a tomato wedge with his fork. A chime went off in his head as he recalled the stub of the boarding pass. "Rhodes? Do they still have any connection to the island?"

Francis shrugged, intent on renewing his assault on the snapper. "Quite possibly. When the Italian Fascists took the island from the Ottomans in the first part of the last century, they encouraged European powers to establish a presence there. With the order's political connections, I wouldn't be surprised if they were included."

Lang picked up his knife. "Very historically informative but what about today's version? I mean, you haven't told me why the order or whatever is anything but ceremonial, right?"

Francis shook his head. "Not necessarily. There are three types of Knights of Malta. First is the one you mentioned, the ones who are knighted because of some outstanding deed . . ."

"Like a major contribution to the church."

"That frequently is the case, yes. The other two types are described as 'chaplains' and 'hospitaliers.' The chaplains are priests and the hospitaliers still tend to the sick and are likely but not necessarily priests, too. The order is governed by the sovereign council, which meets every five years at the Rome priory to elect the grand master. In fact, I believe they'll be convening next week."

"You said something about political connections."

"Interestingly enough, some eighty nations, excluding the US and Great Britain, accord the knights diplomatic status. They even have observer status at the UN."

Lang was chewing slowly, thinking about medieval religious military orders. He had encountered the deadly Pegasus organization and was not eager to face another. But a religious group made sense: the murders that paralleled the martyrdom of saints, an effort to suppress a heretical gospel, the fact they clearly had access to the Vatican's guest quarters.

"That still doesn't explain why they are willing to kill to keep the James Gospel a secret."

Francis held up a cautionary finger. "*If* they are the guilty party. Just because two who might be of their number tried to kidnap Gurt and Manfred doesn't mean the entire order is behind it. I'm not sure, but they number somewhere in excess of fifteen thousand scattered worldwide. For that matter, the two culprits who got arrested might well belong to any number of other organizations."

"You're right. But staging three murders to reflect martyrdom of three saints, trying to suppress the Book of James. *Vere scire est causas scire.*"

"To know truly is to know causes; let's get to the bottom of this. First you're going to have to find out if the Knights of Malta are the ones behind your problems. As you can imagine, they are an *extremely* conservative bunch. Their priests, or chaplains, the ones who run the day-to-day operations, probably are somewhere to the right of the most conservative Jesuits. They wouldn't take kindly to having St. Peter, the first pope, depicted as a malcontent and murderer. Such a major change in the church wouldn't sit well at all. Whether they would go as far as murder and kidnapping, who knows?"

"Well, then," Lang said, "all I have to do is find out."

And he had a pretty good idea of how he was going to do just that.

XI.

High Hampton Inn
Cashiers, North Carolina
Two Days Later

Manfred shrieked in glee as the trout twisted on the hook like molten silver. The contagion of the child's joy had Lang laughing. Here with his son and Gurt, the uglier realities of the world had no place.

Manfred held up his wriggling trophy. "Can we keep him?"

Lang managed a serious face. "Are you going to eat him?"

The child's joy evaporated at the memory of bass from the pond in Lamar County. A lot of bass. "Ugh!"

"Then we better put him back."

"But I want to keep him!"

Lang knelt, bringing his face even with his son's. "Think how sad we would be if you were snatched up like that fish, snatched up and never came back. That little trout has a mommy and daddy, too."

The sociological implications of trout fishing had never occurred to Manfred. He shook his head slowly. "Then we better let him go."

Lang turned to where Gurt was smoking a Marlboro under an oak tree and rubbing Grumps's muzzle, to the dog's obvious delight. Lang winked.

"You could have explained he is too small to keep." She nodded toward a discreet sign the hotel had posted specifying anything under ten inches had to be thrown back. "Or told him it is forbidden to keep such a fish."

Verboten, forbidden, was something the youngest German understood.

Lang would prefer to shield his son against regulations and the arbitrary rules of the law as long as possible. There was already enough unpleasantness in the child's world, what with a kidnapping attempt still fresh in his young mind.

"I like it better my way."

Manfred had watched the exchange. "Does it hurt the fish when we catch him?"

Lang could have explained the difference between warm- and cold-blooded animals or related some arcane argument of the animal rights nuts but decided on another tack. He was ready to give the piscine population a rest for a while. "Would a sharp hook in your mouth hurt?"

Manfred looked at the trout still flopping on the line and then at his father. "Please let him go." He handed the light rod to Lang. "I don't think I want to fish anymore."

Gurt ground out her cigarette. "It is nap time anyway."

Manfred started his usual protest but stopped in mid-sentence with a look from his mother.

Manfred stopped on the way back to the cottage, hand behind his back. "Daddy?"

Lang leaned down. "Yes?"

With a puff, the little boy sent a cloud of dandelion

seeds into his father's face and ran, laughing. In a couple of steps, Lang had him, tickling. Then Lang grabbed a pod of dandelion seeds himself, dusting his son's face with them. Then Manfred found yet another. Grumps knew only that someone was having fun without him. He barked furiously.

"It would perhaps be good for all of you children to take a nap," Gurt observed dryly.

They reached the cottage, Lang holding hands with both Gurt and his son. He could not remember the last time he had been so happy.

He had arrived yesterday. Putting the Porsche through its paces on both interstate and mountain roads had shaken anyone attempting to follow. He had just pulled the car up in front of the cottage when the door exploded open and Manfred ran out, arms outstretched to embrace ... Grumps.

Trying not to show his annoyance at playing second fiddle to the dog, Lang said to Gurt, who had arrived in a somewhat more leisurely fashion than her son, "I'm delighted Manfred and Grumps get along so."

Gurt had smiled that slow, sexy smile and given him a kiss so long Manfred and Grumps were vying for attention. "And did Grumps enjoy the mountain roads as much as did you?"

The truth was the Porsche was designed for serpentine highways but the dog was not. Twice Grumps had whined so loudly at Lang's driving that Lang had had to stop to let the distressed animal get out and throw up.

Lang changed the subject. "How long till he takes a nap? We have some catching up to do."

She had rolled her eyes. "You are badly timed. He just got up. I fear we must wait a while longer."

Lang had sighed his disappointment. "I brought a few toys."

Gurt shook her head in mock disapproval. "More

important you brought him Grumps. You cannot bring gifts every time you come. It will make him rotten."

"Spoiled."

"That, too."

So his arrival had gone, topped with lovemaking so vigorous that night that, upon reflection, Lang wondered they had not awakened the boy. Today had begun with a large breakfast, a walk along shaded mountain paths and a picnic lunch, which had included a few treats for the dog. The fishing idea had been inspired when Manfred noted the supplies available to hotel and cottage guests.

They entered a good imitation of a genuine log cabin, complete with hooked rugs on rough planked floors, beamed ceilings and bent wood furniture, uniformly uncomfortable.

Gurt pointed. "Manfred, go get undressed for your nap."

Obediently, he trudged into a room off the living room, reappearing with a book in his hand which he held out to Lang. "Will you read to me?"

Paternal instinct versus lust for Gurt.

Oh, well, too few kids had interest in books these days, their parents substituting TV for literature.

Lang looked at the volume in his hand. Brothers Grimm. Aptly named. Evil trolls, child-eating witches. Stuff that would be PG-13 if made into movies. No wonder the German people had a dark side.

"Don't suppose you have a copy of Hans Christian Andersen?" he called toward the master bedroom.

"Sissy!" Gurt was standing in the doorway of the bedroom, a bathrobe doing little to conceal the fact it was all she had on.

What was the Grimm brothers' shortest story?

CHAPTER SEVEN

I.

Leonardo da Vinci International Airport
Flumicino
0650 Local Time
Two Days Later

Lang was not surprised to be picked up by a tail the minute he cleared customs. He certainly had made it as easy as possible: an international flight on an airline rather than the Gulfstream booked in advance under his own name. He couldn't bring himself to check his bag and risk spending his time waiting while the airline conducted a fruitless search for luggage that, by that time, could well be in Singapore.

He wanted company.

He was almost certain he had identified his minder, a middle-aged man who had stood behind Lang in the line at the airport's rail terminal to buy a ticket into Rome. The last time Lang had seen an international traveler in coat and tie was when John Wayne nursed his crippled Constellation aircraft across part of the Pacific in *The High and the Mighty* on the late, late movie on TV.

Whatever the movie, the guy behind Lang wore a suit, albeit a cheap one, making himself as conspicuous as if he had worn a tutu. Certainly another amateur. He ordered his rail ticket in Italian, smiled at Lang and went over to the coffee bar to wait. Lang almost lost sight of him in the surge of embarking passengers swimming upstream against those getting off the train. Anywhere else, those boarding would have waited for the cars to empty. Well, maybe a New York subway . . . Lang's tail managed to wedge himself into the same car where he smiled again and stared out of the window.

Gurt had been less than happy with Lang's idea but unable to come up with a better one. After all, Lang had explained, with whom would Manfred be safer? After the shoot-out at Lang's country place, the attempt in Baden-Baden and the most recent kidnap attempt, he could hardly be entrusted to a hired nanny, and no matter how willing the Hendersons, their farm was no longer secure. Any way he looked at it, Lang felt the mountains of North Carolina provided a safe haven by the fact he had no connection with the area whatsoever. If trouble did arrive, he would be hard-pressed to think of a more capable guardian.

Thirty minutes later, he stepped down from the railcar into the bustling mob that was Roma Termini.

Outside, he ignored the cabstand. Only tourists waited in orderly if futile fashion while the experienced traveler walked a block or so farther to catch cabs as they arrived at the station. Lang was aware of the man from the train at his elbow. He stood patiently until the white taxi stopped to unload its passenger and what must have been her entire wardrobe. The cabby yelled for a porter and a dolly was soon loaded with an assortment of mismatched luggage from the largest on bottom to the small overnight case crowned by a . . . what? A rat with a rhinestone collar around its neck? Lang wasn't sure until the creature began to bark crossly. Its mistress's alternating coos and pleas failed to silence the ill-natured canine. Lang pitied the traveler who shared a car with that animal. He could only imagine the haggle involving the porter's tip.

As the porter staggered away under his load, the cabdriver looked expectantly at Lang, who stepped back, indicating the man beside him should have the taxi.

The Italians are a civilized, graceful people.

Except when it comes to the last seat on a bus, train, cab or in a trattoria.

Lang's shadow gaped, uncomprehending. He had two immediate choices: expose his intent to follow the American or accept the offer and lose his mark.

He chose the latter.

Perhaps so he might regale his grandchildren with the story of how someone had voluntarily relinquished a taxi to him.

More likely because he feared a confrontation.

Lang leaned into the next cab, giving his destination and asking the fare. Roman cabdrivers are notorious for bilking strangers to their city. A ride that should consist of a few blocks easily becomes an hour's tour.

The driver held up both hands, ten euro.

Lang shook his head, knowing the distance he would travel. He held up one hand, fingers spread. "Five."

Ultimately reaching an agreement, Lang climbed in. The ride in Roman traffic was the usual blaring horns and ignored traffic signals. It would be impossible to spot a tail in the chaos. As always, Lang was a little surprised to arrive intact.

The cab jolted to a stop at the limit of vehicular traffic at the edge of the crowded Piazza della Rotonda. Lang paid the driver, adding a small tip, retrieved his bag from the trunk and set out across the square. For what might have been the hundredth time, he stopped in front of the Pantheon, Rome's ultimate example of simplicity and symmetry.

Built under the direction of the second-century emperor Hadrian, it had served as a temple to all gods and now as a church and final resting place of Raphael, Marconi and several kings of modern Italy. Its dome of equal height and width had been studied by Michelangelo as a potential model for the new Vatican (the commission for the dome's construction ultimately went to someone else). Unlike other temples, its only natural illumination came from the oculus, the hole at the top of the dome.

With some difficulty, Lang turned his back on the building and continued across the cobblestoned pavement to a glass door bearing a drawing of a smiling sun and gilt letters announcing the Sole al Pantheon. A fifteenth-century palazzo, it was one of the city's oldest hotels. It had been occupied when Columbus first sailed and into its second century long before the rebuilding of the Vatican.

Happily, the plumbing had been updated.

In more contemporary times, it had housed the writers Jean-Paul Sartre and Simone de Beauvoir.

More important for Lang's purposes, it was centrally located, discreet and had a single entrance/exit, one easily monitored from his room's window.

He entered the tiny lobby and submitted his passport to the young man behind the desk. "I'm expecting a package. It should have arrived last night."

Lang faced a small fountain behind a pane of glass at the far end of the room while the clerk glanced around, stooped and retrieved a parcel from beneath the desk before finishing entering Lang's passport into a computer. Declining the use of the hotel's claustrophobic elevator, Lang climbed two flights of winding stairs and walked down a short tiled hall that changed levels every few feet. He unlocked a door and stepped into semidarkness. Crossing the tiled floor, he opened a shuttered window. Sounds of the piazza below as well as light flooded the room.

He had an unobstructed view of the Pantheon and its fountain and obelisk to his left, the same view a resident of the original palazzo might have had.

Except for the McDonald's almost directly below him, an anachronism that had delighted Dawn when they had stayed here a lifetime ago. The whole city had delighted her. From this window, in this room, they had made plans for other trips, plans both would shortly realize would never be fulfilled.

Had he chosen to return here because of a memory, deceiving himself that location and layout were the reasons? No matter; he was here. He sighed deeply as he unwrapped the package, marked MACHINE PARTS. He opened a sturdy cardboard box and removed pieces of the Browning HP 35 he had purchased in Monk's pawnshop and two loaded clips. The risk in having it delivered via FedEx had been minimized by its disassembly. No one part would be recognizable to random X-ray. Besides, security for freight carriers was considerably more lax than at passenger terminals.

He spent the next few minutes reassembling the weapon and then shoved a magazine into place with a decisive click. Removing the holster from his suitcase, he placed the pistol into position in the small of his back, put on a light jacket and went out.

He found a cab where he had left the one in which he had arrived, negotiated a fare and directed the driver to the Via Veneto entrance to the Villa Borghese, Rome's largest park and site of one of its most impressive palaces. Upon arrival, he waited for the taxi to depart before setting off. He wanted whoever had been trying to kill him to know he was in town but making no effort to foil observation might well seem suspicious.

A few blocks from the park he dodged his way across the busy Corso D'Italia, cut down a side street and entered an office of Hertz. Although he still experienced nightmares from the last time he drove in Rome, an automobile was essential to his plan. He had reserved not just any car but a bright red Alfa Romeo two-seat sport model, one that would draw attention.

It would also draw the car thieves for which Italy was famous.

Either way, if his plan worked, Mr. Hertz was never going to see this baby again.

Before getting in the car, he stopped at one of the stands that seemed to have been randomly scattered throughout Rome, selling maps, photographs and prints of the city's attractions. It took him only a minute to find what he wanted.

He returned to the car rental, where a young man was standing over the sports car with the hood raised.

Lang had had enough experience with Italian cars to expect the worst. "Problem?"

"*Si, signore.* She will not start. Perhaps *domani?*"

"Tomorrow won't do."

Lang took a look at the engine compartment, an incomprehensible spaghetti of various colored wires, ducts that seemed to go nowhere and somewhere beneath, an engine block.

The man from the rental agency slid into the driver seat and cranked the car. The starter ground away, the engine turned over once, twice and died. Perhaps that was why the US Department of Transportation no longer allowed importation of Alfas: terminal frustration. That was certainly the reason Lang slammed the hood shut.

The engine purred to life.

Lang was thankful his plan did not call for reliability.

Gritting his teeth and holding the Alfa's steering wheel in a death grip, Lang drove back to the Piazza della Rotonda. He found a narrow space between a Fiat and a subcompact Lancia in front of a conspicuous NO PARKING sign and only a few yards from the open-air seating of one of the piazza's numerous trattorias, where he could keep an eye on the Alfa. The tables were beginning to fill with those seeking to quench the morning's thirst, people-watch or have an early lunch. He had ordered a La Rossa and began to study the reproduced engraving of the Piazza dei Cavalieri he had bought in the stand near the Hertz office. The beer had just arrived when a man sat beside him. There was no mistaking the rancid odor of stale tobacco.

"Hello, Jacob," Lang said.

II.

Piazza della Rotonda

Jacob signaled a waiter with the hand not holding his pipe. The man ignored him. "Bloody guineas! Man could die of thirst before they'd pay attention."

Lang ignored the condemnation of the Italian people, saying mildly, "Looks like there are plenty of other customers. I take it you acquired what you need?"

Jacob was sucking a match's flame into the bowl of the briar. "Yes, yes, of course. The question is where and when."

The waiter finally approached, regretted the menu did not include British ale and took Jacob's reluctant order for whatever Lang was having. Both men waited until the server was out of earshot.

"I'm not sure, but we can get started right now."

Jacob took a puff on his pipe and exhaled, sending acrid blue smoke drifting toward Lang on the day's fitful breeze. "Tell me exactly what you have in mind. You were less than specific on the phone."

When Lang finished, Jacob's beer had arrived. He took the pipe out of his mouth long enough to take a long sip. "Ahh. That settles the dust of travel! Your plan's a bit edgy. I mean, assuming this Knights of Malta lot are the villains, how do we . . . ?"

"Their sovereign council meets every five years. The meeting starts tonight. Drink up and we'll have a look."

"You're just going to bait the lion in his den, are you? Not the method I'd fancy. I'd imagine the blokes'll spot us."

"I hope so."

Jacob wriggled his way into the passenger seat. "You should have gotten a car we rode in, not one we wear."

Lang pulled the hood latch and opened the engine compartment. "You're only young once."

Jacob watched with unspoken curiosity as Lang slammed the hood closed. "That was true some time ago."

Lang got into the driver seat. The car cranked immediately.

III.

Aventine Hill
Via S. Sabina
Fifteen Minutes Later

The street was largely residential. Tops of cypress trees peeked timidly over a high wall, giving evidence of the private piazza within. What little traffic there was consisted of large cars moving sedately, many chauffeured and the occupants shielded by tinted glass. It was as if the sounds of the city were too heavy to float up the steep slope.

Lang pulled the Alfa to the curb and cut the engine, opposite massive wooden doors about fifteen feet high. Their most prominent feature was a huge brass keyhole through which a queue of Japanese tourists were alternately looking and consulting guidebooks.

They parted long enough for the gates to slowly swing open to admit a Mercedes limo. Even through its darkened glass, Lang caught a glimpse of a man in a plumed hat and black robe trimmed in scarlet. The momentary view of the piazza itself was of multiple buildings, two of which looked like churches. Lang strained to see where the Mercedes went, but the doors closed before he could.

"Doesn't look like Dracula's castle to me," Jacob observed. "In fact, the chap in the car looked like he was on his way to perform in a Gilbert and Sullivan operetta."

"More likely to a meeting of the sovereign council."

"So you think the grand pooh-bah himself will be there."

"Grand master, yeah. He presides over the council until they elect a new one."

Jacob was fumbling in his pocket for his pipe and tobacco pouch. "Jolly good show if you can be sure these are the sods that have caused you bother. Bag 'em on the spot." He reached up to touch the convertible's top. "May as well put the lid down."

"Good idea. See if you can give me a hand getting the top down on this hot rod, will you?"

In the course of an hour, Lang watched seven trucks pass through that gate, each bearing the names of foodstuffs. From the designs or pictures on the sides, he guessed at seafood, a butcher, two vegetable suppliers, two pasta makers and a baker. That wasn't counting the vintner.

"Looks like someone is having a party, all right," Jacob commented, "bringing the goodies in by the lorry load."

Lang got out of the car as a van, this one an electrician, pulled up to the gate. "Think I'll have a little look-see."

He waited until the vehicle had been admitted and the gates nearly closed before hurrying across the empty street to put his face against the keyhole. To his left was an ochre-colored building in neoclassic style. From the engraving he had bought at the stand near the Hertz office, he guessed he was looking at the priory church, Santa Maria del Priorato. Across the piazza, he could turn his head to see a somewhat more modest building of gray stone. From the number of windows, he gathered it housed offices or living quarters or both rather than the second church he had thought. After watching a crew carrying folding tables in, he guessed he was looking at the dining area. Several men in chefs' white jackets came out to inspect one of the grocery trucks. Whatever the structure, it was going to be the site of what looked like a major banquet.

Lang returned to the Alfa.

"If you're wanting to be seen, you have been," Jacob said cheerfully. "Chap in a dark suit watched you from down the street, was talking on a cell phone."

Lang turned the key in the ignition. "Good enough. Now let's see what we can flush out."

IV.

Aventine Hill
2100 Local Time

Lang stopped down the hill from the Knights of Malta priory. He let Jacob out into the dusky shadows between streetlights with a clear view of the gates. Parking in the same spot he had that afternoon, Lang scanned the blank walls with binoculars, well aware the lenses would reflect such little light as was available. Once, he got out of the cramped sports car to walk around it, a man stretching his legs during a tedious wait.

Half an hour later, he repeated the process, this time squatting beside the car at the end of his stroll. He slammed the door closed as loudly as possible.

If there was revelry going on inside, the walls muffled it. The only sound Lang could hear was a faint hum of city traffic below punctuated with a honk of distant horns. The cypress trees sighed contentedly with the fresh evening breeze as though thankful to be relieved of the heat of the day.

One or two limousines entered the priory, no doubt carrying latecomers. Nothing else entered or left.

Lang was about to decide he needed another tactic when he heard a sound, something that did not belong among the whispers of the trees or the faraway murmur of distant automobiles. He tensed, his eyes trying to probe the darkness. Shadows of gently moving cypress branches haunted the street. Somewhere down the hill a motor scooter coughed to life.

Then he heard it again, a scuffling, scraping sound, the sound of shoe leather on pavement.

They were on the Alfa almost before Lang saw them, four men, each carrying something.

He hardly had time to guess what before the night was shredded with gunfire. Four sets of muzzle flashes burned into Lang's retinas as his ears rang with what must have been hundreds of rounds from automatic weapons.

Like a living creature, the Alfa shuddered under the impact of the fusillade, bullets shattering glass and piercing metal. The little car seemed to utter a death shudder as it sank on bare rims from which the tires had been shredded.

The storm of gunfire passed as quickly as it had begun. Quiet pressed on Lang's eardrums, relieved only by the hissing of a punctured radiator. The pulsating wail of a siren was growing stronger. There would be no time for the would-be killers to verify their work.

From the shadows in which he had hidden the second time he had gotten out of the car, he watched as the gates across the street swung slowly open to allow the silhouettes of four men entry.

Up and down the street, lights were coming on. The curious and foolhardy were wandering outside. Questions were shouted into the dark.

"I'd say you've gotten your proof."

Lang flinched. He hadn't heard Jacob come up from his post downhill. "I'd say. Now we go to the second part of the plan."

Jacob placed a hand on Lang's shoulder, gently moving him away from the hole-riddled Alfa. "We'd best get along before the coppers show up."

V.

Thirty Minutes Later

Deputy Chief Police Inspector Hanaratti put a hand to his eyes to shade them from the glare of the lights arranged around the ruins of what had been an Alfa Romeo Spyder, the sort of car the inspector would have lusted after twenty years, three children and an ex-wife ago. It was so much scrap metal now. Not a square centimeter of the once sleek coachwork that didn't have a bullet hole in it. Fortunate for the driver he had escaped; he would not have survived the hailstorm of lead.

Hanaratti scowled. This looked very much like a botched Mafia job. Personally, he couldn't care less how many mafiosi bodies littered the streets. Good riddance to bad garbage. The problem was, one shooting usually begat another and another. The criminals could go to mattress as they called it, but the unaware civilian too often got caught in the cross fire.

And a strange location, too. One of the city's more up-scale neighborhoods and right across the street from the Piazza dei Cavalieri di Malta. Could the shooting be related to the fact the order was having some sort of meeting? Like any good policeman, the inspector was suspicious of coincidences.

But it would be absurd to see a connection between some church order and organized crime, particularly the Mafia, which the church had denounced for centuries. He dismissed the idea but it stubbornly refused to vanish.

There was something else tiptoeing around the perimeter of his mind, like a man wary of stepping onto a floor of rotted wood. What . . . ?

"No one inside heard the shots, Inspector."

Hanaratti had not noticed that Manicci was standing

beside him. "It seems those old walls deafen a lot of sound," the junior inspector said.

It would take walls a lot thicker to prevent the sound of so much gunfire, Hanaratti thought sourly. The precinct had gotten telephone calls from as far as nearly a kilometer away. The priestly members of the order should set a better example than trying to evade cooperating with an investigation, no matter how important their meeting.

The priests.

The thought stirred something, an idea a little less reticent to step forward.

"From the license plate, we have learned the car was rented," Manicci continued.

We? Hanaratti thought. The inspector was a master of claiming credit due others, equally adept at passing along blame like a soup bowl too hot to hold. The perfect bureaucrat but not someone Hanaratti would have chosen for this particularly brazen crime. But he didn't get to choose with whom he worked. Manicci was married to the daughter of the chief inspector's wife's first cousin.

In Italy, nepotism was a matter of family pride.

"We have already located the Hertz office and the manager will meet one of my men there to ascertain the name of the person renting it."

Opportunity knocked.

"One of your men? It is too important to entrust to an underling. Go yourself."

Hanaratti tried not to smile as he savored the disappointment on Manicci's face at being banished from the crime scene where he might seize the accolades for someone's discovery of an important bit of evidence. It was only as he was watching Manicci reluctantly climb into the blue and white Fiat that the idea he had been toying with solidified.

Priests.

A religious order.

It had been only a few weeks since that Greek Orthodox priest had been fished out of the Tiber after Hanaratti had investigated some sort of gun battle at his apartment near the Vatican.

Connection?

Tenuous at best, but priests were not the type one would ordinarily connect with violent acts, certainly not as perpetrators and usually not as victims.

Coincidences.

"Inspector?"

One of the uniforms was at his elbow.

"We have just received a report that the car, the Alfa there, was stolen from near the Pantheon."

Hanaratti felt his gut clinch as he saw the most obvious clue in this shooting begin to fade. "Stolen?"

"Yes, sir. It was rented to an American who is staying at a hotel near there."

"When?"

The officer looked confused. "'When'?"

The deputy chief inspector swallowed the urge to scream at the man. "When was it stolen?"

The policeman shrugged. "The American doesn't know. He went into a restaurant and when he came out, the car was gone."

Perfect.

At least Hanaratti would have the pleasure of assigning Manicci to a mundane car theft. After all, it was connected to a shooting, and interviewing the American would keep the junior inspector out of the main investigation for at least half of tomorrow.

Even misfortune had its bright side.

VI.

Piazza dei Cavalieri di Malta
Aventine Hill
The Next Morning

It had taken most of the morning for Lang and Jacob to find a truck from the electrician they had seen entering the piazza yesterday. A few euro liberally spread among the two-man crew and Lang and Jacob were dressed in the same coveralls as the two legitimate workers. A little more money and the van was in front of the wooden gates, honking for admission.

The one electrician who spoke English was explaining in Italian that they were here to check on yesterday's job and, no, there would be no additional costs involved for the service. Once inside, Lang and Jacob, toolboxes in hand, split up to explore the multiwindowed gray stone building.

Their hopes the uniforms would give them the invisibility of anonymity proved to be correct. Cooks, serving personnel as well as a few workmen filled the hallways with good-natured confusion. The five-year meeting of the council had the air of a country fair. No one gave the two electricians a second look.

The larger offices were deserted, leaving only what Lang guessed was salaried administrative staff. Members and officials would be attending the meeting of the grand council in the church next door.

Jacob peered around the corner of the largest office either he or Lang had found. "Boss's digs, I'd bet."

Standing in the hall, Lang nervously looked both ways. "So?"

"So, we take a look."

Jacob was inside while Lang stood sentry in the hall.

Jacob picked up the phone on the desk, pushing all four

buttons on its base one by one. Nodding as though confirming an undivulged theory, he followed the line to the
wall plug, where he inserted an instrument resembling a
thermometer.

"Got it."

"Got what?" Lang asked.

"The private line."

"But why . . . ?"

"Later, lad. Let's go. Right after . . ."

Jacob produced a package about the size of a bar of soap
and stuck it to the bottom of the desktop with a wad of
putty. "We're done."

Outside, Lang learned his friend's reconnaissance revealed the upper floors were residential. From the clothing
Jacob had noted in the closets, almost all rooms were occupied by priests, the hospitaliers and chaplains of the
Rome priory, no doubt.

The two collected the real electricians and left.

On the way back to the hotel, Jacob produced what
looked like some sort of schedule or program printed in
Italian, English, German and some language Lang did not
recognize. "Tonight is the time," he said. "The visiting
members of the council have a special dinner at the Vatican."

Lang looked at him. "So?"

"So, the professionals, the full-time people, should still
be at the priory. Reduce the chance of collateral damage."

A euphemism for civilian casualties.

Lang thought of the terror on Manfred's face as bullets
tore through the thin wooden walls of a farmhouse in Georgia, of his son's frightened face in Atlanta.

"Vatti, I was so scared!"

For just an instant, Lang couldn't have cared less about
collateral damage.

VII.

Piazza della Rotonda
Sole al Pantheon
Fifteen Minutes Later

Lang and Jacob entered their hotel and stopped just inside the doorway. The man sitting in one of the two ornately carved, silver-painted chairs in the microscopic lobby reeked of police.

The man rose, exhibiting a police badge. "Which one of you is Mr. Langford Reilly?" he asked in English.

Lang studied the badge before answering. "I am."

The policeman favored him with a humorless smile. "I am Inspector Antonio Manicci and am here to inquire about the car you reported stolen."

He didn't offer a hand.

An inspector chasing down stolen cars? In Italy where few European insurance companies would write car theft coverage because the crime was endemic to the country? The fact the vehicle had been recovered looking like it had been used by Bonnie and Clyde was the likely explanation.

Lang became uncomfortably aware both of the weight of the Browning in the small of his back and the severe penalties meted out for possession of firearms in Italy.

The inspector looked around, searching for a place to talk. The two carved chairs were it.

The desk clerk said something in Italian and Manicci gave that same dead smile. "*Grazie.* He tells me we may use the bar."

Like most rooms here, the bar was not level with the lobby but two or three steps down to the left. A single table with four chairs sat in front of a wooden bar whose shelves were largely bare. The dim light created atmosphere, but anyone looking for a nightcap other than grappa or brandy would be deeply disappointed.

Seated, Manicci put a small tape recorder on the table. "Where was the car when stolen?"

Lang pointed as though the walls were not there. "Right along this edge of the piazza."

The Italian frowned. "Parking is forbidden there."

"No doubt the thief was merely enforcing the law."

"How did you know the car had been stolen and not, dragged . . ."

"Towed?"

"Towed. How do you know the car was not towed rather than stolen?"

Lang looked at him blankly. "When is the last time you saw a car towed in this city for parking in a no-parking space?"

The inspector made a noise that had equal chances of being a laugh, cough or clearing his throat. He leaned forward, studying Lang's face. "It was found on the Aventine shot full of holes. Do you have an idea who would do this?"

Lang hoped he was successful in demonstrating surprise. "Perhaps someone frustrated when he couldn't get the car started?"

"You make the joke, Mr. Reilly. My investigation is serious."

Lang leaned back, hoping the shadows helped obscure his face. "I apologize. I have no idea who would shoot that car."

Uncertain of the sincerity of the admission of fault, the inspector continued. "You are in Rome on business?"

"I come almost every year to enjoy the museums, the churches, the architecture. One cannot live long enough to see it all."

"And how much longer will you remain?"

"Several more days at least. But I doubt I'll rent a car."

"And you have no guess as to who would shoot the car?"

"None. Perhaps the thief had enemies."

"Why did you rent the car, Mr. Reilly? Is not Rome's bus and metro good enough?"

"I had hoped to drive out to Hadrian's villa. I understand it is both interesting and beautiful."

Lang was certain the man was more interested in studying his face than asking fruitless questions.

He stood. "Inspector, I know nothing of what happened on the Aventine. I do know I have a lunch date with a business associate. I'd prefer not to keep him waiting."

Manicci stood also, stuffing the recorder in his pocket, an admission the interview was unproductive. "Very well then. I may wish to contact you again."

"I'll be right here."

Jacob and Lang watched the policeman's departure through the hotel's glass door.

"From what I heard from the lobby, the copper didn't learn a thing," Jacob observed.

Lang was still looking out into the piazza. "After the first few minutes, it wasn't information he was after."

"Oh?"

"Remember, I told you about the gunfire in the priest's apartment building, the one where I gave last rites in the priest's cassock before disappearing?"

"So?"

"That cop, Manicci, was one of the investigating officers."

"You're sure he saw you there?"

"Your people took the same course in face recognition we did, hours of looking at different photos, different views of the same person. Yep, that's him. He kept trying to get a better look at my face. Sooner or later, he'll place me."

Jacob stuck his pipe in his mouth. "Bloody hell! I'd say it's jolly well time to bid farewell to this place before he comes back. As our Froggie friends would say, *tout suite.*"

VIII.

Piazza Venezia
Minutes Later

Inspector Antonio Manicci was oblivious to the huge Monument Victor Emmanuel that filled the unmarked Fiat's windshield. Referred to by irreverent Romans as the Typewriter or the Wedding Cake because of its tiered structure and mass of white Brescian marble, it was completed in 1911 in honor of Victor Emmanuel II of Savoy, the first king of a unified Italy. Also commemorated were architectural bad taste, self-importance and insensitivity to the ocher tones of surrounding buildings.

Instead of the universal loathing of the thing, Manicci's mind was occupied with the man he had just interrogated. He had seen Reilly before. He was sure. Remembering faces went with his job.

But where?

He swung left, south, onto the Via del Teatro di Marcello. Michelangelo's steep staircase, the Cordonata, stretched up to his Piazza del Campidogli at the top of the Capitoline Hill. Tour buses blocked the first of the northbound lanes and Roman motorists, ever impatient, were honking their disapproval.

Where would he have met the American?

The wooded flanks of the hill were on his left now but he didn't notice. Instead, his eyes fixed on three priests walking along the sidewalk.

Priests!

That Greek priest whose apartment had been the scene of some sort of gun battle, a Wild West shoot-out like something in the American Western films.

Another priest, one who had murmured last rites over the dead man on the stairs and then disappeared.

The realization was as violent as an electrical shock, so disconcerting he had to jam on the Fiat's brakes at the last moment to avoid running over a young woman on a Vespa. A young woman whose small dog had been riding at her feet. The animal turned to snarl his anger at the inspector, an expression that closely matched that on his mistress's face.

That priest had been the American, Langford Reilly. He was certain of it.

He fought the temptation to attempt a U-turn, aware such a move would likely be fatal even with his siren and lights hidden in the grille turned on. Instead, he pulled his cell phone from its holder on his belt and scrolled down before punching in a number. He ignored the chorus of horns behind him.

He identified himself, then, "I want you to check the immigration records for the last three months for Langford Reilly, an American. He should have entered the country recently, but more important, I want the date he entered *before*. Entry and exit."

He listened for a moment of protest.

"I don't care if the office is closed until 1600; the computer records aren't!"

He pushed the disconnect button among a cavalcade of more excuses.

If he were right, if Lang Reilly had been in the country when the shooting took place—and the Greek priest subsequently found dead—the American would have a lot more questions to answer.

IX.

Via Campania
An Hour Later

The safe house Jacob had managed to scrounge from his former colleagues on short notice was no more than a third-floor suite of three rooms, a bath and a tiny kitchen. Were it not for the tedious sameness shared by safe houses, Lang could have sworn this was the apartment he had shared with Jacob and Gurt for a few days during the Pegasus affair. Through a pair of grime-streaked windows, he could see just over the top of the ancient city wall, where a strip of green denoted the park of the Villa Borghese, the only thing remotely cheerful in sight.

Two chairs and a sofa that Goodwill would have rejected were placed against walls bare of any decoration other than cracks in the plaster. A wooden table, its surface scarred by cigarette burns, stood forlornly between the main room and a two-burner stove, sink and small refrigerator that seemed to be gasping its last breaths.

Lang was thankful they would be there only a few hours. Jacob seemed to be taking contentment from his pipe, which he had smoked continually since their arrival.

The place was not only dismal, now it stunk.

Jacob looked at his watch. "Suppose the inspector has made the connection by now?"

Lang tossed down a two-month-old copy of *Der Spiegel*. "I wouldn't have wanted to hang around the hotel and find out."

Jacob gently puffed a smoke ring. It shimmered across the floor before dissolving against a table leg. "Too bad we can't be at the airport. If he's noodled out who you are, the place will be rife with coppers. Bright idea, that: making reservations on the next flight back to Atlanta."

"Should keep him busy while we attend to unfinished

business. Tell me again, what time will the visiting members of the council be at the Vatican?"

"1900. I'd say give it an hour to make sure it's dark."

X.

Piazza della Rotonda
Sole al Pantheon
At the Same Time

The two policeman stood at the desk shifting their weight from foot to foot.

Deputy Chief Police Inspector Hanaratti leaned over to put his face as close to the clerk's as possible. "Checked out? The man said he would be here a few more days!"

He looked at Manicci, who attested to the truth of the statement with a nod.

Unruffled, the desk clerk thumbed his guest ledger. "He was scheduled to stay." He shrugged, his expression saying the coming and going of guests was hardly his affair. "Then he and his friend asked for their passports and checked out unexpectedly."

"Did he say where they were going?" Hanaratti asked.

"One of them told the cabdriver to take them to the airport."

"They have not arrived there, yet," Manicci said. "I have a number of men waiting for them." He smiled the smile of a man way ahead in the game. "I ran Reilly's name through reservations lists. He has a return flight to Atlanta, Georgia, via New York this evening."

Skeptical, Hanaratti checked his watch. "They have had time to get to Flumicino." He turned back to the clerk. "Do you know this driver?"

"Of course, Inspector. The hotel would not enlist someone it did not know to serve our guests."

Or who would not pay a fee for the referral.

"Call this cabdriver. I wish to speak to him," Hanaratti ordered.

A few minutes later, he put down the phone. "The driver says the two changed their minds and instructed him to drop them off at Stazione Termini."

"They could be on a train headed almost anywhere," observed Manicci, always a spokesman for the obvious.

Hanaratti thought for a moment. "Call headquarters. Find out every train that has departed in the last hour and a half. Have the local *poliza* board each at the next stop."

"And how will Reilly and his companion be identified?" Manicci asked. "We have no pictures of them."

The senior inspector hadn't thought of that. "Every male passenger from twenty-five to fifty will have to show papers if it comes to it."

Manicci could only imagine the bureaucratic turf war with *Ferrovie dello Stato*, the Italian state railway, that would ignite.

XI.

Questure di Aventine
(Aventine Precinct Police Station)
Via di San Teodoro
Two Hours Later

Deputy Chief Inspector Hanaratti stood behind a series of desks where computers blinked as they scrolled lists. The national railway agency had been surprising cooperative. Or at least they had not been obstructionist. It had been the local police stations that had balked. Only a connection with a higher up in the Carabiniere, the national military police, had produced the manpower to board each of more than a dozen trains. That favor would cost the deputy chief inspector dearly.

So far, the search had produced two Bulgarians who had entered the country illegally, one man with a warrant outstanding for a minor crime and a woman smuggling cigarettes. Hardly a major war against crime. Manicci's men at the airport had lingered until after the flight on which Reilly had reservations had departed.

The net was, so far, empty.

Hanaratti lit his first cigarette in three years, ignoring the signs depicting a cigarette with a red line drawn through it. The first puff made him giddy. Perhaps it was the tobacco that gave him the idea.

"Manicci," he said. "The airline reservation was intended to throw us off the trail, do you not agree?"

Unsurprisingly, the junior inspector did.

"Why, then, would not getting off at Termini also be intended to mislead?"

Manicci was not one to risk giving answers that might conflict with what a superior had in mind. "But, then how would this Reilly man and his companion leave the city? We have sent warnings to the rental car agencies."

Well, perhaps the registered ones. A number of entrepreneurs rented a selection of automobiles out of storefronts or their homes to evade the numerous and burdensome taxes.

"I was thinking," Hanaratti continued, "they might not have left Rome at all."

"Quite possible," Manicci agreed, trying not to make a show of fanning away the cigarette smoke. "But to what end?"

Hanaratti dropped the smoldering butt into a coffee cup, where it hissed angrily. "We do not yet know. The only real connection Reilly has here was the rental car."

"In which he was going to visit Hadrian's villa."

The senior inspector nodded, a teacher encouraging a

not-so-bright pupil. "Perhaps, perhaps not. Perhaps he was the one who drove the car to the place it was destroyed."

"To what end? He could have been killed."

"But he wasn't."

Manicci knew better than to ask the point of his superior's rambling. He said nothing.

"Perhaps he had a reason to have the car so shot up. Or a reason to have it where it was."

"Do we know what that might be?" Manicci ventured.

"No, but I think it might be in order to go back to the Knights of Malta, ask more pointed questions. I do not believe they neither heard nor saw anything last night. Someone must have at least heard gunfire. Someone would have at least looked out of a window. They are a large and wealthy organization. It would not surprise me if they had enemies, enemies who wished to make them appear in a less than favorable light. Having a crime committed on their doorstep might achieve that."

Manicci failed to see how having a sports car shot up outside the priory could reflect anything, good or bad, but he knew better than to admit it. "Shall I call for an appointment? With whom?"

Hanaratti picked up a newspaper. "Happily for us, the media has taken an interest in an event that takes place only every five years." He held up a page, showing a picture of a procession of men in what looked like seventeenth-century attire. "Even publish schedules for the various meetings. Visiting members of their supreme council will be at a function at the Vatican this evening. That should leave the grand master and full-time staff at the priory. I think that would be an ideal time for a surprise visit."

XII.

Circo Massimo Metro Station
Via del Circo Massimo
1830 Local Time

Lang and Jacob had chosen the anonymity of public transportation but now had the long uphill trudge to the priory before them. As they climbed the stairs out of the station, they faced west. Across the Tiber, a bloodred balloon of a setting sun limned the domes and towers of the Trastevere in picture postcard perfection.

Lang was more interested in the steep hill to his left. "How far do we have to go?"

Jacob puckered his lips. "I'd say a kilometer and a half. If you don't think you've recovered enough, lad, I can go it alone."

"Not a chance. How close do we have to get?"

"Hard to say. You saw where I put the device but exactly how close . . ."

Lang's legs were already complaining of the climb. "Explain it to me again."

Jacob took out his pipe, thought better of it and returned it to a pocket. "We had three choices: We could have tossed something nasty over the wall that would have wreaked bloody hell. That was a bit of a dice because we wanted to make sure we eliminated the people most likely involved in trying to suppress the James Gospel by killing you or nicking someone close to you. That would most likely be the grand master and his full-time staff. Once we located where they might be, we could have left a timed device, except we had no way of knowing *when* the sodding grand master and his henchmen would be where. So, the little gem I left can be set off with this."

He held up a small black box.

Lang squinted in the fading light. "Looks like a an automatic garage-door opener to me."

"Right you are! That's exactly what it is. It works by sending out a low-frequency signal that activates the receiver, usually attached to your garage door. The question is, how close to the blooming door do we have to get for the signal to reach?"

Lang paused to bend over and massage his calves. "And we find that out how?"

Jacob paused, too, puffing from the climb. "By the most common of scientific methods: trial and error."

"And suppose the wall prevents us from getting close enough?"

"Well, now, that would be a spot of bother. But it shouldn't. The ad on the telly said this bugger worked up to fifty meters."

Lang began the uphill climb again. "And if it doesn't, you get your money back?"

Jacob looked puzzled for a moment. "Well yes, I suppose I do."

Swell.

XIII.

Aventine Hill
At the Same Time

The dark, unmarked Alfa Romeo sedan pulled up to the massive wooden gates. The driver, a uniformed policeman, got out and rang the buzzer. After a prolonged exchange, the gates swung open and the car drove inside.

"Bloody hell!" Jacob spat. "The sodding coppers are here! Now what?"

Lang stepped back into the shadows that now consumed almost everything at street level. "We'll just have to wait."

"Wait? How long? The visiting council members will be back from tea with the pope or whatever they're at."

"I know, but we can't just ignore the fact the police are inside, probably in the building."

"I thought collateral damage wasn't a concern."

"It is where cops are concerned. Kill one of them and every law enforcement officer in Europe will be on our ass."

Jacob shook his head. "I wasn't planning on claiming credit for this any more than I was expecting the sodding Nobel Peace Prize. We either get this done soon or there'll be a lot more people likely to get hurt."

Lang thought a minute. "OK, here's what we're gonna do . . ."

Two minutes later, Lang crossed the street like a man without a care in the world. He pushed the buzzer by the gate as casually as though he were a guest invited to a dinner party. The response was immediate if unintelligible.

"Please tell the police that Langford Reilly wants to see them."

There was a pause before more Italian squawked through the speaker box, then, "Langford Reilly? Police?"

"Yes, *si.*"

It was as if someone had been expecting him. The giant gates began to rumble open. By the time they had parted wide enough, two plainclothesmen and a uniform squeezed through.

Lang easily recognized Manicci. "I understand you're looking for me?"

Across the street, Jacob dialed a number on his cell phone and waited. Two rings later the call was answered. *"Prego?"*

"The grand master," Jacob said.

The voice switched to English. "How did you get this number?"

"That doesn't matter. Tell the grand master Lang Reilly wishes to speak with him."

Pause.

"*Momento*, just a moment."

The second voice came so quickly the grand master must have been in the room when the call came through. "Yes?"

Jacob pushed the button on his garage-door opener and winced.

Nothing.

Bloody hell! He had tested the tiny battery before he left London. He pushed the button again with the same lack of result.

"Hello?" The grand master was getting impatient. He wasn't going to hang on the line forever. If he left the room, the explosive device might not do the job.

Across the street, the policeman approached Lang.

"Ah, Mr. Reilly," the older of the two men in plain clothes said in accented English, "we are indeed looking for you. But I am curious, how did you know Inspector Manicci and I would be here?"

"Lucky guess."

The policeman nodded his head slightly. "Perhaps so. Will you be so kind as to step inside? We have much to talk about."

Lang took a step back. "If it is all the same to you, I'd rather talk out here."

Another nod, this time to the uniformed officer. Arms reached around Lang, pulling his hands behind him.

"I regret we cannot accommodate you, Mr. Reilly," the older inspector said. "But I'm sure you understand."

Lang was shoved toward the open gate.

Jacob looked at the device in his hand as though he could actually see it in the dark.

"Mr. Reilly?" the voice on the other end of the line asked.

"Reilly here. I think we might have something to talk about."

Stall, keep the man on the line before he hung up and left the room.

Jacob was holding the phone with one hand, fumbling with the door opener with the other. If the problem wasn't the battery, it must be the contact point. Blindly, his fingers searched for the seam in the plastic casing. He thought he had found it when the thing slipped from his hand. It was pure luck it fell at his feet. It took only seconds to retrieve, but from what he saw across the street, there weren't any seconds to waste.

Lang shoved back. "Look, there's no reason we can't talk out here."

Delay, stall. Standard agency tactics. When things are going badly, make your opponent spend time he hadn't planned on. There's always the chance something will happen. In this case, Lang knew exactly what. But he couldn't figure out why it hadn't already. According to Jacob's announced plan, there should have been an explosion several minutes ago. Lang had a sinking feeling at the bottom of his stomach. Now was not the time for one of his friend's concoctions to fail.

"If you prefer," the older man said, "we can handcuff you and have you bodily carried to a proper place to ask you questions. The grand master has kindly consented to give us an office for the purpose."

Hardly good news.

At the moment, there were only three possibilities, none attractive: Either he would be inside the building when Jacob's contraption went off or he was about to meet the grand master himself. Or both. Lang doubted he would be greeted with anything resembling traditional hospitality.

"And what did you have in mind, Mr. Reilly?" the voice on Jacob's cell phone asked. "I'm not sure I know why you called."

"I think you have a bleeding good notion," Jacob said as

he managed to insert a thumbnail into the seam between the two plastic parts of the door opener's plastic casing. Taking care not to drop it again, or dislodge the battery, he pried the two halves apart and blew gently. If condensation on the contact point had been the problem, that should take care of it. If not, Lang was in for a spot of bother.

"What's that you say?" The grand master's temper was getting shorter and shorter.

As slowly as he could manage, Lang let himself be pushed through the gates. The piazza was tastefully lit, hidden lights accenting a number of monuments as well as the facades of buildings. A double file of cypress trees were columns reaching into infinity. In the distance, Rome's lights sparkled like a handful of jewels.

He was being taken to the building he and Jacob had entered that morning.

"I said, we have something to talk about." Jacob fumbled in the dark, trying to get the two halves back together. Across the street, those formidable doors were beginning to swing shut.

He forced himself to take a deep breath. Somewhere there was a catch. He ran fingers made clumsy by anxiety around the edge, found the protruding piece of plastic.

With a snap, the device closed.

Lang and the police were less than fifty yards away from the building.

"Ah, Mr. Reilly?" A man was standing in the open door. "Then who is the grand master talking to . . . ?"

He turned to dash inside.

"I'm curious how the grand master of the Knights of Malta knew who you were," one of the policemen said.

Lang wondered. Did the order's power reach into the police, too?

He would never know.

At that moment, night became day, a day with the light of a dozen suns. A wall of heat knocked Lang over as an explosion clapped silencing hands over his ears.

Groggy, he got to his knees, able to see only streaks of light as though someone had fired a flashbulb in his face. His ears felt pressure as if he were in a rapidly descending aircraft. The grip on his arms was gone. He could only guess at the direction of the way out of the piazza and stumbled that way.

Blurs of vision were returning as he reached the gates and squeezed through before they completely shut.

He felt a hand on his arm. "This way, lad!"

His last sight of the piazza was of blazing rubble where the building had been. The flames reflected from the windows of the nearby church. Not a one had been damaged. Then the gates clicked shut, sealing off pursuit.

Lang's sight and hearing had returned by the time they reached the bottom of the hill, just in time to hear the wail of fire trucks on the way. He turned and looked behind him to see a flickering glow that turned the Aventine into a contemporary Vesuvius. The curious, singly and in small groups, were already filling the street as they hurried uphill to see what had happened.

Minutes later, Lang and Jacob were on the metro again.

"You destroyed the entire building," Lang finally said in wonderment, "but I saw not even a crack in the church's windows."

Jacob was sucking on an empty pipe. Public transportation was one of the few places in Rome where smoking bans were actually enforced. "Better bomb than I thought. Artistry is not confined to painting and sculpture."

Lang believed him.

They got off at different stations, since the police, if the two inspectors reacted in time, would be looking for two men rather a single traveler. Jacob at Termini, where they had paid a porter to keep a watchful eye on their suitcases. Lang went on to Tiburtina, from where he would take an Appian Line bus to Venice, cross over into Slovenia and, eventually, to Vienna and a flight to Paris and then home.

XIV.

Excerpt from the next day's *International Herald Tribune*:

EXPLOSION ROCKS ROME LANDMARK

ROME—A building at the headquarters of the Order of St. James, internationally known as the Knights of Malta, was destroyed yesterday in a blast that killed the grand master and a number of full-time rank-and-file members.

The order's headquarters, known as a "priory," was filled with members visiting Rome for the every-fifth-year election of leadership and members of the supreme council. Fortunately, all the visiting members were attending a function at the Vatican at the time of the explosion or the casualty list would have been far greater, according to a spokesman for the order who declined to be identified.

Also unharmed were three members of Rome's police force who were on the premises at the time. The police declined to state why they were present.

The same spokesman for the order attributed the explosion to a leaking gas main.

The Order of St. James became known as the Knights of Malta . . .

XV.

472 LaFayette Drive
Atlanta
A Month Later

Lang and Gurt stood on a grassy lawn, looking at the house. Lang thought it had vaguely Victorian lines; Gurt saw something slightly more contemporary. Either way, it was typical of Ansley Park, Atlanta's upscale, midtown neighborhood where mansions of frame and shingle were as common as Craftsman cottages. Built in the first decades of the last century, The Park, as it was known to its residents, featured towering oaks, winding streets, a number of parks and grassy squares and a small-town atmosphere. You always knew your neighbors and they always knew your business.

Lang had spent a lot of time at his sister's home only a short distance away. Janice and Jeff, her adopted son, had loved the area. Lang had often thought if he ever had a child of his own, this would be a good place to live. Now he had a son who had already made himself at home on the swing set in the backyard before the final papers had been signed.

The condominium at Park Place had sold for somewhat more than Lang had anticipated. The new buyer loved the fixtures, those that had actually been paid for and installed. The deliveries from Home Depot, as far as Lang knew, continued. Lang suspected the decline in the price of the company's stock might well be attributable to the sizable inventory overflowing Park Place's storage space. For certain, any needs for his future residence would be fulfilled by Sears, Lowe's or some other vendor that did not view itself as a cornucopia of unordered and unwanted merchandise.

"It is good, no?" Gurt said.

Lang reached out to take her hand. "It is good, yes. Manfred seems to like it."

"Few European children have a room and bath of their own."

"Neither does Manfred, not unless he can get Grumps to sleep elsewhere."

Neither spoke, enjoying the euphoria of travelers who have finally managed to return from a long and perilous journey. The homely shingled two-story was surrounded on three sides by a porch, the roof of which ran just below the upstairs windows. The effect was of the house having the beetle-browed expression of the genetically witless. But then, the sheer ugliness of most of the neighboring houses gave the area its unique character. Still, it had a certain cozy charm that had infected both Lang and Gurt. They had not debated buying it; they both knew this was home the minute they walked in.

Behind them, a car door opened. As one, they turned to see Francis climbing out of the church's six-year-old Toyota.

"Hi! Was visiting parishioners and thought I'd stop by!"

Lang smiled. The chances of overwhelmingly white, protestant Ansley Park inhabitants leaving their million-dollar homes to attend a Catholic church, mostly black, poor and in south Atlanta was a stretch, even for the wildly liberal views professed by many of the residents.

Francis was meddling. Lang had no doubt his friend had his and Gurt's best interests at heart, at least as the priest perceived those interests to be, but meddling nonetheless.

Lang and Gurt exchanged glances, knowing what was coming.

Francis, hands behind his back, joined them in viewing the house. "A fine place for Manfred to grow up."

Silence.

The priest cleared his throat. "Exactly when do you two plan to get married?"

Deeper silence.

Undeterred, Francis cleared his throat again and continued. "It would be difficult but I might, just might, be able to get a special dispensation to allow me to perform the ceremony. I mean, with neither of you being practicing Catholics . . ."

"There's no one I'd rather have marry us," Lang said.

"*If* we got married," Gurt added.

"But you must." Now Francis was facing them. "Think of your obligation to your son. You want the other children snickering behind his back when he starts school? Do you want—"

"If I wanted a husband, it would be one who does not bring danger to his family," Gurt said with finality. "A man who doesn't become a target."

The remark was patently unfair. Danger had followed Lang like an unwanted stray dog. He had never sought trouble. Well, almost never. Besides, Gurt enjoyed the thrill of life-and-death action as much as he.

Motherhood, he thought, had changed her viewpoint, a she-bear protective of her cub.

But he kept his mouth shut.

Francis looked from one to the other, well aware of the facts. "Suppose both of you disavow violence, promise each other to live like normal people?"

Boring people.

Gurt shrugged nonchalantly. "If he so agrees, so will I."

Lang wasn't sure he had heard correctly. "You mean you'll quit working for the agency, come live permanently in the United States?"

Gurt grinned, the first evidence she was enjoying the exchange. "With a rich husband I should work?"

Francis touched his clerical collar, a gesture of which he was unaware. "Good! Then it's all settled."

Lang was far from sure but hoped so. He wasn't, as they say, getting any younger and a little peace and quiet might even do him some good. And spending every day with the two people he loved more than anything was a prospect of nothing but joy.

His BlackBerry chimed as though to remind him of the real world outside Ansley Park. Without taking it out of his pocket, he turned it off.

The real world could wait.

Author's Note

Thirteen books of the Nag Hammadi Library were recovered. The bedouins who found them were uncertain how many their mother had actually used to start cooking fires nor were the authorities ever completely sure none of the volumes were sold on Cairo's thriving antiquities black market.

Most city building codes prohibit use of gas in high-rise buildings, an effort to prevent what happened to Lang occurring by accident. Atlanta allows exceptions upon special permit.

Honesty requires acknowledgment of sources even if used in fictionalized form. Additionally, readers frequently e-mail me, requesting the place they can find more on some of the historical facts that form the basis of plots.

For both reasons, I include the following:

Ron Cameron's translation of the text of the Secret Book of James was most helpful, although I took considerable liberties with it to make the plotline work. I used Paul Tobin's *The Rejection of Pascal's Wager: A Skeptic's Guide to Christianity* and *James the Brother of Jesus* by Robert Eisenman in dealing with James as the blood brother of Jesus and the perpetual virginity of Mary. The description of the discovery of the Nag Hammadi Library is based on Elaine Pagels's *The Gnostic Gospels.*

I would be ungrateful as well as in deep trouble if I didn't also note here that my wife, Suzanne, constantly frequents history's curio shop in search of dusty and forgotten scraps of the past.

My agent, Mary Jack Wald, has infinite patience, certainly more than I deserve. Don D'Auria and his wonderful artistic, publicity and editing staff at Dorchester deserve a great deal of credit for any success of the Lang Reilly yarns.

G.L.

February 5, 2008

INTERACT WITH DORCHESTER ONLINE!

Want to learn more about your favorite books and authors?
Want to talk with other readers that like to read the same books as you?
Want to see up-to-the-minute Dorchester news?

VISIT DORCHESTER AT:
DorchesterPub.com
Twitter.com/DorchesterPub
Facebook.com (Search Pages)

DISCUSS DORCHESTER'S NOVELS AT:
Dorchester Forums at DorchesterPub.com
GoodReads.com
LibraryThing.com
Myspace.com/books
Shelfari.com
WeRead.com